W9-BZD-122

T-MINUS
the race to the moon

jim OTTAVIANI   zander CANNON   kevin CANNON

Aladdin
New York   London   Toronto   Sydney

This book is a work of historical fiction. Any references to historical events, real people, or real locales are used fictitiously. Other names, characters, places, and incidents are the product of the author's imagination, and any resemblance to actual events or locales or persons, living or dead, is entirely coincidental.

ALADDIN
An imprint of Simon & Schuster Children's Publishing Division
1230 Avenue of the Americas, New York, NY 10020

Designed by Zander Cannon and Kevin Cannon
Manufactured in the United States of America
First Aladdin edition May 2009
10 9 8 7 6 5 4 3 2 1
Library of Congress Control Number 2009920999
ISBN: 978-1-4169-8682-9 (hc)
ISBN: 978-1-4169-4960-2 (pbk)

To my parents, who let me stay up past my bedtime to watch the first humans walk around on another world.
—Jim Ottaviani

To Julie and Jin-Seo
—Zander Cannon

For R. A.
—Kevin Cannon

Thanks to Kevin, Zander, Liesa, the folks at NASA, the astronauts who answered questions, and everyone who helped make this book possible (not quite 400,000, but close).—J. O.

The astronauts may be famous for going to the moon, but it took tens of thousands of people working behind the scenes to get them there. Likewise, *T-Minus* wouldn't exist without many talented people working behind the scenes. Jim Ottaviani wrote a fantastic script, but he also patiently answered our many artistic and reference questions in the form of late-night e-mails. It has been a thrill and an honor to work on another book with Jim, and if our luck holds out, this will be the second of many more to come. Liesa Abrams believed in this project from the start, and, with the help of her crack team at Aladdin, produced the gorgeous book you're now holding. Bob Mecoy, our agent, and Matt Madden, our editor, have been encouraging, insightful, and even dogged (when necessary) during this project's long and exciting journey. We also owe thanks to the photographers, writers, website producers, and museum curators whose enthusiasm for the space race shines through in their work and who have indirectly helped this extremely research-heavy book come to fruition. And finally, we'd like to thank our friends and family for being with us as we slowly counted down to T-minus 0.—Z. C. and K. C.

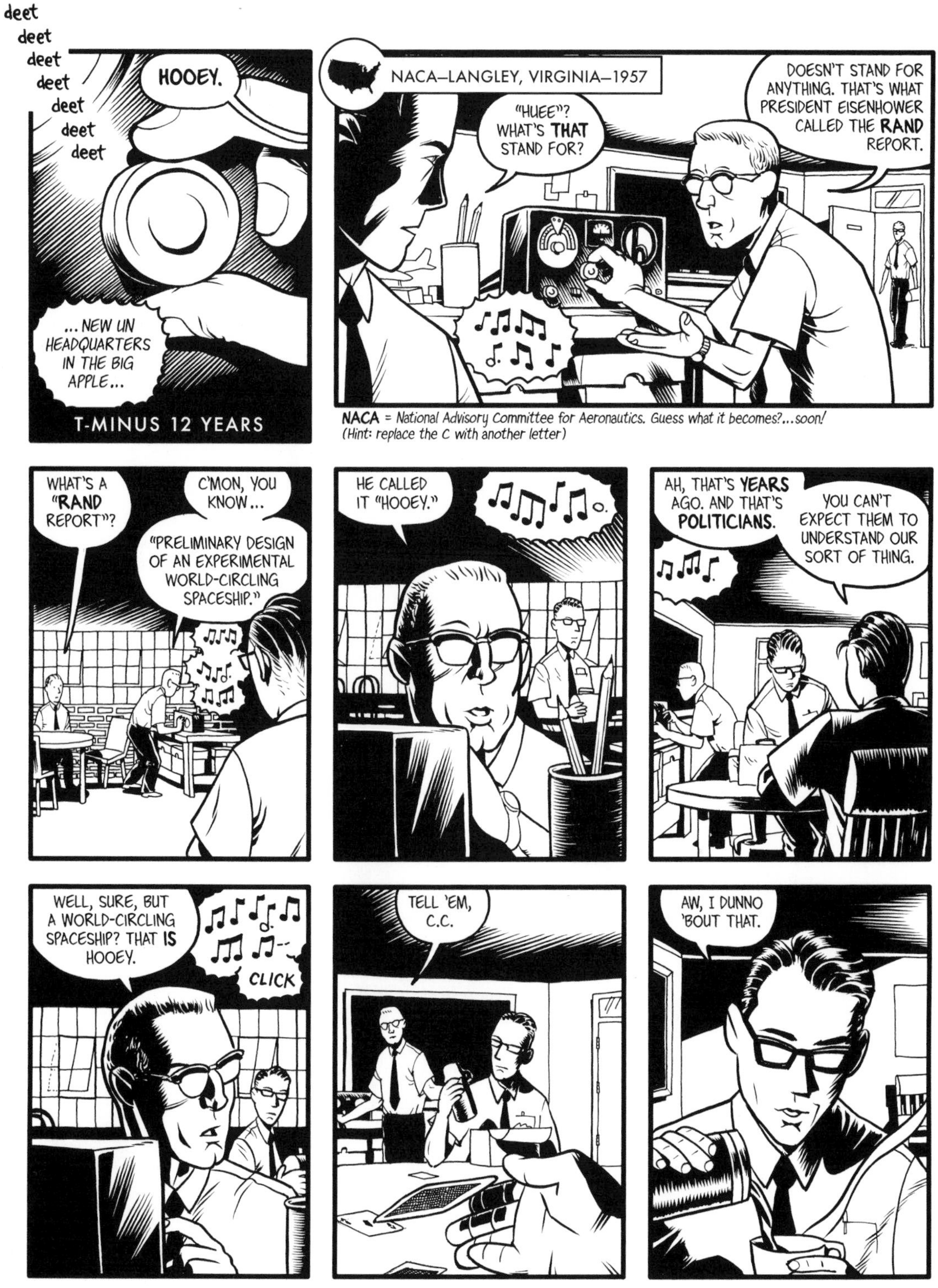
deet deet deet deet deet deet deet
HOOEY.
...NEW UN HEADQUARTERS IN THE BIG APPLE...
T-MINUS 12 YEARS
NACA–LANGLEY, VIRGINIA–1957
"HUEE"? WHAT'S THAT STAND FOR?
DOESN'T STAND FOR ANYTHING. THAT'S WHAT PRESIDENT EISENHOWER CALLED THE RAND REPORT.
NACA = National Advisory Committee for Aeronautics. Guess what it becomes?...soon! (Hint: replace the C with another letter)
WHAT'S A "RAND REPORT"?
C'MON, YOU KNOW... "PRELIMINARY DESIGN OF AN EXPERIMENTAL WORLD-CIRCLING SPACESHIP."
HE CALLED IT "HOOEY."
AH, THAT'S YEARS AGO. AND THAT'S POLITICIANS.
YOU CAN'T EXPECT THEM TO UNDERSTAND OUR SORT OF THING.
WELL, SURE, BUT A WORLD-CIRCLING SPACESHIP? THAT IS HOOEY.
CLICK
TELL 'EM, C.C.
AW, I DUNNO 'BOUT THAT.

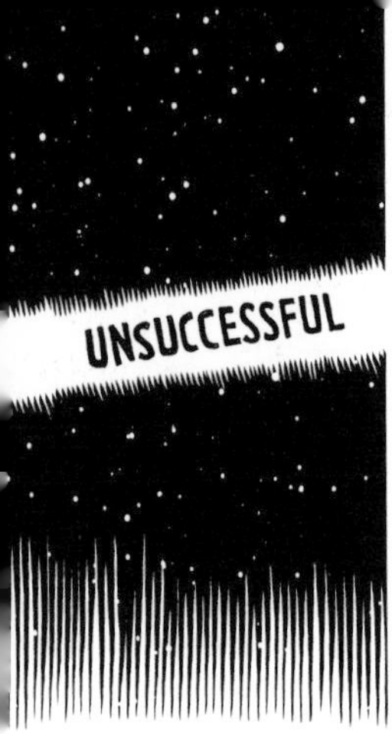
UNSUCCESSFUL

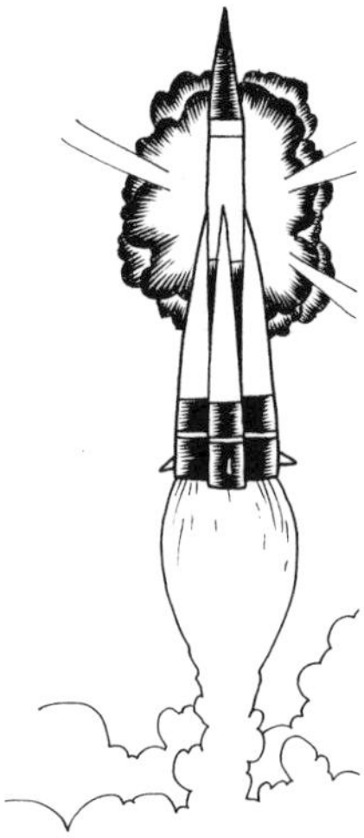

R-7 Semyorka
May 15, 1957
T-Minus 12 Years
Flight duration:
20 seconds

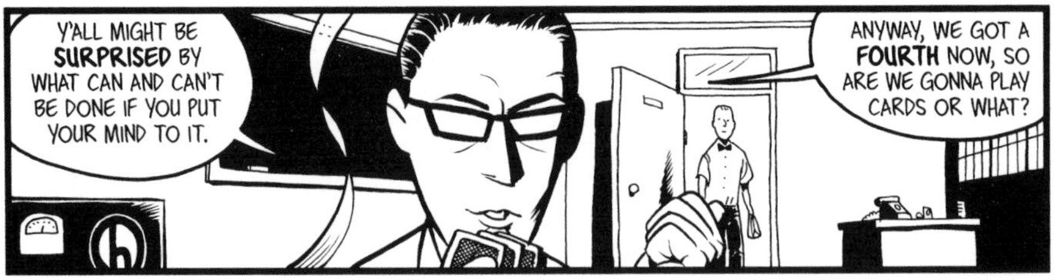
Y'ALL MIGHT BE **SURPRISED** BY WHAT CAN AND CAN'T BE DONE IF YOU PUT YOUR MIND TO IT.
ANYWAY, WE GOT A **FOURTH** NOW, SO ARE WE GONNA PLAY CARDS OR WHAT?

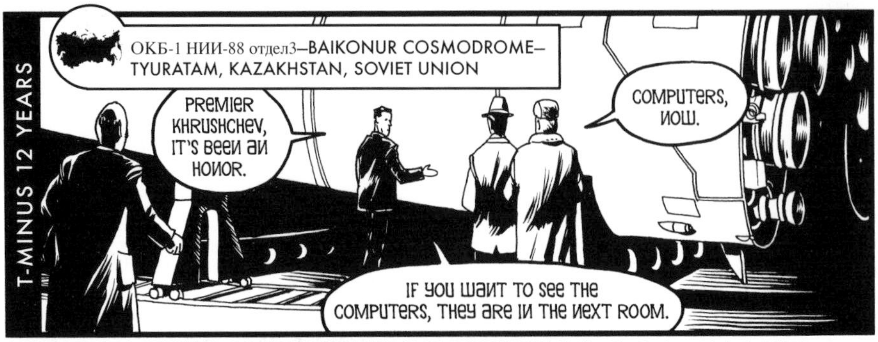
T-MINUS 12 YEARS
ОКБ-1 НИИ-88 отдел3—BAIKONUR COSMODROME—TYURATAM, KAZAKHSTAN, SOVIET UNION
PREMIER KHRUSHCHEV, IT'S BEEN AN HONOR.
COMPUTERS, NOW.
IF YOU WANT TO SEE THE COMPUTERS, THEY ARE IN THE NEXT ROOM.

DESIGN BUREAU 1, SCIENTIFIC-RESEARCH INSTITUTE NO. 88, DEPARTMENT NO. 3. = The Russian equivalent of NASA.

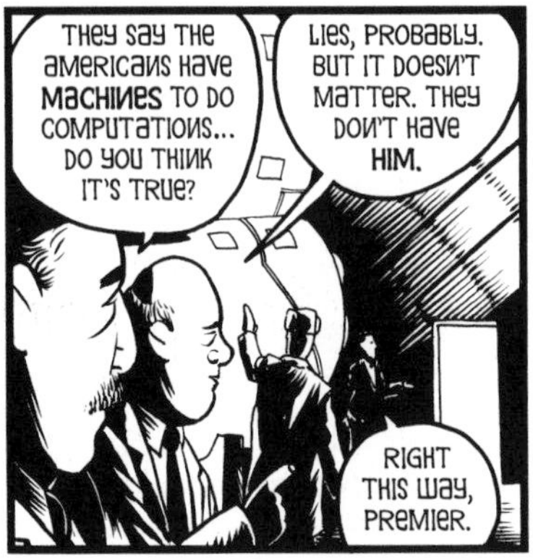
THEY SAY THE AMERICANS HAVE **MACHINES** TO DO COMPUTATIONS... DO YOU THINK IT'S TRUE?
LIES, PROBABLY. BUT IT DOESN'T MATTER. THEY DON'T HAVE **HIM.**
RIGHT THIS WAY, PREMIER.

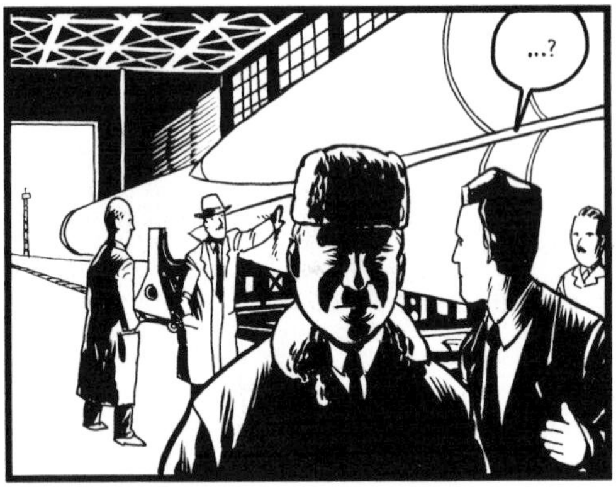
...?

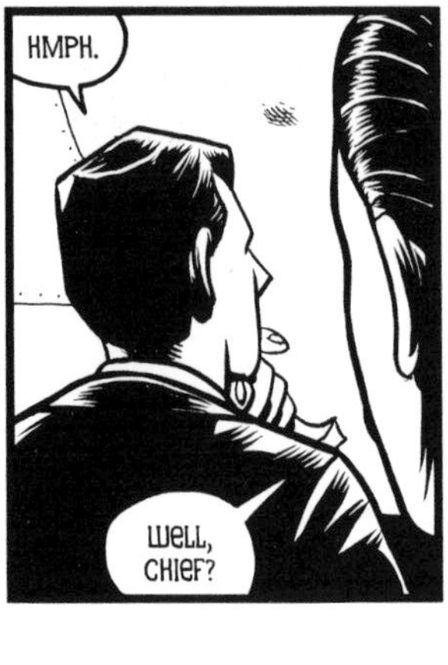
HMPH.
WELL, CHIEF?

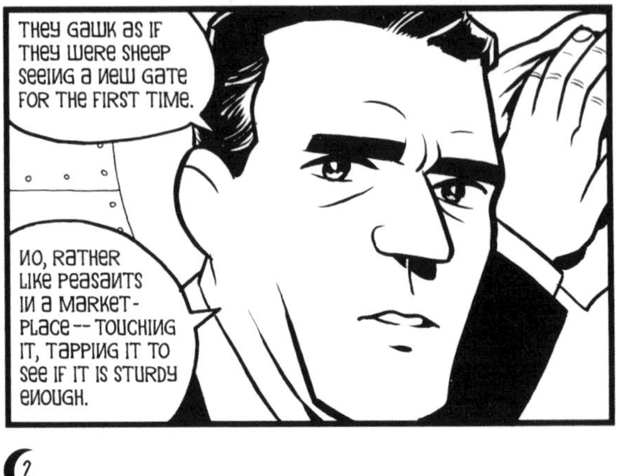
THEY GAWK AS IF THEY WERE SHEEP SEEING A NEW GATE FOR THE FIRST TIME.
NO, RATHER LIKE PEASANTS IN A MARKET-PLACE -- TOUCHING IT, TAPPING IT TO SEE IF IT IS STURDY ENOUGH.

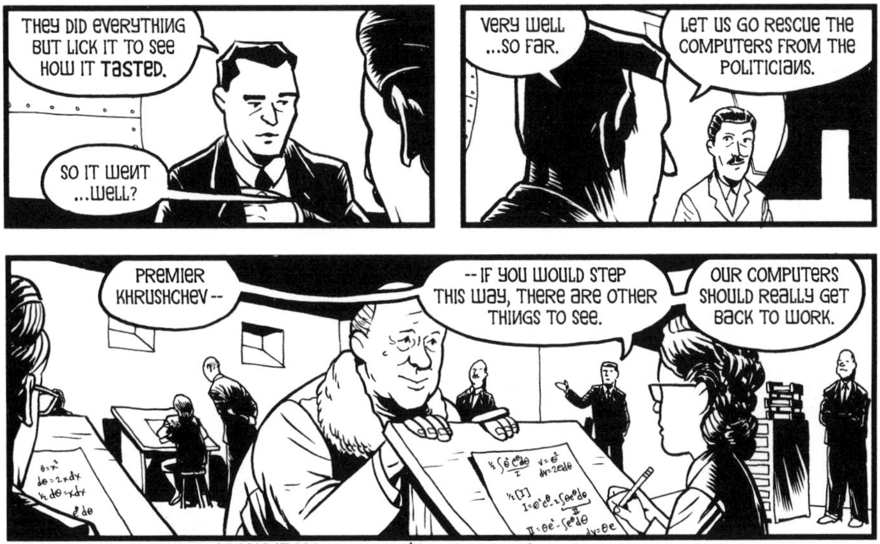
THEY DID EVERYTHING BUT LICK IT TO SEE HOW IT **TASTED**.
SO IT WENT ...WELL?
VERY WELL ...SO FAR.
LET US GO RESCUE THE COMPUTERS FROM THE POLITICIANS.
PREMIER KHRUSHCHEV --
-- IF YOU WOULD STEP THIS WAY, THERE ARE OTHER THINGS TO SEE.
OUR COMPUTERS SHOULD REALLY GET BACK TO WORK.

That's right -- in 1950s Russia, a **"COMPUTER"** was a person! (Usually a woman.)

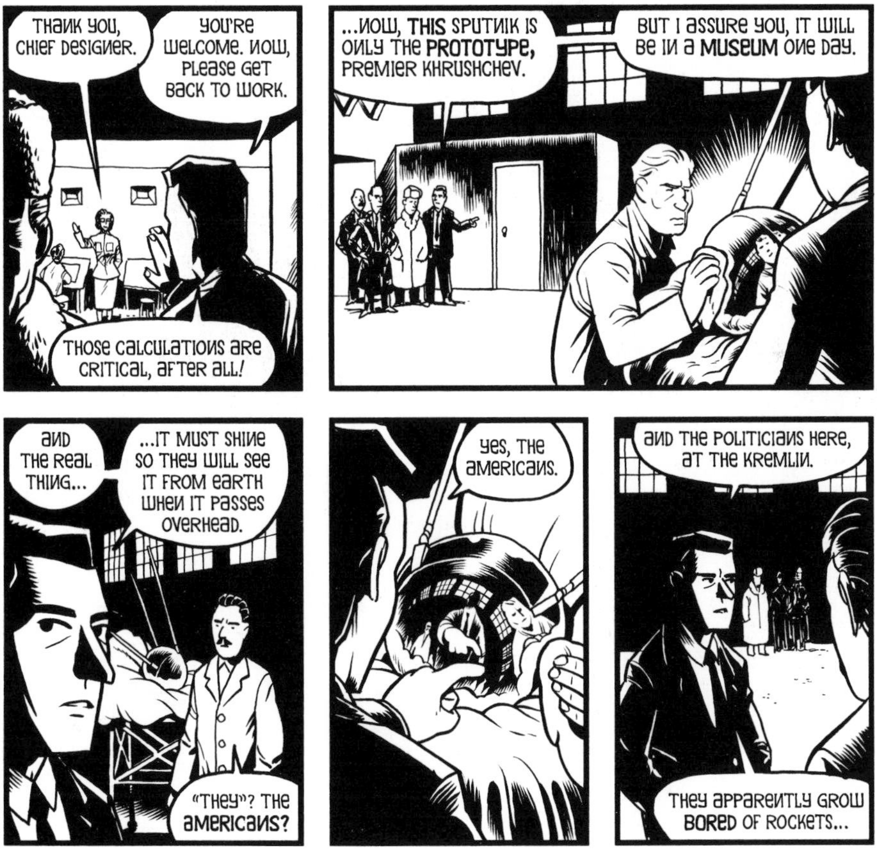
THANK YOU, CHIEF DESIGNER.
YOU'RE WELCOME. NOW, PLEASE GET BACK TO WORK.
THOSE CALCULATIONS ARE CRITICAL, AFTER ALL!
...NOW, **THIS** SPUTNIK IS ONLY THE **PROTOTYPE,** PREMIER KHRUSHCHEV.
BUT I ASSURE YOU, IT WILL BE IN A **MUSEUM** ONE DAY.
AND THE REAL THING...
...IT MUST SHINE SO THEY WILL SEE IT FROM EARTH WHEN IT PASSES OVERHEAD.
"THEY"? THE **AMERICANS?**
YES, THE AMERICANS.
AND THE POLITICIANS HERE, AT THE KREMLIN.
THEY APPARENTLY GROW **BORED** OF ROCKETS...

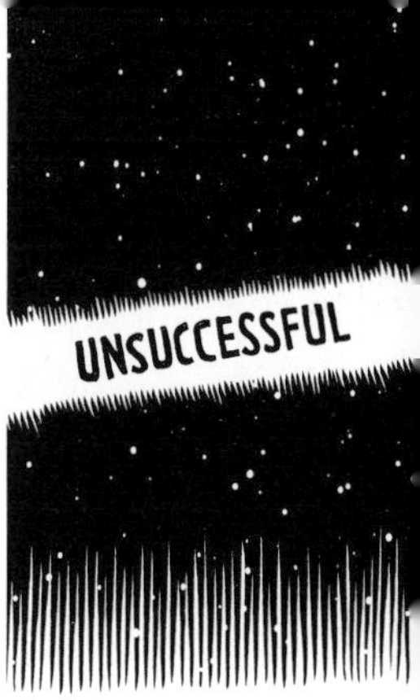
UNSUCCESSFUL

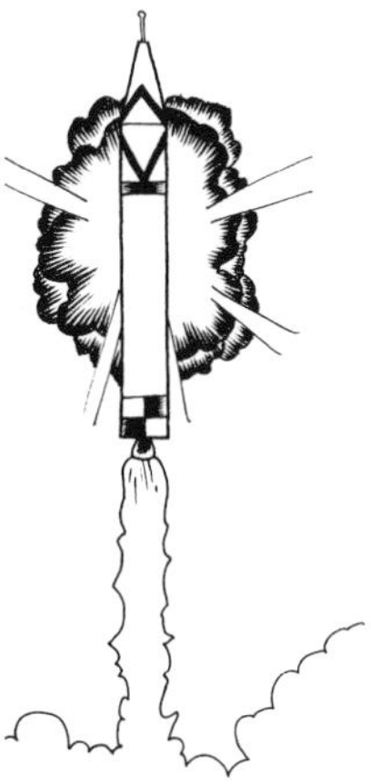

Jupiter AM-1A
March 1, 1957
T-Minus 12 Years
Flight duration:
7.4 seconds

THE REAL SPUTNIK WILL FIX THAT.
AND AFTER SPUTNIK...
...WHO KNOWS?
MEANWHILE, BACK IN THE U.S....
WELL...
YOU GUYS CAN JAW ALL DAY, BUT I'M GETTIN' BACK TO WORK.
GAME OVER, THEN?
NAH...
...BUT I WANTED TO GET BACK TO WORK TOO.
SAY--
YOU LOOK REAL FAMILIAR. DID WE MEET IN THE NAVY? AT LOUISIANA STATE?
I DON'T THINK I EVER...

WAIT.

YEAH, I THINK WE DID MEET AT THAT.

BACK IN '35.

MODEL-AIRPLANE COMPETITION.

MAX, RIGHT?

THAT'S RIGHT. MAX.

YEAH?

HEARD O' YOU. I'M CALDWELL.

IT'S PRONOUNCED "CADWELL"...

"...BUT YOU CAN CALL ME C.C."

RIGHT. COUNTRY BOY.

ME AND MY PLANE WHUPPED YOU BUT GOOD, DIDN'T WE?

THAT AIN'T THE WAY I REMEMBER IT ...COLLEGE BOY.

ANYWAY, THAT'S HISTORY. I GOT WORK TO DO.

YEAH, WELL, THIS DOESN'T LOOK LIKE AN AIRPLANE DESIGN.

THAT'S 'CAUSE IT AIN'T.

...

RIGHT.

RIGHT. SEE YOU 'ROUND.

COUNT ON IT.

AND WHEN YOU HAVE A MOMENT, YOU MIGHT LIKE TO C'MON OVER TO **PARD**... SEE WHAT WE'RE UP TO.

PARD = Pilotless Aircraft Research Division... in other words, rockets!

WELL, THAT'S WHAT I HEARD. THE RUSSKIES, THEY --

AH, DON'T YOU BELIEVE IT. IF OUR BOY VON BRAUN CAN'T EVEN GET HIS **JUPITER ROCKET** TO LAUNCH, HOW CAN THE RUSSKIES PUT UP A **SATELLITE**?

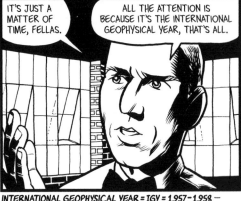

IT'S JUST A MATTER OF TIME, FELLAS.

ALL THE ATTENTION IS BECAUSE IT'S THE INTERNATIONAL GEOPHYSICAL YEAR, THAT'S ALL.

INTERNATIONAL GEOPHYSICAL YEAR = IGY = 1957-1958 —
A year when scientists around the world agreed to study the Earth, from pole to pole.

A MADE-UP THING -- HECK!

IT'S NOT EVEN A YEAR. IT'S A YEAR AND A HALF.

HA HA HA HA HA HA HA

IT'S TRUE -- *the IGY was eighteen months long. Those crazy scientists...*

WHAT DO YOU THINK, C.C.?

'BOUT WHAT -- ROCKETS? SATELLITES?

THIS IS WHAT I THINK: WHY DON'T WE PUT A **MAN** ON TOP O' ONE OF 'EM?

HA HA HA HA HA HA HA HA HA HA HA HA HA HA HA HA HA HA HA HA

HA HA HA HA

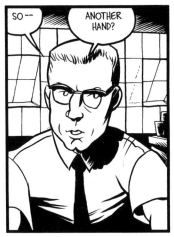

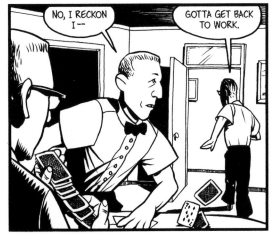

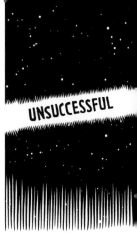

SO--
ANOTHER HAND?
NO, I RECKON I--
GOTTA GET BACK TO WORK.
I WAS THINKING THE SAME THING.
I MEAN...
...I WONDER HOW SMALL WE COULD MAKE A NOSE CONE AND STILL GET A MAN IN IT...
YOU KNOW, IF WE, UM...
SCRUNCHED HIM UP SOME?
T-MINUS 11 YEARS, 9 MONTHS
BAIKONUR COSMODROME

UNSUCCESSFUL

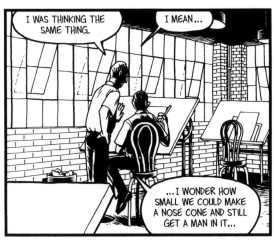

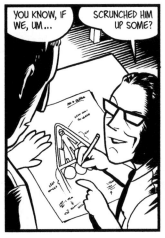

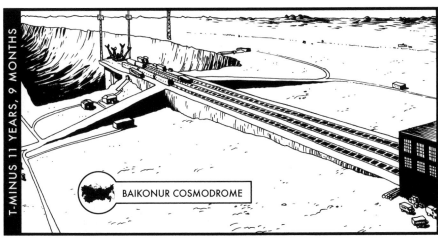

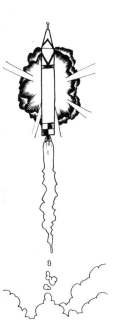

Jupiter AM-1B
April 26, 1957
T-Minus 12 Years
Flight duration:
93 seconds

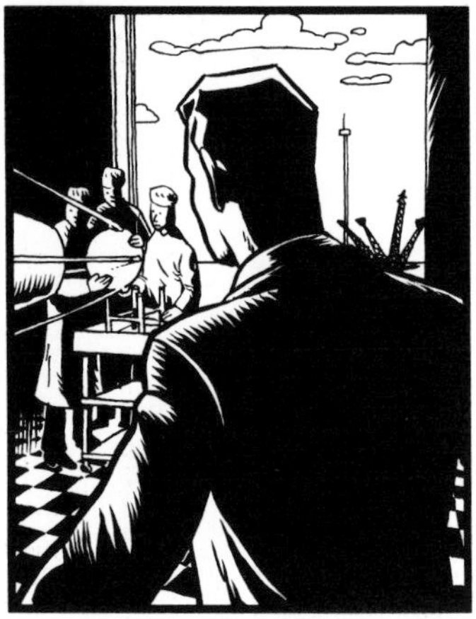

The real **SPUTNIK 1,** *not the model, weighed 184 lb.*

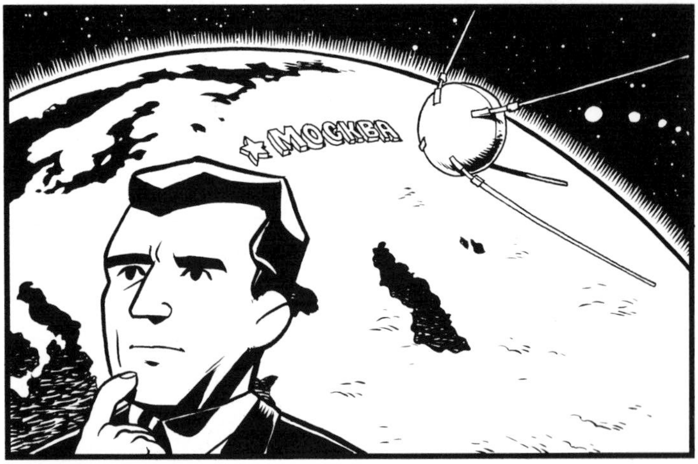
МОСКВА

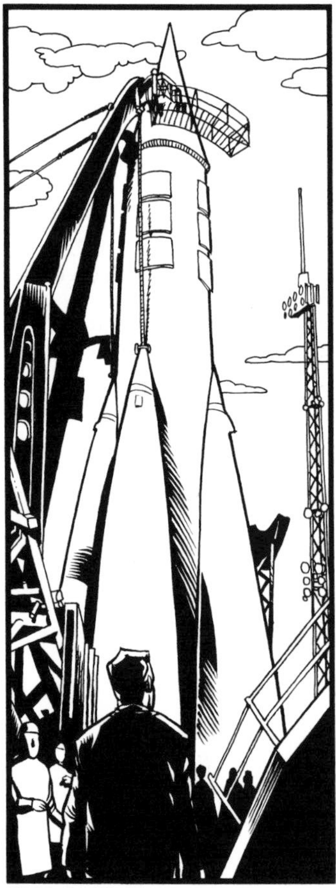

THE R-7 ROCKET:
An impressive 100 ft. tall and 280 tons -- but only one successful launch so far.

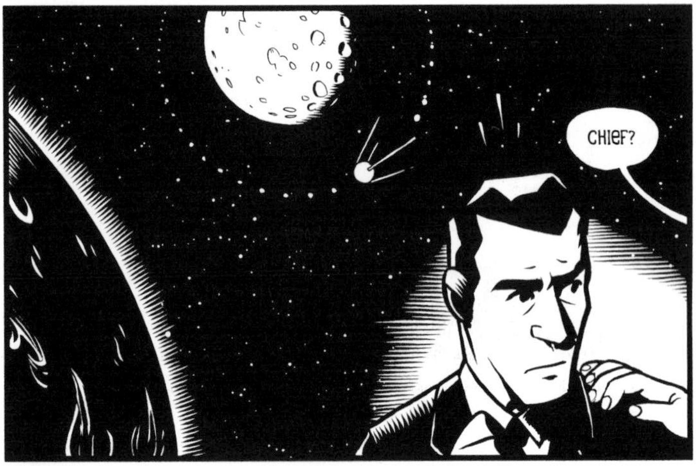
CHIEF?

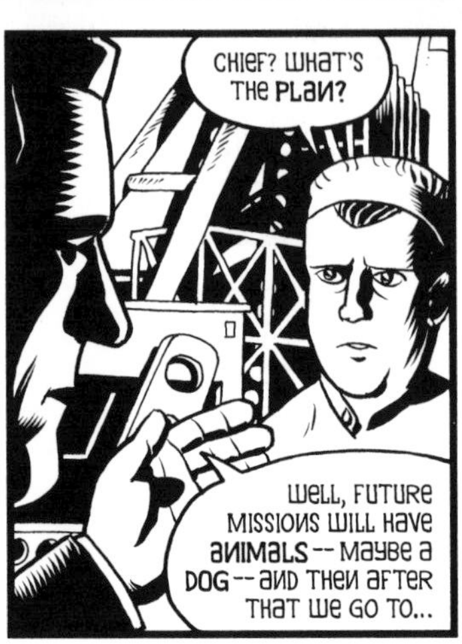
CHIEF? WHAT'S THE **PLAN?**
WELL, FUTURE MISSIONS WILL HAVE **ANIMALS** -- MAYBE A **DOG** -- AND THEN AFTER THAT WE GO TO...

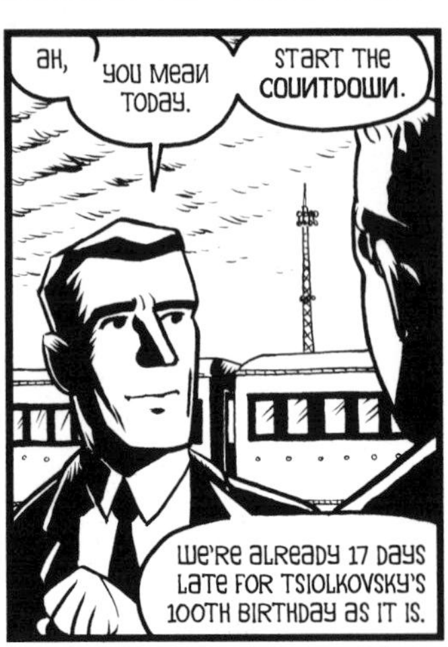
AH,
YOU MEAN TODAY.
START THE **COUNTDOWN.**
WE'RE ALREADY 17 DAYS LATE FOR TSIOLKOVSKY'S 100TH BIRTHDAY AS IT IS.

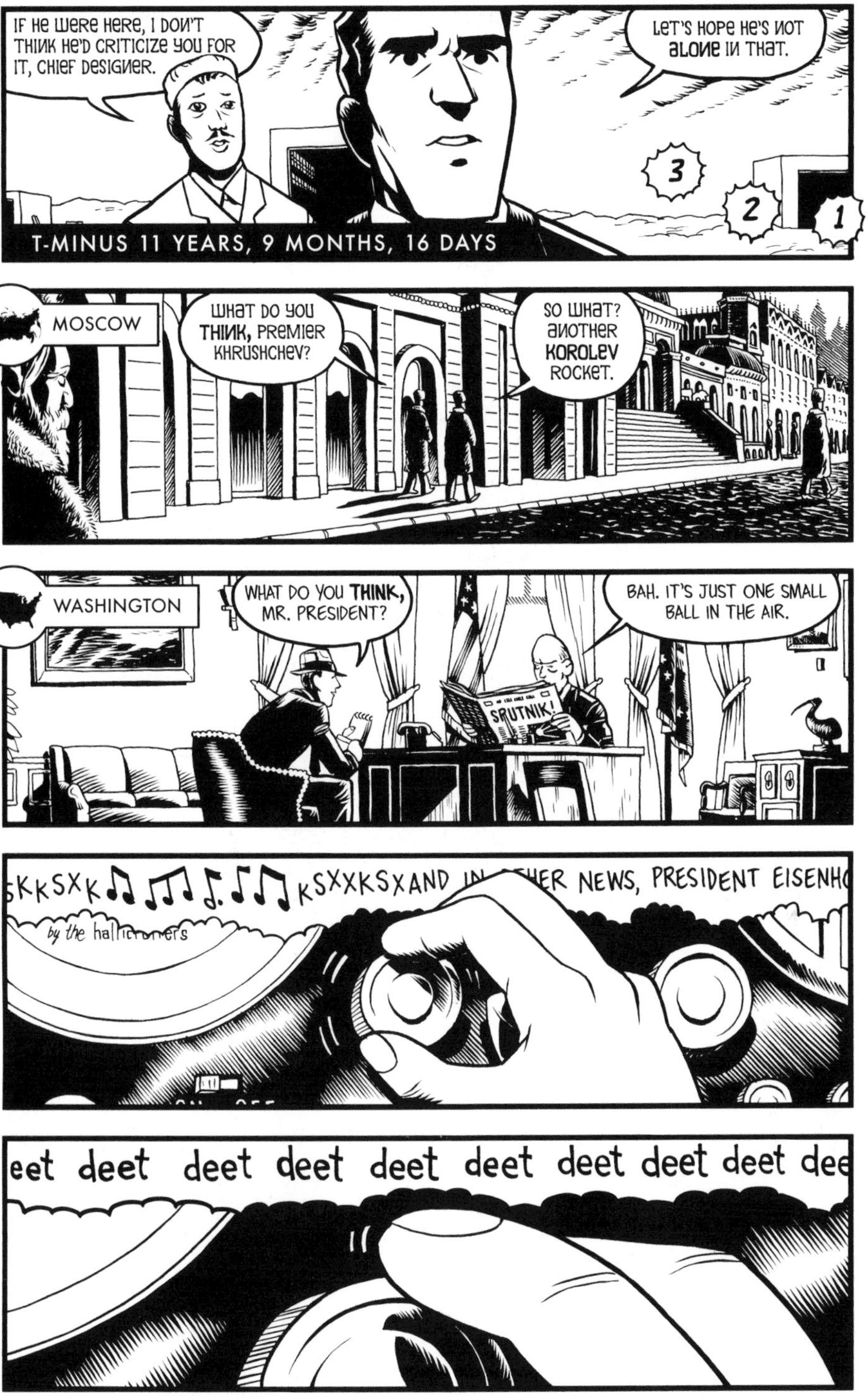
IF HE WERE HERE, I DON'T THINK HE'D CRITICIZE YOU FOR IT, CHIEF DESIGNER.
LET'S HOPE HE'S NOT **ALONE** IN THAT.
3
2
1
T-MINUS 11 YEARS, 9 MONTHS, 16 DAYS
MOSCOW
WHAT DO YOU **THINK,** PREMIER KHRUSHCHEV?
SO WHAT? ANOTHER **KOROLEV** ROCKET.
WASHINGTON
WHAT DO YOU **THINK,** MR. PRESIDENT?
BAH. IT'S JUST ONE SMALL BALL IN THE AIR.
SKKSXK KSXXKSXAND IN OTHER NEWS, PRESIDENT EISENH
by the hallicrafters
eet deet deet deet deet deet deet deet deet dee

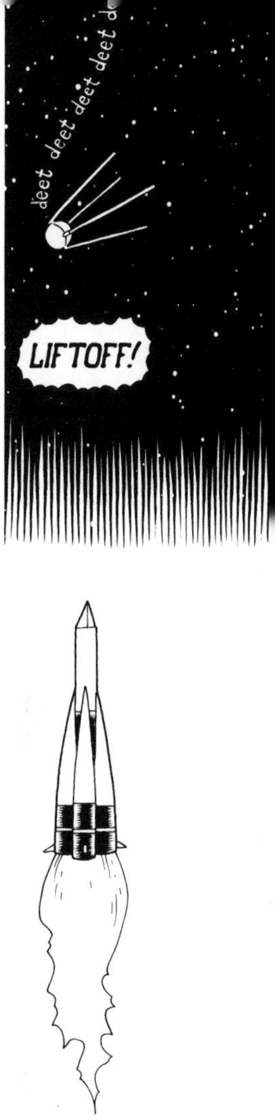
deet deet deet deet deet d
LIFTOFF!

R-7/Sputnik 1
October 4, 1957
T-Minus 11 Years,
9 months, 16 days
Flight duration:
3 months

deet deet deet deet deet deet deet deet
POLITICIANS ARE SAYING THEY CAN'T BELIEVE IT--
--TOOK 'EM BY **SURPRISE.**
THAT'S **CRAZY.**
deet deet deet deet deet deet deet
"THE RUSSKIES PUBLISHED THE **FREQUENCY** IN AMATEUR **RADIO** MAGAZINES...
deet deet deet
наука ящик
...SO **KIDS** COULD TUNE IN TO SPUTNIK'S **SIGNAL.**"
N A C A
deet deet deet deet deet deet
WELL, NOBODY'S HAVING ANY OF THAT KIND OF FUN OVER **HERE.**
deet deet
AND THE THING OF IT IS, WE COULDA DONE IT FIRST.
WELL, I'LL BE A...!

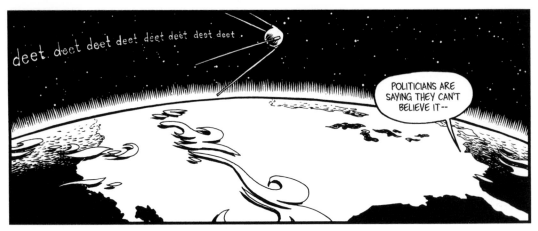

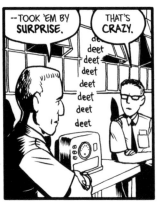

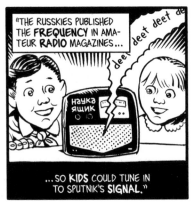

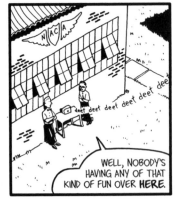

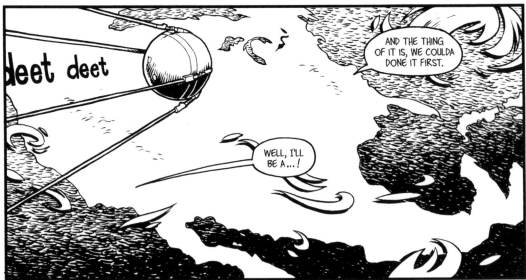

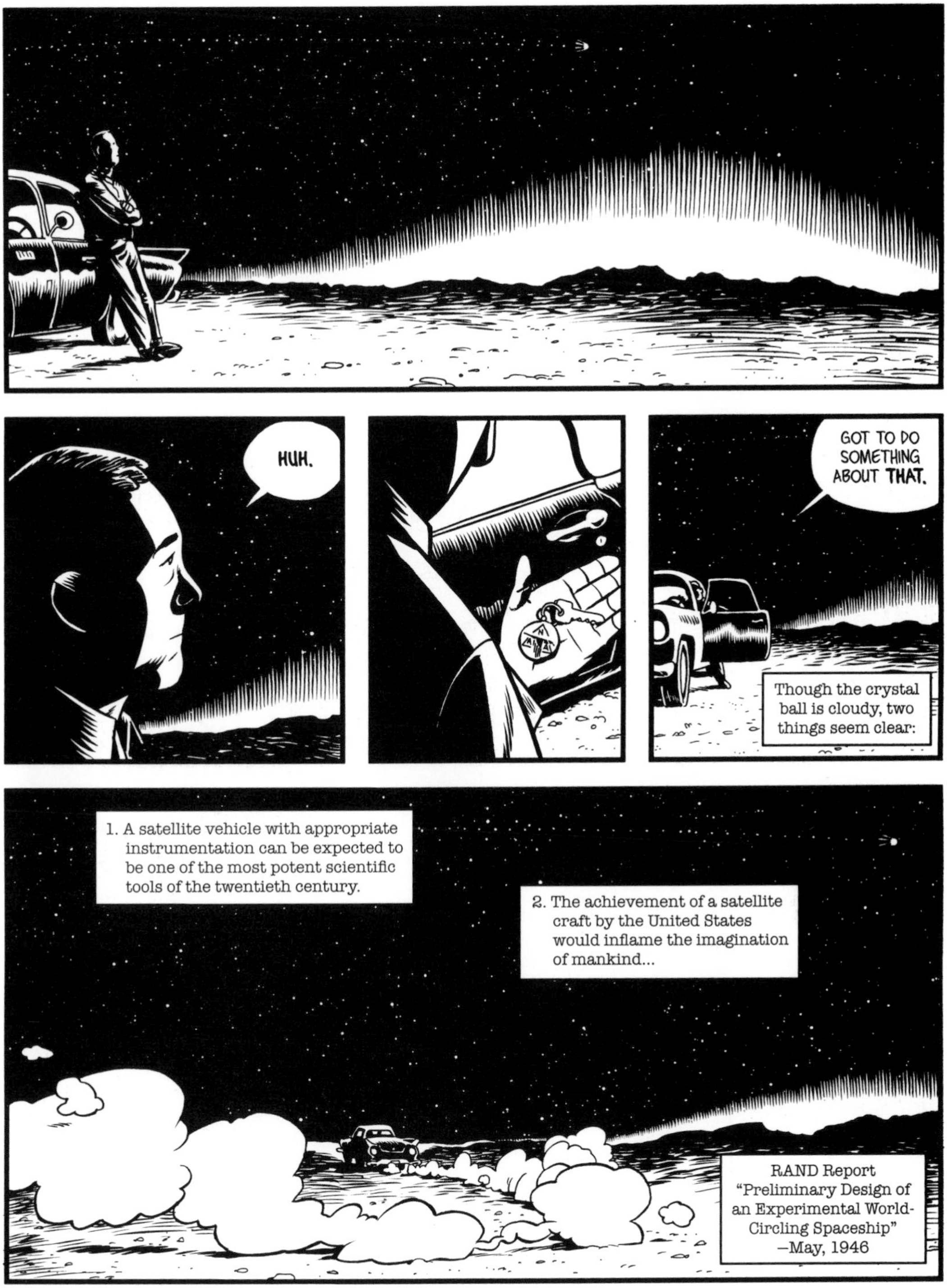
HUH.
GOT TO DO SOMETHING ABOUT THAT.
Though the crystal ball is cloudy, two things seem clear:
1. A satellite vehicle with appropriate instrumentation can be expected to be one of the most potent scientific tools of the twentieth century.
2. The achievement of a satellite craft by the United States would inflame the imagination of mankind...
RAND Report "Preliminary Design of an Experimental World-Circling Spaceship" —May, 1946

INFLAMED IMAGINATION

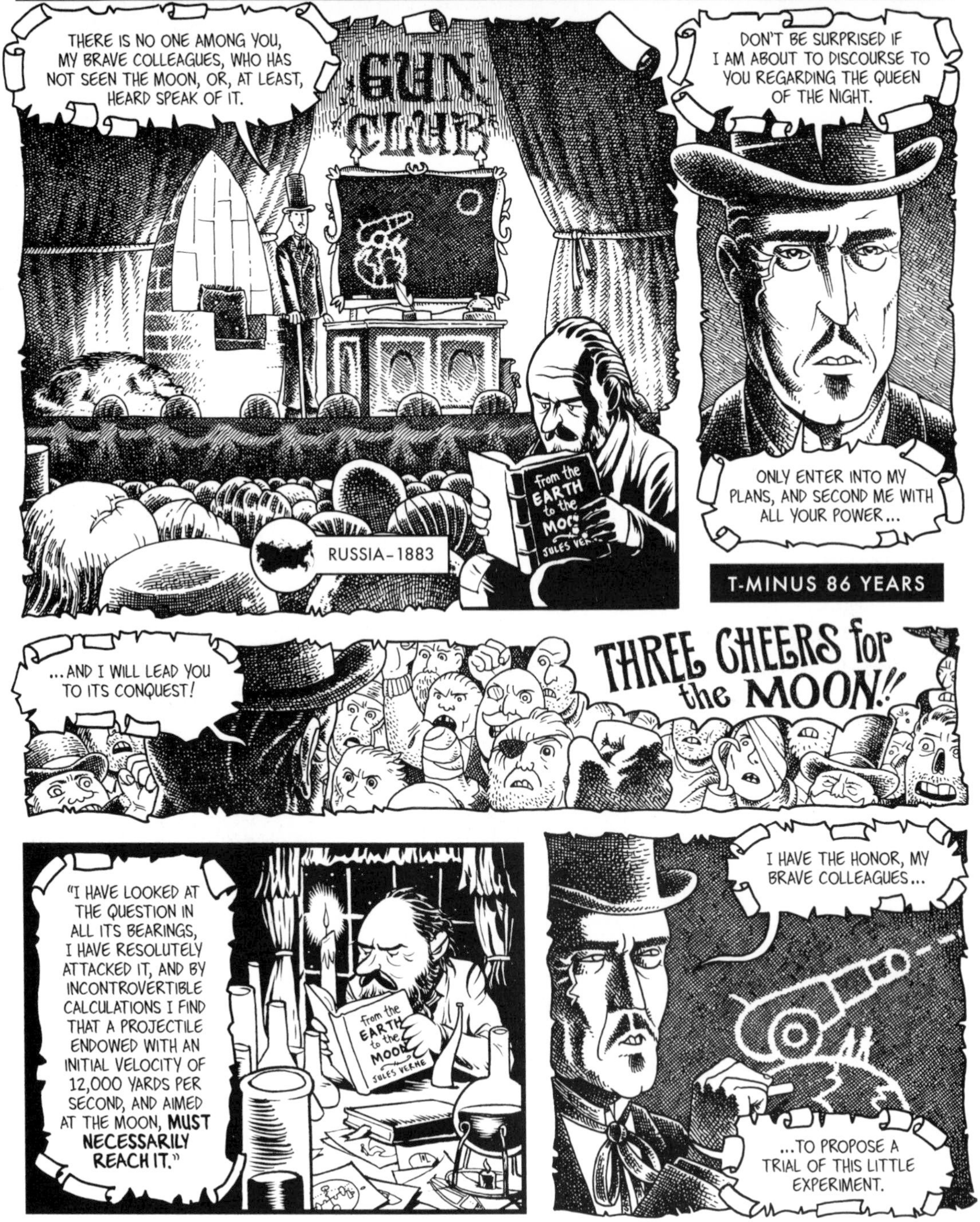
THERE IS NO ONE AMONG YOU, MY BRAVE COLLEAGUES, WHO HAS NOT SEEN THE MOON, OR, AT LEAST, HEARD SPEAK OF IT.
GUN CLUB
from the EARTH to the MOO JULES VER
RUSSIA–1883
DON'T BE SURPRISED IF I AM ABOUT TO DISCOURSE TO YOU REGARDING THE QUEEN OF THE NIGHT.
ONLY ENTER INTO MY PLANS, AND SECOND ME WITH ALL YOUR POWER...
T-MINUS 86 YEARS
...AND I WILL LEAD YOU TO ITS CONQUEST!
THREE CHEERS for the MOON!!
"I HAVE LOOKED AT THE QUESTION IN ALL ITS BEARINGS, I HAVE RESOLUTELY ATTACKED IT, AND BY INCONTROVERTIBLE CALCULATIONS I FIND THAT A PROJECTILE ENDOWED WITH AN INITIAL VELOCITY OF 12,000 YARDS PER SECOND, AND AIMED AT THE MOON, MUST NECESSARILY REACH IT."
from the EARTH to the MOON JULES VERNE
I HAVE THE HONOR, MY BRAVE COLLEAGUES...
...TO PROPOSE A TRIAL OF THIS LITTLE EXPERIMENT.

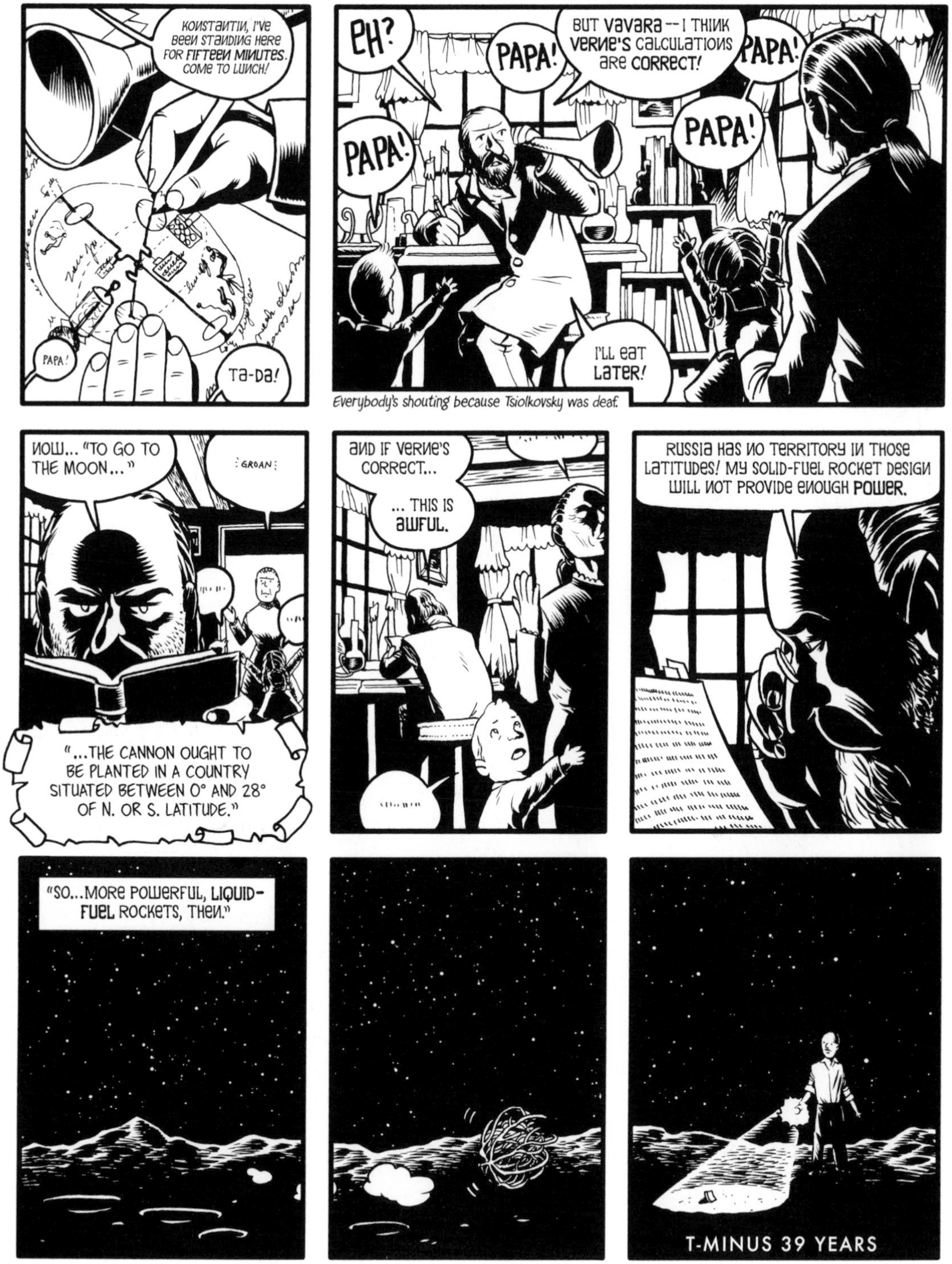
KONSTANTIN, I'VE BEEN STANDING HERE FOR FIFTEEN MINUTES. COME TO LUNCH!
PAPA!
TA-DA!
EH?
PAPA!
BUT VAVARA -- I THINK VERNE'S CALCULATIONS ARE CORRECT!
PAPA!
PAPA!
PAPA!
I'LL EAT LATER!
Everybody's shouting because Tsiolkovsky was deaf.
NOW... "TO GO TO THE MOON..."
GROAN
"...THE CANNON OUGHT TO BE PLANTED IN A COUNTRY SITUATED BETWEEN 0° AND 28° OF N. OR S. LATITUDE."
AND IF VERNE'S CORRECT...
... THIS IS AWFUL.
RUSSIA HAS NO TERRITORY IN THOSE LATITUDES! MY SOLID-FUEL ROCKET DESIGN WILL NOT PROVIDE ENOUGH POWER.
"SO...MORE POWERFUL, LIQUID-FUEL ROCKETS, THEN."
T-MINUS 39 YEARS

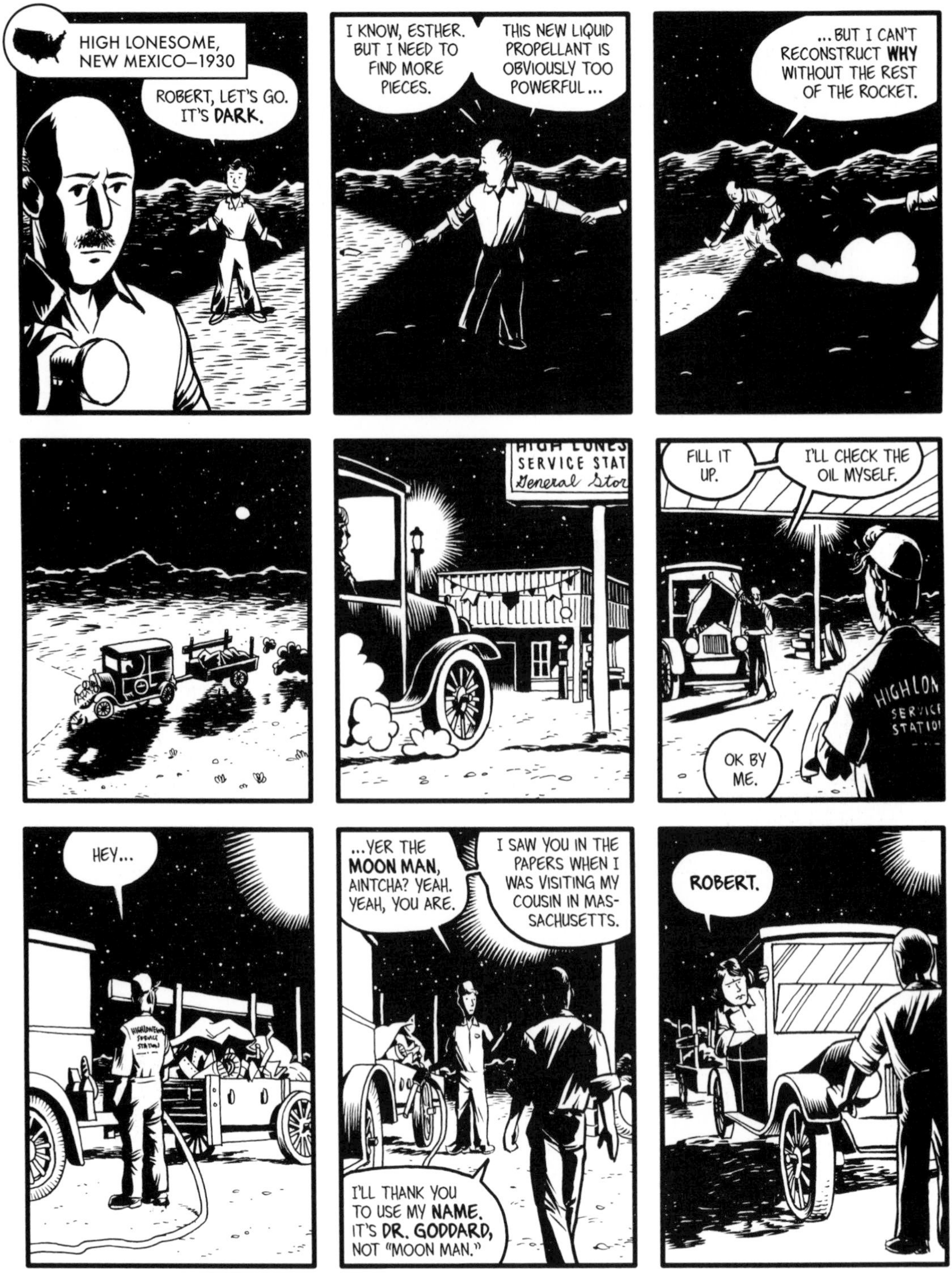
HIGH LONESOME, NEW MEXICO—1930
ROBERT, LET'S GO. IT'S **DARK**.
I KNOW, ESTHER. BUT I NEED TO FIND MORE PIECES.
THIS NEW LIQUID PROPELLANT IS OBVIOUSLY TOO POWERFUL...
...BUT I CAN'T RECONSTRUCT **WHY** WITHOUT THE REST OF THE ROCKET.
FILL IT UP.
I'LL CHECK THE OIL MYSELF.
OK BY ME.
HEY...
...YER THE **MOON MAN**, AINTCHA? YEAH. YEAH, YOU ARE.
I SAW YOU IN THE PAPERS WHEN I WAS VISITING MY COUSIN IN MASSACHUSETTS.
I'LL THANK YOU TO USE MY **NAME**. IT'S **DR. GODDARD**, NOT "MOON MAN."
ROBERT.

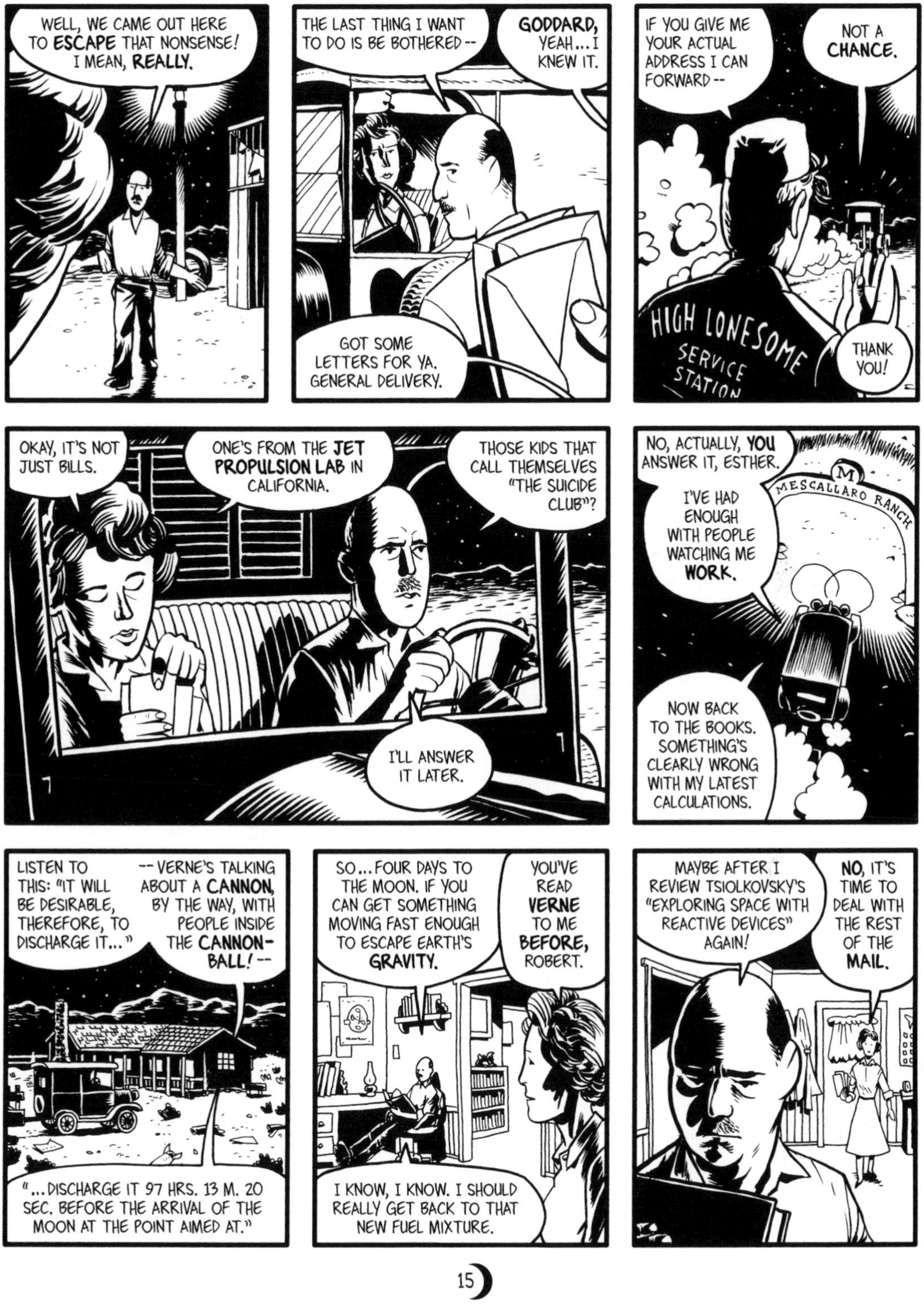
WELL, WE CAME OUT HERE TO **ESCAPE** THAT NONSENSE! I MEAN, **REALLY.**
THE LAST THING I WANT TO DO IS BE BOTHERED --
GODDARD, YEAH... I KNEW IT.
GOT SOME LETTERS FOR YA. GENERAL DELIVERY.
IF YOU GIVE ME YOUR ACTUAL ADDRESS I CAN FORWARD --
NOT A **CHANCE.**
HIGH LONESOME SERVICE STATION
THANK YOU!
OKAY, IT'S NOT JUST BILLS.
ONE'S FROM THE **JET PROPULSION LAB** IN CALIFORNIA.
THOSE KIDS THAT CALL THEMSELVES "THE SUICIDE CLUB"?
I'LL ANSWER IT LATER.
NO, ACTUALLY, **YOU** ANSWER IT, ESTHER.
MESCALLARO RANCH
I'VE HAD ENOUGH WITH PEOPLE WATCHING ME **WORK.**
NOW BACK TO THE BOOKS. SOMETHING'S CLEARLY WRONG WITH MY LATEST CALCULATIONS.
LISTEN TO THIS: "IT WILL BE DESIRABLE, THEREFORE, TO DISCHARGE IT..."
-- VERNE'S TALKING ABOUT A **CANNON,** BY THE WAY, WITH PEOPLE INSIDE THE **CANNON-BALL!** --
"...DISCHARGE IT 97 HRS. 13 M. 20 SEC. BEFORE THE ARRIVAL OF THE MOON AT THE POINT AIMED AT."
SO... FOUR DAYS TO THE MOON. IF YOU CAN GET SOMETHING MOVING FAST ENOUGH TO ESCAPE EARTH'S **GRAVITY.**
YOU'VE READ **VERNE** TO ME **BEFORE,** ROBERT.
I KNOW, I KNOW. I SHOULD REALLY GET BACK TO THAT NEW FUEL MIXTURE.
MAYBE AFTER I REVIEW TSIOLKOVSKY'S "EXPLORING SPACE WITH REACTIVE DEVICES" AGAIN!
NO, IT'S TIME TO DEAL WITH THE REST OF THE **MAIL.**

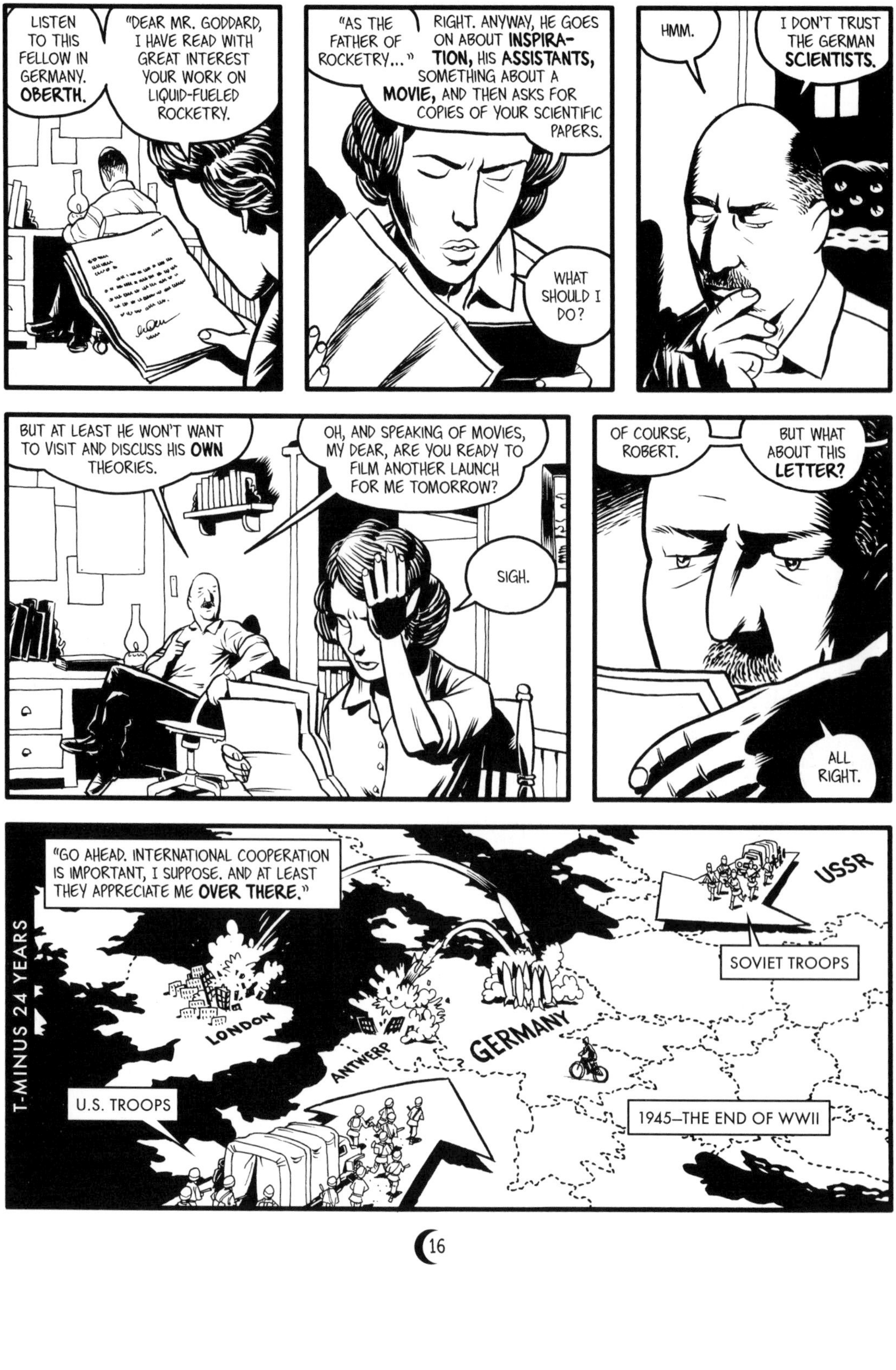
LISTEN TO THIS FELLOW IN GERMANY. OBERTH.
"DEAR MR. GODDARD, I HAVE READ WITH GREAT INTEREST YOUR WORK ON LIQUID-FUELED ROCKETRY.
"AS THE FATHER OF ROCKETRY..."
RIGHT. ANYWAY, HE GOES ON ABOUT INSPIRATION, HIS ASSISTANTS, SOMETHING ABOUT A MOVIE, AND THEN ASKS FOR COPIES OF YOUR SCIENTIFIC PAPERS.
WHAT SHOULD I DO?
HMM.
I DON'T TRUST THE GERMAN SCIENTISTS.
BUT AT LEAST HE WON'T WANT TO VISIT AND DISCUSS HIS OWN THEORIES.
OH, AND SPEAKING OF MOVIES, MY DEAR, ARE YOU READY TO FILM ANOTHER LAUNCH FOR ME TOMORROW?
SIGH.
OF COURSE, ROBERT.
BUT WHAT ABOUT THIS LETTER?
ALL RIGHT.
T-MINUS 24 YEARS
"GO AHEAD. INTERNATIONAL COOPERATION IS IMPORTANT, I SUPPOSE. AND AT LEAST THEY APPRECIATE ME OVER THERE."
USSR
SOVIET TROOPS
LONDON
ANTWERP
GERMANY
U.S. TROOPS
1945—THE END OF WWII

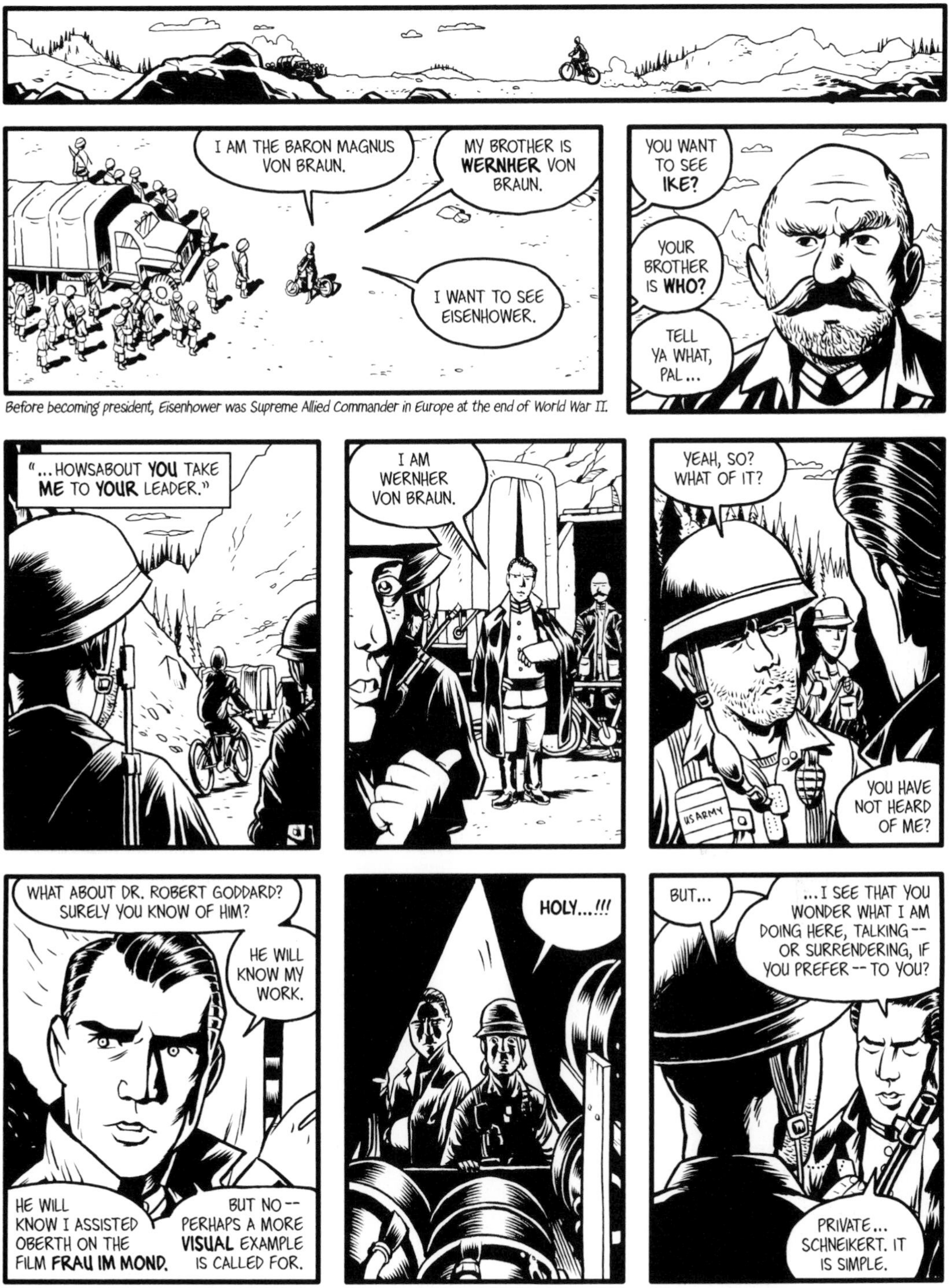
I AM THE BARON MAGNUS VON BRAUN.
MY BROTHER IS **WERNHER** VON BRAUN.
I WANT TO SEE EISENHOWER.
YOU WANT TO SEE **IKE?**
YOUR BROTHER IS **WHO?**
TELL YA WHAT, PAL...
"...HOWSABOUT **YOU** TAKE **ME** TO **YOUR** LEADER."
I AM WERNHER VON BRAUN.
YEAH, SO? WHAT OF IT?
US ARMY
YOU HAVE NOT HEARD OF ME?
WHAT ABOUT DR. ROBERT GODDARD? SURELY YOU KNOW OF HIM?
HE WILL KNOW MY WORK.
HE WILL KNOW I ASSISTED OBERTH ON THE FILM **FRAU IM MOND.**
BUT NO -- PERHAPS A MORE **VISUAL** EXAMPLE IS CALLED FOR.
HOLY...!!!
BUT...
...I SEE THAT YOU WONDER WHAT I AM DOING HERE, TALKING -- OR SURRENDERING, IF YOU PREFER -- TO YOU?
PRIVATE... SCHNEIKERT. IT IS SIMPLE.

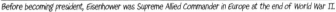

Before becoming president, Eisenhower was Supreme Allied Commander in Europe at the end of World War II.

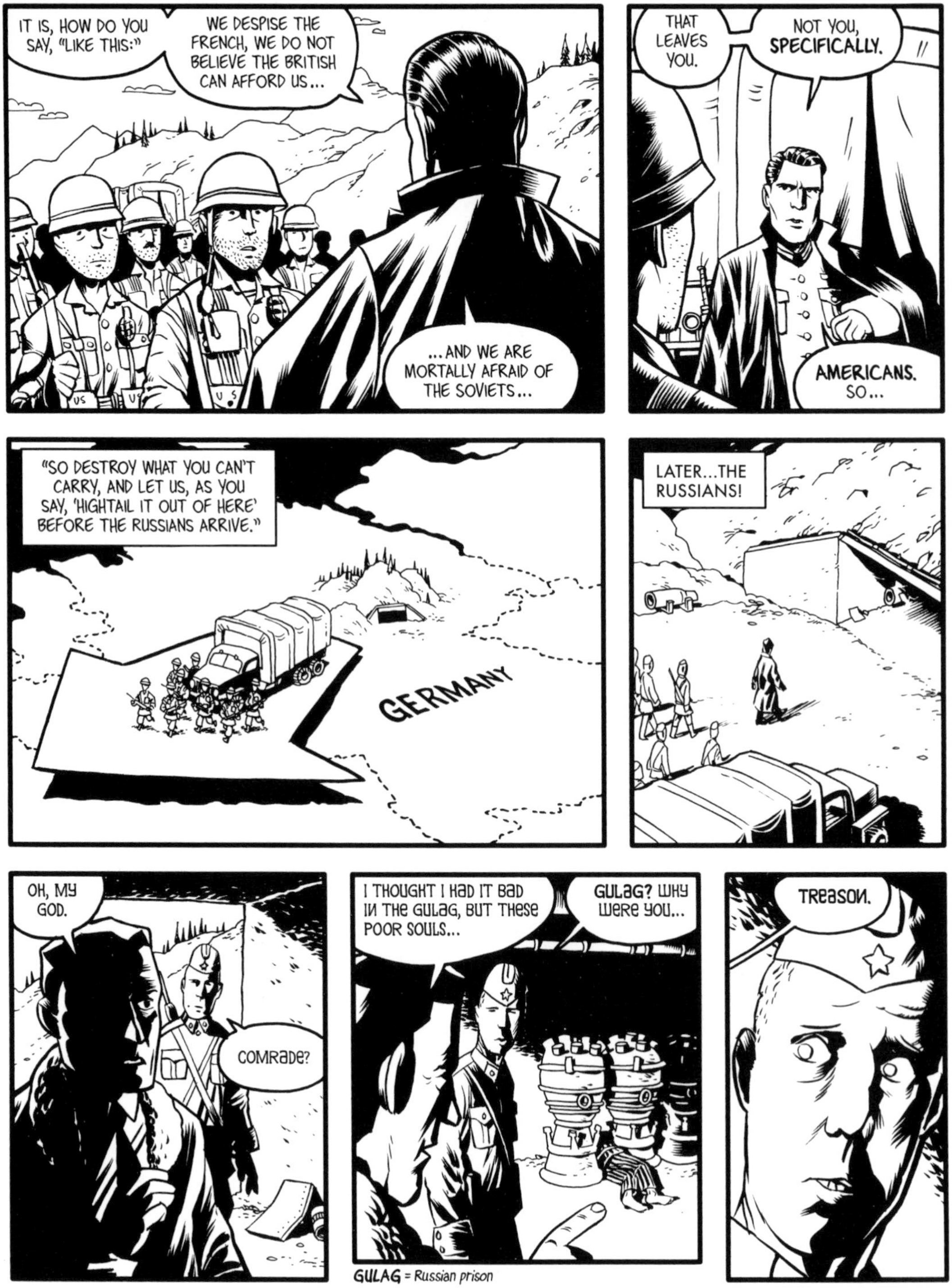
IT IS, HOW DO YOU SAY, "LIKE THIS:"
WE DESPISE THE FRENCH, WE DO NOT BELIEVE THE BRITISH CAN AFFORD US...
...AND WE ARE MORTALLY AFRAID OF THE SOVIETS...
THAT LEAVES YOU.
NOT YOU, **SPECIFICALLY.**
AMERICANS. SO...
"SO DESTROY WHAT YOU CAN'T CARRY, AND LET US, AS YOU SAY, 'HIGHTAIL IT OUT OF HERE' BEFORE THE RUSSIANS ARRIVE."
GERMANY
LATER...THE RUSSIANS!
OH, MY GOD.
COMRADE?
I THOUGHT I HAD IT BAD IN THE GULAG, BUT THESE POOR SOULS...
GULAG? WHY WERE YOU...
TREASON.
GULAG = *Russian prison*

RELAX, SOLDIER.

I SIMPLY ADVOCATED LIQUID-FUEL ROCKETS WHEN MY BOSSES WANTED SOLID-FUEL ROCKETS.

THEY FINALLY LET ME OUT TO DESIGN NEW WEAPONS FOR THEM.

AND THEY SEND ME TO THIS FORSAKEN PLACE TO PICK THROUGH NAZI GARBAGE FOR ROCKET SCRAPS.

COMRADE?

The Chief Designer's looking at the A4-Fibel, the V-2 rocket launch manual for German soldiers. It had cartoons on most pages.

I'VE SEEN ENOUGH.

PACK THIS UP AND GET IT OUT OF HERE BEFORE THE AMERICANS RETURN TO DESTROY THE REST.

THEY HAVE VON BRAUN, THOUGH...

...SO THEY MAY NOT BOTHER.

T-MINUS 12 YEARS

LANGLEY, VIRGINIA – SATURDAY AFTERNOON

MANY YEARS LATER...

HEY! HEY!

WOULD YOU GUYS STOP FOOLING AROUND?

WE'RE JUST ABOUT READY TO EAT...

...HERE.

...

THAT'S IT!

BE RIGHT BACK.

ER...MAYBE NOT.

MAX?

DON'T WAIT UP. SORRY!

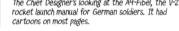

NACA

SO, WHADDAYA HAVE THAT'S SO IMPORTANT THAT YOU COULDN'T WAIT UNTIL MONDAY?

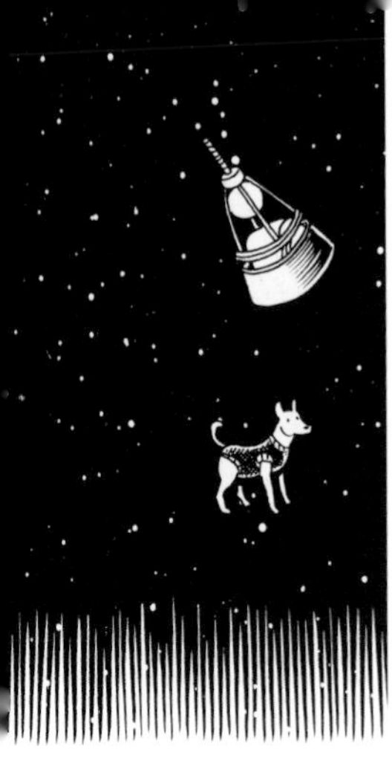

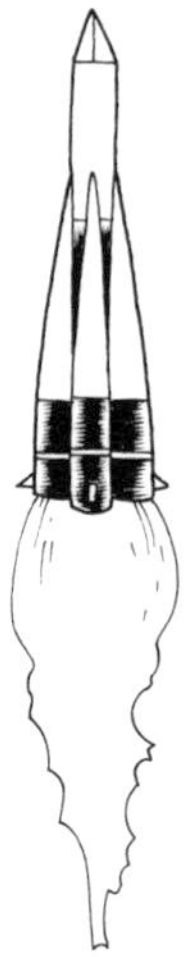

R-7/Sputnik 2
November 3, 1957
T-Minus 12 Years
Flight duration:
162 days
Laika orbits
the Earth

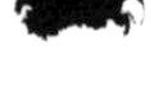

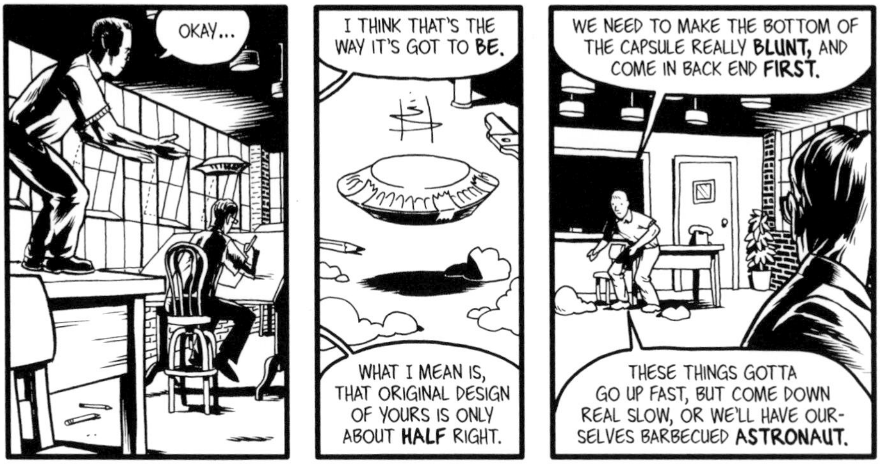
OKAY...
I THINK THAT'S THE WAY IT'S GOT TO **BE.**
WHAT I MEAN IS, THAT ORIGINAL DESIGN OF YOURS IS ONLY ABOUT **HALF** RIGHT.
WE NEED TO MAKE THE BOTTOM OF THE CAPSULE REALLY **BLUNT,** AND COME IN BACK END **FIRST.**
THESE THINGS GOTTA GO UP FAST, BUT COME DOWN REAL SLOW, OR WE'LL HAVE OURSELVES BARBECUED **ASTRONAUT.**

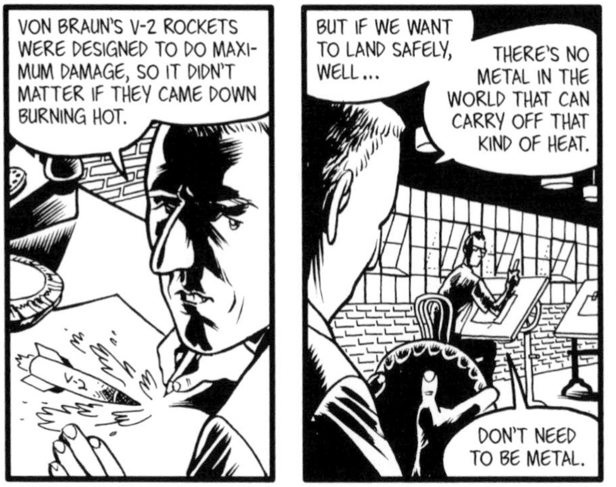
VON BRAUN'S V-2 ROCKETS WERE DESIGNED TO DO MAXIMUM DAMAGE, SO IT DIDN'T MATTER IF THEY CAME DOWN BURNING HOT.
V-2
BUT IF WE WANT TO LAND SAFELY, WELL...
THERE'S NO METAL IN THE WORLD THAT CAN CARRY OFF THAT KIND OF HEAT.
DON'T NEED TO BE METAL.

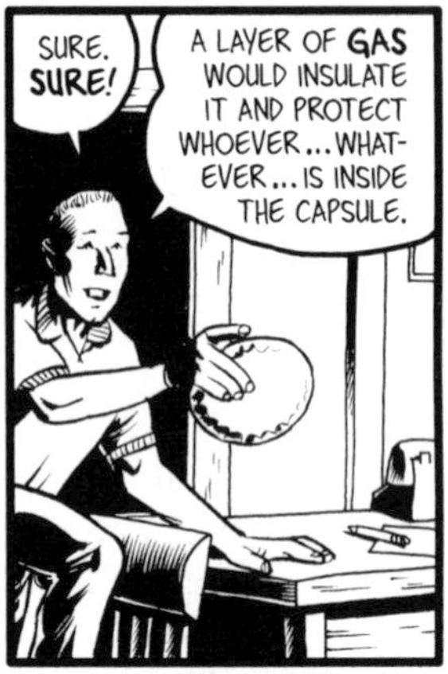
SURE. **SURE!**
A LAYER OF **GAS** WOULD INSULATE IT AND PROTECT WHOEVER... WHATEVER... IS INSIDE THE CAPSULE.

*Max is right: a **LAYER OF GAS** would absorb almost **90%** of the heat!*

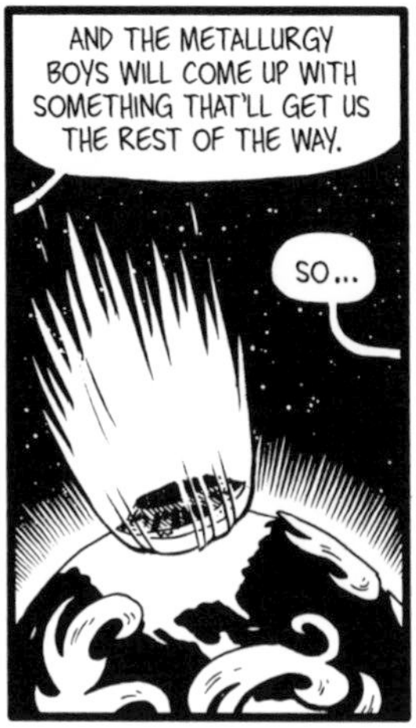
AND THE METALLURGY BOYS WILL COME UP WITH SOMETHING THAT'LL GET US THE REST OF THE WAY.
SO...

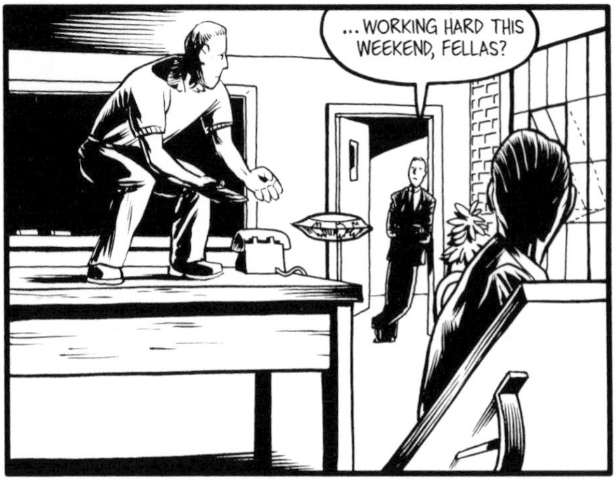
...WORKING HARD THIS WEEKEND, FELLAS?

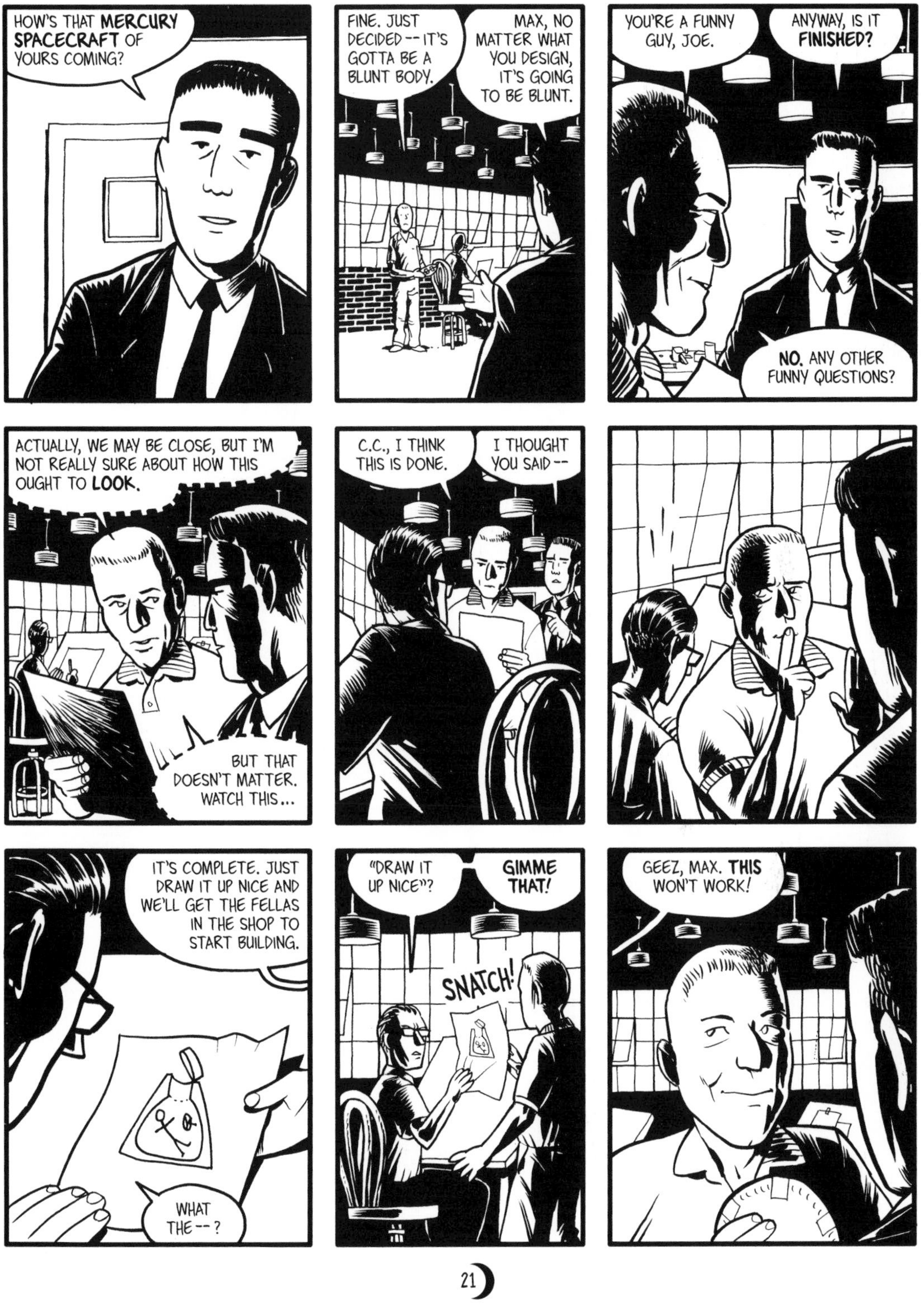
HOW'S THAT **MERCURY SPACECRAFT** OF YOURS COMING?
FINE. JUST DECIDED -- IT'S GOTTA BE A BLUNT BODY.
MAX, NO MATTER WHAT YOU DESIGN, IT'S GOING TO BE BLUNT.
YOU'RE A FUNNY GUY, JOE.
ANYWAY, IS IT **FINISHED?**
NO. ANY OTHER FUNNY QUESTIONS?
ACTUALLY, WE MAY BE CLOSE, BUT I'M NOT REALLY SURE ABOUT HOW THIS OUGHT TO **LOOK.**
BUT THAT DOESN'T MATTER. WATCH THIS...
C.C., I THINK THIS IS DONE.
I THOUGHT YOU SAID--
IT'S COMPLETE. JUST DRAW IT UP NICE AND WE'LL GET THE FELLAS IN THE SHOP TO START BUILDING.
WHAT THE--?
"DRAW IT UP NICE"?
GIMME THAT!
SNATCH!
GEEZ, MAX. **THIS** WON'T WORK!

AND WHAT WERE YOU THINKING **HERE?**

I CAN'T BELIEVE YOU DIDN'T ALLOW FOR...

THAT'S THE WAY YOU DO IT. PUT IN SOME SUPER-FLUOUS DETAILS...

...TELL C.C. IT'S DONE...

AND YOU'RE GUARANTEED IT **WILL** BE DONE...

...WHEN **HE'S** FINISHED WITH IT!

AND BY THE WAY, MERCURY IS GOING TO BE MORE LIKE AN **ESCAPE** CAPSULE THAN ANYTHING ELSE.

WON'T BE A **SPACECRAFT** UNTIL THE ASTRONAUT CAN STEER IT.

OKAY, SO...

MOST OF WHAT HAPPENS UP THERE WILL HAVE TO BE DIRECTED FROM A CONTROL ROOM.

ANY IDEA HOW **THAT'S** GOING TO LOOK?

PRETTY MUCH LIKE MY SECRETARY'S DESK OVER THERE. MAYBE ANOTHER PHONE OR TWO... AND A TELEPRINTER.

TELEPRINTER = like email, only with gears and a typewriter-like printer (no screen). No graphics, but lots of sound.

  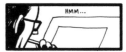

HMM...

A FEW **PHONES?**

YOU'RE **NUTS.**

MAYBE THAT'S OKAY FOR A SIMPLE UP-AND-DOWN FLIGHT.

BUT...

...IF WE PUT SOMEBODY IN **ORBIT...**

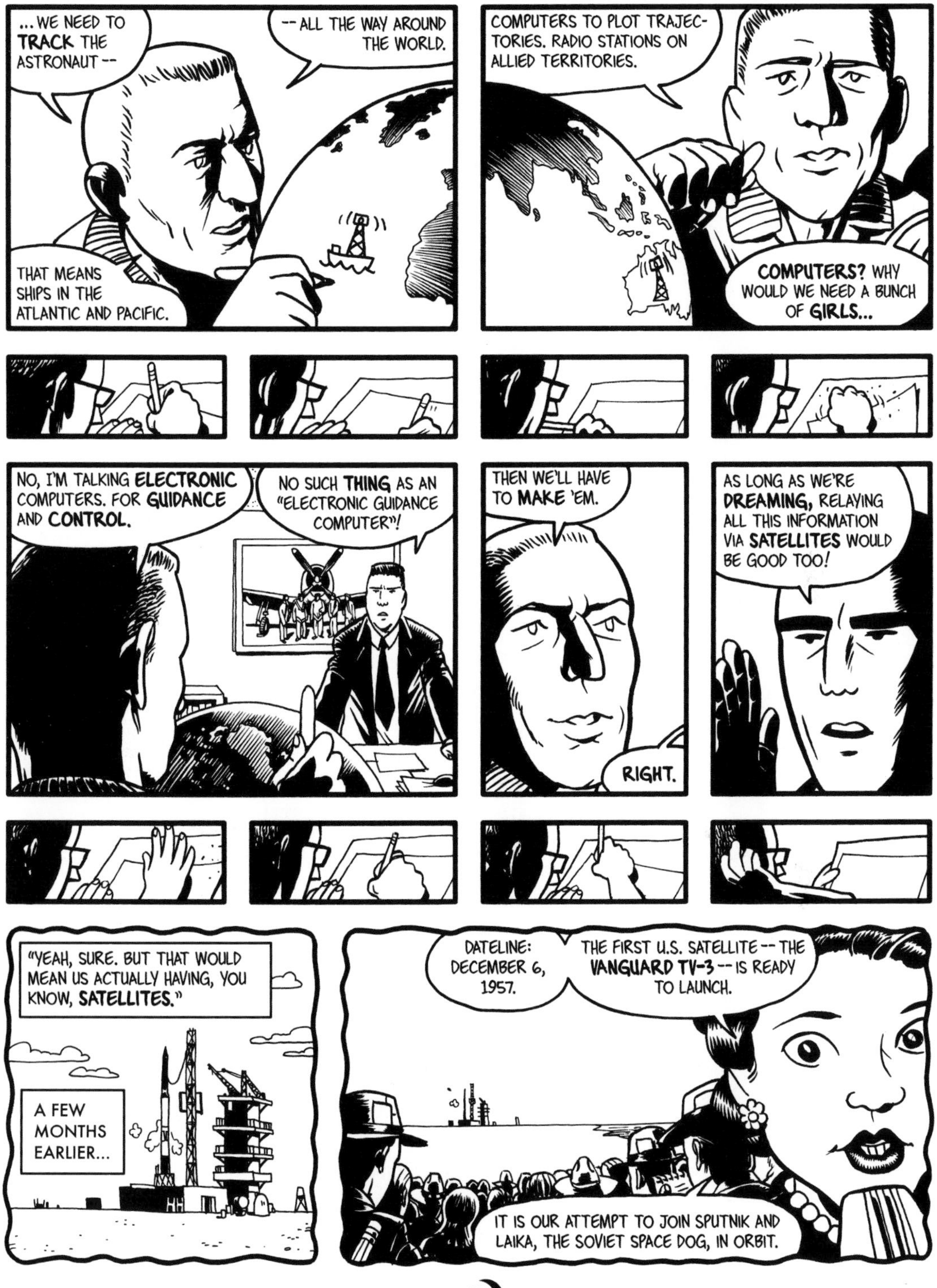

...WE NEED TO TRACK THE ASTRONAUT--
--ALL THE WAY AROUND THE WORLD.
THAT MEANS SHIPS IN THE ATLANTIC AND PACIFIC.
COMPUTERS TO PLOT TRAJECTORIES. RADIO STATIONS ON ALLIED TERRITORIES.
COMPUTERS? WHY WOULD WE NEED A BUNCH OF GIRLS...
NO, I'M TALKING ELECTRONIC COMPUTERS. FOR GUIDANCE AND CONTROL.
NO SUCH THING AS AN "ELECTRONIC GUIDANCE COMPUTER"!
THEN WE'LL HAVE TO MAKE 'EM.
RIGHT.
AS LONG AS WE'RE DREAMING, RELAYING ALL THIS INFORMATION VIA SATELLITES WOULD BE GOOD TOO!
"YEAH, SURE. BUT THAT WOULD MEAN US ACTUALLY HAVING, YOU KNOW, SATELLITES."
A FEW MONTHS EARLIER...
DATELINE: DECEMBER 6, 1957.
THE FIRST U.S. SATELLITE -- THE VANGUARD TV-3 -- IS READY TO LAUNCH.
IT IS OUR ATTEMPT TO JOIN SPUTNIK AND LAIKA, THE SOVIET SPACE DOG, IN ORBIT.

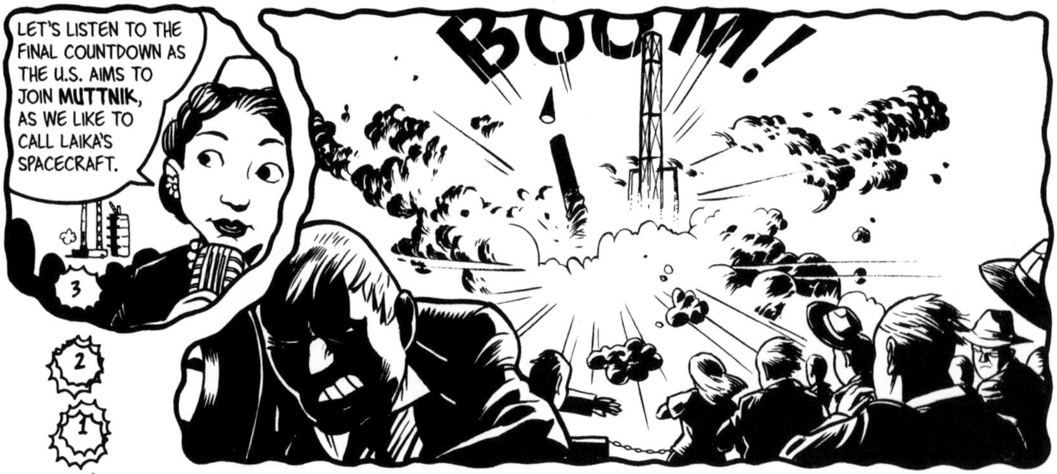
LET'S LISTEN TO THE FINAL COUNTDOWN AS THE U.S. AIMS TO JOIN **MUTTNIK**, AS WE LIKE TO CALL LAIKA'S SPACECRAFT.
3
BOOM!
2
1

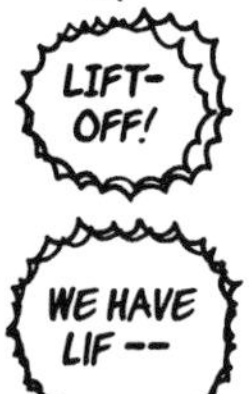
LIFT-OFF!
WE HAVE LIF --

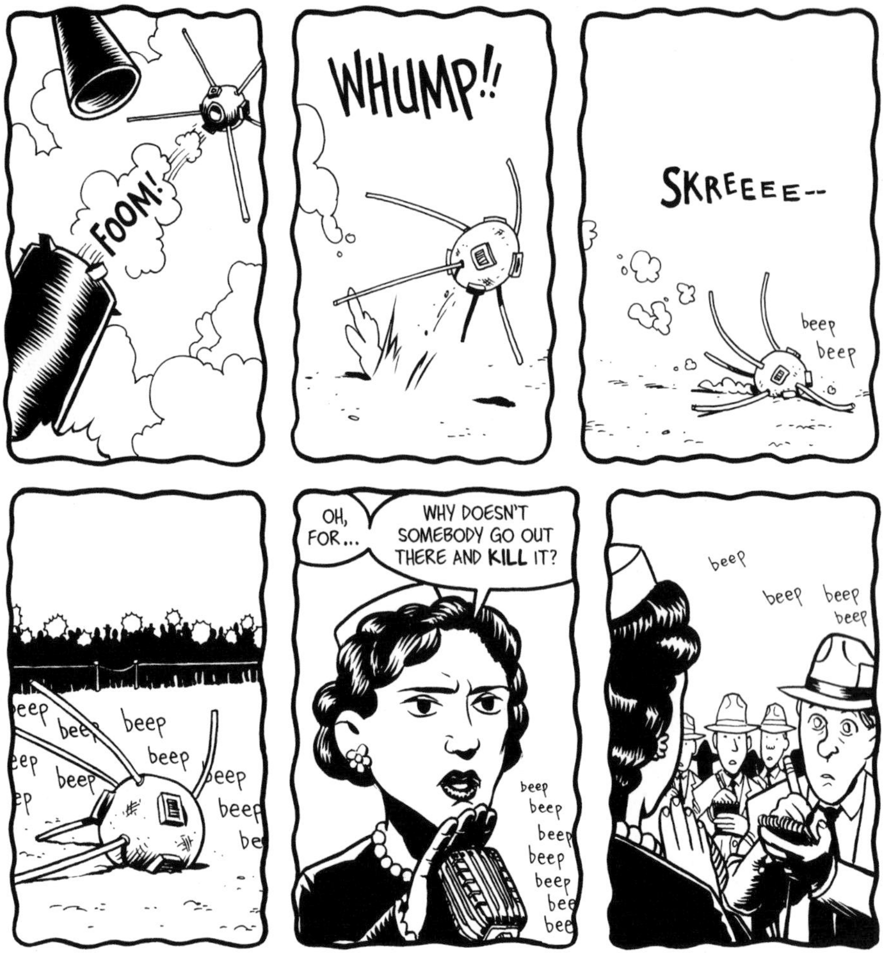
FOOM!
WHUMP!!
SKREEEE--
beep
beep
beep
beep
beep
beep
beep
beep
OH, FOR...
WHY DOESN'T SOMEBODY GO OUT THERE AND **KILL** IT?
beep
beep
beep
beep
beep
beep
beep
beep
beep

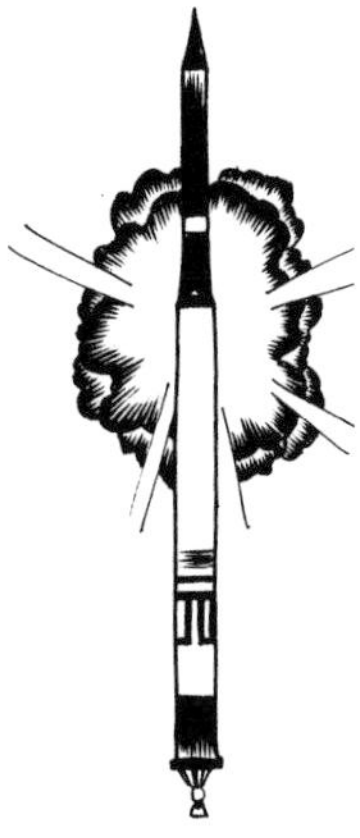

Vanguard TV3
December 6, 1957
T-Minus 12 Years
Flight Duration:
2 seconds

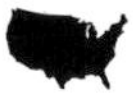

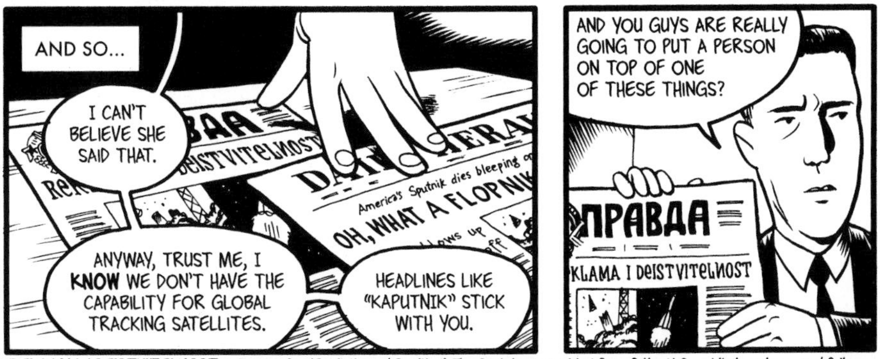
AND SO...
I CAN'T BELIEVE SHE SAID THAT.
America's Sputnik dies bleeping on
OH, WHAT A FLOPNIK
ANYWAY, TRUST ME, I **KNOW** WE DON'T HAVE THE CAPABILITY FOR GLOBAL TRACKING SATELLITES.
HEADLINES LIKE "KAPUTNIK" STICK WITH YOU.
AND YOU GUYS ARE REALLY GOING TO PUT A PERSON ON TOP OF ONE OF THESE THINGS?
ПРАВДА
REKLAMA I DEISTVITELNOST

REKLAMA I DEISTVITELNOST = *Russian for "Publicity and Reality." The Soviets are making fun of the U.S. public launches...and failures.*

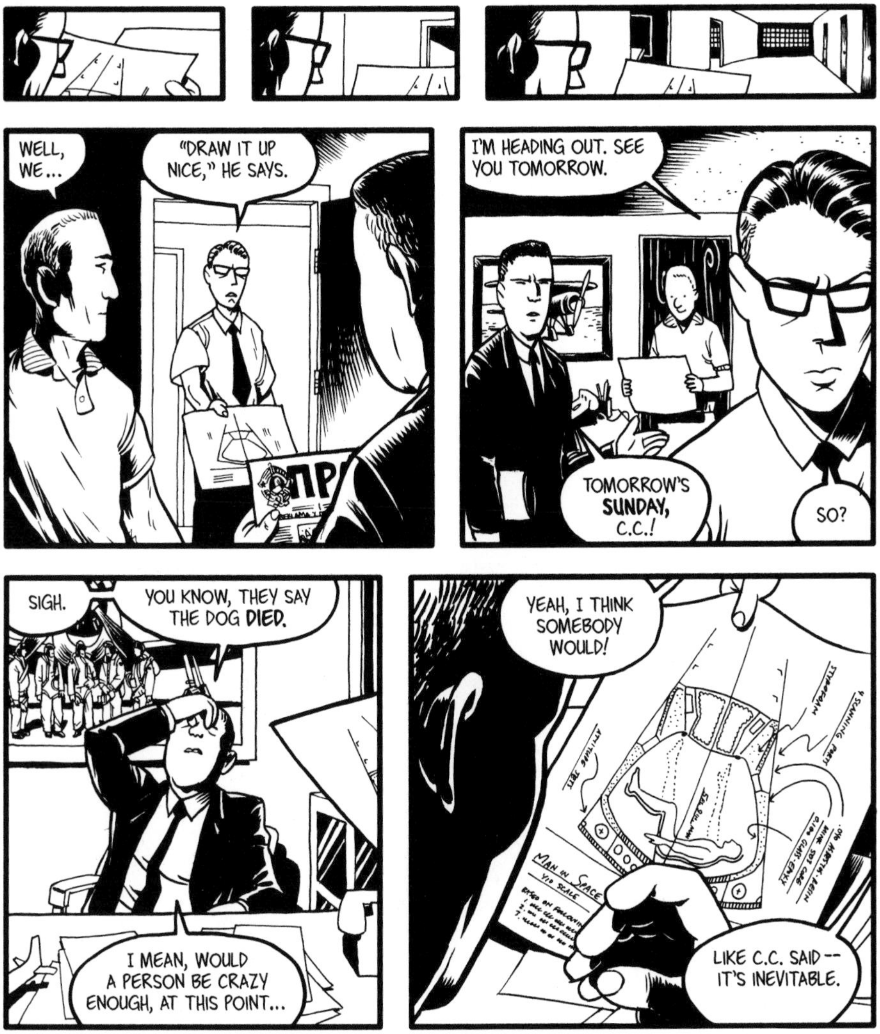
WELL, WE...
"DRAW IT UP NICE," HE SAYS.
I'M HEADING OUT. SEE YOU TOMORROW.
TOMORROW'S **SUNDAY,** C.C.!
SO?
SIGH.
YOU KNOW, THEY SAY THE DOG **DIED.**
I MEAN, WOULD A PERSON BE CRAZY ENOUGH, AT THIS POINT...
YEAH, I THINK SOMEBODY WOULD!
MAN IN SPACE
LIKE C.C. SAID -- IT'S INEVITABLE.

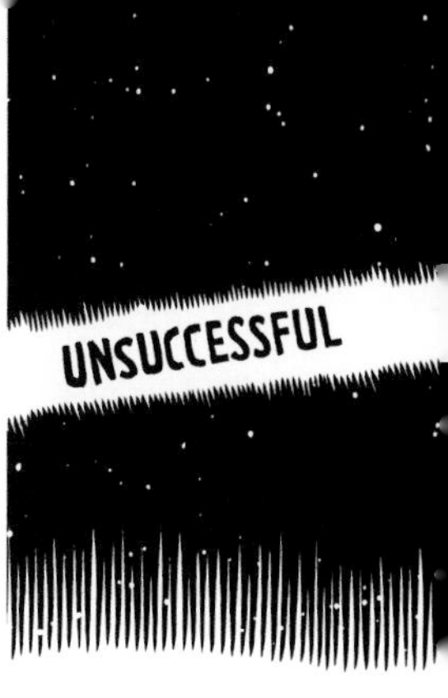
UNSUCCESSFUL

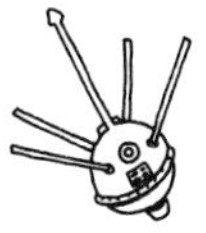

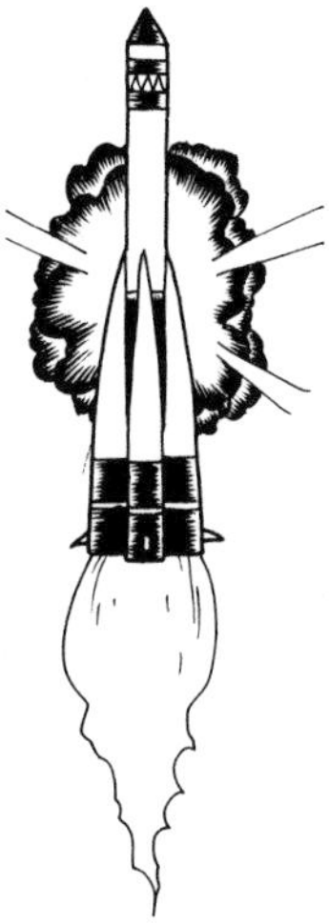

E-1 Luna Probe,
1st Attempt: 1958
T-Minus 11 Years
Flight Duration:
93 Seconds

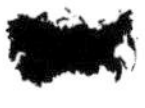

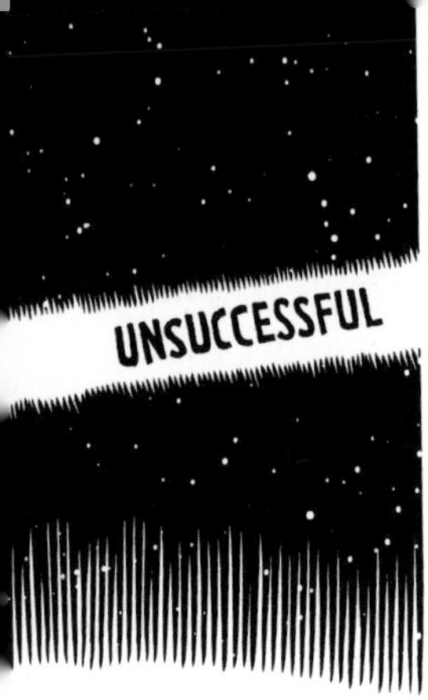
UNSUCCESSFUL

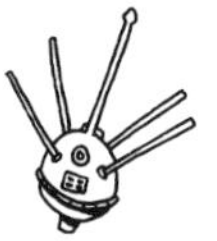

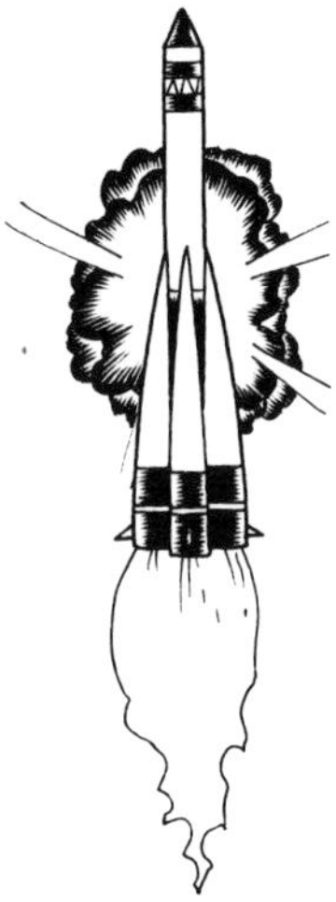

E-1 Luna Probe,
2nd Attempt: 1958
T-Minus 11 Years
Flight Duration:
104 Seconds

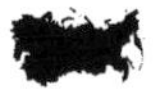

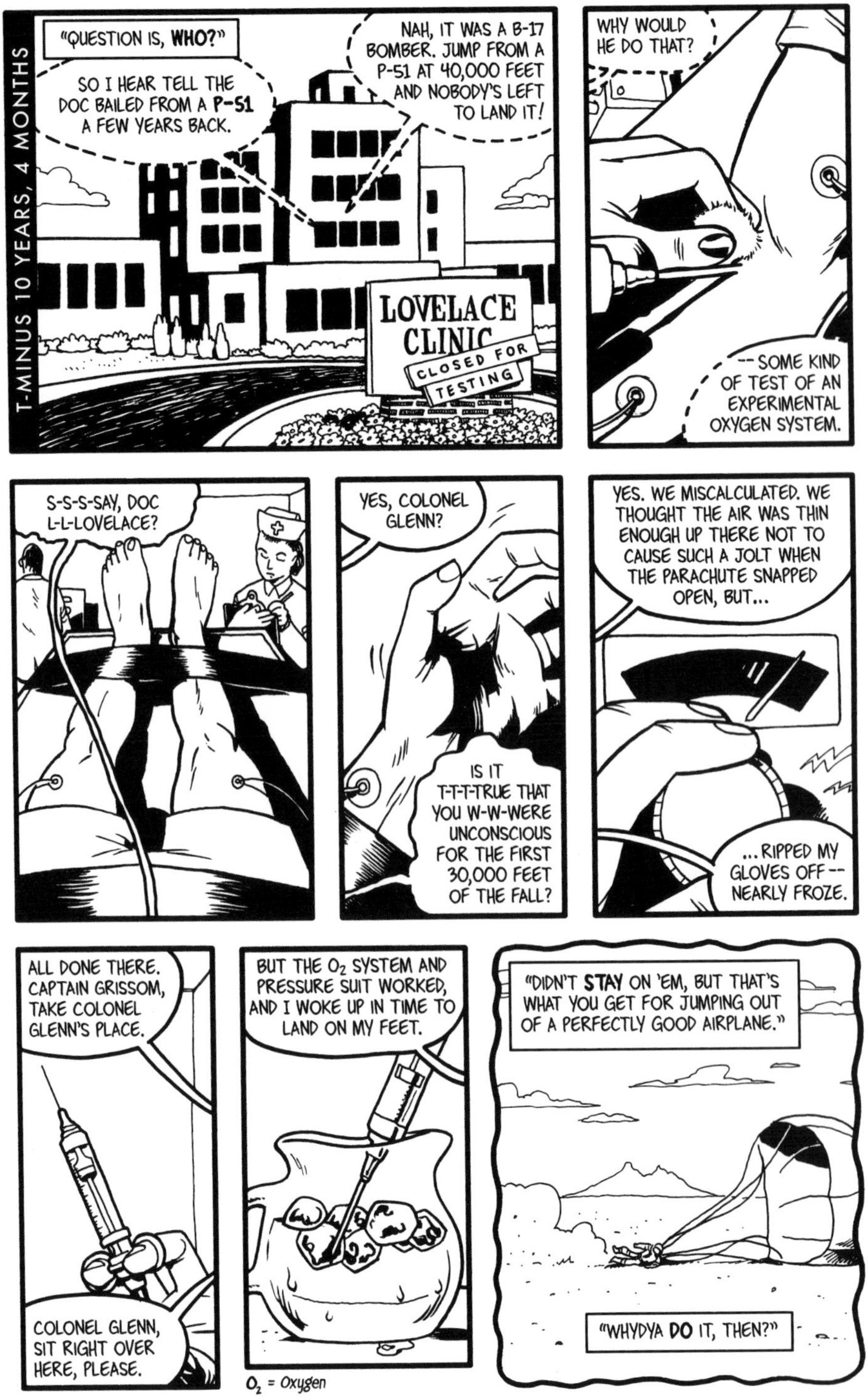
T-MINUS 10 YEARS, 4 MONTHS
"QUESTION IS, WHO?"
SO I HEAR TELL THE DOC BAILED FROM A P-51 A FEW YEARS BACK.
NAH, IT WAS A B-17 BOMBER. JUMP FROM A P-51 AT 40,000 FEET AND NOBODY'S LEFT TO LAND IT!
LOVELACE CLINIC
CLOSED FOR TESTING
WHY WOULD HE DO THAT?
--SOME KIND OF TEST OF AN EXPERIMENTAL OXYGEN SYSTEM.
S-S-S-SAY, DOC L-L-LOVELACE?
YES, COLONEL GLENN?
IS IT T-T-T-TRUE THAT YOU W-W-WERE UNCONSCIOUS FOR THE FIRST 30,000 FEET OF THE FALL?
YES. WE MISCALCULATED. WE THOUGHT THE AIR WAS THIN ENOUGH UP THERE NOT TO CAUSE SUCH A JOLT WHEN THE PARACHUTE SNAPPED OPEN, BUT...
...RIPPED MY GLOVES OFF-- NEARLY FROZE.
ALL DONE THERE. CAPTAIN GRISSOM, TAKE COLONEL GLENN'S PLACE.
COLONEL GLENN, SIT RIGHT OVER HERE, PLEASE.
BUT THE O_2 SYSTEM AND PRESSURE SUIT WORKED, AND I WOKE UP IN TIME TO LAND ON MY FEET.
"DIDN'T STAY ON 'EM, BUT THAT'S WHAT YOU GET FOR JUMPING OUT OF A PERFECTLY GOOD AIRPLANE."
"WHYDYA DO IT, THEN?"

O_2 = *Oxygen*

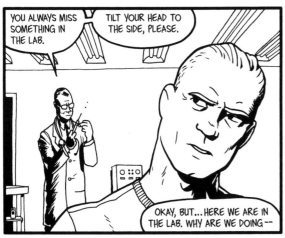

YOU ALWAYS MISS SOMETHING IN THE LAB.
TILT YOUR HEAD TO THE SIDE, PLEASE.
OKAY, BUT... HERE WE ARE IN THE LAB. WHY ARE WE DOING--
...AAH!!
--DOING THIS?
SQUIRT
WELL, YOU DON'T MISS **EVERYTHING** IN THE LAB. NOW, THIS MIGHT CAUSE SOME DISCOMFORT.
T-MINUS 9 YEARS, 8 MONTHS
"BUT DON'T WORRY--'SOME DISCOMFORT' IS PRETTY MUCH THE POINT."
FASTER.
MOSCOW'S KHODYNKA (FRUNZE) AIRFIELD-MOSCOW-1959
FASTER!
19G
20G
G-FORCE — Force on the body measured relative to gravity. If you weigh 100 lb, at 20g you actually feel like you weigh a ton (2,000 lb).
AND, FASTER... NO. WE'RE DONE--
HE'S PASSED OUT.
STOP THE TEST.
LEONOV, YOU NEXT, FOLLOWED BY KOMAROV.
GAGARIN, OVER TO THE PRESSURE CHAMBER.

UNSUCCESSFUL
USAF

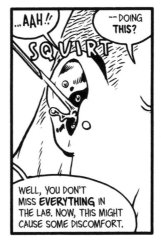

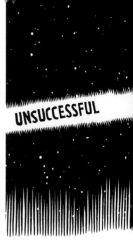

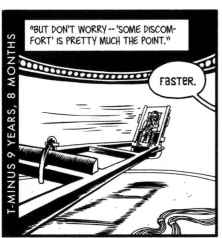

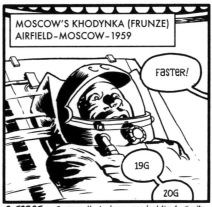

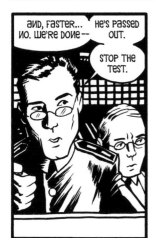

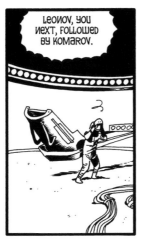

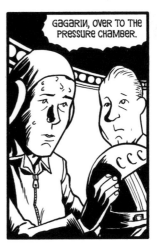

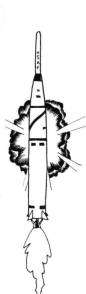

Thor-Able/Pioneer
Lunar Probe:
August 17, 1958
T-Minus 11 Years
Flight Duration:
77 Seconds

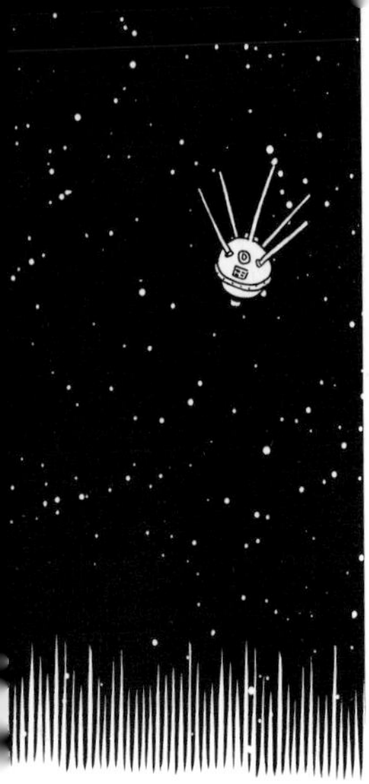

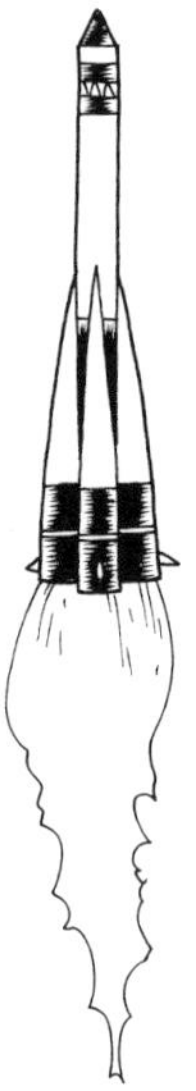

E-1 Luna Probe,
3rd Attempt: 1958
T-Minus 11 Years
Flight Duration:
245 Seconds

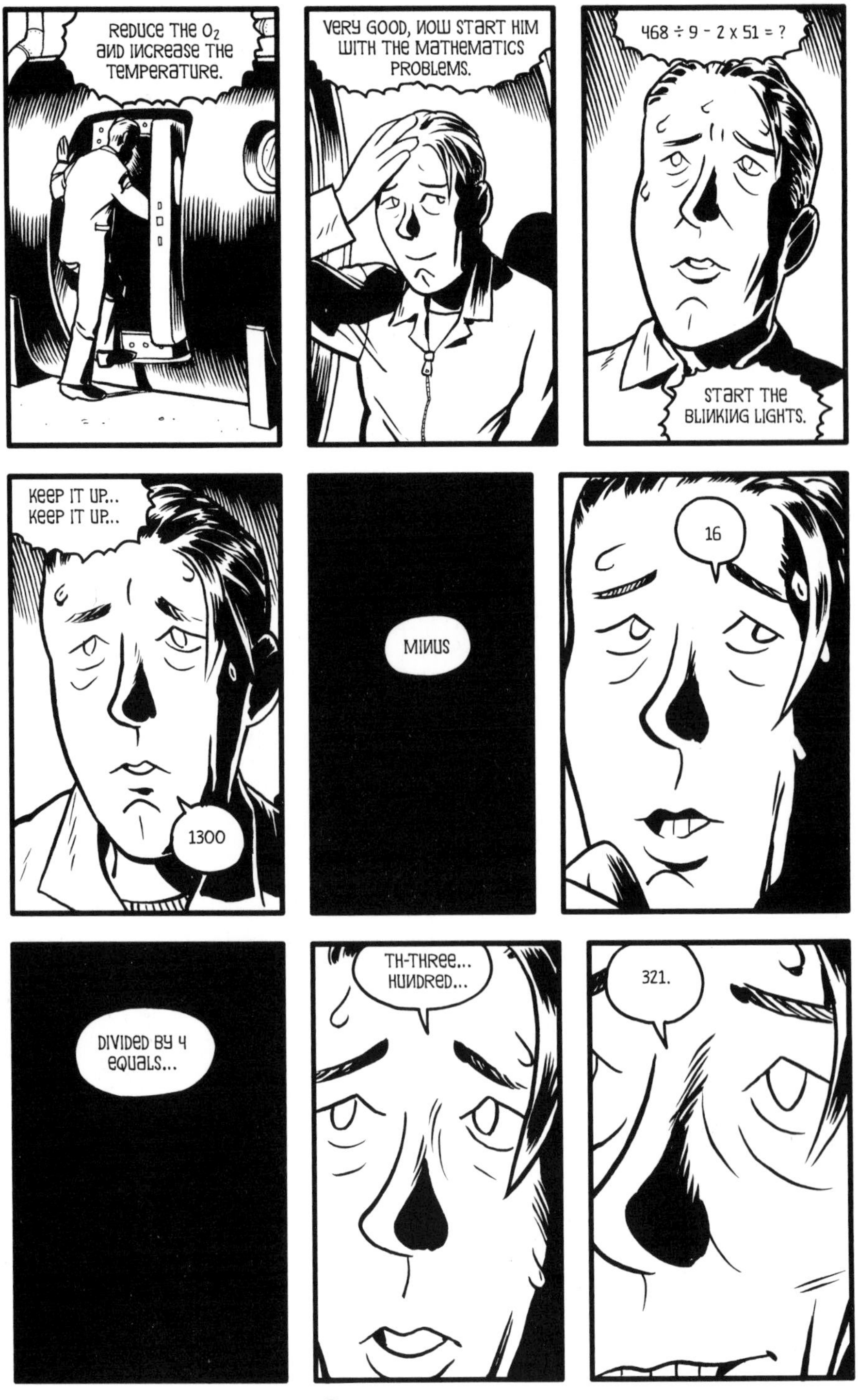
REDUCE THE O_2 AND INCREASE THE TEMPERATURE.
VERY GOOD, NOW START HIM WITH THE MATHEMATICS PROBLEMS.
468 ÷ 9 - 2 x 51 = ?
START THE BLINKING LIGHTS.
KEEP IT UP... KEEP IT UP...
1300
MINUS
16
DIVIDED BY 4 EQUALS...
TH-THREE... HUNDRED...
321.

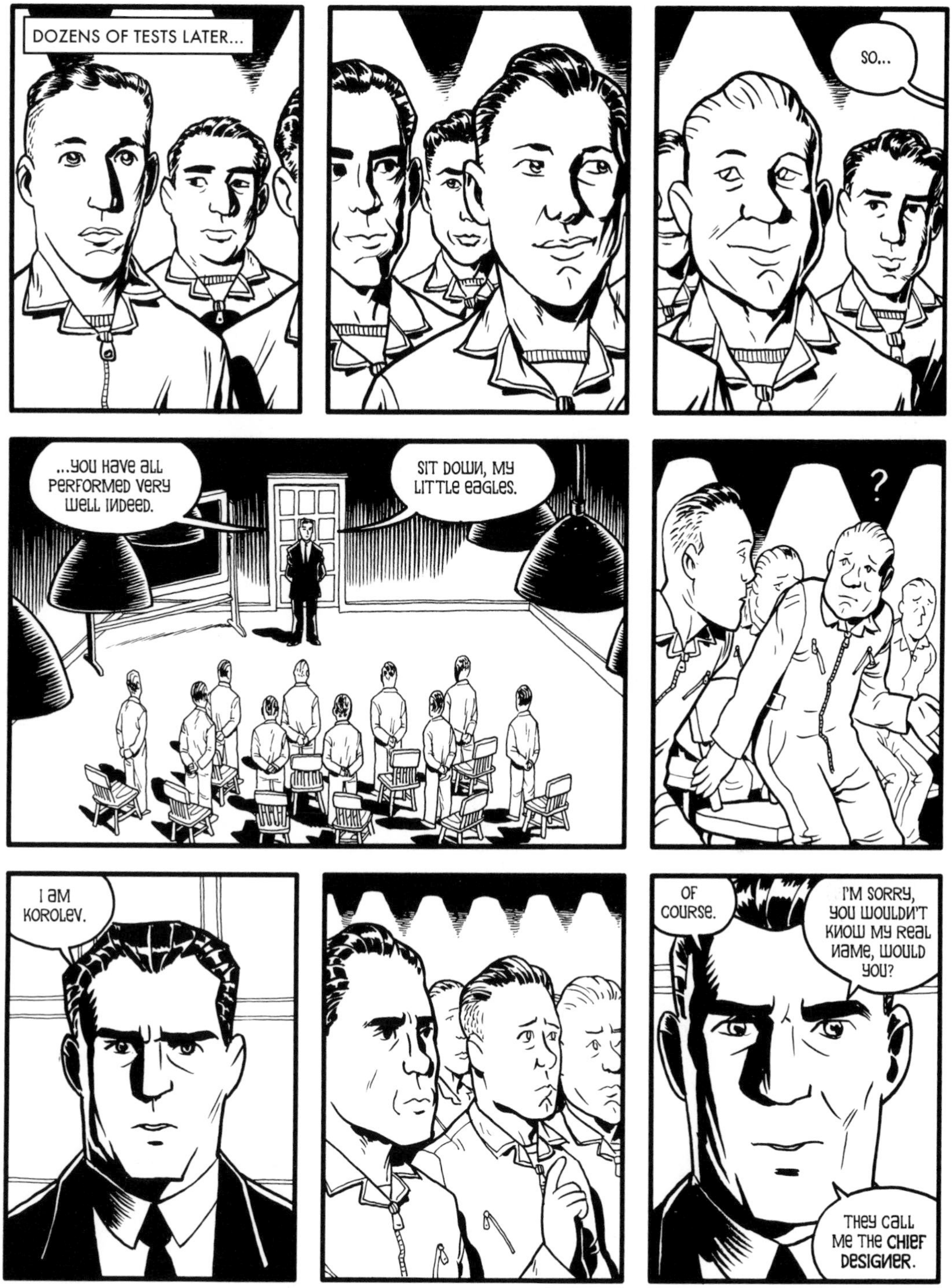
DOZENS OF TESTS LATER...
SO...
...YOU HAVE ALL PERFORMED VERY WELL INDEED.
SIT DOWN, MY LITTLE EAGLES.
?
I AM KOROLEV.
OF COURSE.
I'M SORRY, YOU WOULDN'T KNOW MY REAL NAME, WOULD YOU?
THEY CALL ME THE **CHIEF DESIGNER**.

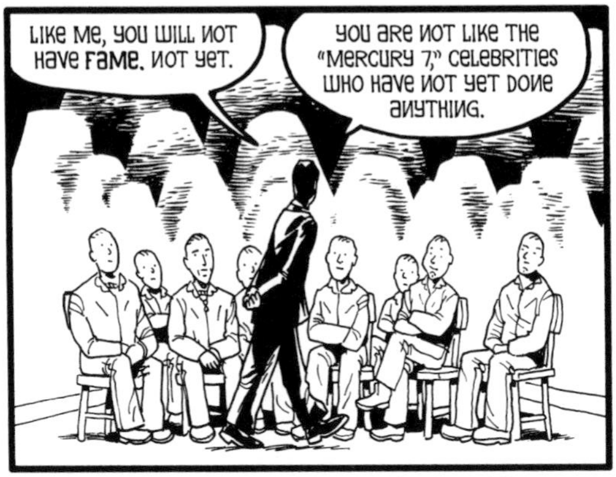
LIKE ME, YOU WILL NOT HAVE **FAME.** NOT YET.
YOU ARE NOT LIKE THE "MERCURY 7," CELEBRITIES WHO HAVE NOT YET DONE ANYTHING.

The American Mercury astronauts had a magazine deal that paid them $500,000 over three years for their stories. Russian cosmonauts made about $100 each month.

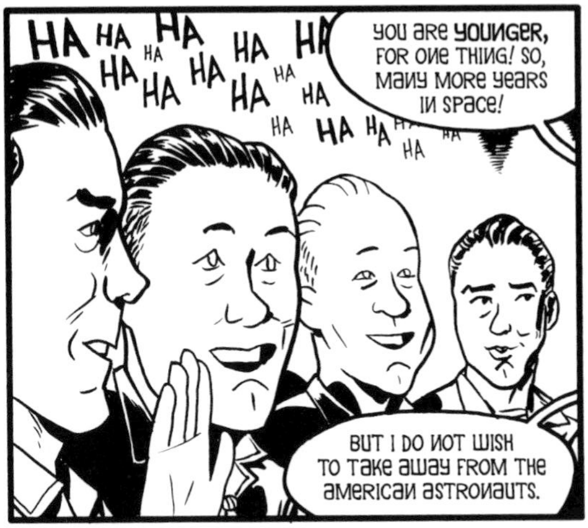
HA HA HA HA HA HA HA HA HA HA HA HA HA HA HA HA
YOU ARE **YOUNGER,** FOR ONE THING! SO, MANY MORE YEARS IN SPACE!
BUT I DO NOT WISH TO TAKE AWAY FROM THE AMERICAN ASTRONAUTS.

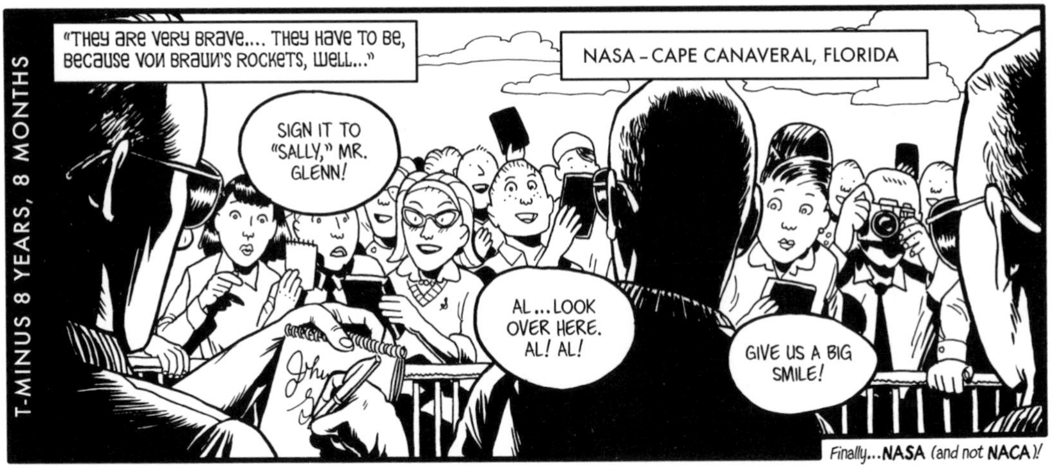
T-MINUS 8 YEARS, 8 MONTHS
"THEY ARE VERY BRAVE.... THEY HAVE TO BE, BECAUSE VON BRAUN'S ROCKETS, WELL..."
NASA – CAPE CANAVERAL, FLORIDA
SIGN IT TO "SALLY," MR. GLENN!
AL... LOOK OVER HERE. AL! AL!
GIVE US A BIG SMILE!

Finally... ***NASA*** *(and not* ***NACA****)!*

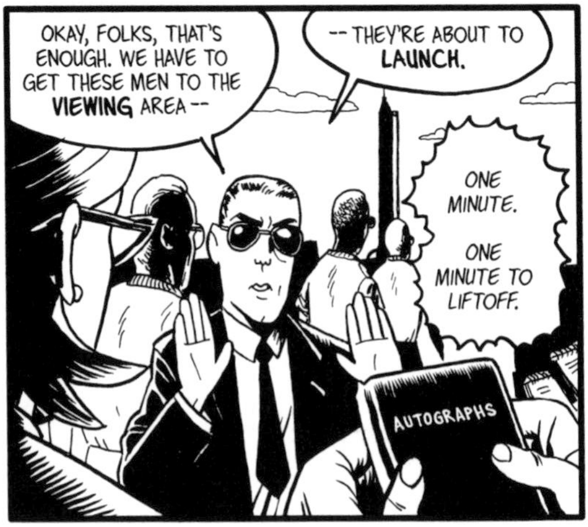
OKAY, FOLKS, THAT'S ENOUGH. WE HAVE TO GET THESE MEN TO THE **VIEWING** AREA--
--THEY'RE ABOUT TO **LAUNCH.**
ONE MINUTE.
ONE MINUTE TO LIFTOFF.
AUTOGRAPHS

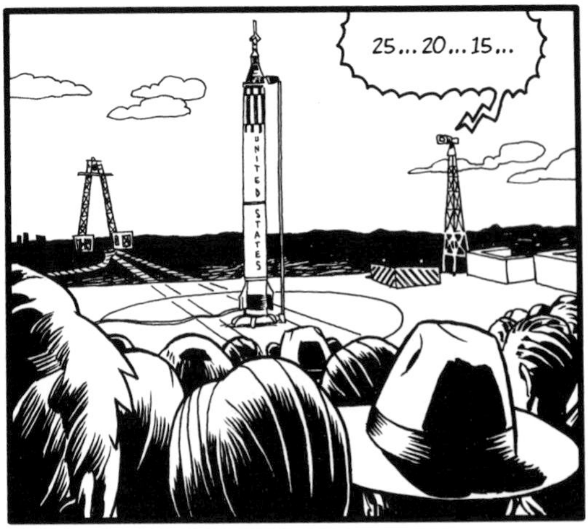
25... 20... 15...
UNITED STATES

LIFTOFF!

WHERE--

POP!

UNITED STAT

FFFFSSSSSSSSS

UNITED STAT

WHOOSH!

UNITED

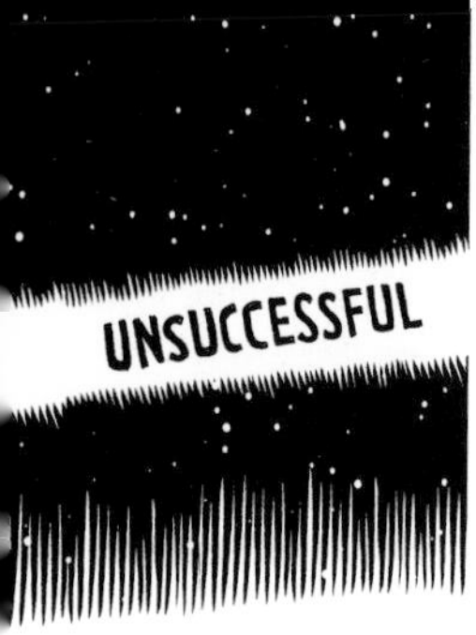
UNSUCCESSFUL

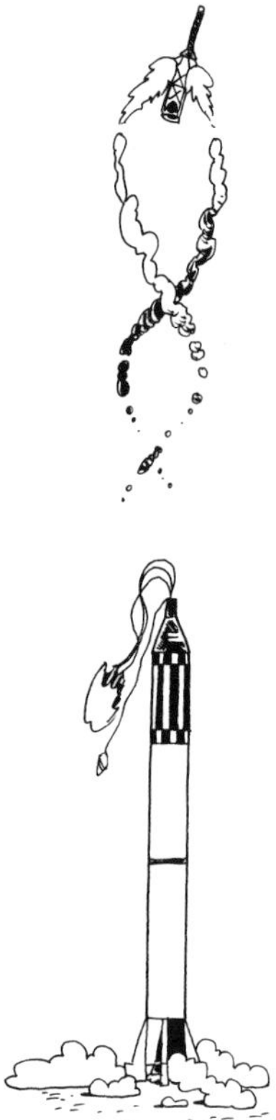

Mercury-Redstone 1:
November 21, 1960
T-Minus 8 Years,
8 Months
Flight Duration:
2 Seconds
Altitude: 4 inches

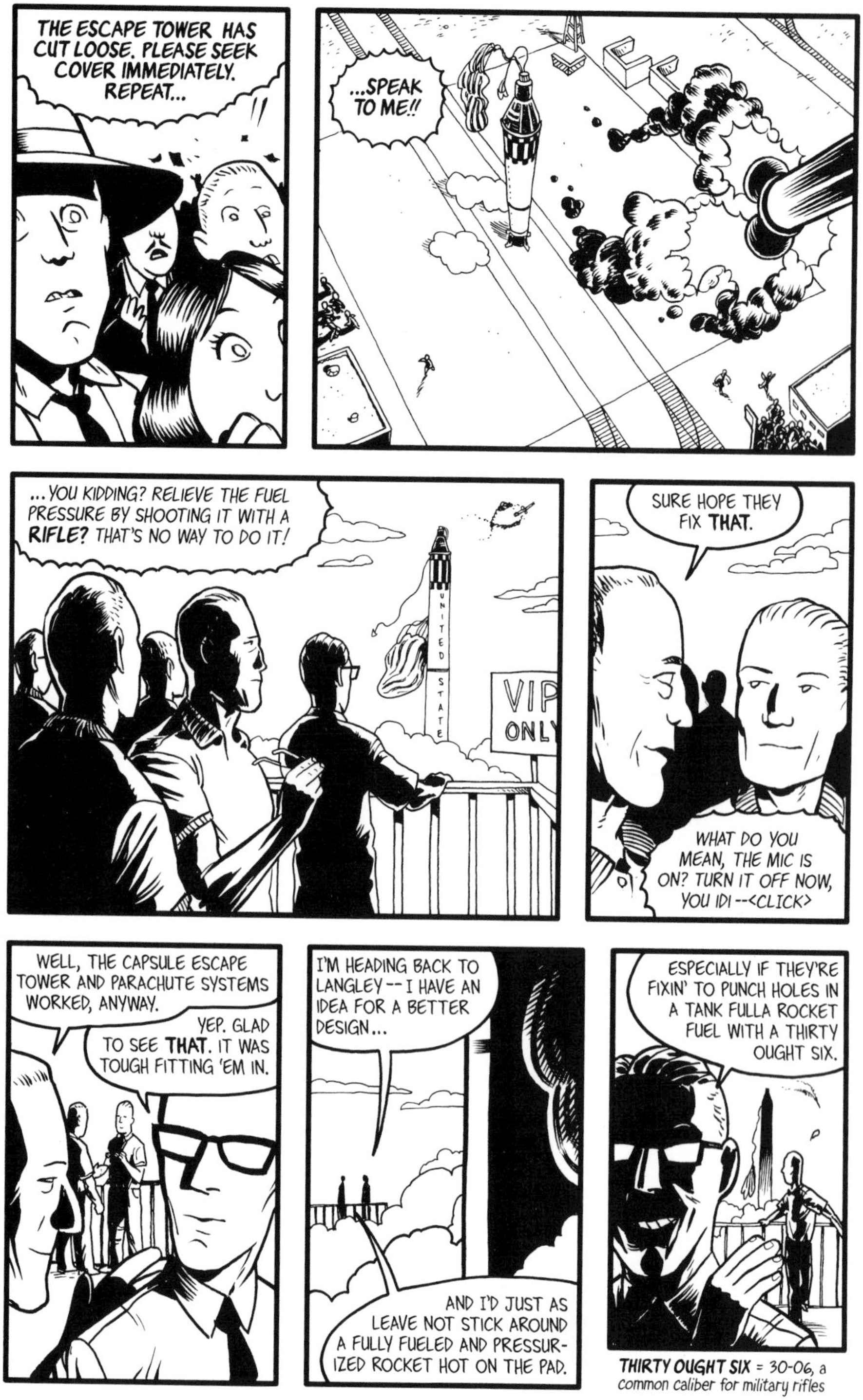
THE ESCAPE TOWER HAS CUT LOOSE. PLEASE SEEK COVER IMMEDIATELY. REPEAT...
...SPEAK TO ME!!
...YOU KIDDING? RELIEVE THE FUEL PRESSURE BY SHOOTING IT WITH A RIFLE? THAT'S NO WAY TO DO IT!
UNITED STATE
VIP ONLY
SURE HOPE THEY FIX THAT.
WHAT DO YOU MEAN, THE MIC IS ON? TURN IT OFF NOW, YOU IDI --<CLICK>
WELL, THE CAPSULE ESCAPE TOWER AND PARACHUTE SYSTEMS WORKED, ANYWAY.
YEP. GLAD TO SEE THAT. IT WAS TOUGH FITTING 'EM IN.
I'M HEADING BACK TO LANGLEY -- I HAVE AN IDEA FOR A BETTER DESIGN...
AND I'D JUST AS LEAVE NOT STICK AROUND A FULLY FUELED AND PRESSURIZED ROCKET HOT ON THE PAD.
ESPECIALLY IF THEY'RE FIXIN' TO PUNCH HOLES IN A TANK FULLA ROCKET FUEL WITH A THIRTY OUGHT SIX.

THIRTY OUGHT SIX = 30-06, a common caliber for military rifles

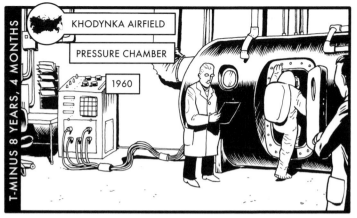

KHODYNKA AIRFIELD

PRESSURE CHAMBER

1960

CLANK

PSI 0 16

PSI 0 16

PSI 0 16

"NO ONE!"

"I REPEAT -- NO ONE MUST KNOW!"

WHAT --?

WHOOM

NO --

OH GOD --

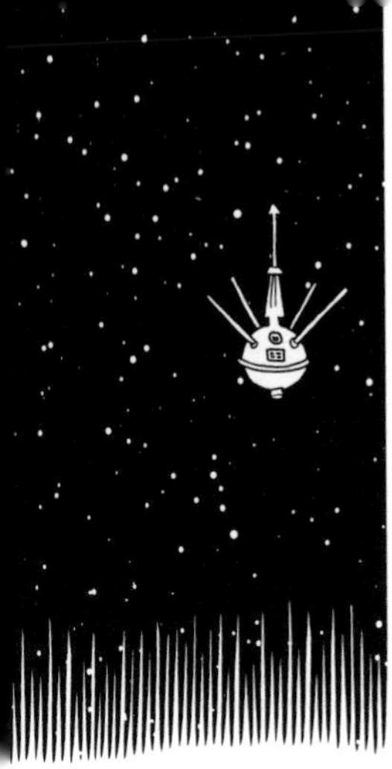

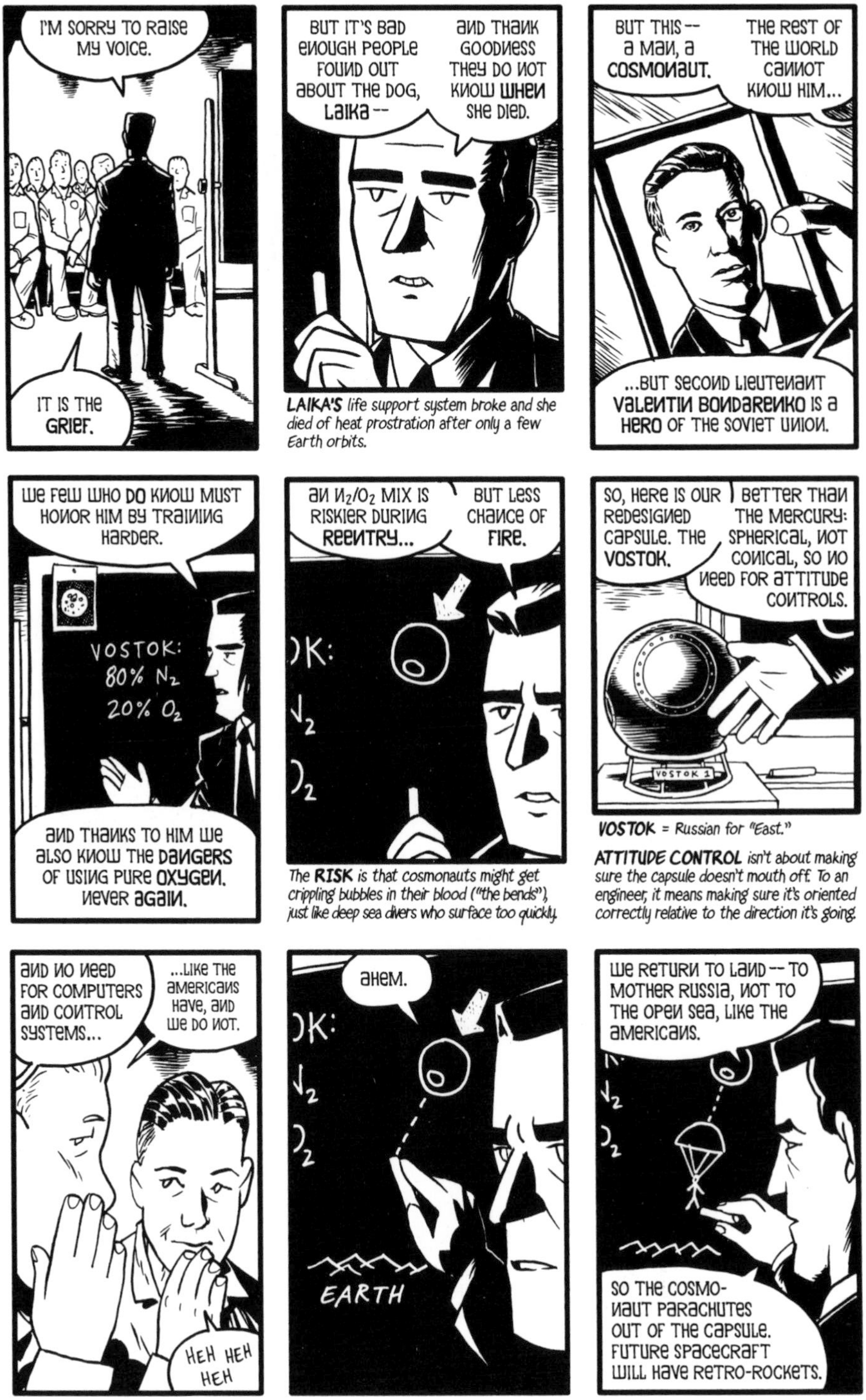

I'M SORRY TO RAISE MY VOICE.
IT IS THE GRIEF.
BUT IT'S BAD ENOUGH PEOPLE FOUND OUT ABOUT THE DOG, LAIKA --
AND THANK GOODNESS THEY DO NOT KNOW WHEN SHE DIED.
LAIKA'S life support system broke and she died of heat prostration after only a few Earth orbits.
BUT THIS -- A MAN, A COSMONAUT.
THE REST OF THE WORLD CANNOT KNOW HIM...
...BUT SECOND LIEUTENANT VALENTIN BONDARENKO IS A HERO OF THE SOVIET UNION.
WE FEW WHO DO KNOW MUST HONOR HIM BY TRAINING HARDER.
VOSTOK: 80% N_2 20% O_2
AND THANKS TO HIM WE ALSO KNOW THE DANGERS OF USING PURE OXYGEN. NEVER AGAIN.
AN N_2/O_2 MIX IS RISKIER DURING REENTRY...
BUT LESS CHANCE OF FIRE.
The RISK is that cosmonauts might get crippling bubbles in their blood ("the bends"), just like deep sea divers who surface too quickly.
SO, HERE IS OUR REDESIGNED CAPSULE. THE VOSTOK.
BETTER THAN THE MERCURY: SPHERICAL, NOT CONICAL, SO NO NEED FOR ATTITUDE CONTROLS.
VOSTOK 1
VOSTOK = Russian for "East."
ATTITUDE CONTROL isn't about making sure the capsule doesn't mouth off. To an engineer, it means making sure it's oriented correctly relative to the direction it's going.
AND NO NEED FOR COMPUTERS AND CONTROL SYSTEMS...
...LIKE THE AMERICANS HAVE, AND WE DO NOT.
HEH HEH HEH
AHEM.
EARTH
WE RETURN TO LAND -- TO MOTHER RUSSIA, NOT TO THE OPEN SEA, LIKE THE AMERICANS.
SO THE COSMONAUT PARACHUTES OUT OF THE CAPSULE. FUTURE SPACECRAFT WILL HAVE RETRO-ROCKETS.

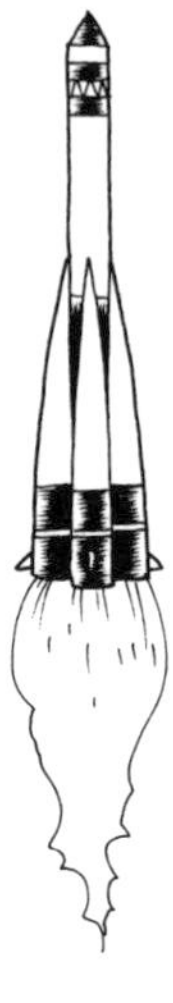

E-2 Luna Probe: 1959
T-Minus 10 Years,
Flight Duration:
33.5 Hours
It made it to the
moon in a planned
crash landing!

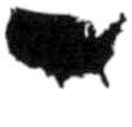

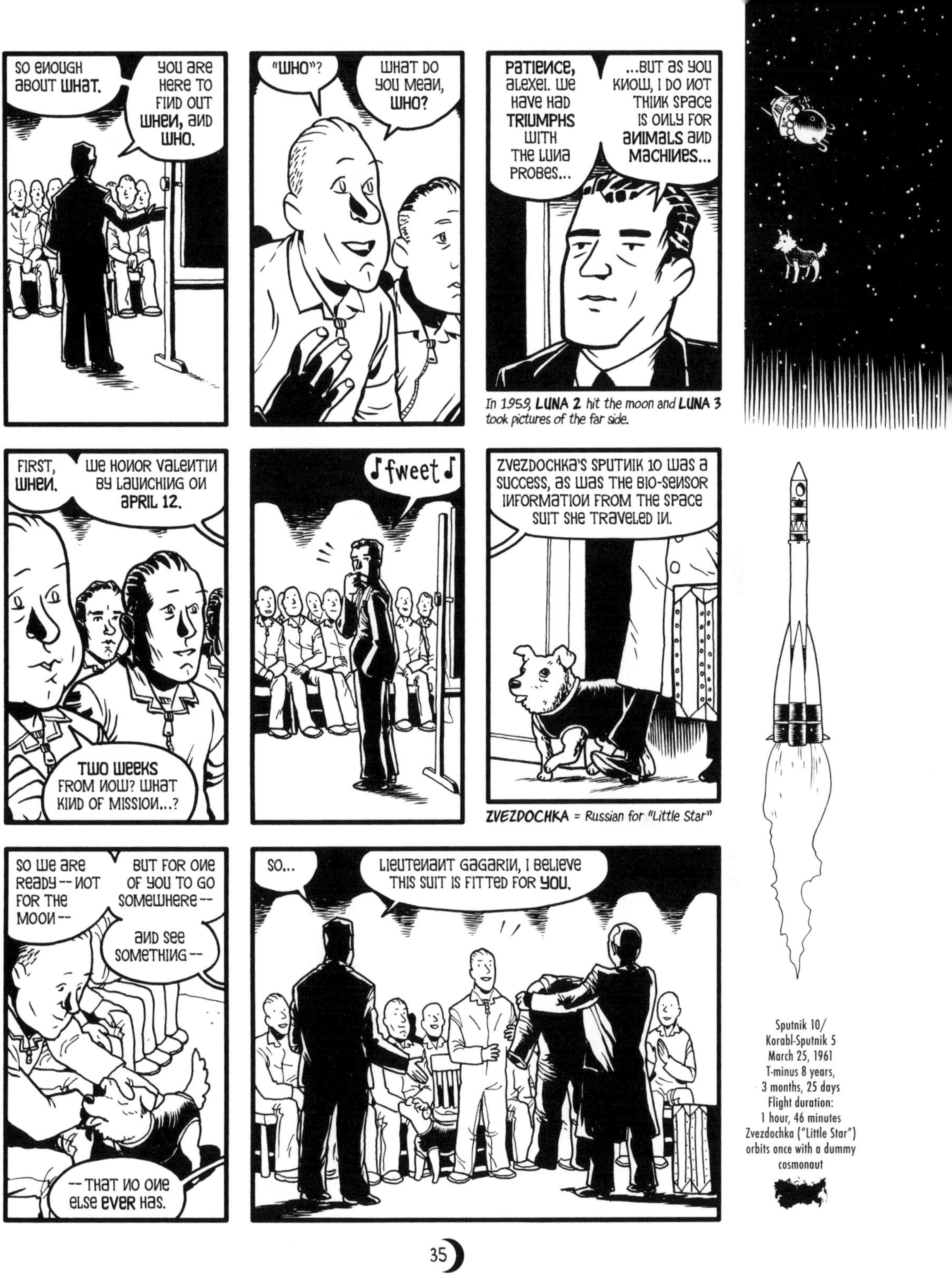

SO ENOUGH ABOUT WHAT.
YOU ARE HERE TO FIND OUT WHEN, AND WHO.
"WHO"?
WHAT DO YOU MEAN, WHO?
PATIENCE, ALEXEI. WE HAVE HAD TRIUMPHS WITH THE LUNA PROBES...
...BUT AS YOU KNOW, I DO NOT THINK SPACE IS ONLY FOR ANIMALS AND MACHINES...
In 1959, LUNA 2 hit the moon and LUNA 3 took pictures of the far side.
FIRST, WHEN.
WE HONOR VALENTIN BY LAUNCHING ON APRIL 12.
TWO WEEKS FROM NOW? WHAT KIND OF MISSION...?
♪fweet♪
ZVEZDOCHKA'S SPUTNIK 10 WAS A SUCCESS, AS WAS THE BIO-SENSOR INFORMATION FROM THE SPACE SUIT SHE TRAVELED IN.
ZVEZDOCHKA = Russian for "Little Star"
SO WE ARE READY -- NOT FOR THE MOON --
BUT FOR ONE OF YOU TO GO SOMEWHERE --
AND SEE SOMETHING --
-- THAT NO ONE ELSE EVER HAS.
SO...
LIEUTENANT GAGARIN, I BELIEVE THIS SUIT IS FITTED FOR YOU.
Sputnik 10/
Korabl-Sputnik 5
March 25, 1961
T-minus 8 years, 3 months, 25 days
Flight duration:
1 hour, 46 minutes
Zvezdochka ("Little Star") orbits once with a dummy cosmonaut

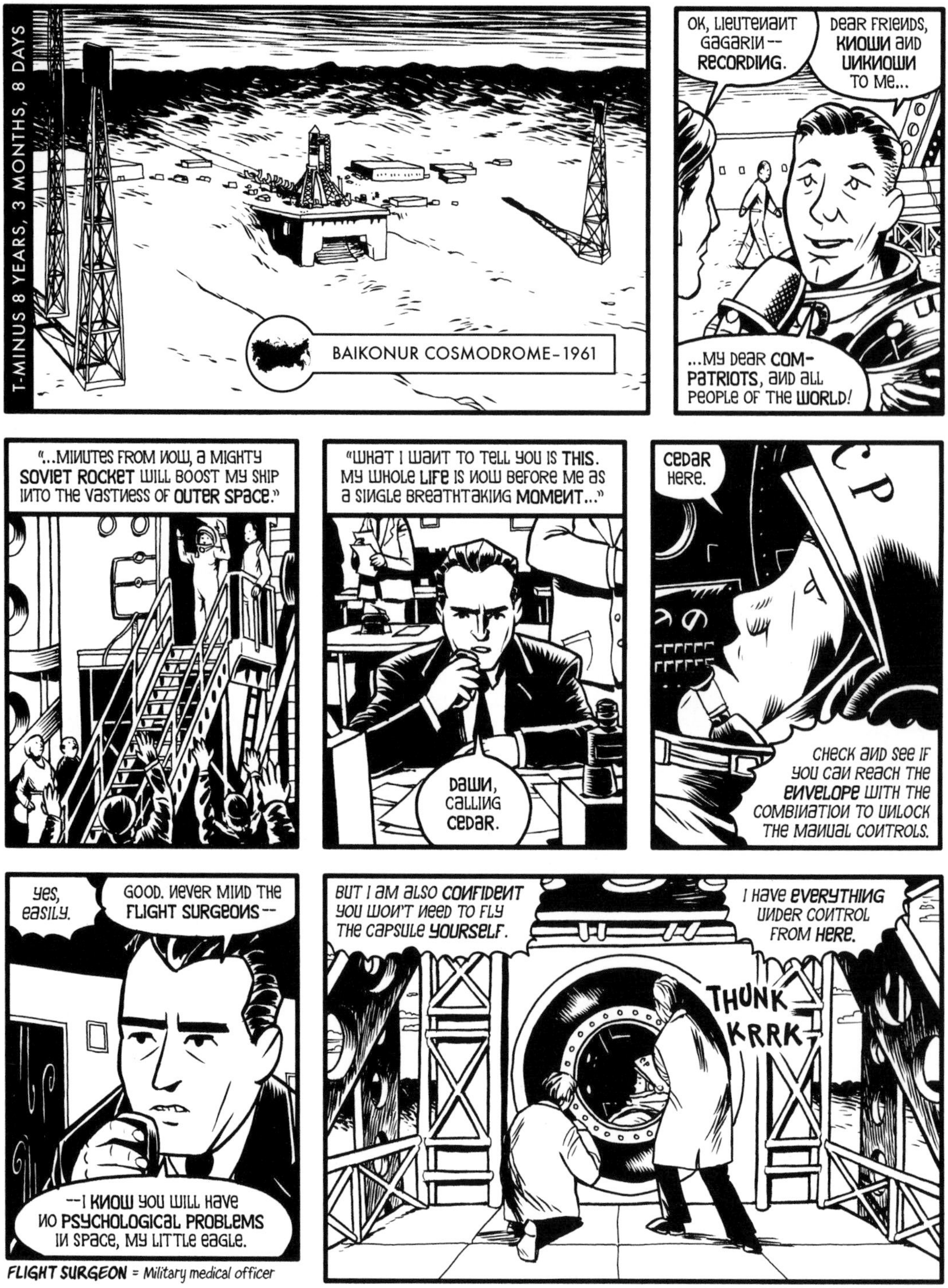

T-MINUS 8 YEARS, 3 MONTHS, 8 DAYS
BAIKONUR COSMODROME-1961
OK, LIEUTENANT GAGARIN -- RECORDING.
DEAR FRIENDS, KNOWN AND UNKNOWN TO ME...
...MY DEAR COMPATRIOTS, AND ALL PEOPLE OF THE WORLD!
"...MINUTES FROM NOW, A MIGHTY SOVIET ROCKET WILL BOOST MY SHIP INTO THE VASTNESS OF OUTER SPACE."
"WHAT I WANT TO TELL YOU IS THIS. MY WHOLE LIFE IS NOW BEFORE ME AS A SINGLE BREATHTAKING MOMENT..."
DAWN, CALLING CEDAR.
CEDAR HERE.
CHECK AND SEE IF YOU CAN REACH THE ENVELOPE WITH THE COMBINATION TO UNLOCK THE MANUAL CONTROLS.
YES, EASILY.
GOOD. NEVER MIND THE FLIGHT SURGEONS--
--I KNOW YOU WILL HAVE NO PSYCHOLOGICAL PROBLEMS IN SPACE, MY LITTLE EAGLE.
BUT I AM ALSO CONFIDENT YOU WON'T NEED TO FLY THE CAPSULE YOURSELF.
I HAVE EVERYTHING UNDER CONTROL FROM HERE.
THUNK
KRRK-

FLIGHT SURGEON = *Military medical officer*

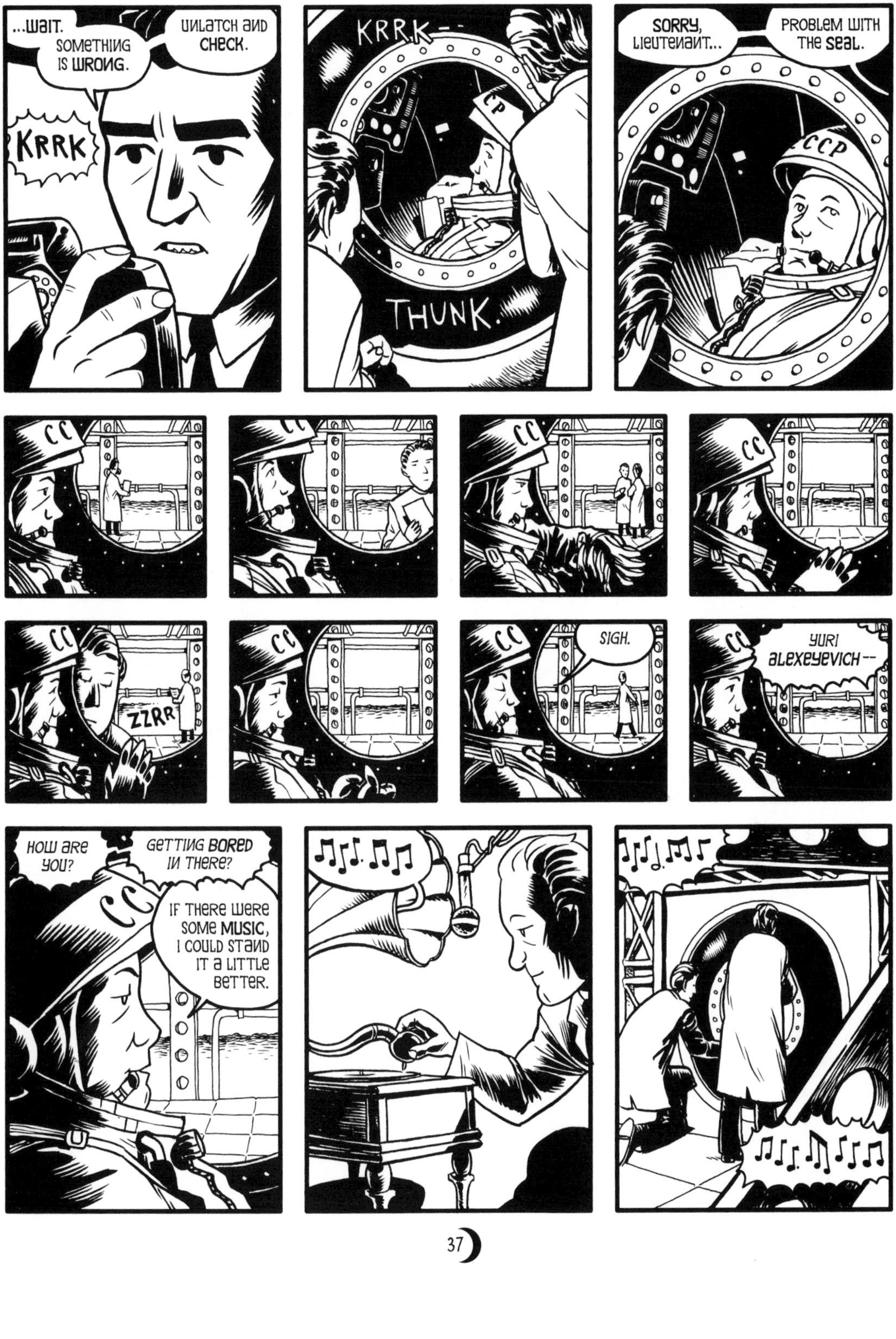
...WAIT. SOMETHING IS WRONG.
UNLATCH AND CHECK.
KRRK
KRRK--
THUNK.
SORRY, LIEUTENANT...
PROBLEM WITH THE SEAL.
ZZRR
SIGH.
YURI ALEXEYEVICH--
HOW ARE YOU?
GETTING BORED IN THERE?
IF THERE WERE SOME MUSIC, I COULD STAND IT A LITTLE BETTER.

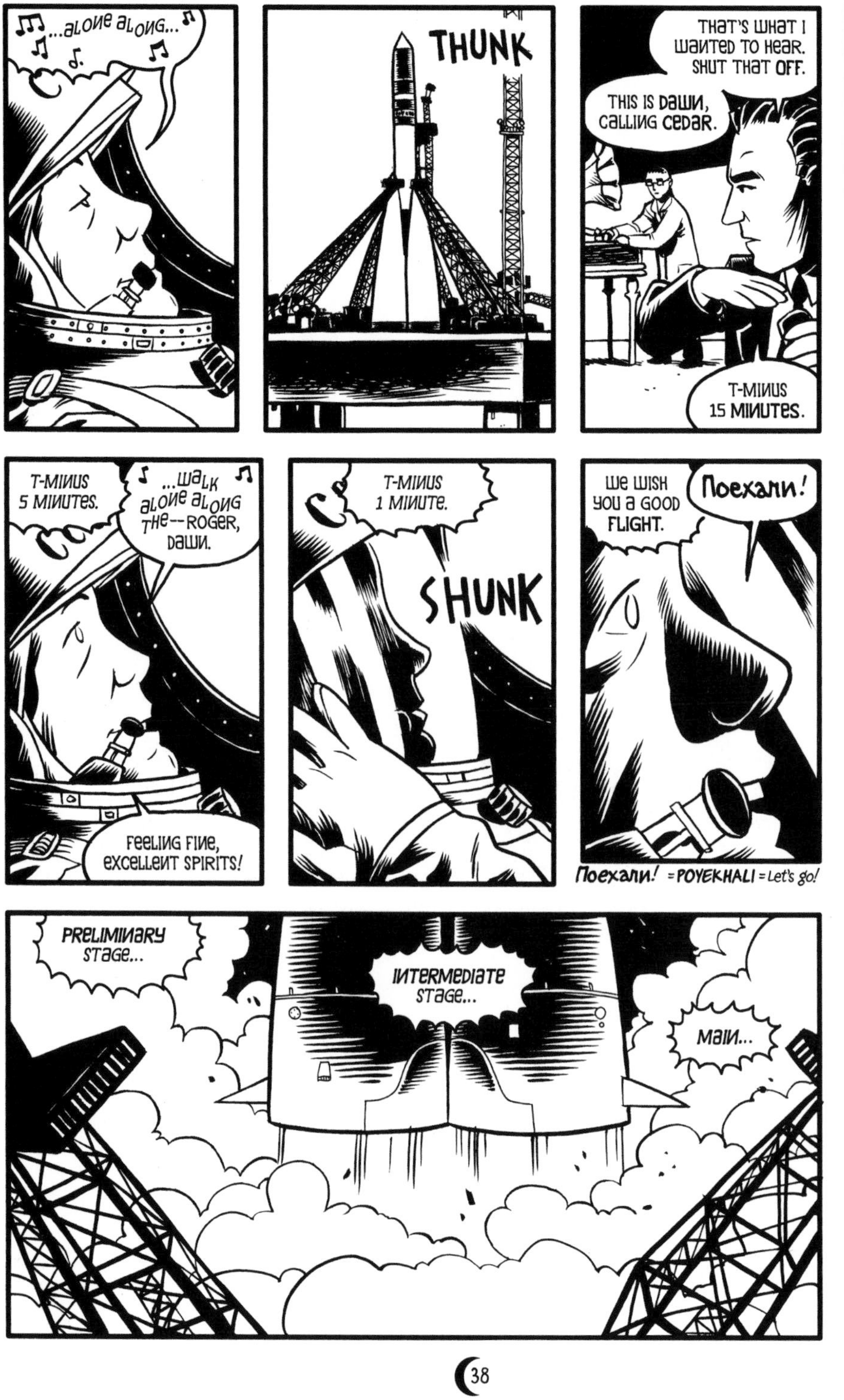
...alone along...
That's what I wanted to hear. Shut that off.
This is Dawn, calling Cedar.
T-minus 15 minutes.
T-minus 5 minutes.
...walk alone along the--Roger, Dawn.
Feeling fine, excellent spirits!
T-minus 1 minute.
SHUNK
We wish you a good flight.
Поехали!
Поехали! = POYEKHALI = Let's go!
Preliminary stage...
Intermediate stage...
Main...

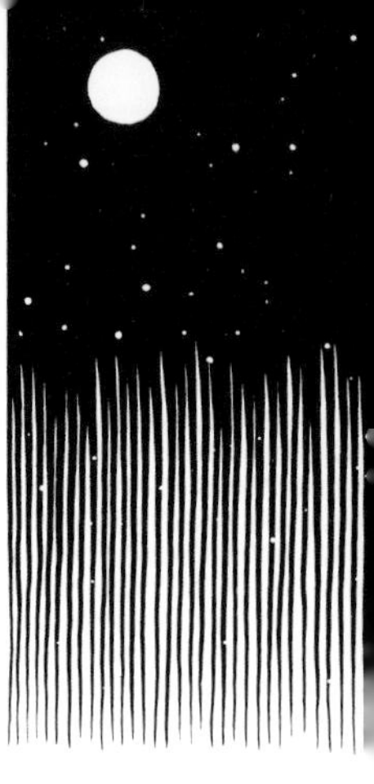

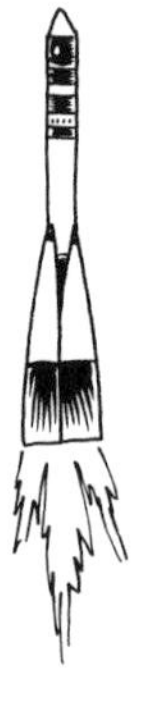

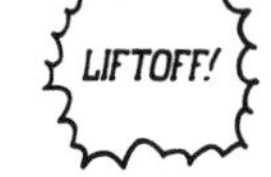
LIFTOFF!

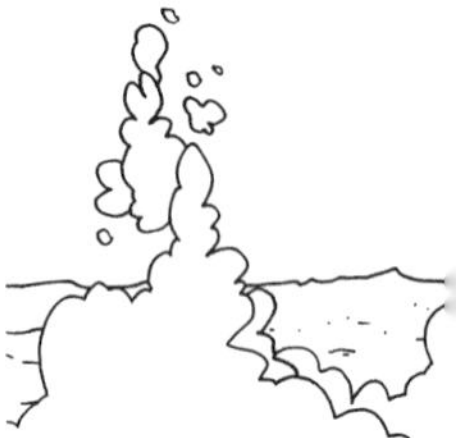

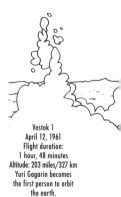

Vostok 1
April 12, 1961
Flight duration:
1 hour, 48 minutes
Altitude: 203 miles/327 km
Yuri Gagarin becomes
the first person to orbit
the earth.

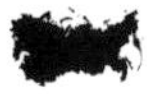

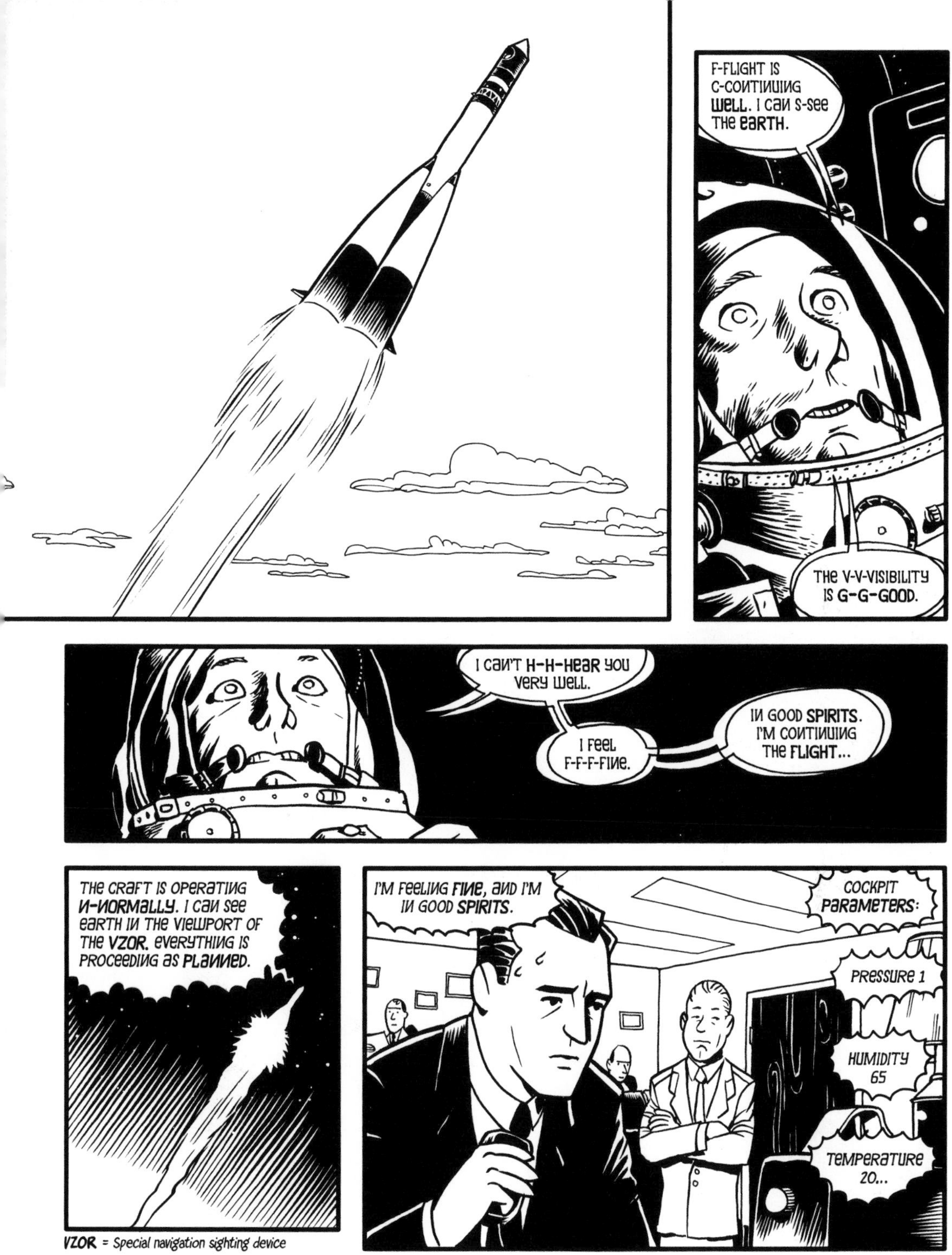
F-FLIGHT IS C-CONTINUING WELL. I CAN S-SEE THE EARTH.
THE V-V-VISIBILITY IS G-G-GOOD.
I CAN'T H-H-HEAR YOU VERY WELL.
I FEEL F-F-FINE.
IN GOOD SPIRITS. I'M CONTINUING THE FLIGHT...
THE CRAFT IS OPERATING N-NORMALLY. I CAN SEE EARTH IN THE VIEWPORT OF THE VZOR. EVERYTHING IS PROCEEDING AS PLANNED.
I'M FEELING FINE, AND I'M IN GOOD SPIRITS.
COCKPIT PARAMETERS:
PRESSURE 1
HUMIDITY 65
TEMPERATURE 20...

VZOR = *Special navigation sighting device*

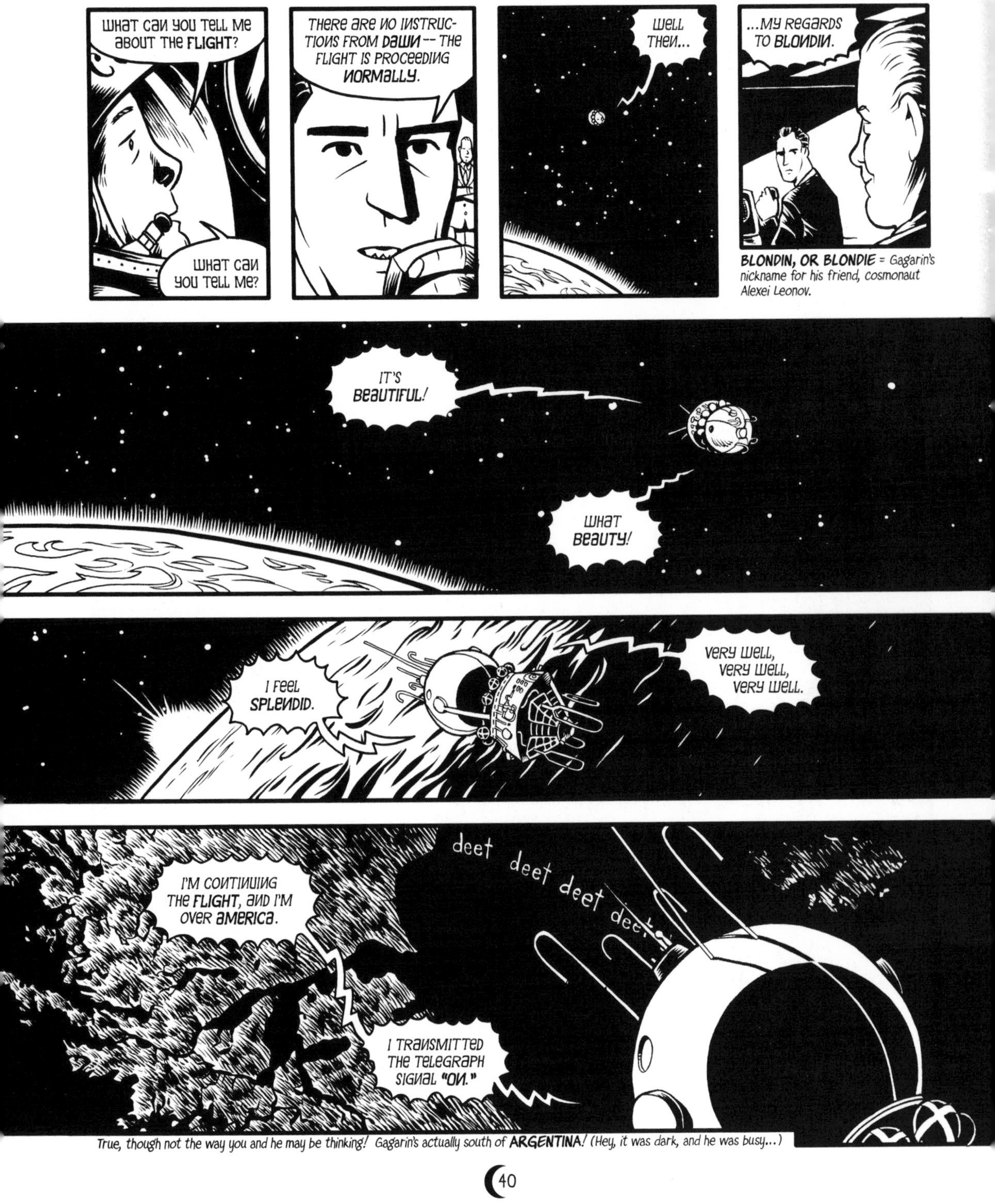
WHAT CAN YOU TELL ME ABOUT THE **FLIGHT**?
WHAT CAN YOU TELL ME?
THERE ARE NO INSTRUCTIONS FROM **DAWN** -- THE FLIGHT IS PROCEEDING **NORMALLY**.
WELL THEN...
...MY REGARDS TO **BLONDIN**.
BLONDIN, OR BLONDIE = Gagarin's nickname for his friend, cosmonaut Alexei Leonov.
IT'S **BEAUTIFUL**!
WHAT **BEAUTY**!
I FEEL **SPLENDID**.
VERY WELL, VERY WELL, VERY WELL.
I'M CONTINUING THE **FLIGHT**, AND I'M OVER **AMERICA**.
deet deet deet deet
I TRANSMITTED THE TELEGRAPH SIGNAL **"ON."**
True, though not the way you and he may be thinking! Gagarin's actually south of **ARGENTINA**! *(Hey, it was dark, and he was busy...)*

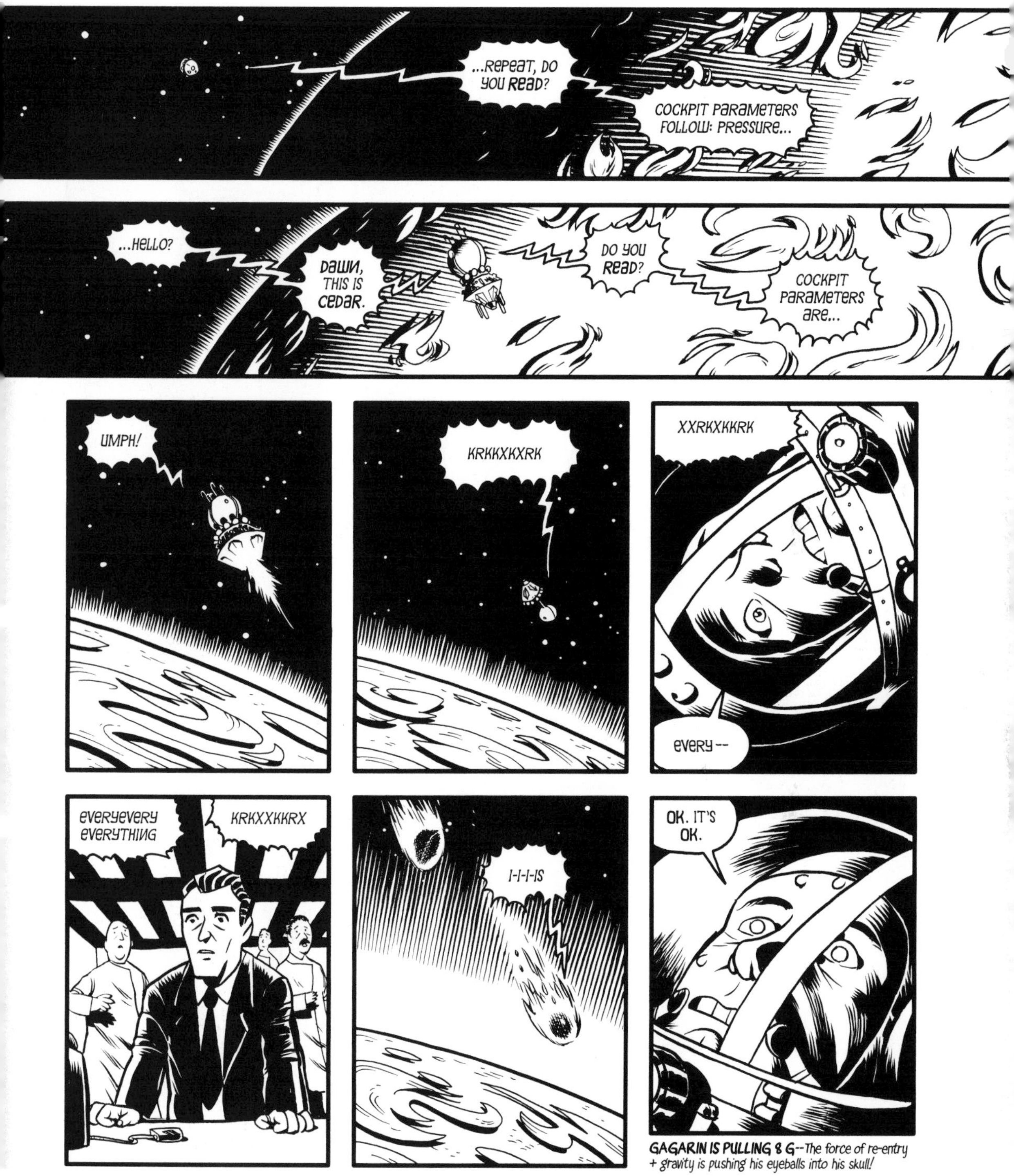
...REPEAT, DO YOU READ?
COCKPIT PARAMETERS FOLLOW: PRESSURE...
...HELLO?
DAWN, THIS IS CEDAR.
DO YOU READ?
COCKPIT PARAMETERS ARE...
UMPH!
KRKKXKXRK
XXRKXKKRK
EVERY --
EVERYEVERY EVERYTHING
KRKXXKKRX
I-I-I-IS
OK. IT'S OK.

GAGARIN IS PULLING 8 G--*The force of re-entry + gravity is pushing his eyeballs into his skull!*

KCHAK

WHUMP!

OOF!

DON'T BE
AFRAID!

I'M ONE
OF YOURS...a
SOVIET!

I HAVE
COME FROM
SPACE.

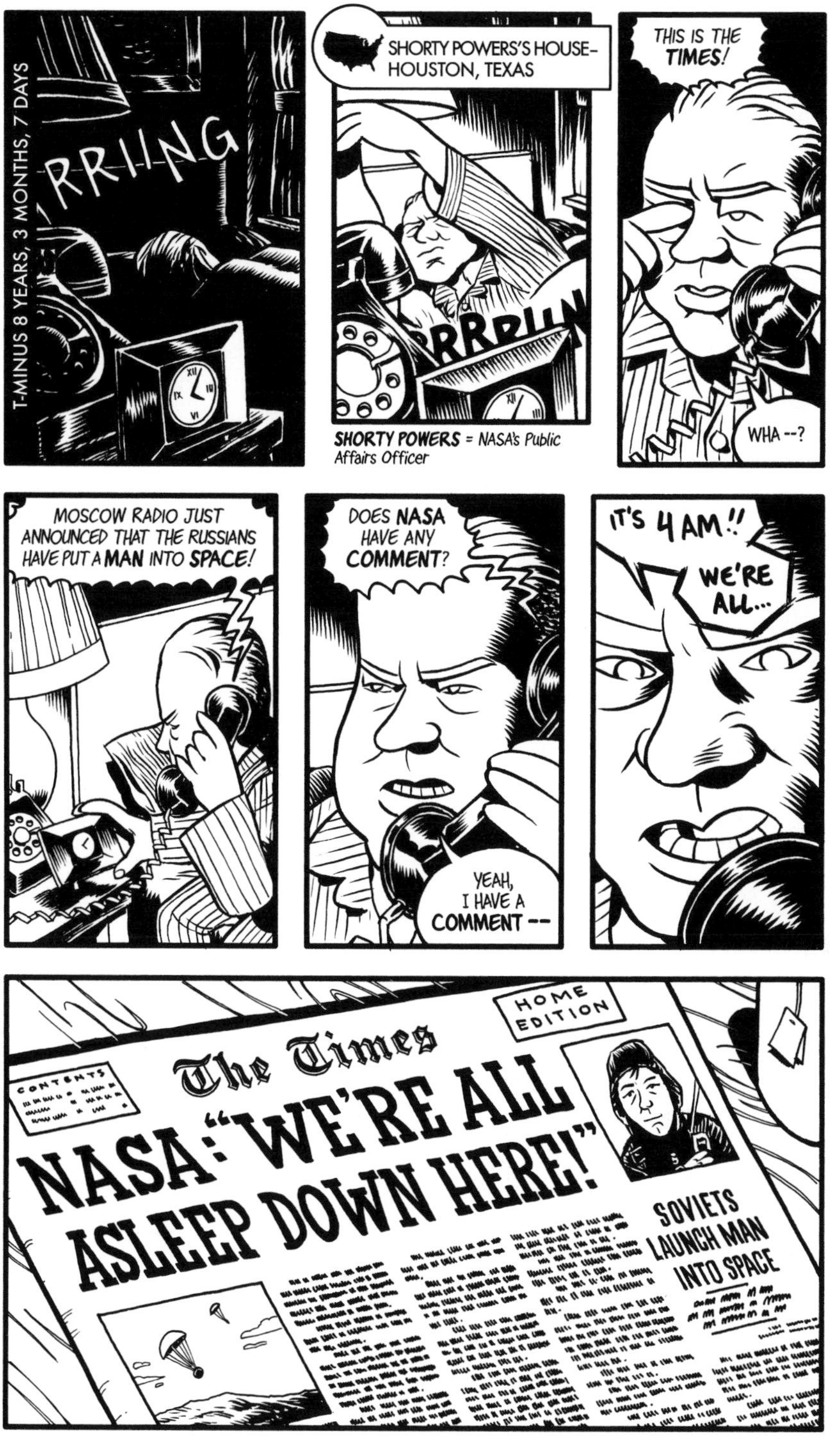
T-MINUS 8 YEARS, 3 MONTHS, 7 DAYS
RRIING
SHORTY POWERS'S HOUSE-HOUSTON, TEXAS
RRRRIIN
SHORTY POWERS = NASA's Public Affairs Officer
THIS IS THE TIMES!
WHA --?
MOSCOW RADIO JUST ANNOUNCED THAT THE RUSSIANS HAVE PUT A MAN INTO SPACE!
DOES NASA HAVE ANY COMMENT?
YEAH, I HAVE A COMMENT --
IT'S 4 AM!!
WE'RE ALL...
HOME EDITION
The Times
CONTENTS
NASA: "WE'RE ALL ASLEEP DOWN HERE!"
SOVIETS LAUNCH MAN INTO SPACE

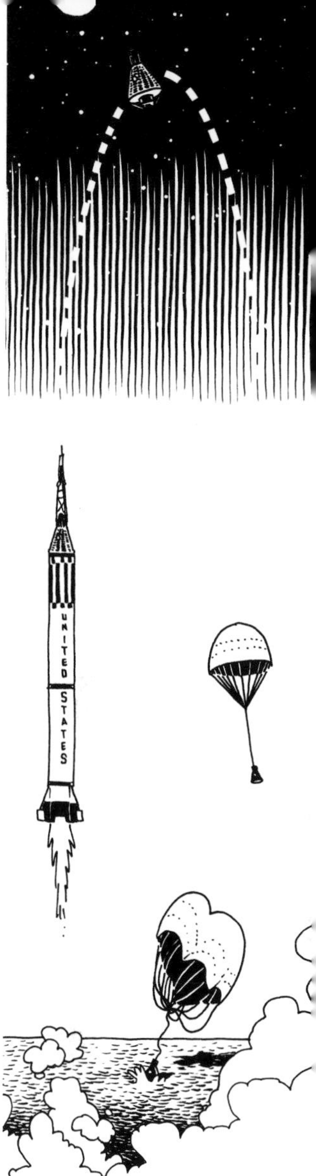
UNITED STATES

Mercury-Redstone 3/
Freedom 7:
May 5, 1961
T-Minus 8 Years,
2 Months, 15 Days
Flight duration:
15 minutes, 22 seconds
Altitude: 116 miles/
187 km. (Suborbital)
Alan Shepard, first
American in space

T-MINUS 8 YEARS, 1 MONTH, 25 DAYS

THE DRAMATIC ACHIEVEMENTS IN **SPACE** WHICH OCCURRED IN RECENT WEEKS SHOULD HAVE MADE CLEAR TO US ALL, AS DID THE **SPUTNIK** IN **1957,** THE IMPACT OF THIS ADVENTURE ON THE MINDS OF MEN EVERYWHERE.

JOINT SESSION OF CONGRESS- WASHINGTON D.C.-MAY 25, 1961

NOW IT IS TIME TO TAKE LONGER **STRIDES.** TIME FOR A GREAT NEW AMERICAN **ENTERPRISE...**

JOHN F. KENNEDY

TIME FOR THIS NATION TO TAKE A CLEARLY LEADING **ROLE** IN SPACE **ACHIEVEMENT...**

...WHICH IN MANY WAYS MAY HOLD THE KEY TO OUR **FUTURE** ON EARTH.

HOW CAN HE **SAY** THAT?

CLAP CLAP CLAP CLAP CLAP

PRESIDENT **KENNEDY**? HELL, I DON'T KNOW.

NAH, I MEAN **SHORTY POWERS.** WE AREN'T **ASLEEP** OVER HERE.

I BELIEVE WE POSSESS ALL THE **RESOURCES** AND **TALENTS** NECESSARY.

BUT THE **FACTS** OF THE MATTER ARE THAT WE HAVE NEVER MADE THE NATIONAL **DECISIONS** REQUIRED FOR SUCH LEADERSHIP.

RECOGNIZING THE **HEAD START** OBTAINED BY THE SOVIETS...

...WHILE WE CANNOT GUARANTEE THAT WE SHALL ONE DAY BE **FIRST,** WE CAN **GUARANTEE** THAT ANY **FAILURE** TO MAKE THIS EFFORT WILL MAKE US **LAST.**

I BELIEVE THAT THIS NATION SHOULD COMMIT ITSELF TO ACHIEVING THE **GOAL,** BEFORE THIS **DECADE** IS **OUT,** OF LANDING A **MAN ON THE MOON** AND RETURNING HIM SAFELY TO THE **EARTH.**

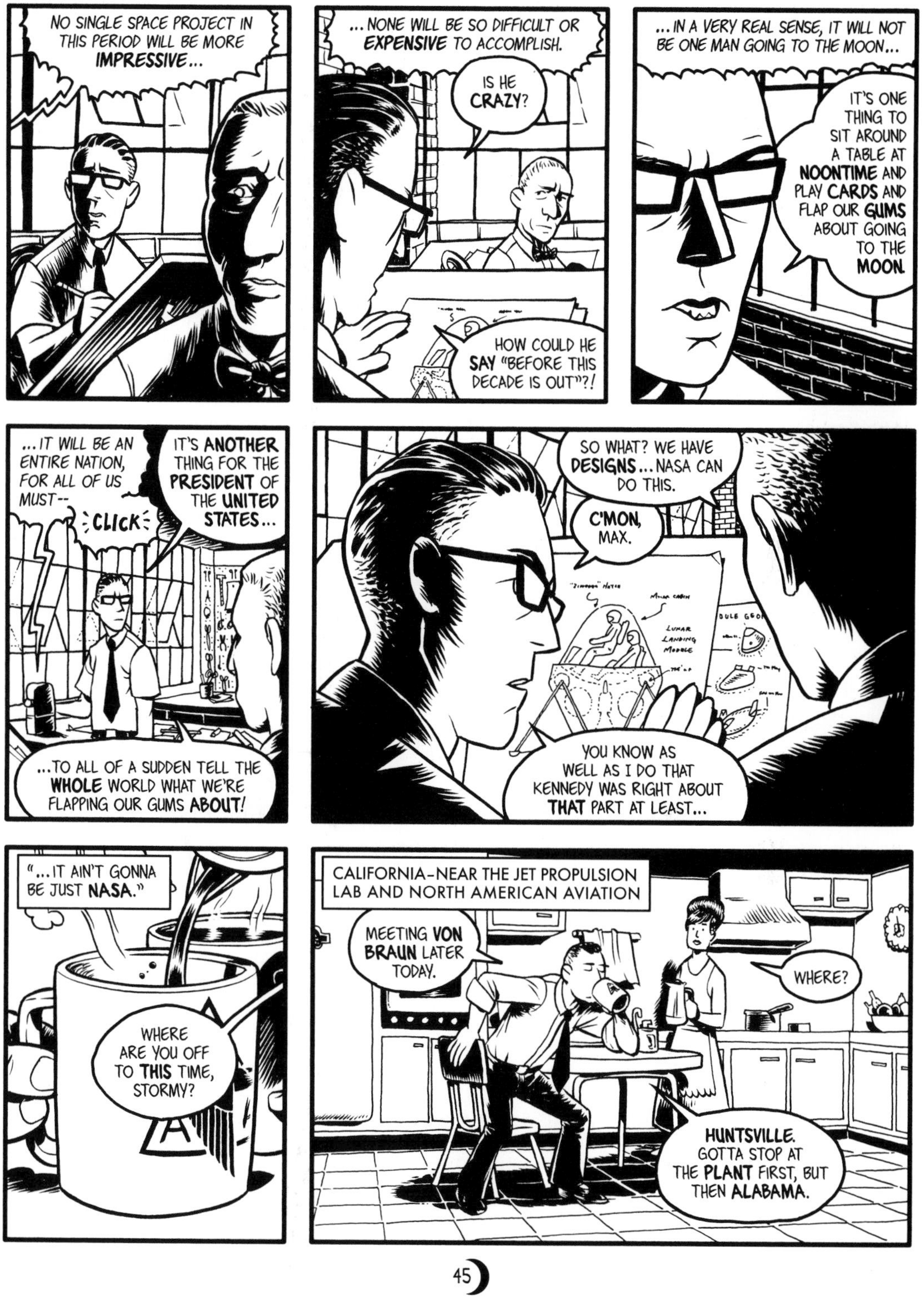
NO SINGLE SPACE PROJECT IN THIS PERIOD WILL BE MORE IMPRESSIVE...
...NONE WILL BE SO DIFFICULT OR EXPENSIVE TO ACCOMPLISH.
IS HE CRAZY?
HOW COULD HE SAY "BEFORE THIS DECADE IS OUT"?!
...IN A VERY REAL SENSE, IT WILL NOT BE ONE MAN GOING TO THE MOON...
IT'S ONE THING TO SIT AROUND A TABLE AT NOONTIME AND PLAY CARDS AND FLAP OUR GUMS ABOUT GOING TO THE MOON.
...IT WILL BE AN ENTIRE NATION, FOR ALL OF US MUST--
CLICK
IT'S ANOTHER THING FOR THE PRESIDENT OF THE UNITED STATES...
...TO ALL OF A SUDDEN TELL THE WHOLE WORLD WHAT WE'RE FLAPPING OUR GUMS ABOUT!
SO WHAT? WE HAVE DESIGNS... NASA CAN DO THIS.
C'MON, MAX.
YOU KNOW AS WELL AS I DO THAT KENNEDY WAS RIGHT ABOUT THAT PART AT LEAST...
"...IT AIN'T GONNA BE JUST NASA."
WHERE ARE YOU OFF TO THIS TIME, STORMY?
CALIFORNIA–NEAR THE JET PROPULSION LAB AND NORTH AMERICAN AVIATION
MEETING VON BRAUN LATER TODAY.
WHERE?
HUNTSVILLE. GOTTA STOP AT THE PLANT FIRST, BUT THEN ALABAMA.

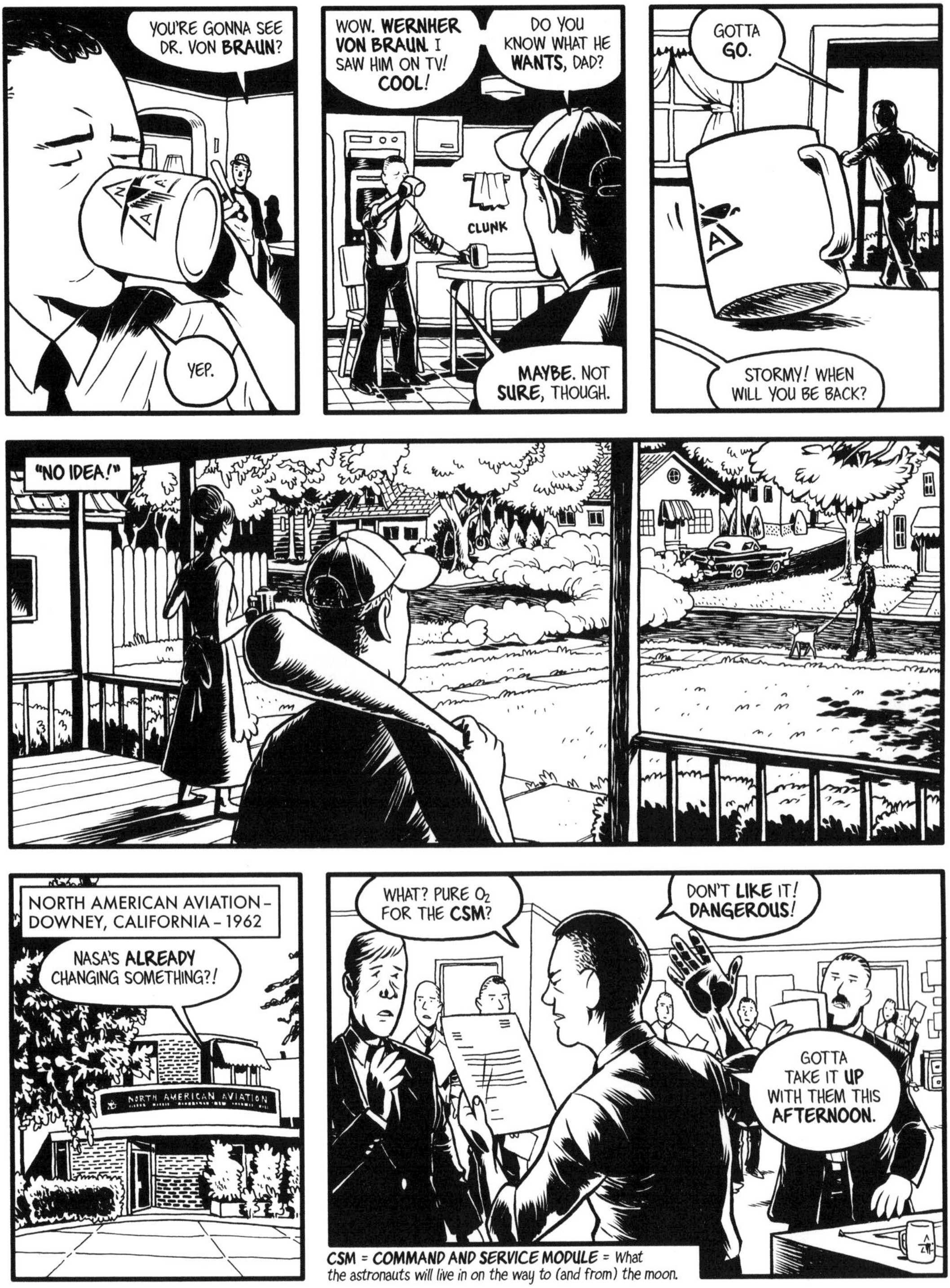

YOU'RE GONNA SEE DR. VON **BRAUN**?
YEP.
WOW. **WERNHER VON BRAUN.** I SAW HIM ON TV! **COOL**!
DO YOU KNOW WHAT HE **WANTS**, DAD?
CLUNK
MAYBE. NOT **SURE**, THOUGH.
GOTTA **GO**.
STORMY! WHEN WILL YOU BE BACK?
"NO IDEA!"
NORTH AMERICAN AVIATION – DOWNEY, CALIFORNIA – 1962
NASA'S **ALREADY** CHANGING SOMETHING?!
NORTH AMERICAN AVIATION
WHAT? PURE O_2 FOR THE **CSM**?
DON'T **LIKE** IT! **DANGEROUS**!
GOTTA TAKE IT **UP** WITH THEM THIS **AFTERNOON**.

CSM = COMMAND AND SERVICE MODULE = *What the astronauts will live in on the way to (and from) the moon.*

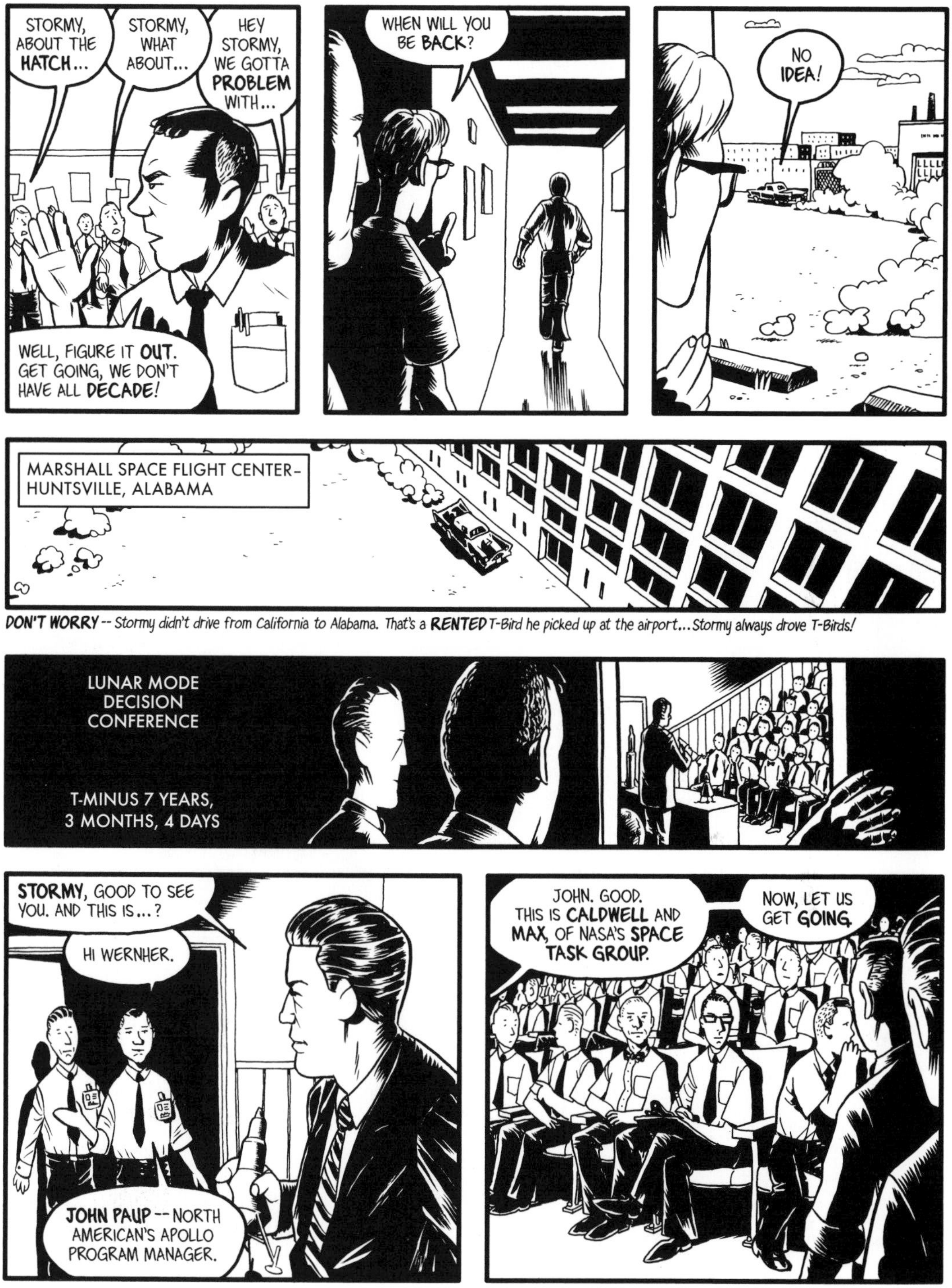

STORMY, ABOUT THE **HATCH**...
STORMY, WHAT ABOUT...
HEY STORMY, WE GOTTA **PROBLEM** WITH...
WELL, FIGURE IT **OUT**. GET GOING, WE DON'T HAVE ALL **DECADE**!
WHEN WILL YOU BE **BACK**?
NO **IDEA**!
MARSHALL SPACE FLIGHT CENTER–HUNTSVILLE, ALABAMA
DON'T WORRY -- *Stormy didn't drive from California to Alabama. That's a* **RENTED** *T-Bird he picked up at the airport*... *Stormy always drove T-Birds!*
LUNAR MODE DECISION CONFERENCE
T-MINUS 7 YEARS, 3 MONTHS, 4 DAYS
STORMY, GOOD TO SEE YOU. AND THIS IS...?
HI WERNHER.
JOHN PAUP -- NORTH AMERICAN'S APOLLO PROGRAM MANAGER.
JOHN. GOOD. THIS IS **CALDWELL** AND **MAX**, OF NASA'S **SPACE TASK GROUP**.
NOW, LET US GET **GOING**.

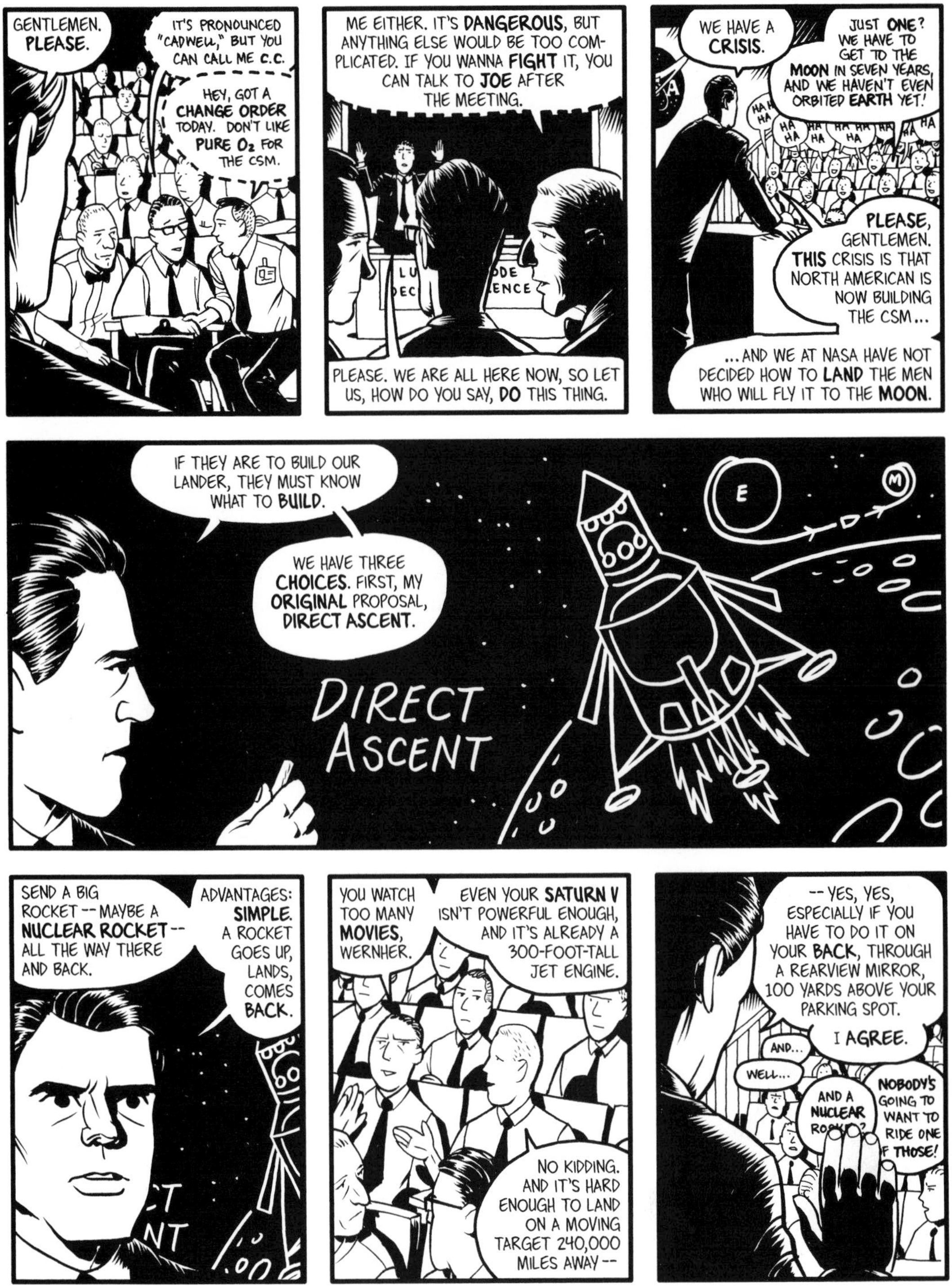
GENTLEMEN. PLEASE.
IT'S PRONOUNCED "CADWELL," BUT YOU CAN CALL ME C.C.
HEY, GOT A CHANGE ORDER TODAY. DON'T LIKE PURE O2 FOR THE CSM.
ME EITHER. IT'S DANGEROUS, BUT ANYTHING ELSE WOULD BE TOO COMPLICATED. IF YOU WANNA FIGHT IT, YOU CAN TALK TO JOE AFTER THE MEETING.
PLEASE. WE ARE ALL HERE NOW, SO LET US, HOW DO YOU SAY, DO THIS THING.
WE HAVE A CRISIS.
JUST ONE? WE HAVE TO GET TO THE MOON IN SEVEN YEARS, AND WE HAVEN'T EVEN ORBITED EARTH YET!
HA HA
HA HA
PLEASE, GENTLEMEN. THIS CRISIS IS THAT NORTH AMERICAN IS NOW BUILDING THE CSM...
...AND WE AT NASA HAVE NOT DECIDED HOW TO LAND THE MEN WHO WILL FLY IT TO THE MOON.
IF THEY ARE TO BUILD OUR LANDER, THEY MUST KNOW WHAT TO BUILD.
WE HAVE THREE CHOICES. FIRST, MY ORIGINAL PROPOSAL, DIRECT ASCENT.
DIRECT ASCENT
E
M
SEND A BIG ROCKET -- MAYBE A NUCLEAR ROCKET -- ALL THE WAY THERE AND BACK.
ADVANTAGES: SIMPLE. A ROCKET GOES UP, LANDS, COMES BACK.
YOU WATCH TOO MANY MOVIES, WERNHER.
EVEN YOUR SATURN V ISN'T POWERFUL ENOUGH, AND IT'S ALREADY A 300-FOOT-TALL JET ENGINE.
NO KIDDING. AND IT'S HARD ENOUGH TO LAND ON A MOVING TARGET 240,000 MILES AWAY --
-- YES, YES, ESPECIALLY IF YOU HAVE TO DO IT ON YOUR BACK, THROUGH A REARVIEW MIRROR, 100 YARDS ABOVE YOUR PARKING SPOT.
I AGREE.
AND...
WELL...
AND A NUCLEAR
NOBODY'S GOING TO WANT TO RIDE ONE F THOSE!

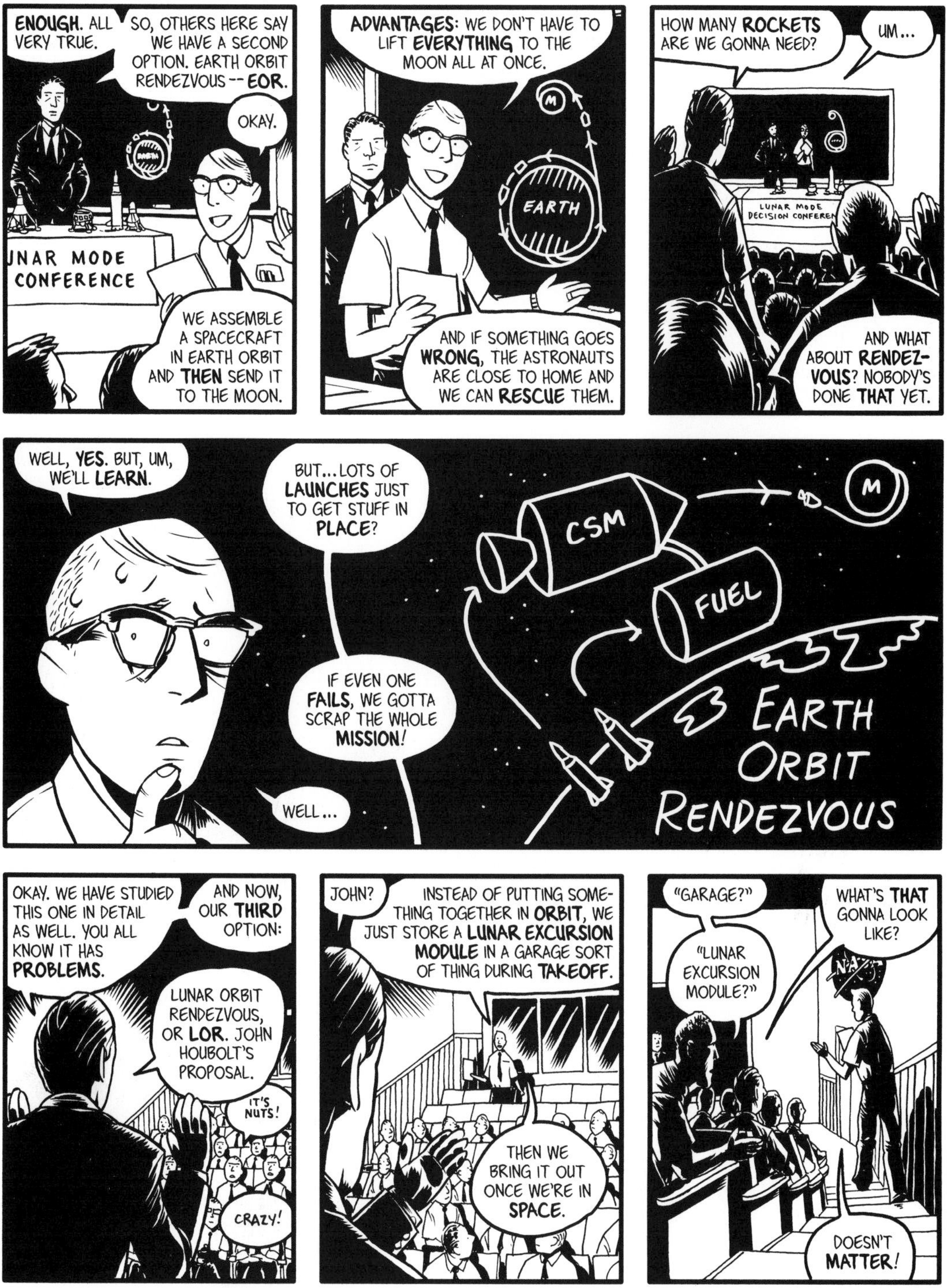
ENOUGH. ALL VERY TRUE.
SO, OTHERS HERE SAY WE HAVE A SECOND OPTION. EARTH ORBIT RENDEZVOUS -- EOR.
OKAY.
EARTH
UNAR MODE CONFERENCE
WE ASSEMBLE A SPACECRAFT IN EARTH ORBIT AND THEN SEND IT TO THE MOON.
ADVANTAGES: WE DON'T HAVE TO LIFT EVERYTHING TO THE MOON ALL AT ONCE.
M
EARTH
AND IF SOMETHING GOES WRONG, THE ASTRONAUTS ARE CLOSE TO HOME AND WE CAN RESCUE THEM.
HOW MANY ROCKETS ARE WE GONNA NEED?
UM...
LUNAR MODE DECISION CONFEREN
AND WHAT ABOUT RENDEZ-VOUS? NOBODY'S DONE THAT YET.
WELL, YES. BUT, UM, WE'LL LEARN.
BUT... LOTS OF LAUNCHES JUST TO GET STUFF IN PLACE?
IF EVEN ONE FAILS, WE GOTTA SCRAP THE WHOLE MISSION!
WELL...
CSM
M
FUEL
EARTH ORBIT RENDEZVOUS
OKAY. WE HAVE STUDIED THIS ONE IN DETAIL AS WELL. YOU ALL KNOW IT HAS PROBLEMS.
AND NOW, OUR THIRD OPTION:
LUNAR ORBIT RENDEZVOUS, OR LOR. JOHN HOUBOLT'S PROPOSAL.
IT'S NUTS!
CRAZY!
JOHN?
INSTEAD OF PUTTING SOMETHING TOGETHER IN ORBIT, WE JUST STORE A LUNAR EXCURSION MODULE IN A GARAGE SORT OF THING DURING TAKEOFF.
THEN WE BRING IT OUT ONCE WE'RE IN SPACE.
"GARAGE?"
"LUNAR EXCURSION MODULE?"
WHAT'S THAT GONNA LOOK LIKE?
DOESN'T MATTER!

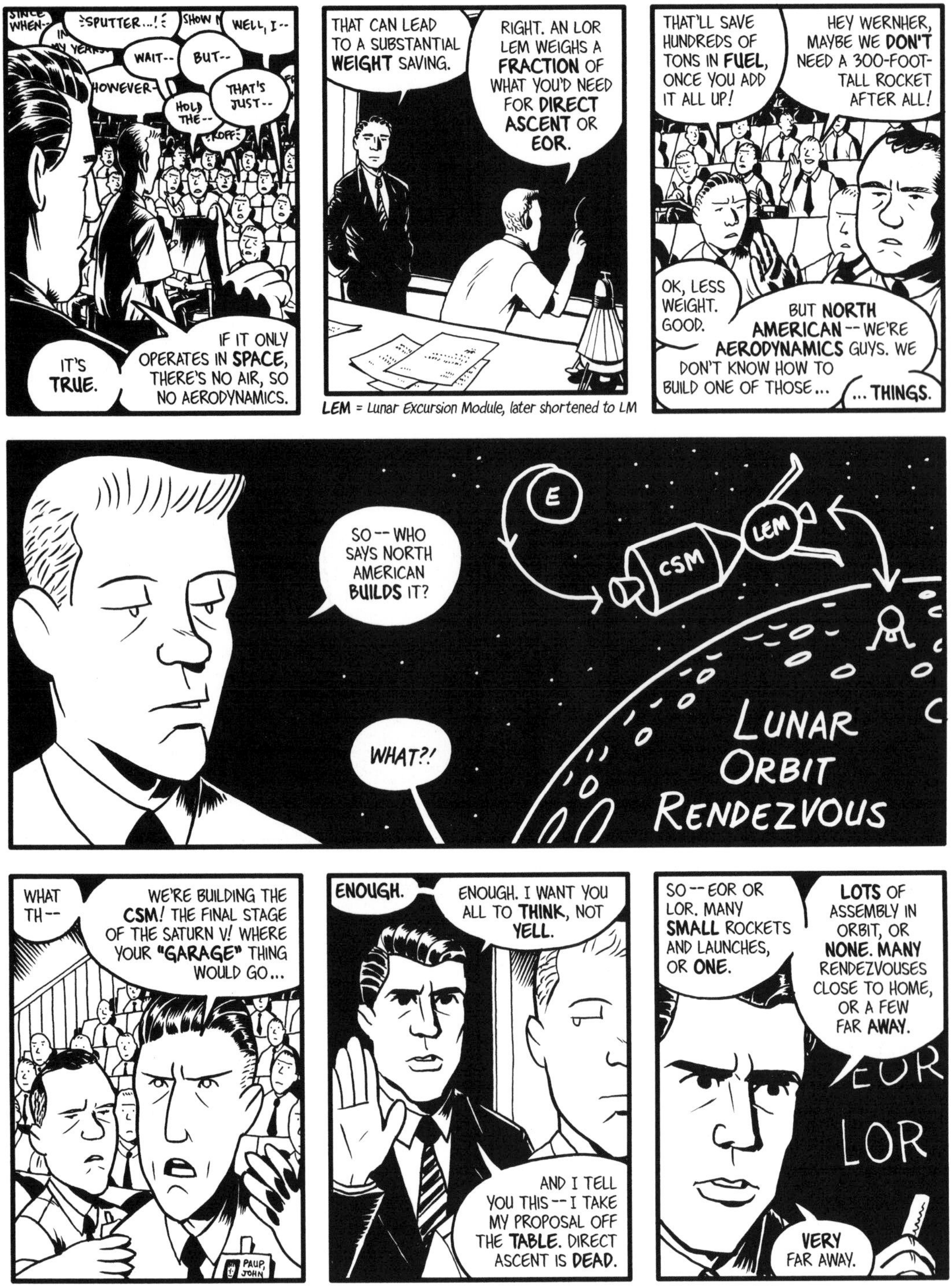
WHEN--
SPUTTER...!
WELL, I--
WAIT--
BUT--
HOWEVER-
HOLD THE--
THAT'S JUST--
KOFF
IT'S TRUE.
IF IT ONLY OPERATES IN SPACE, THERE'S NO AIR, SO NO AERODYNAMICS.
THAT CAN LEAD TO A SUBSTANTIAL WEIGHT SAVING.
RIGHT. AN LOR LEM WEIGHS A FRACTION OF WHAT YOU'D NEED FOR DIRECT ASCENT OR EOR.
LEM = Lunar Excursion Module, later shortened to LM
THAT'LL SAVE HUNDREDS OF TONS IN FUEL, ONCE YOU ADD IT ALL UP!
HEY WERNHER, MAYBE WE DON'T NEED A 300-FOOT-TALL ROCKET AFTER ALL!
OK, LESS WEIGHT. GOOD.
BUT NORTH AMERICAN--WE'RE AERODYNAMICS GUYS. WE DON'T KNOW HOW TO BUILD ONE OF THOSE...
...THINGS.
SO--WHO SAYS NORTH AMERICAN BUILDS IT?
WHAT?!
E
CSM
LEM
LUNAR ORBIT RENDEZVOUS
WHAT TH--
WE'RE BUILDING THE CSM! THE FINAL STAGE OF THE SATURN V! WHERE YOUR "GARAGE" THING WOULD GO...
PAUP, JOHN
ENOUGH.
ENOUGH. I WANT YOU ALL TO THINK, NOT YELL.
AND I TELL YOU THIS--I TAKE MY PROPOSAL OFF THE TABLE. DIRECT ASCENT IS DEAD.
SO--EOR OR LOR. MANY SMALL ROCKETS AND LAUNCHES, OR ONE.
LOTS OF ASSEMBLY IN ORBIT, OR NONE. MANY RENDEZVOUSES CLOSE TO HOME, OR A FEW FAR AWAY.
EOR
LOR
VERY FAR AWAY.

"DISCUSS. WE DECIDE TODAY."

...WE DON'T GET TO BUILD THE **LUNAR EXCURSION MODULE** IF WE CHOOSE THIS.

IT'S BAD FOR THE **COMPANY**.

YEAH, BUT...

...THE WHOLE APOLLO PROGRAM, YOU KNOW?

YEAH, I **KNOW**.

ALL RIGHT. **DECISION.** C.C.? MAX?

THE **SPACE TASK GROUP** THINKS LOR IS THE WAY TO **GO**.

SPEAKING FOR THE **ROCKET LAUNCH** AND **BOOSTER** GROUPS HERE AT **MARSHALL**, I AGREE.

STORMS, CAN NORTH AMERICAN BUILD US A **LUNAR EXCURSION MODULE** FOR LOR?

LUNAR MODE DECISION CONFERENCE

NOPE. CAN'T DO IT.

≥GASP!!≤

DOESN'T **MATTER** THOUGH -- WE'LL **GET** YOU THERE. SOMEONE ELSE WILL BUILD THE... THING...THAT LANDS.

THE POINT IS TO **DO** IT!

SO, ANY **IDIOTS** OUT THERE THINKING LOR **ISN'T** THE RIGHT THING?

IN TERMS OF--

I CAN'T--

SINCE CAN'T--

FOR HOW LONG--

HOW WILL--

WHAT

BUT HOW THE--

BUT THAT'S A--

WHERE WILL WE--

UNB ABLE

LUNAR MODE DECISION CONFERENCE

OK, THEN IT IS **SETTLED**.

I WILL WRITE THE **MEMO** AND GET IT **APPROVED.** YOU PEOPLE GET BACK TO **WORK**...AND GET IT **DONE.**

LET US **GO!**

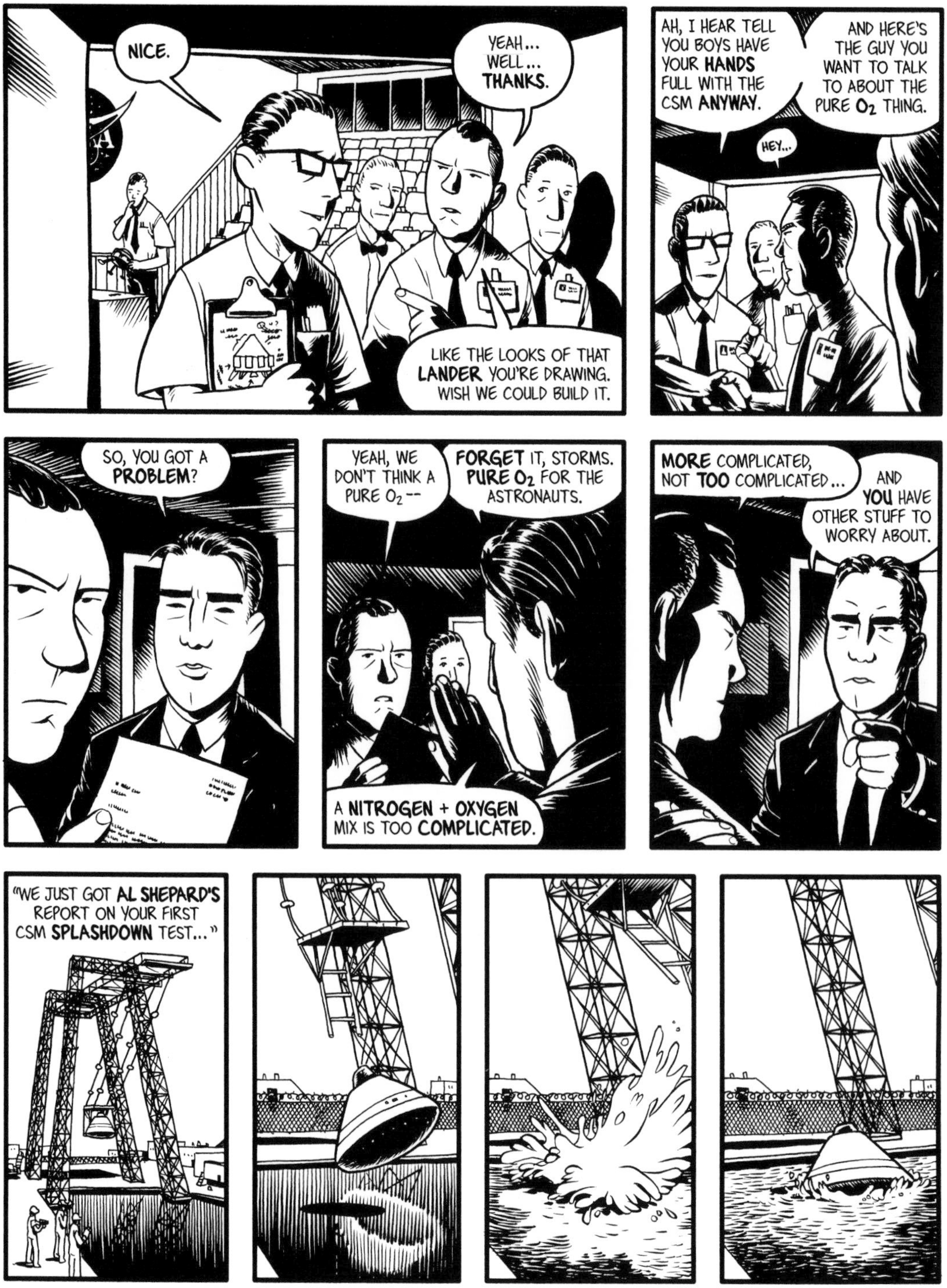
NICE.
YEAH... WELL... THANKS.
LIKE THE LOOKS OF THAT LANDER YOU'RE DRAWING. WISH WE COULD BUILD IT.
AH, I HEAR TELL YOU BOYS HAVE YOUR HANDS FULL WITH THE CSM ANYWAY.
AND HERE'S THE GUY YOU WANT TO TALK TO ABOUT THE PURE O_2 THING.
HEY...
SO, YOU GOT A PROBLEM?
YEAH, WE DON'T THINK A PURE O_2 --
FORGET IT, STORMS. PURE O_2 FOR THE ASTRONAUTS.
A NITROGEN + OXYGEN MIX IS TOO COMPLICATED.
MORE COMPLICATED, NOT TOO COMPLICATED...
AND YOU HAVE OTHER STUFF TO WORRY ABOUT.
"WE JUST GOT AL SHEPARD'S REPORT ON YOUR FIRST CSM SPLASHDOWN TEST..."

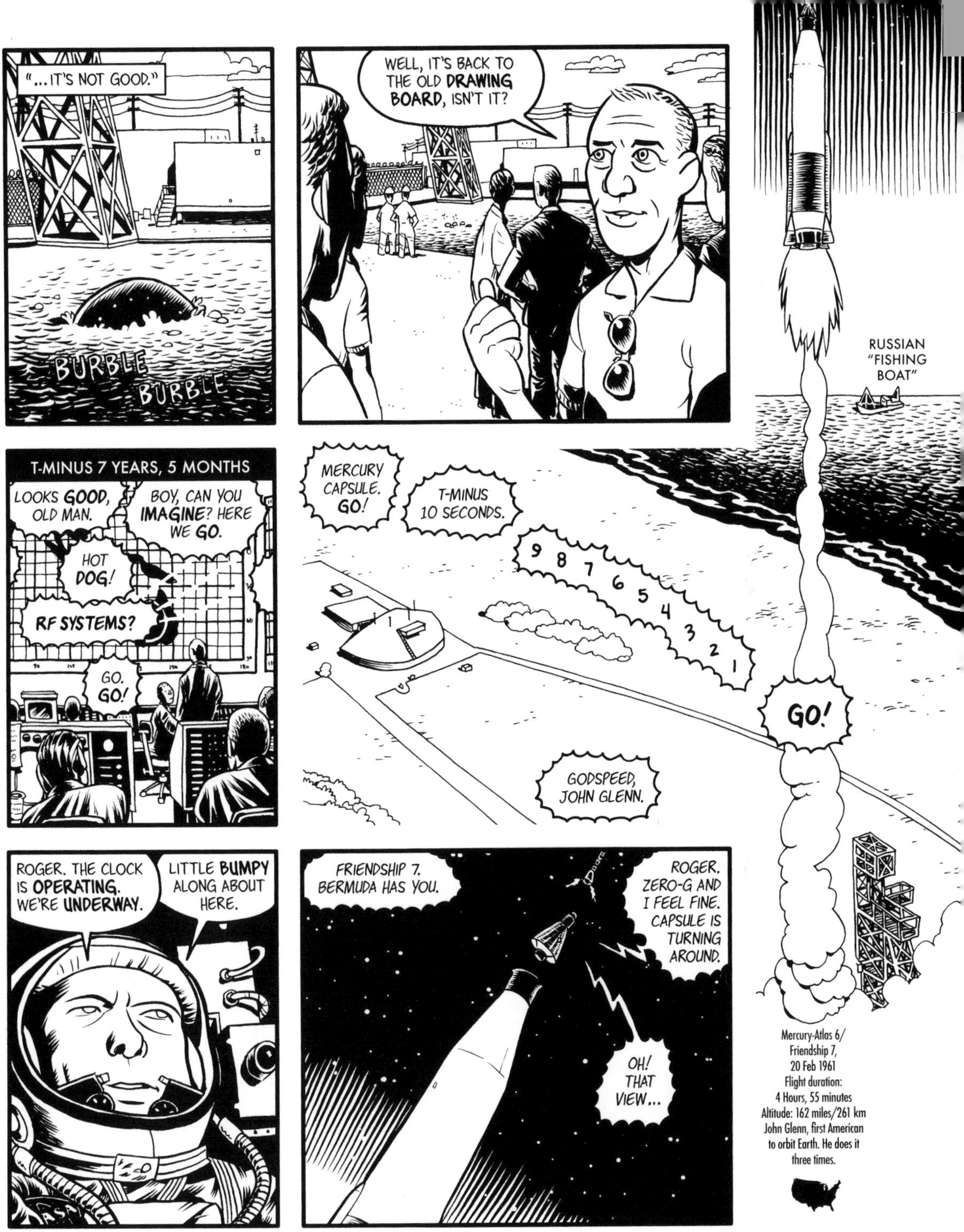
"...IT'S NOT GOOD."
BURBLE BURBLE
WELL, IT'S BACK TO THE OLD DRAWING BOARD, ISN'T IT?
RUSSIAN "FISHING BOAT"
T-MINUS 7 YEARS, 5 MONTHS
LOOKS GOOD, OLD MAN.
BOY, CAN YOU IMAGINE? HERE WE GO.
HOT DOG!
RF SYSTEMS?
GO. GO!
MERCURY CAPSULE. GO!
T-MINUS 10 SECONDS.
9 8 7 6 5 4 3 2 1
GO!
GODSPEED, JOHN GLENN.
ROGER. THE CLOCK IS OPERATING. WE'RE UNDERWAY.
LITTLE BUMPY ALONG ABOUT HERE.
FRIENDSHIP 7. BERMUDA HAS YOU.
ROGER. ZERO-G AND I FEEL FINE. CAPSULE IS TURNING AROUND.
OH! THAT VIEW...

Mercury-Atlas 6/
Friendship 7,
20 Feb 1961
Flight duration:
4 Hours, 55 minutes
Altitude: 162 miles/261 km
John Glenn, first American to orbit Earth. He does it three times.

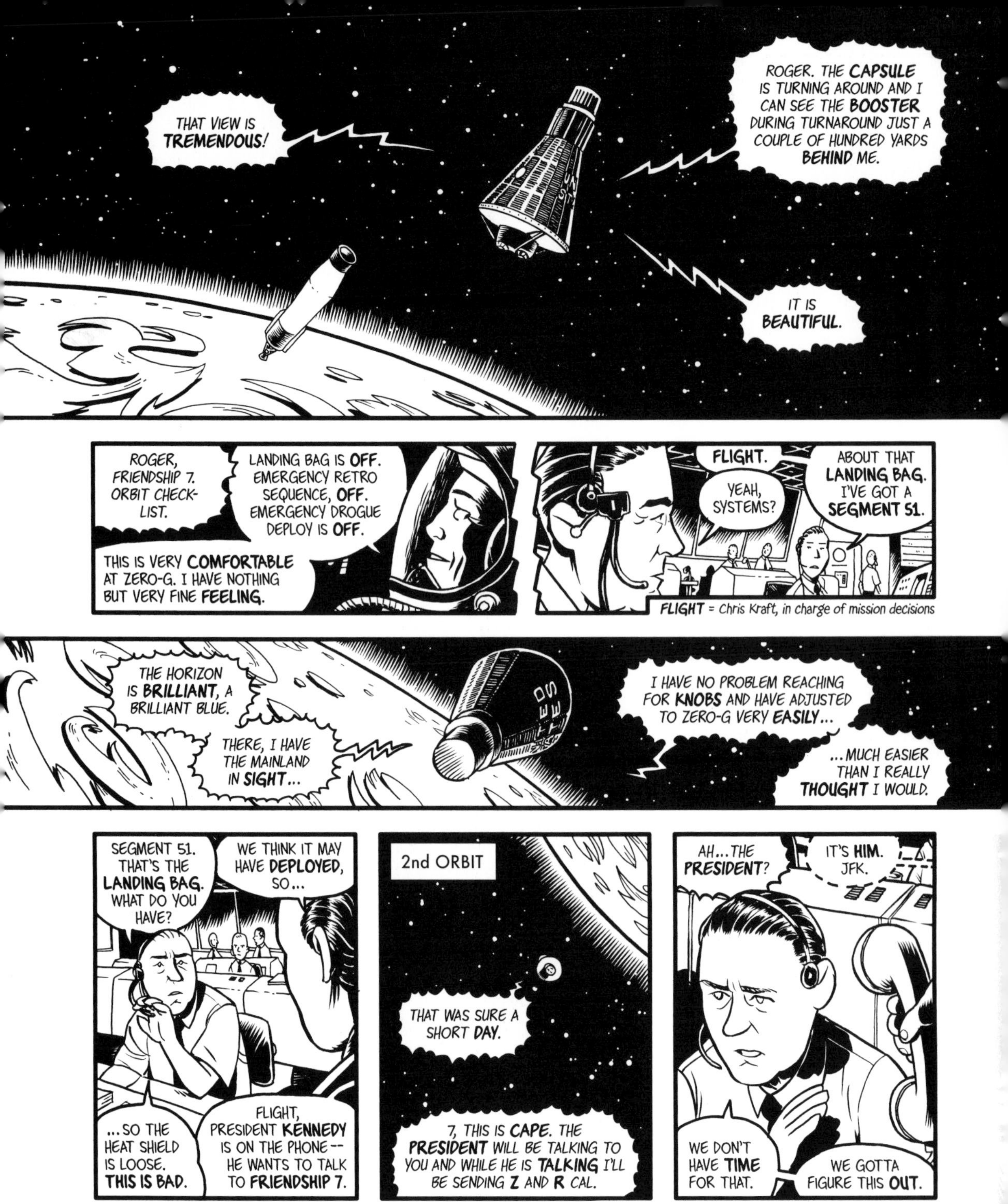
THAT VIEW IS **TREMENDOUS**!
ROGER. THE **CAPSULE** IS TURNING AROUND AND I CAN SEE THE **BOOSTER** DURING TURNAROUND JUST A COUPLE OF HUNDRED YARDS **BEHIND** ME.
IT IS **BEAUTIFUL**.
ROGER, FRIENDSHIP 7. ORBIT CHECK-LIST.
LANDING BAG IS **OFF**. EMERGENCY RETRO SEQUENCE, **OFF**. EMERGENCY DROGUE DEPLOY IS **OFF**.
THIS IS VERY **COMFORTABLE** AT ZERO-G. I HAVE NOTHING BUT VERY FINE **FEELING**.
FLIGHT.
YEAH, SYSTEMS?
ABOUT THAT **LANDING BAG**. I'VE GOT A **SEGMENT 51**.
THE HORIZON IS **BRILLIANT**, A BRILLIANT BLUE.
THERE, I HAVE THE MAINLAND IN **SIGHT**...
I HAVE NO PROBLEM REACHING FOR **KNOBS** AND HAVE ADJUSTED TO ZERO-G VERY **EASILY**...
...MUCH EASIER THAN I REALLY **THOUGHT** I WOULD.
SEGMENT 51. THAT'S THE **LANDING BAG**. WHAT DO YOU HAVE?
WE THINK IT MAY HAVE **DEPLOYED**, SO...
...SO THE HEAT SHIELD IS LOOSE. **THIS IS BAD**.
FLIGHT, PRESIDENT **KENNEDY** IS ON THE PHONE-- HE WANTS TO TALK TO **FRIENDSHIP** 7.
2nd ORBIT
THAT WAS SURE A SHORT **DAY**.
7, THIS IS **CAPE**. THE **PRESIDENT** WILL BE TALKING TO YOU AND WHILE HE IS **TALKING** I'LL BE SENDING **Z** AND **R** CAL.
AH... THE **PRESIDENT**?
IT'S **HIM**. JFK.
WE DON'T HAVE **TIME** FOR THAT.
WE GOTTA FIGURE THIS **OUT**.

FLIGHT = *Chris Kraft, in charge of mission decisions*

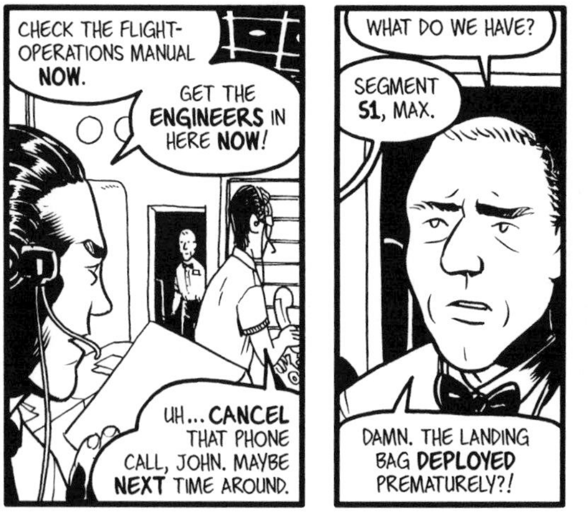
CHECK THE FLIGHT-OPERATIONS MANUAL **NOW**.
GET THE **ENGINEERS** IN HERE **NOW**!
UH... **CANCEL** THAT PHONE CALL, JOHN. MAYBE **NEXT** TIME AROUND.
WHAT DO WE HAVE?
SEGMENT **51**, MAX.
DAMN. THE LANDING BAG **DEPLOYED** PREMATURELY?!

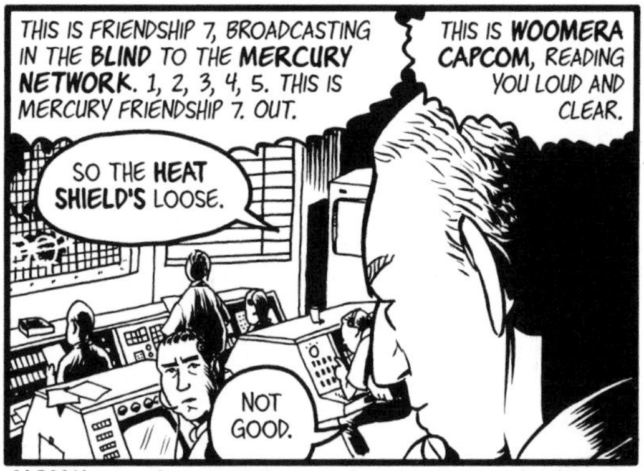
THIS IS FRIENDSHIP 7, BROADCASTING IN THE **BLIND** TO THE **MERCURY NETWORK**. 1, 2, 3, 4, 5. THIS IS MERCURY FRIENDSHIP 7. OUT.
THIS IS **WOOMERA CAPCOM**, READING YOU LOUD AND CLEAR.
SO THE **HEAT SHIELD'S** LOOSE.
NOT GOOD.

CAPCOM = *Capsule Communicator = an astronaut on the ground, and the only person who talks directly with the astronaut in flight.*

WOOMERA = *A city in Australia--CAPCOMs were stationed all over the world for orbital missions. (P.S. Look up the meaning of "woomera"!)*

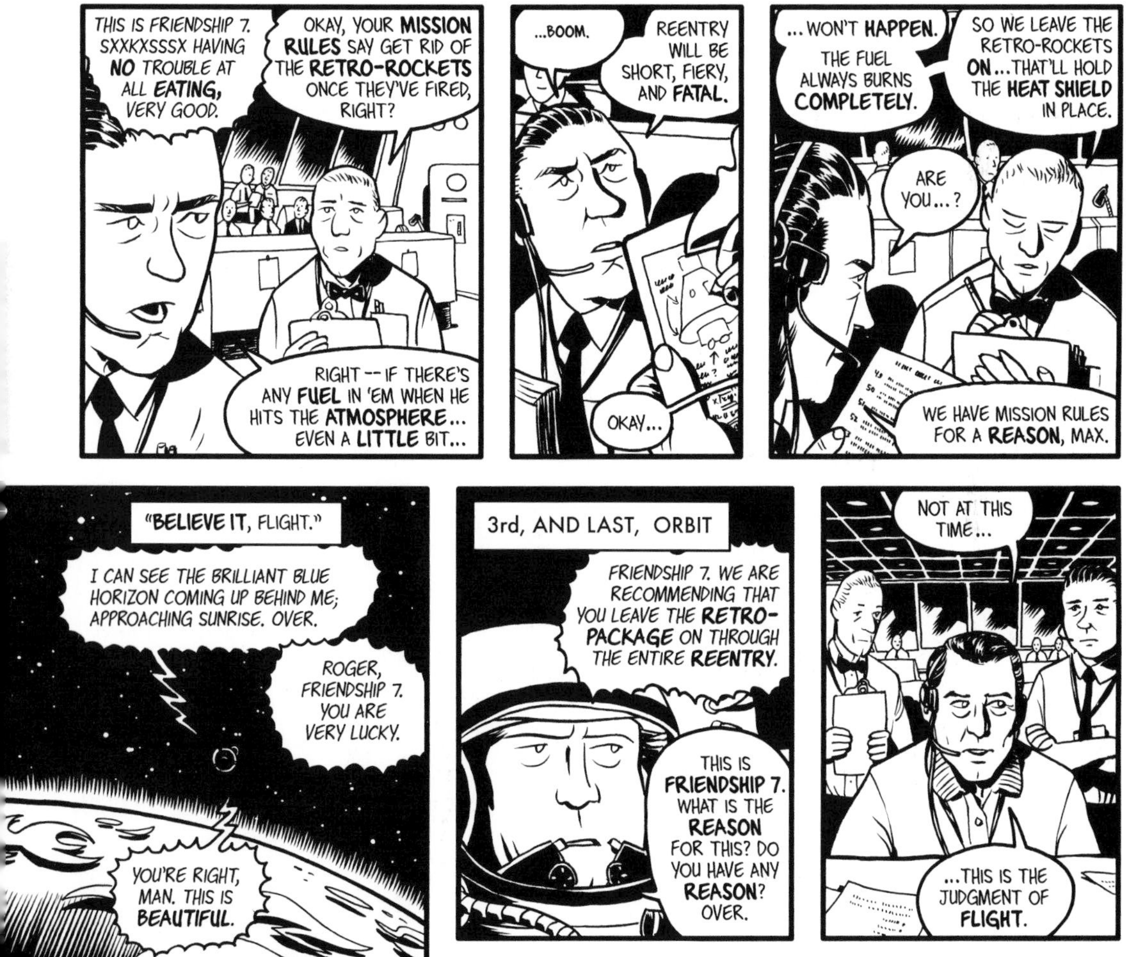
THIS IS FRIENDSHIP 7. SXXKXSSSX HAVING **NO** TROUBLE AT ALL **EATING**, VERY GOOD.
OKAY, YOUR **MISSION RULES** SAY GET RID OF THE **RETRO-ROCKETS** ONCE THEY'VE FIRED, RIGHT?
RIGHT -- IF THERE'S ANY **FUEL** IN 'EM WHEN HE HITS THE **ATMOSPHERE**... EVEN A **LITTLE** BIT...
...BOOM.
REENTRY WILL BE SHORT, FIERY, AND **FATAL**.
OKAY...
... WON'T **HAPPEN**.
THE FUEL ALWAYS BURNS **COMPLETELY**.
SO WE LEAVE THE RETRO-ROCKETS **ON**... THAT'LL HOLD THE **HEAT SHIELD** IN PLACE.
ARE YOU...?
WE HAVE MISSION RULES FOR A **REASON**, MAX.
"**BELIEVE IT**, FLIGHT."
I CAN SEE THE BRILLIANT BLUE HORIZON COMING UP BEHIND ME; APPROACHING SUNRISE. OVER.
ROGER, FRIENDSHIP 7. YOU ARE VERY LUCKY.
YOU'RE RIGHT, MAN. THIS IS **BEAUTIFUL**.
3rd, AND LAST, ORBIT
FRIENDSHIP 7. WE ARE RECOMMENDING THAT YOU LEAVE THE **RETRO-PACKAGE** ON THROUGH THE ENTIRE **REENTRY**.
THIS IS **FRIENDSHIP 7**. WHAT IS THE **REASON** FOR THIS? DO YOU HAVE ANY **REASON**? OVER.
NOT AT THIS TIME...
...THIS IS THE JUDGMENT OF **FLIGHT**.

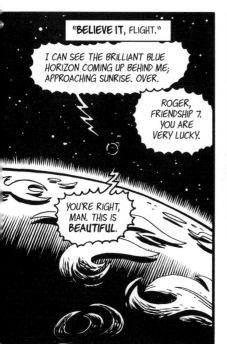

WHY THE...? HMM.

SAY AGAIN YOUR **INSTRUCTIONS** PLEASE. OVER.

WE ARE RECOM-MENDING THAT THE RETRO-PACKAGE NOT, I SAY AGAIN, **NOT** BE JETTISONED.

ROGER, UNDERSTAND. I WILL HAVE TO MAKE A MANUAL 0.05 G ENTRY WHEN IT OCCURS... IS THAT **AFFIRM**?

THAT IS **AFFIRMATIVE,** FRIENDSHIP 7.

SXXKX -- SHIP 7 XKSSX PACK SKXXXS LET GO.

THIS IS **FRIEND** -- SKSSKX XXKSS REAL FIRE SKKXXX OUTSIDE

7, THIS IS **CAPE.** WHAT'S YOUR GENERAL CONDITION?

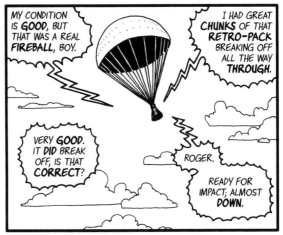

MY CONDITION IS **GOOD,** BUT THAT WAS A REAL **FIREBALL,** BOY.

I HAD GREAT **CHUNKS** OF THAT **RETRO-PACK** BREAKING OFF ALL THE WAY **THROUGH.**

VERY **GOOD.** IT **DID** BREAK OFF, IS THAT **CORRECT**?

ROGER.

READY FOR IMPACT; ALMOST **DOWN.**

CONDITION **OK.** DOES THE **CAPSULE** LOOK LIKE IT'S OK? OVER.

FRIENDSHIP 7, REFERENCE YOUR LAST -- **AFFIRMATIVE.**

CAPSULE LOOKS GOOD FROM **HERE.** OVER.

ОКОЛО

ROGER, UNDERSTAND THEY WANT ME TO STAY IN THE **CAPSULE** UNTIL **RESCUE**...

HA. RESCUE! THEY NEED TO **RESCUE** THEIR COSMONAUTS.

THE **CHIEF DESIGNER** WILL FIND THIS MOST **INTERESTING.**

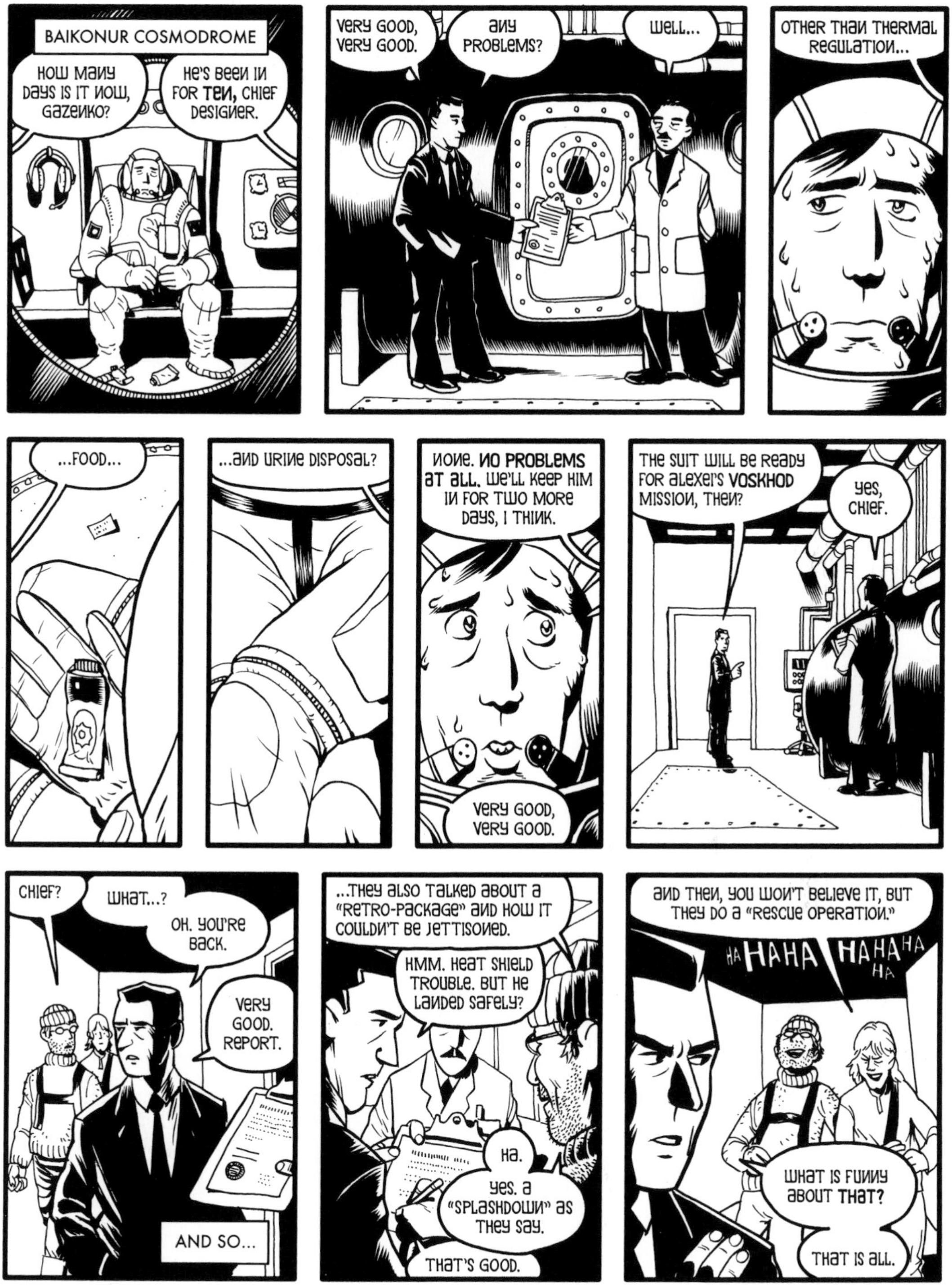
BAIKONUR COSMODROME
HOW MANY DAYS IS IT NOW, GAZENKO?
HE'S BEEN IN FOR TEN, CHIEF DESIGNER.
VERY GOOD, VERY GOOD.
ANY PROBLEMS?
WELL...
OTHER THAN THERMAL REGULATION...
...FOOD...
...AND URINE DISPOSAL?
NONE. NO PROBLEMS AT ALL. WE'LL KEEP HIM IN FOR TWO MORE DAYS, I THINK.
VERY GOOD, VERY GOOD.
THE SUIT WILL BE READY FOR ALEXEI'S VOSKHOD MISSION, THEN?
YES, CHIEF.
CHIEF?
WHAT...?
OH. YOU'RE BACK.
VERY GOOD. REPORT.
AND SO...
...THEY ALSO TALKED ABOUT A "RETRO-PACKAGE" AND HOW IT COULDN'T BE JETTISONED.
HMM. HEAT SHIELD TROUBLE. BUT HE LANDED SAFELY?
HA.
YES. A "SPLASHDOWN" AS THEY SAY.
THAT'S GOOD.
AND THEN, YOU WON'T BELIEVE IT, BUT THEY DO A "RESCUE OPERATION."
HA HAHA
HAHAHA HA HA
WHAT IS FUNNY ABOUT THAT?
THAT IS ALL.

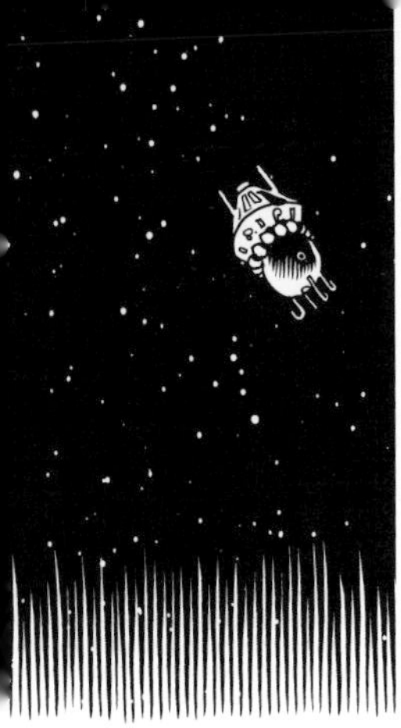

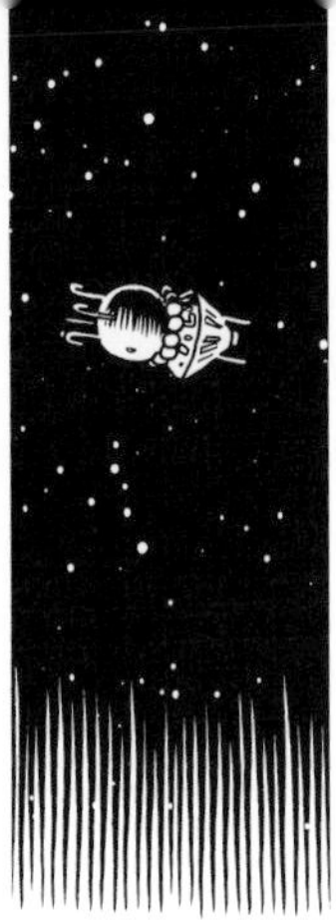

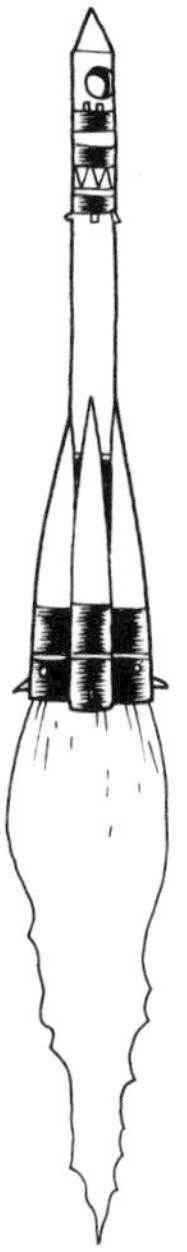

R-7 Semyorka/Vostok 5,
June 14–19, 1963
T-Minus 6 Years, 1 Month, 1 Day
Flight duration: 4 days, 23 hours, 7 minutes
Altitude: 108 miles/175 km
Valery Bykovsky, first long-duration mission

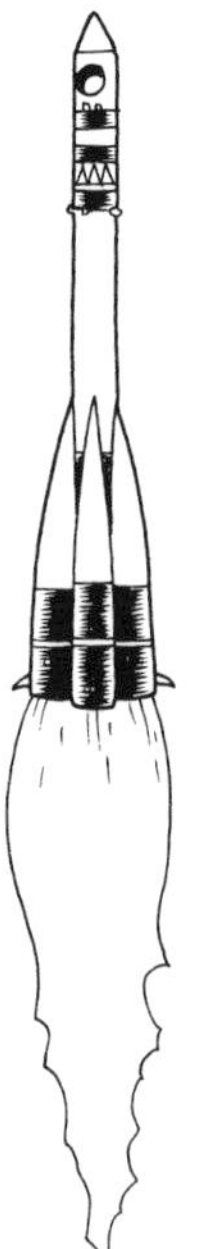

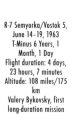

R-7 Semyorka/Vostok 6,
June 16–19, 1963
T-Minus 6 Years, 1 Month, 1 Day
Flight duration: 2 days, 22 hours, 50 minutes
Altitude: 112 miles/181 km
Valentina Tereshkova, the first woman in space

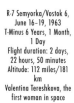

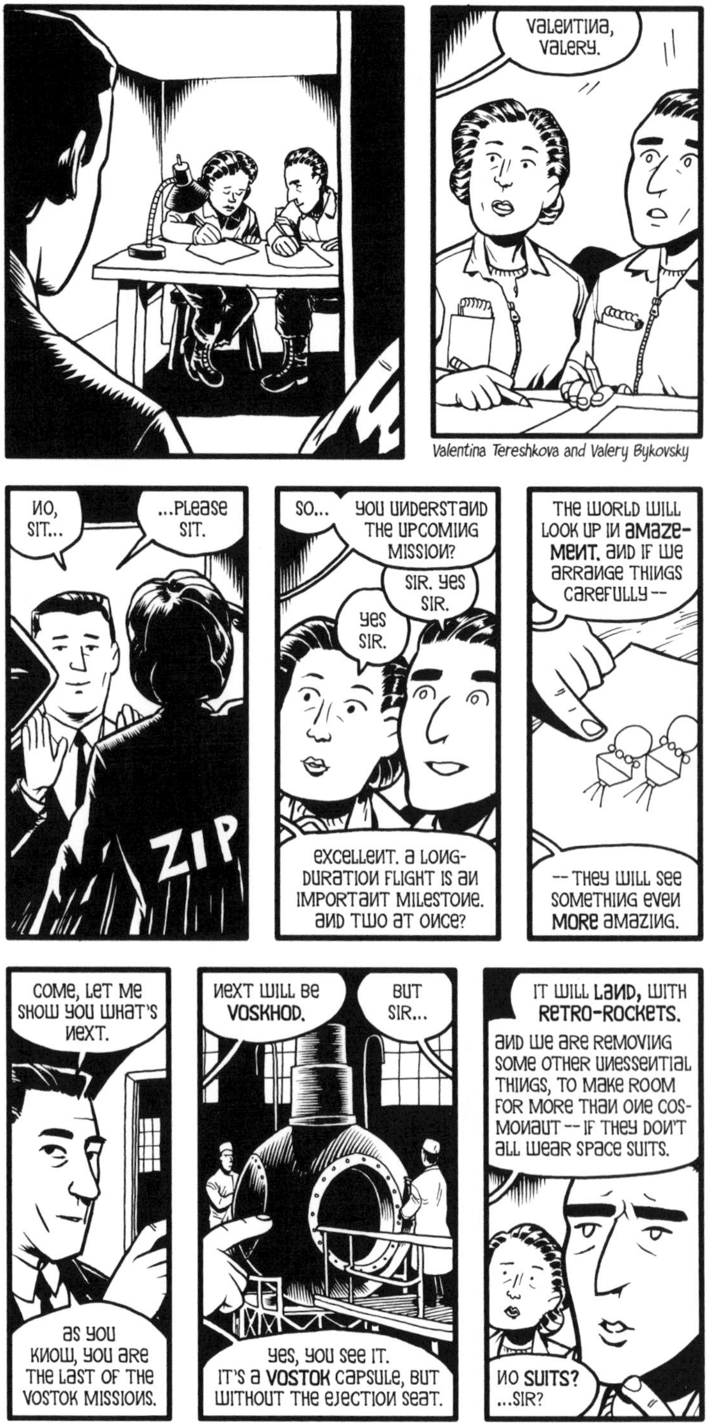
VALENTINA, VALERY.
Valentina Tereshkova and Valery Bykovsky
NO, SIT...
...PLEASE SIT.
ZIP
SO...
YOU UNDERSTAND THE UPCOMING MISSION?
SIR. YES SIR.
YES SIR.
EXCELLENT. A LONG-DURATION FLIGHT IS AN IMPORTANT MILESTONE. AND TWO AT ONCE?
THE WORLD WILL LOOK UP IN AMAZEMENT. AND IF WE ARRANGE THINGS CAREFULLY --
-- THEY WILL SEE SOMETHING EVEN MORE AMAZING.
COME, LET ME SHOW YOU WHAT'S NEXT.
AS YOU KNOW, YOU ARE THE LAST OF THE VOSTOK MISSIONS.
NEXT WILL BE VOSKHOD.
BUT SIR...
YES, YOU SEE IT. IT'S A VOSTOK CAPSULE, BUT WITHOUT THE EJECTION SEAT.
IT WILL LAND, WITH RETRO-ROCKETS.
AND WE ARE REMOVING SOME OTHER NONESSENTIAL THINGS, TO MAKE ROOM FOR MORE THAN ONE COSMONAUT -- IF THEY DON'T ALL WEAR SPACE SUITS.
NO SUITS? ...SIR?

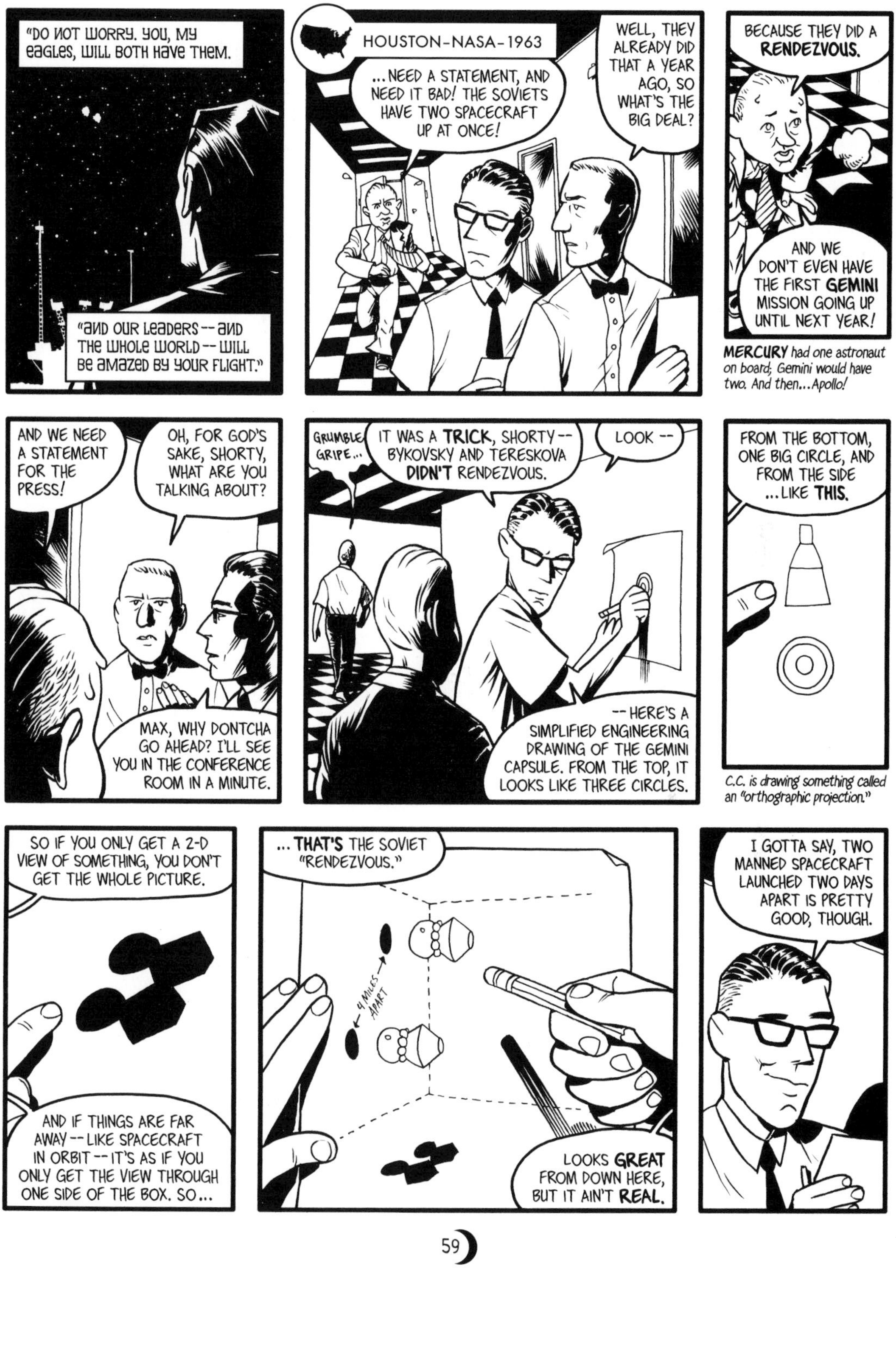
"DO NOT WORRY. YOU, MY EAGLES, WILL BOTH HAVE THEM.
"AND OUR LEADERS -- AND THE WHOLE WORLD -- WILL BE AMAZED BY YOUR FLIGHT."
HOUSTON-NASA-1963
...NEED A STATEMENT, AND NEED IT BAD! THE SOVIETS HAVE TWO SPACECRAFT UP AT ONCE!
WELL, THEY ALREADY DID THAT A YEAR AGO, SO WHAT'S THE BIG DEAL?
BECAUSE THEY DID A **RENDEZVOUS.**
AND WE DON'T EVEN HAVE THE FIRST **GEMINI** MISSION GOING UP UNTIL NEXT YEAR!
MERCURY had one astronaut on board; Gemini would have two. And then...Apollo!
AND WE NEED A STATEMENT FOR THE PRESS!
OH, FOR GOD'S SAKE, SHORTY, WHAT ARE YOU TALKING ABOUT?
MAX, WHY DONTCHA GO AHEAD? I'LL SEE YOU IN THE CONFERENCE ROOM IN A MINUTE.
GRUMBLE GRIPE...
IT WAS A **TRICK**, SHORTY -- BYKOVSKY AND TERESKOVA **DIDN'T** RENDEZVOUS.
LOOK --
-- HERE'S A SIMPLIFIED ENGINEERING DRAWING OF THE GEMINI CAPSULE. FROM THE TOP, IT LOOKS LIKE THREE CIRCLES.
FROM THE BOTTOM, ONE BIG CIRCLE, AND FROM THE SIDE ...LIKE **THIS.**
C.C. is drawing something called an "orthographic projection."
SO IF YOU ONLY GET A 2-D VIEW OF SOMETHING, YOU DON'T GET THE WHOLE PICTURE.
AND IF THINGS ARE FAR AWAY -- LIKE SPACECRAFT IN ORBIT -- IT'S AS IF YOU ONLY GET THE VIEW THROUGH ONE SIDE OF THE BOX. SO...
...**THAT'S** THE SOVIET "RENDEZVOUS."
4 MILES APART
LOOKS **GREAT** FROM DOWN HERE, BUT IT AIN'T **REAL.**
I GOTTA SAY, TWO MANNED SPACECRAFT LAUNCHED TWO DAYS APART IS PRETTY GOOD, THOUGH.

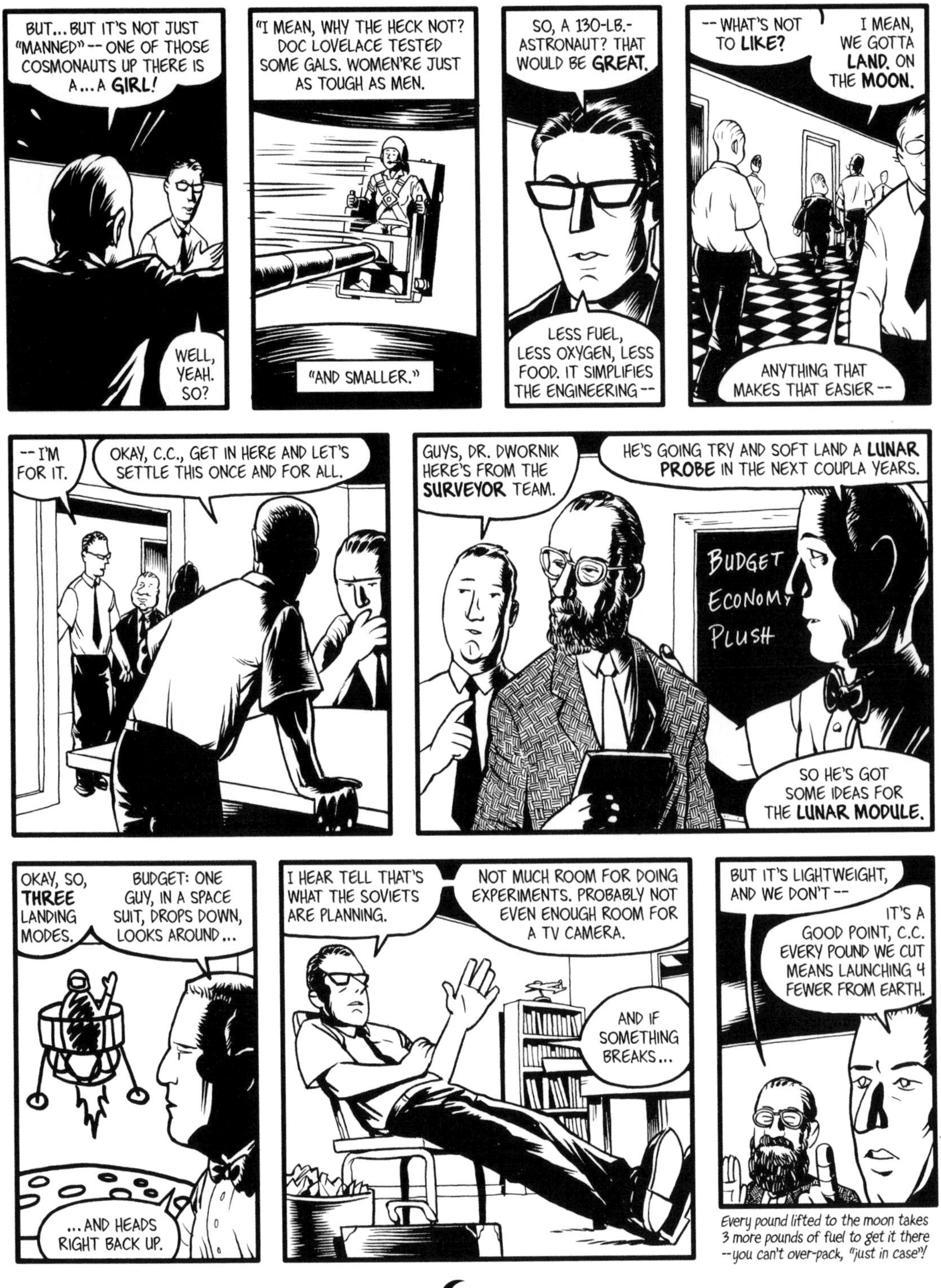
BUT... BUT IT'S NOT JUST "MANNED" -- ONE OF THOSE COSMONAUTS UP THERE IS A... A GIRL!
WELL, YEAH. SO?
"I MEAN, WHY THE HECK NOT? DOC LOVELACE TESTED SOME GALS. WOMEN'RE JUST AS TOUGH AS MEN.
"AND SMALLER."
SO, A 130-LB.-ASTRONAUT? THAT WOULD BE GREAT.
LESS FUEL, LESS OXYGEN, LESS FOOD. IT SIMPLIFIES THE ENGINEERING --
-- WHAT'S NOT TO LIKE?
I MEAN, WE GOTTA LAND. ON THE MOON.
ANYTHING THAT MAKES THAT EASIER --
-- I'M FOR IT.
OKAY, C.C., GET IN HERE AND LET'S SETTLE THIS ONCE AND FOR ALL.
GUYS, DR. DWORNIK HERE'S FROM THE SURVEYOR TEAM.
HE'S GOING TRY AND SOFT LAND A LUNAR PROBE IN THE NEXT COUPLA YEARS.
BUDGET
ECONOMY
PLUSH
SO HE'S GOT SOME IDEAS FOR THE LUNAR MODULE.
OKAY, SO, THREE LANDING MODES.
BUDGET: ONE GUY, IN A SPACE SUIT, DROPS DOWN, LOOKS AROUND...
...AND HEADS RIGHT BACK UP.
I HEAR TELL THAT'S WHAT THE SOVIETS ARE PLANNING.
NOT MUCH ROOM FOR DOING EXPERIMENTS. PROBABLY NOT EVEN ENOUGH ROOM FOR A TV CAMERA.
AND IF SOMETHING BREAKS...
BUT IT'S LIGHTWEIGHT, AND WE DON'T --
IT'S A GOOD POINT, C.C. EVERY POUND WE CUT MEANS LAUNCHING 4 FEWER FROM EARTH.
Every pound lifted to the moon takes 3 more pounds of fuel to get it there --you can't over-pack, "just in case"!

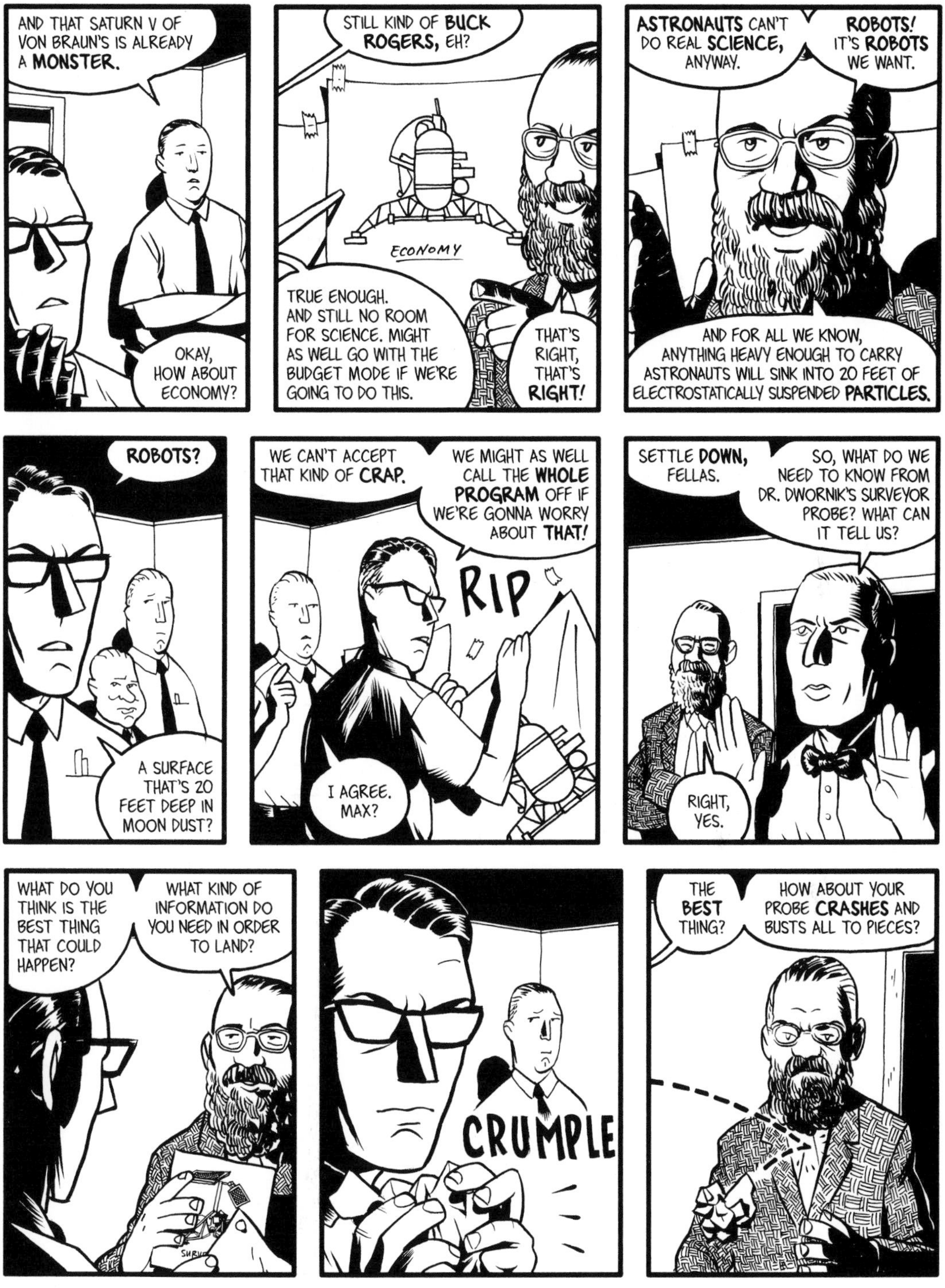
AND THAT SATURN V OF VON BRAUN'S IS ALREADY A MONSTER.
OKAY, HOW ABOUT ECONOMY?
STILL KIND OF BUCK ROGERS, EH?
ECONOMY
TRUE ENOUGH. AND STILL NO ROOM FOR SCIENCE. MIGHT AS WELL GO WITH THE BUDGET MODE IF WE'RE GOING TO DO THIS.
THAT'S RIGHT, THAT'S RIGHT!
ASTRONAUTS CAN'T DO REAL SCIENCE, ANYWAY.
ROBOTS! IT'S ROBOTS WE WANT.
AND FOR ALL WE KNOW, ANYTHING HEAVY ENOUGH TO CARRY ASTRONAUTS WILL SINK INTO 20 FEET OF ELECTROSTATICALLY SUSPENDED PARTICLES.
ROBOTS?
A SURFACE THAT'S 20 FEET DEEP IN MOON DUST?
WE CAN'T ACCEPT THAT KIND OF CRAP.
WE MIGHT AS WELL CALL THE WHOLE PROGRAM OFF IF WE'RE GONNA WORRY ABOUT THAT!
RIP
I AGREE. MAX?
SETTLE DOWN, FELLAS.
SO, WHAT DO WE NEED TO KNOW FROM DR. DWORNIK'S SURVEYOR PROBE? WHAT CAN IT TELL US?
RIGHT, YES.
WHAT DO YOU THINK IS THE BEST THING THAT COULD HAPPEN?
WHAT KIND OF INFORMATION DO YOU NEED IN ORDER TO LAND?
CRUMPLE
THE BEST THING?
HOW ABOUT YOUR PROBE CRASHES AND BUSTS ALL TO PIECES?

THEN WE'LL KNOW THE SURFACE ISN'T SOME FAIRY CASTLE STRUCTURE.
I'LL TAKE THAT UNDER ADVISEMENT.
SMOOTH
The first SURVEYOR landed on the moon just fine, but the second did crash! And neither sunk in....
AND THEY CALL ME BLUNT.
FIGURE IT OUT, FELLAS. I'M GOING TO GO MAKE NICE.
SO.
THE MOON'S SURFACE.
ARIZONA.
CAN'T BE LIKE NOWHERE ELSE--
--SO LET'S DESIGN A LANDING GEAR FOR, YOU KNOW, HIGH LONESOME-LIKE COUNTRY.
BUDGET AND ECONOMY MODES. WHO NEEDS 'EM?
WELL, THEN.
...WE DON'T NEED THOSE AERODYNAMICS EITHER, C.C.
NO AIR UP THERE, AFTER ALL!
GOOD POINT. GET RID OF THAT OLD DRAWING OF MINE AND WE'LL START AGAIN...
"...STRIP THINGS BACK TO THE ESSENTIALS."
MOSCOW, RUSSIA—1965
HM.
THIS MIGHT NOT GO DOWN TOO WELL WITH MY SUPERIORS.

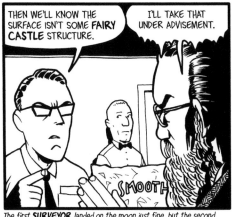

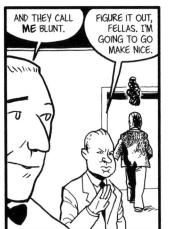

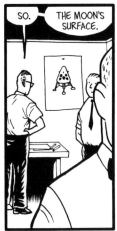

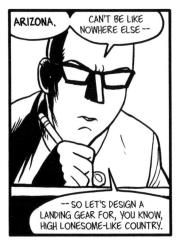

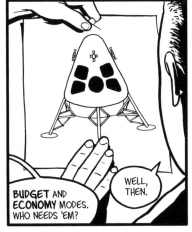

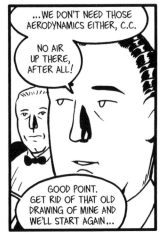

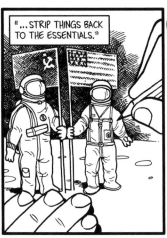

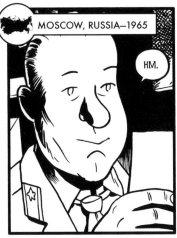

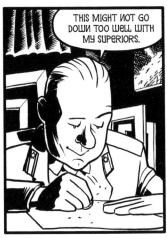

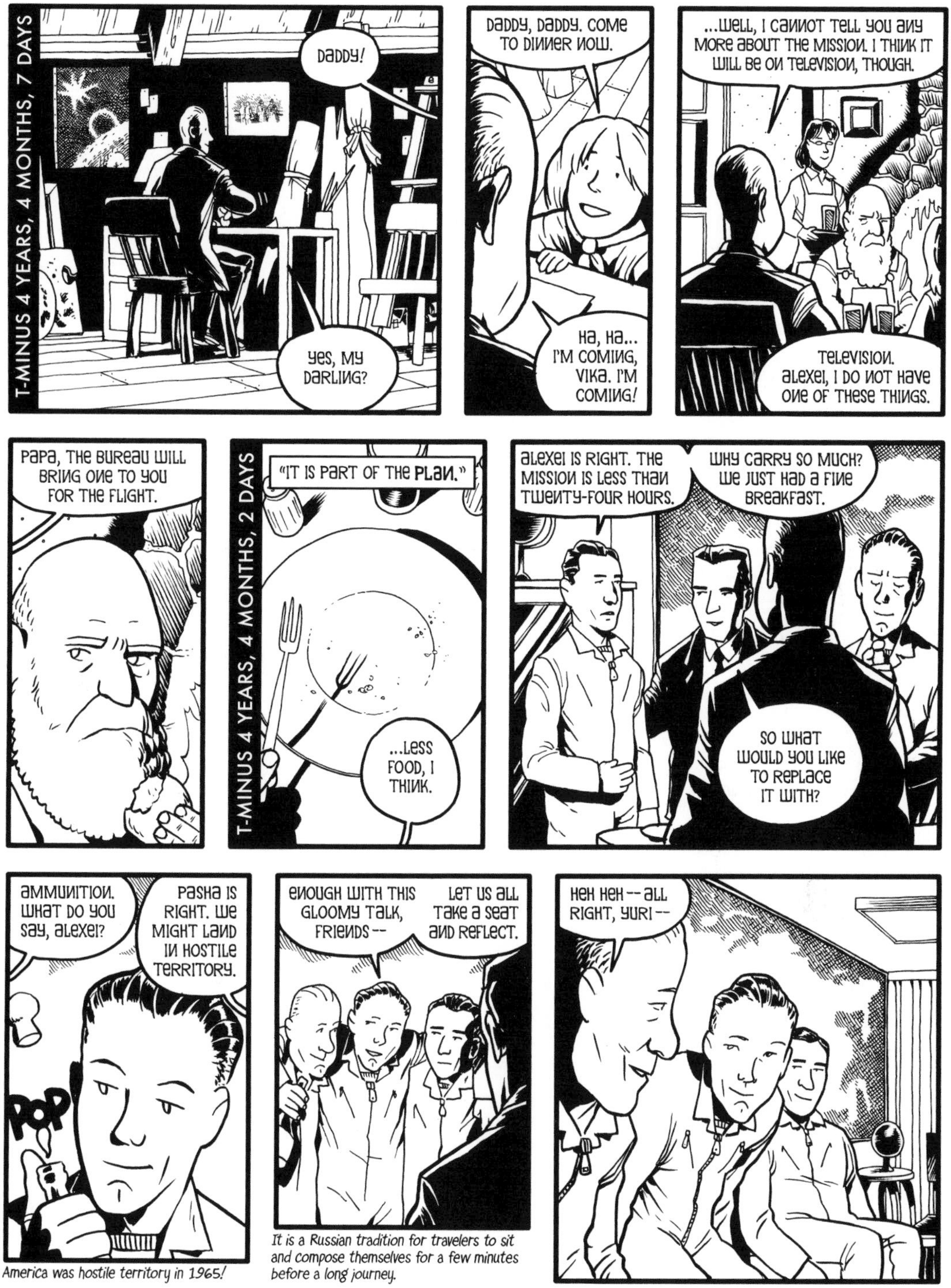
T-MINUS 4 YEARS, 4 MONTHS, 7 DAYS
DADDY!
YES, MY DARLING?
DADDY, DADDY. COME TO DINNER NOW.
HA, HA... I'M COMING, VIKA. I'M COMING!
...WELL, I CANNOT TELL YOU ANY MORE ABOUT THE MISSION. I THINK IT WILL BE ON TELEVISION, THOUGH.
TELEVISION. ALEXEI, I DO NOT HAVE ONE OF THESE THINGS.
PAPA, THE BUREAU WILL BRING ONE TO YOU FOR THE FLIGHT.
T-MINUS 4 YEARS, 4 MONTHS, 2 DAYS
"IT IS PART OF THE PLAN."
...LESS FOOD, I THINK.
ALEXEI IS RIGHT. THE MISSION IS LESS THAN TWENTY-FOUR HOURS.
WHY CARRY SO MUCH? WE JUST HAD A FINE BREAKFAST.
SO WHAT WOULD YOU LIKE TO REPLACE IT WITH?
AMMUNITION. WHAT DO YOU SAY, ALEXEI?
PASHA IS RIGHT. WE MIGHT LAND IN HOSTILE TERRITORY.
POP
ENOUGH WITH THIS GLOOMY TALK, FRIENDS --
LET US ALL TAKE A SEAT AND REFLECT.
HEH HEH -- ALL RIGHT, YURI --

America was hostile territory in 1965!

It is a Russian tradition for travelers to sit and compose themselves for a few minutes before a long journey.

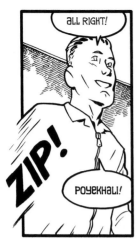

ALL RIGHT!
ZIP!
POYEKHALI!
HA HA HA HA HA HA HA HA
YES!
"WHAT ARE WE WAITING FOR?!"
MY KIDS -- THEY WISH I WAS A FARMER. "WHY CAN'T WE HAVE PIGS AND CHICKENS, DADDY?!"
HA HA HA HA HA
HA, MY DAUGHTER VIKA THINKS MY JOB IS DRIVING THE BUS TO THE LAUNCH SITE.
CCCP
MY FATHER THINKS THAT WOULD BE BETTER TOO...SITTING ON TOP OF A ROCKET?
"THAT'S NO WORK FOR A GROWN MAN!"
HA HA HA HA HA HA HA HA HA HA
AND DON'T FORGET TO STOW THAT GUN.
WHY YOU DIDN'T WANT EXTRA FOOD...
THEY MIGHT UNDERSTAND...
...IF THEY'D EVER TRIED TO EAT IN HERE.
THE SMELL OF PAINT AND SPECIAL GLUE NO. 88 MIXED WITH BEETS...
IT'S ENOUGH TO MAKE A MAN PU --
"DIAMOND ONE," "DIAMOND TWO." YOUR MIC IS LIVE.
CCCP
AHEM
BEGIN COUNTDOWN.
THEY'RE READY.

Q: *Why the empty seat?* **A:** *Voskhod 1 carried three cosmonauts ... if they didn't need space suits! But this time Alexei's going to need his!*

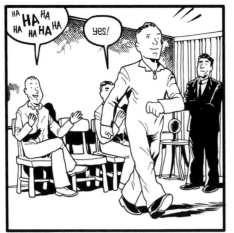

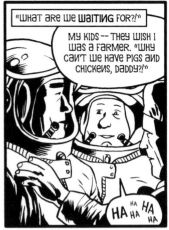

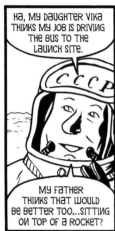

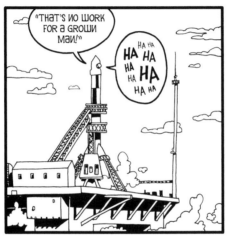

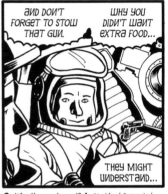

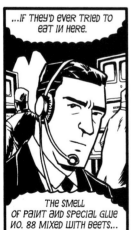

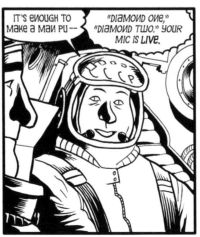

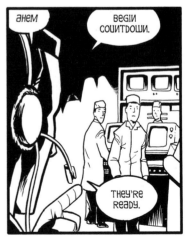

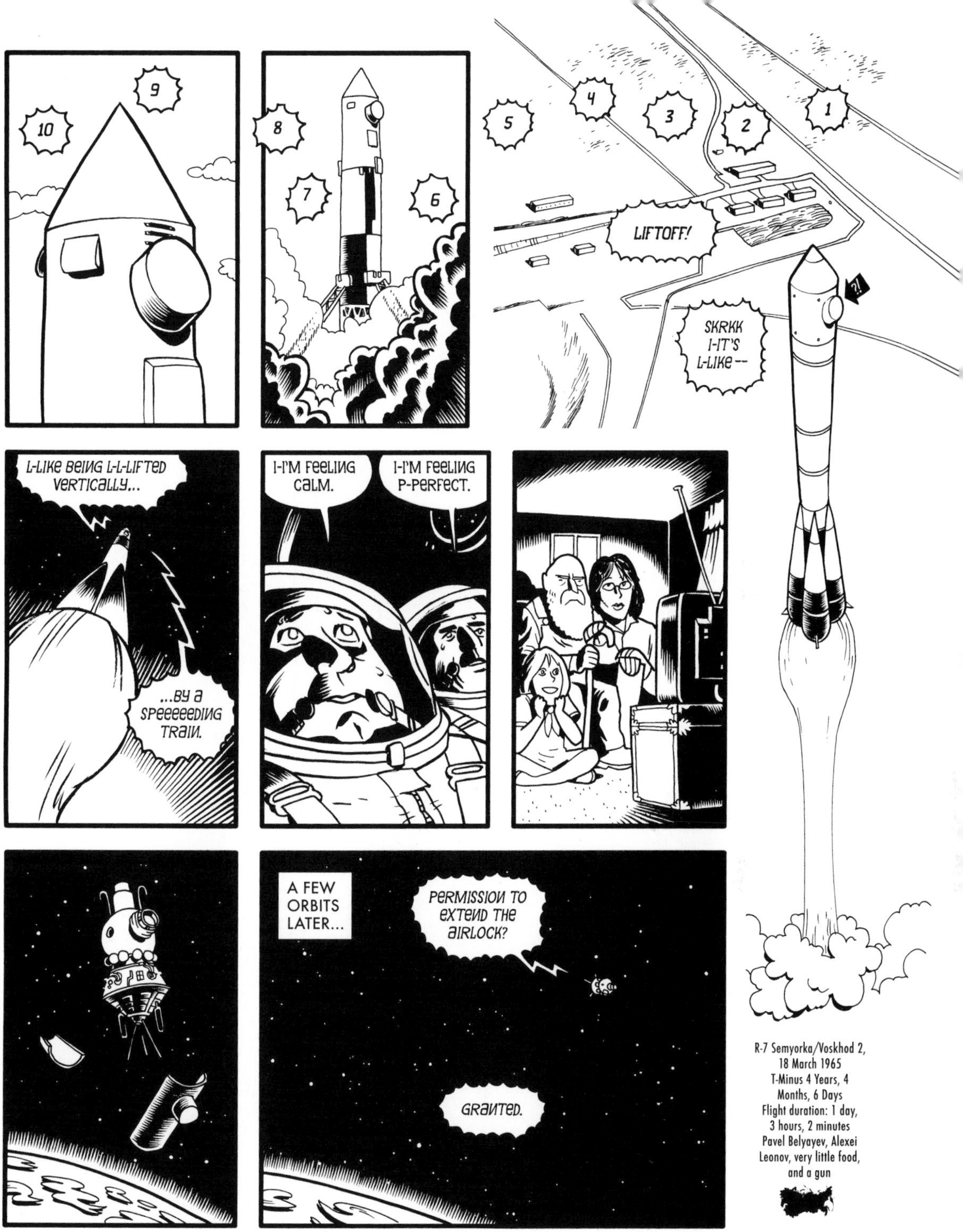
10
9
8
7
6
5
4
3
2
1
LIFTOFF!
SKRKK I-IT'S L-LIKE --
?!
L-LIKE BEING L-L-LIFTED VERTICALLY...
...BY A SPEEEEEDING TRAIN.
I-I'M FEELING CALM.
I-I'M FEELING P-PERFECT.
A FEW ORBITS LATER...
PERMISSION TO EXTEND THE AIRLOCK?
GRANTED.

R-7 Semyorka/Voskhod 2,
18 March 1965
T-Minus 4 Years, 4 Months, 6 Days
Flight duration: 1 day, 3 hours, 2 minutes
Pavel Belyayev, Alexei Leonov, very little food, and a gun

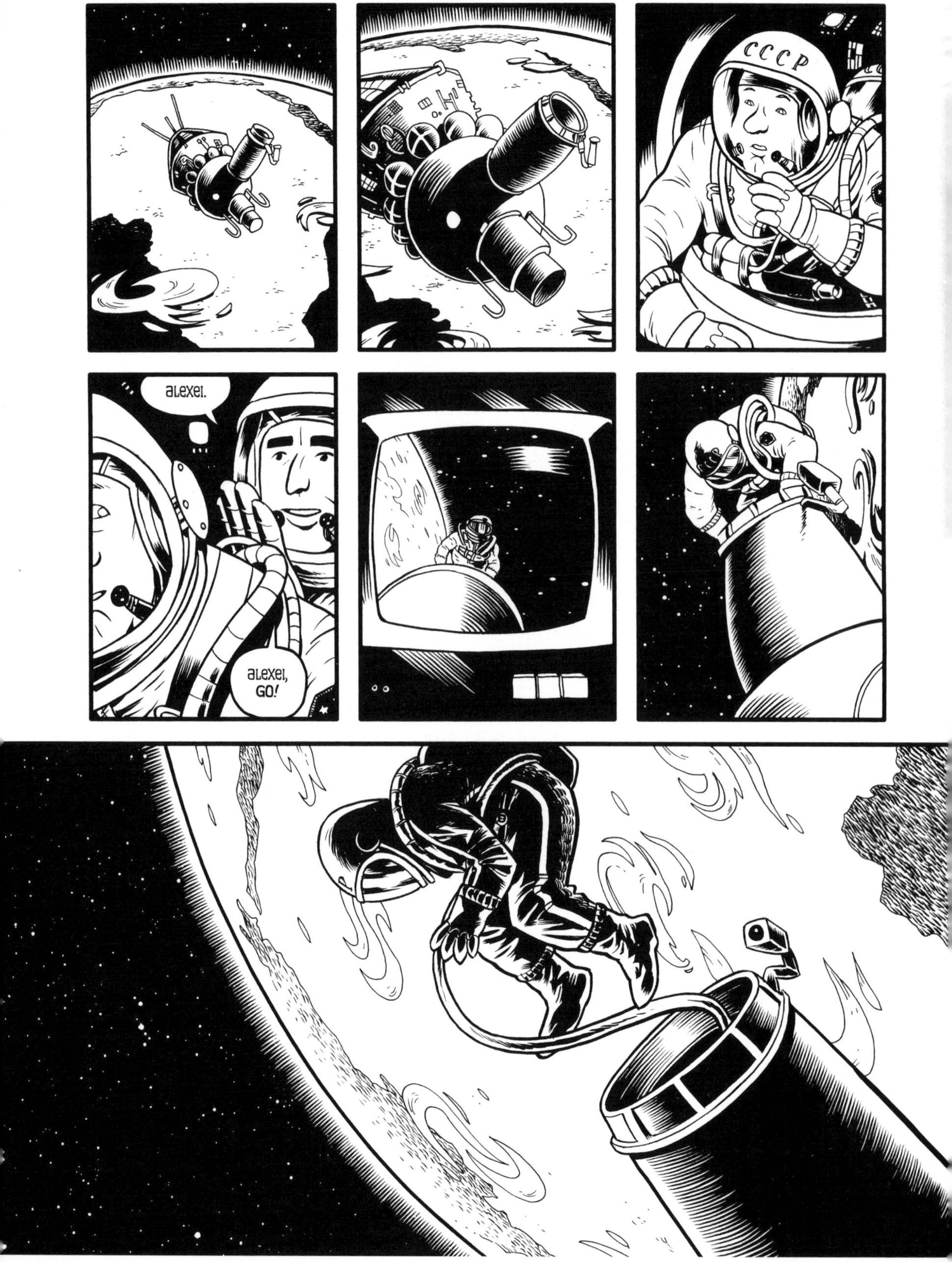
CCCP
alexei.
alexei, GO!

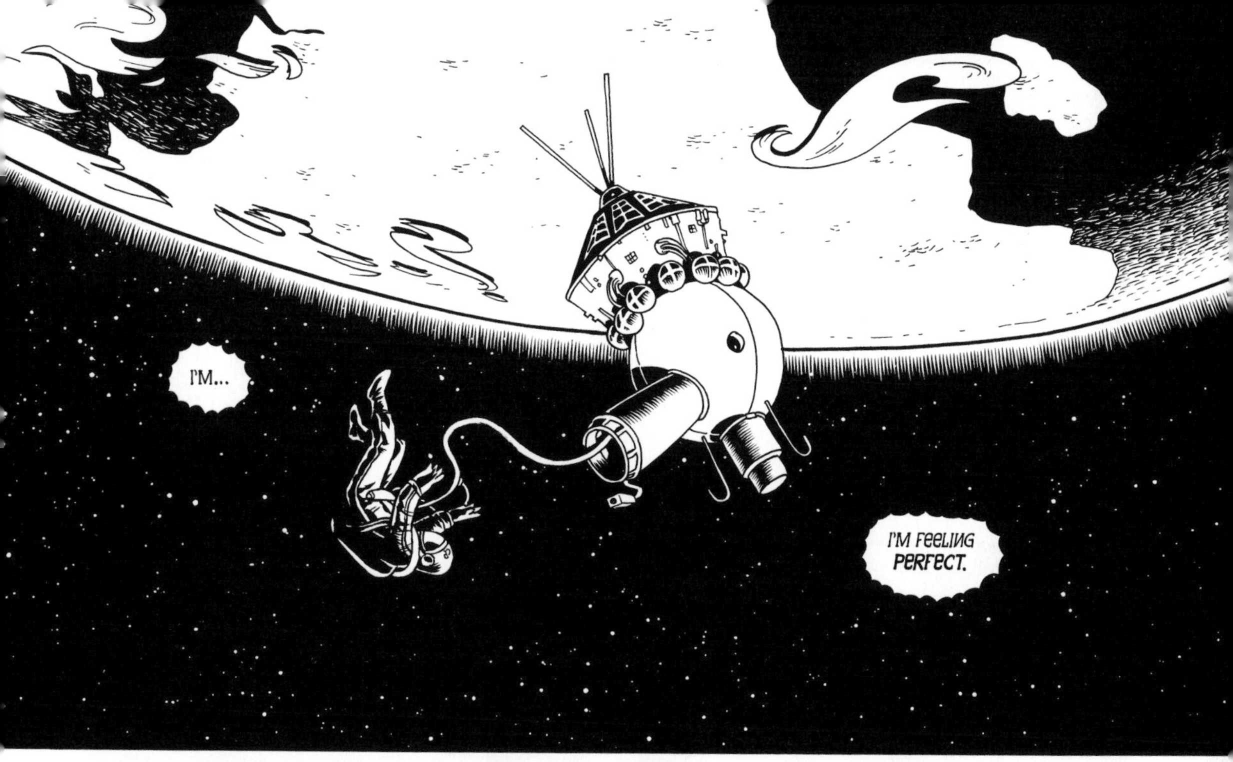
I'M...
I'M FEELING PERFECT.

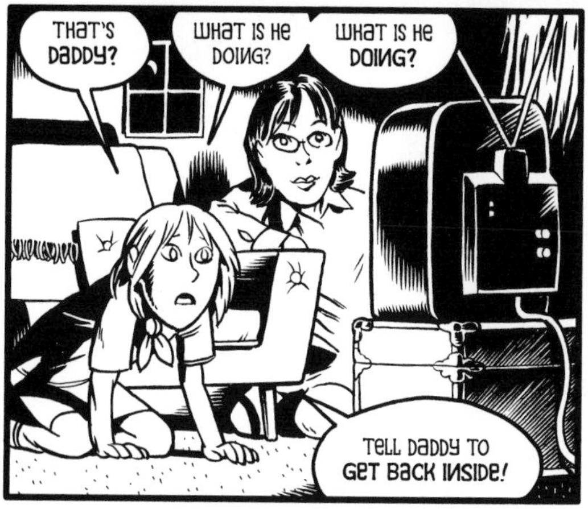
THAT'S DADDY?
WHAT IS HE DOING?
WHAT IS HE DOING?
TELL DADDY TO GET BACK INSIDE!

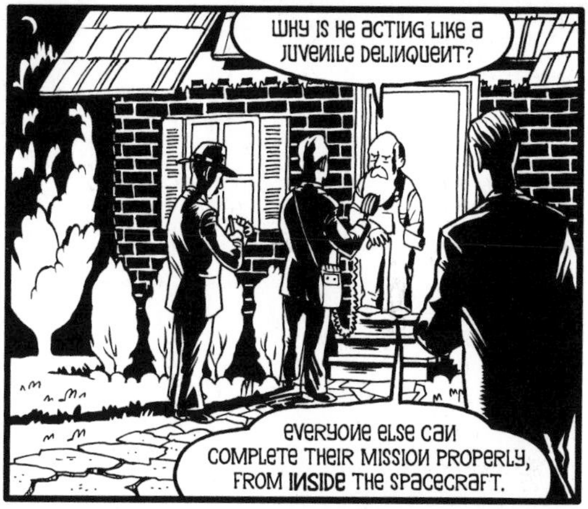
WHY IS HE ACTING LIKE A JUVENILE DELINQUENT?
EVERYONE ELSE CAN COMPLETE THEIR MISSION PROPERLY, FROM INSIDE THE SPACECRAFT.

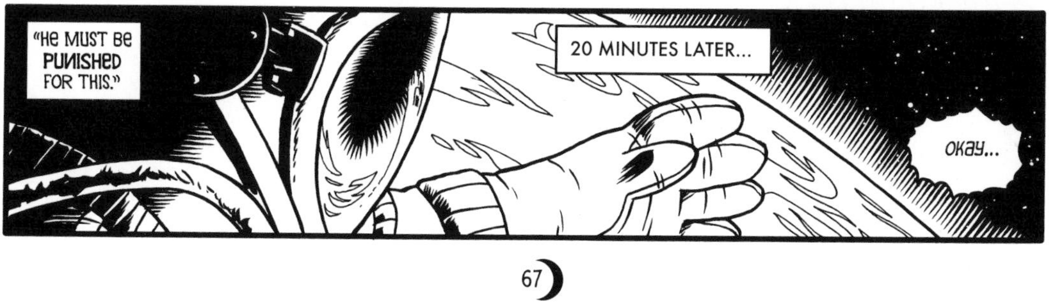
"HE MUST BE PUNISHED FOR THIS."
20 MINUTES LATER...
OKAY...

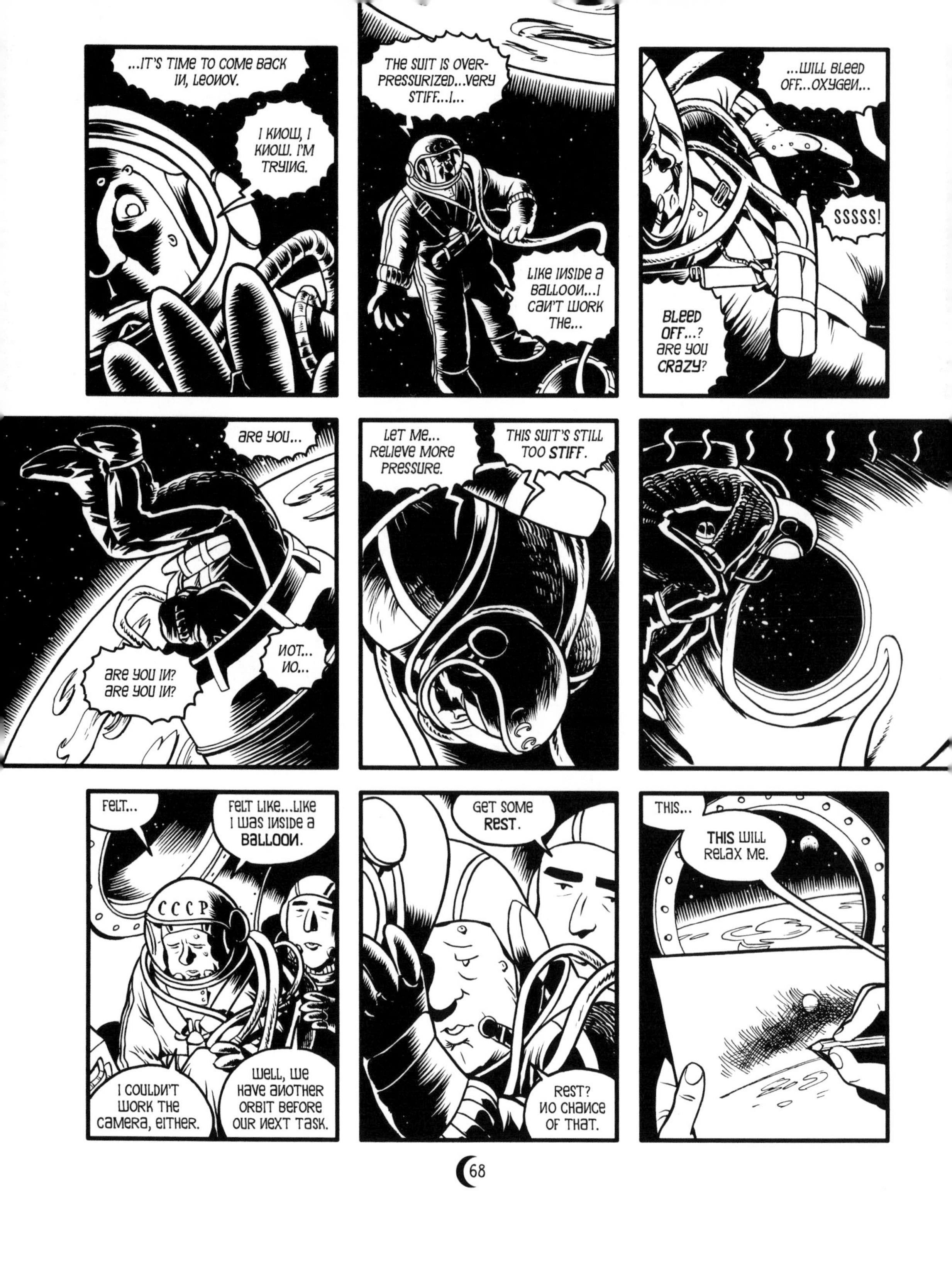
...IT'S TIME TO COME BACK IN, LEONOV.
I KNOW, I KNOW. I'M TRYING.
THE SUIT IS OVER-PRESSURIZED...VERY STIFF...I...
LIKE INSIDE A BALLOON...I CAN'T WORK THE...
...WILL BLEED OFF...OXYGEN...
SSSSS!
BLEED OFF...? ARE YOU CRAZY?
ARE YOU...
ARE YOU IN? ARE YOU IN?
NOT... NO...
LET ME... RELIEVE MORE PRESSURE.
THIS SUIT'S STILL TOO STIFF.
FELT...
FELT LIKE...LIKE I WAS INSIDE A BALLOON.
CCCP
I COULDN'T WORK THE CAMERA, EITHER.
WELL, WE HAVE ANOTHER ORBIT BEFORE OUR NEXT TASK.
GET SOME REST.
REST? NO CHANCE OF THAT.
THIS...
THIS WILL RELAX ME.

MANY UNEVENTFUL ORBITS LATER, IT'S TIME TO RETURN HOME...

OK...

I'M...

GOING...

TO...

ACTIVATE...

THE...

...AUTOMATIC...

PLINK

...LANDING SYSTEM?

HOW ARE YOU BLONDIN? WHERE DID YOU LAND?

DIDN'T.

WE HAD TO TURN OFF THE AUTOMATIC LANDING SYSTEM, YURI. INOPERABLE.

WE'RE VERY LOW ON FUEL -- WE HAVE ENOUGH FOR ONE ATTEMPT AT REENTRY, TO LAND AT...

CCCP

CCCP

WELL, THIS ORBIT TAKES US RIGHT OVER MOSCOW. HOW DOES RED SQUARE SOUND?

ALEXEI...

KIDDING. I'M THINKING JUST OVER THE URAL MOUNTAINS, IN SIBERIA.

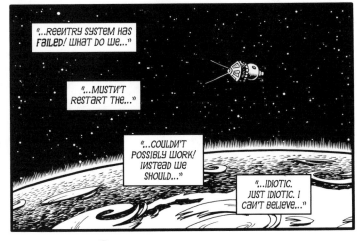

"...REENTRY SYSTEM HAS FAILED! WHAT DO WE..."

"...MUSTN'T RESTART THE..."

"...COULDN'T POSSIBLY WORK! INSTEAD WE SHOULD..."

"...IDIOTIC. JUST IDIOTIC. I CAN'T BELIEVE..."

69

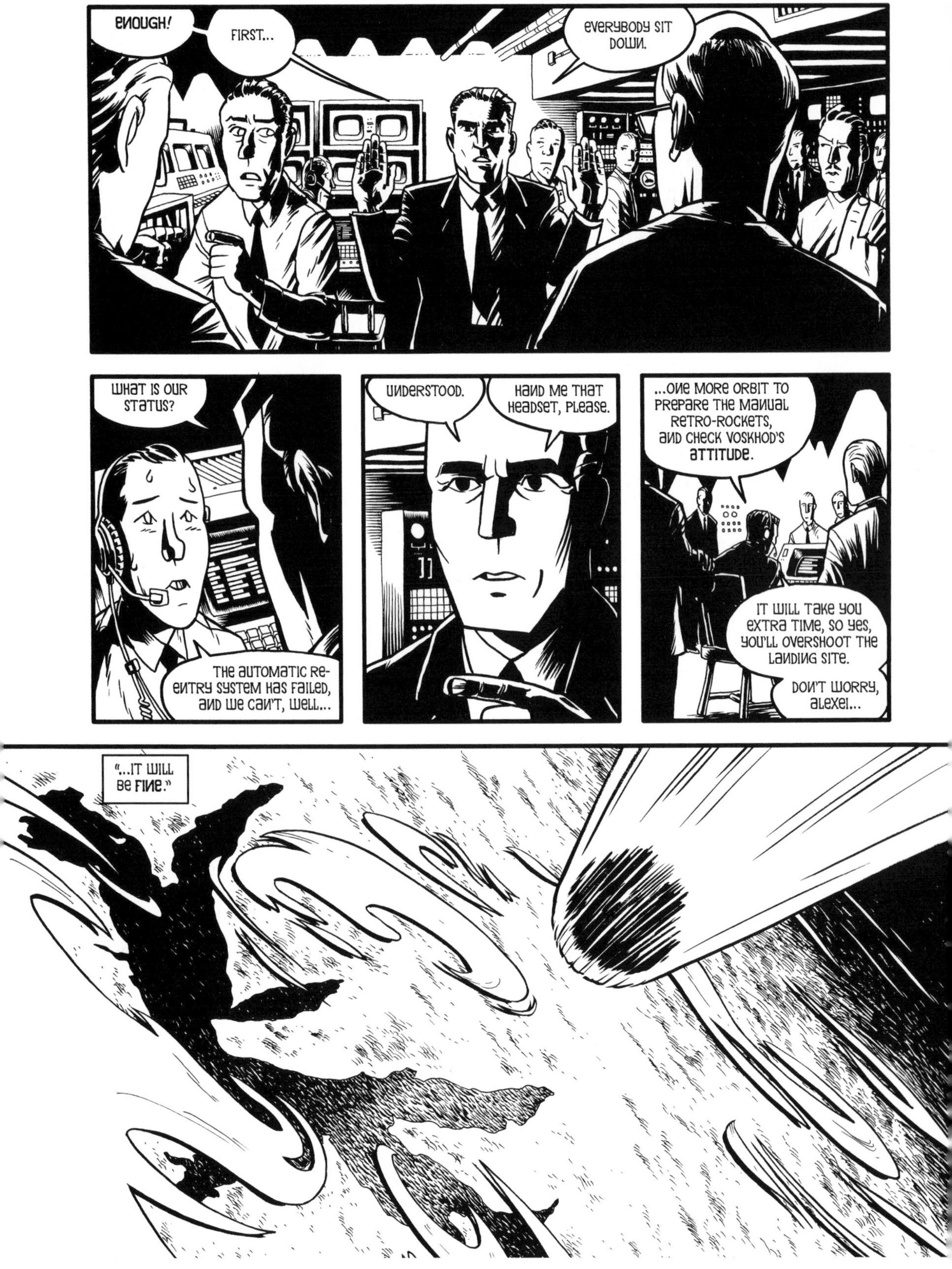
ENOUGH!
FIRST...
EVERYBODY SIT DOWN.
WHAT IS OUR STATUS?
THE AUTOMATIC RE-ENTRY SYSTEM HAS FAILED, AND WE CAN'T, WELL...
UNDERSTOOD.
HAND ME THAT HEADSET, PLEASE.
...ONE MORE ORBIT TO PREPARE THE MANUAL RETRO-ROCKETS, AND CHECK VOSKHOD'S **ATTITUDE**.
IT WILL TAKE YOU EXTRA TIME, SO YES, YOU'LL OVERSHOOT THE LANDING SITE.
DON'T WORRY, ALEXEI...
"...IT WILL BE **FINE**."

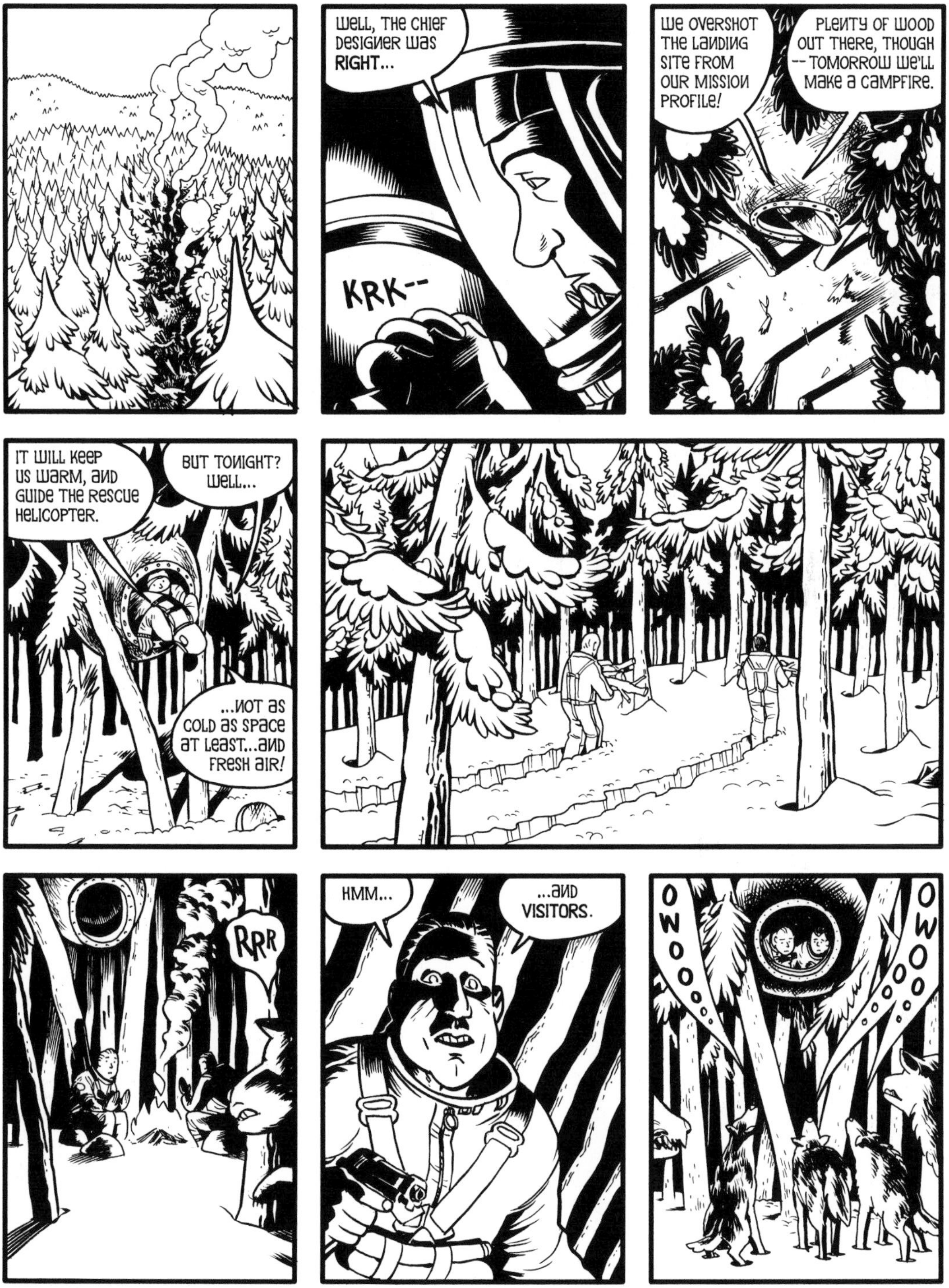
WELL, THE CHIEF DESIGNER WAS RIGHT...
KRK--
WE OVERSHOT THE LANDING SITE FROM OUR MISSION PROFILE!
PLENTY OF WOOD OUT THERE, THOUGH -- TOMORROW WE'LL MAKE A CAMPFIRE.
IT WILL KEEP US WARM, AND GUIDE THE RESCUE HELICOPTER.
BUT TONIGHT? WELL...
...NOT AS COLD AS SPACE AT LEAST...AND FRESH AIR!
RRR
HMM...
...AND VISITORS.
OWOOOooo
OWOOOOOO

T-MINUS 4 YEARS, 3 MONTHS, 27 DAYS

...NO, NO...

...WE **CONGRATULATE** THE SOVIETS ON THEIR SPECTACULAR SUCCESS.

IT'S A **REMARKABLE** ACHIEVEMENT.

HOW DOES THIS CHANGE THE PLANS FOR GEMINI 3?

NO CHANGE. JOHN AND GUS ARE GONNA FLY THE MISSION THEY TRAINED FOR, WHICH IS TO CHECK OUT THEIR SPACECRAFT.

THEY'LL MAKE SURE IT'S READY FOR SOMETHING **BIG** IN GEMINI 4.

GEMINI = John Young and Gus Grissom

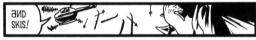

Here are some supplies!

aw...

SOMETHING **BIG? WHAT?!**

THANKS BOYS. THAT'S ALL.

WE **DO** HAVE A **SURPRISE,** DON'T WE?

WE'LL HAVE TO COME UP WITH ONE.

SPACE TASK GROUP'S NEW HEADQUARTERS—HOUSTON, TEXAS

GEMINI 4

EVA

GENTLEMEN, WE WERE PLANNING A "MINI EVA" SCHEDULED FOR YOUR GEMINI 4 FLIGHT.

BUT IN LIGHT OF RECENT EVENTS, WE THINK IT PRUDENT TO REEVALUATE THE SITUATION.

EVA = extravehicular activity

and SKIS!

OWO0000O...

AS SUCH, THE PROFILE HAS UNDERGONE RIGOROUS AND DETAILED --

SAY IT **PLAIN,** JOE!

IF I'M NOT JUST POKING MY HEAD OUT THE **DOOR,** WHAT'LL IT **BE?**

Ed White: Pilot

YEAH, IF YOU'RE NOT GONNA HAVE US DO MEDICAL EXPERIMENTS, TESTS, AND OTHER ASSORTED JUNK...

...THEN WHAT?

Jim McDivitt: Command pilot

YOU'LL GET SOME **NEW** ASSORTED JUNK.

BUT ED'S GONNA GET A NEW SUIT, AND A **GUN.**

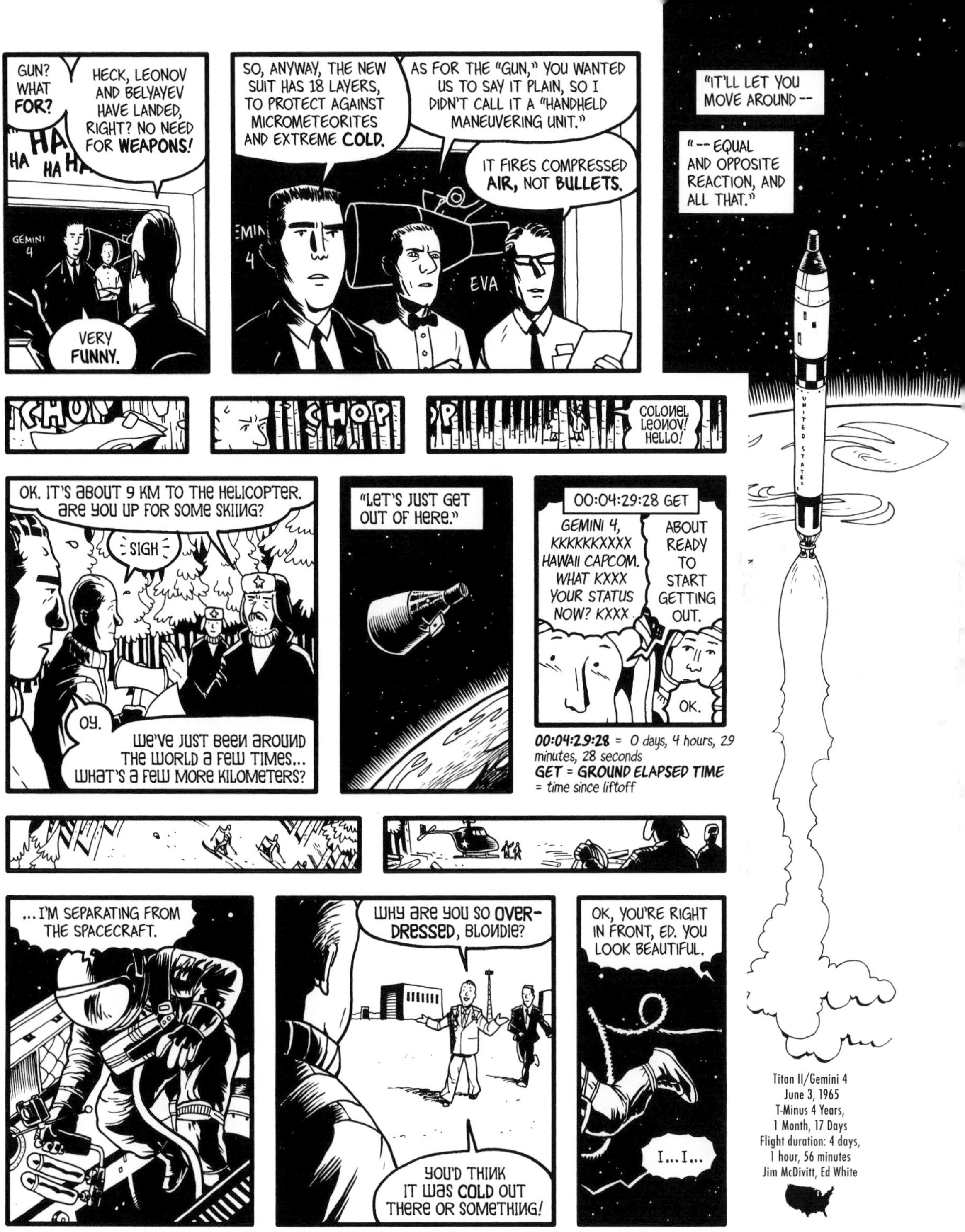

GUN? WHAT FOR?
HECK, LEONOV AND BELYAYEV HAVE LANDED, RIGHT? NO NEED FOR WEAPONS!
HA HA HA HA HA
GEMINI 4
VERY FUNNY.
SO, ANYWAY, THE NEW SUIT HAS 18 LAYERS, TO PROTECT AGAINST MICROMETEORITES AND EXTREME COLD.
AS FOR THE "GUN," YOU WANTED US TO SAY IT PLAIN, SO I DIDN'T CALL IT A "HANDHELD MANEUVERING UNIT."
IT FIRES COMPRESSED AIR, NOT BULLETS.
EVA
CHOP
CHOP
COLONEL LEONOV! HELLO!
OK. IT'S ABOUT 9 KM TO THE HELICOPTER. ARE YOU UP FOR SOME SKIING?
SIGH
OY.
WE'VE JUST BEEN AROUND THE WORLD A FEW TIMES... WHAT'S A FEW MORE KILOMETERS?
"LET'S JUST GET OUT OF HERE."
00:04:29:28 GET
GEMINI 4, KKKKKKXXXX HAWAII CAPCOM. WHAT KXXX YOUR STATUS NOW? KXXX.
ABOUT READY TO START GETTING OUT.
OK.
00:04:29:28 = 0 days, 4 hours, 29 minutes, 28 seconds
GET = GROUND ELAPSED TIME
= time since liftoff
...I'M SEPARATING FROM THE SPACECRAFT.
WHY ARE YOU SO OVER-DRESSED, BLONDIE?
YOU'D THINK IT WAS COLD OUT THERE OR SOMETHING!
OK, YOU'RE RIGHT IN FRONT, ED. YOU LOOK BEAUTIFUL.
I...I...
"IT'LL LET YOU MOVE AROUND --
"-- EQUAL AND OPPOSITE REACTION, AND ALL THAT."
UNITED STATES

Titan II/Gemini 4
June 3, 1965
T-Minus 4 Years, 1 Month, 17 Days
Flight duration: 4 days, 1 hour, 56 minutes
Jim McDivitt, Ed White

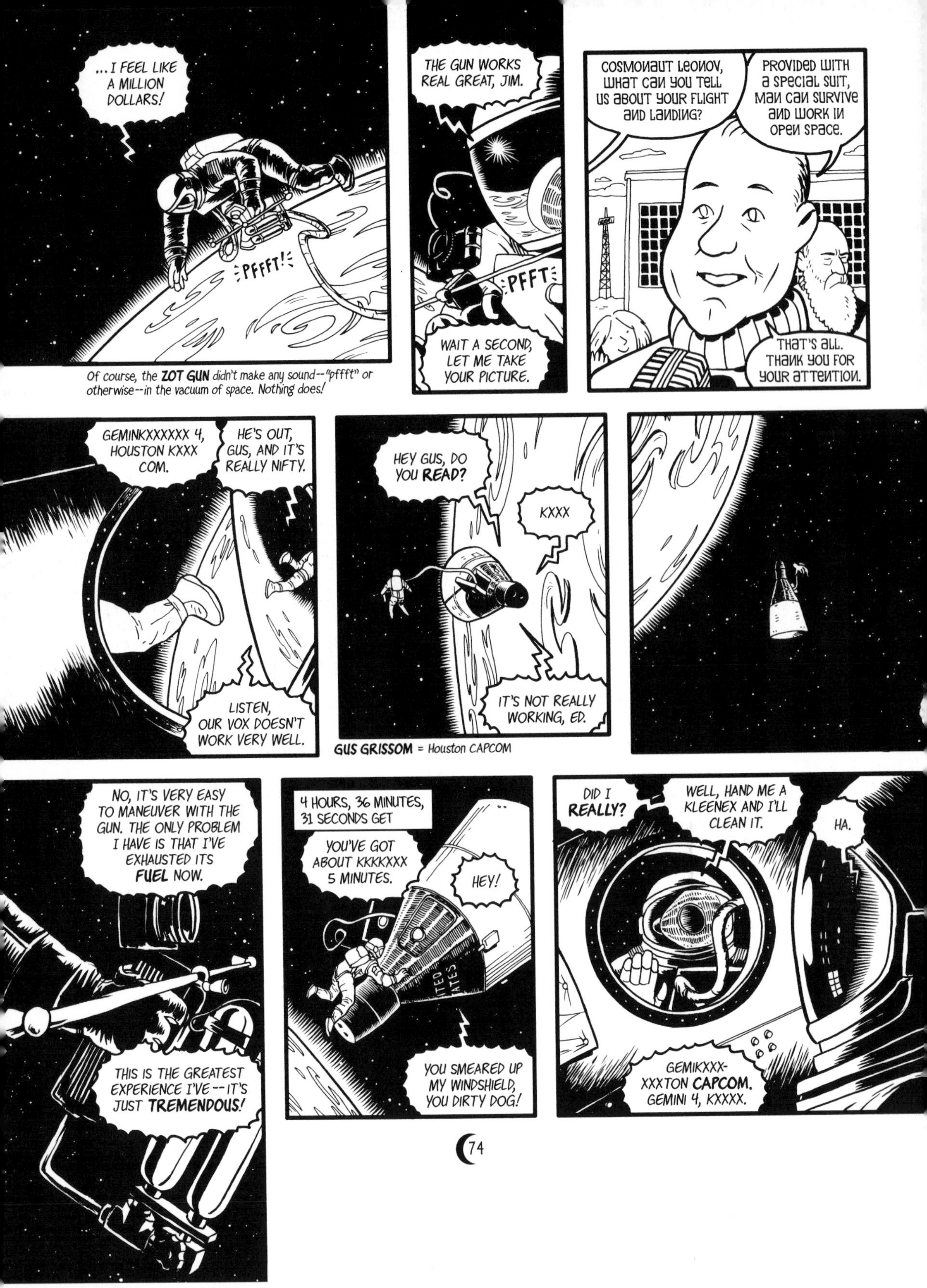
...I FEEL LIKE A MILLION DOLLARS!
PFFFT!
Of course, the ZOT GUN didn't make any sound--"pffft" or otherwise--in the vacuum of space. Nothing does!
THE GUN WORKS REAL GREAT, JIM.
PFFT
WAIT A SECOND, LET ME TAKE YOUR PICTURE.
COSMONAUT LEONOV, WHAT CAN YOU TELL US ABOUT YOUR FLIGHT AND LANDING?
PROVIDED WITH A SPECIAL SUIT, MAN CAN SURVIVE AND WORK IN OPEN SPACE.
THAT'S ALL. THANK YOU FOR YOUR ATTENTION.
GEMINKXXXXXX 4, HOUSTON KXXX COM.
HE'S OUT, GUS, AND IT'S REALLY NIFTY.
LISTEN, OUR VOX DOESN'T WORK VERY WELL.
HEY GUS, DO YOU READ?
KXXX
IT'S NOT REALLY WORKING, ED.
GUS GRISSOM = Houston CAPCOM
NO, IT'S VERY EASY TO MANEUVER WITH THE GUN. THE ONLY PROBLEM I HAVE IS THAT I'VE EXHAUSTED ITS FUEL NOW.
THIS IS THE GREATEST EXPERIENCE I'VE--IT'S JUST TREMENDOUS!
4 HOURS, 36 MINUTES, 31 SECONDS GET
YOU'VE GOT ABOUT KKKKXXX 5 MINUTES.
HEY!
YOU SMEARED UP MY WINDSHIELD, YOU DIRTY DOG!
DID I REALLY?
WELL, HAND ME A KLEENEX AND I'LL CLEAN IT.
HA.
GEMIKXXX-XXXTON CAPCOM. GEMINI 4, KXXXX.

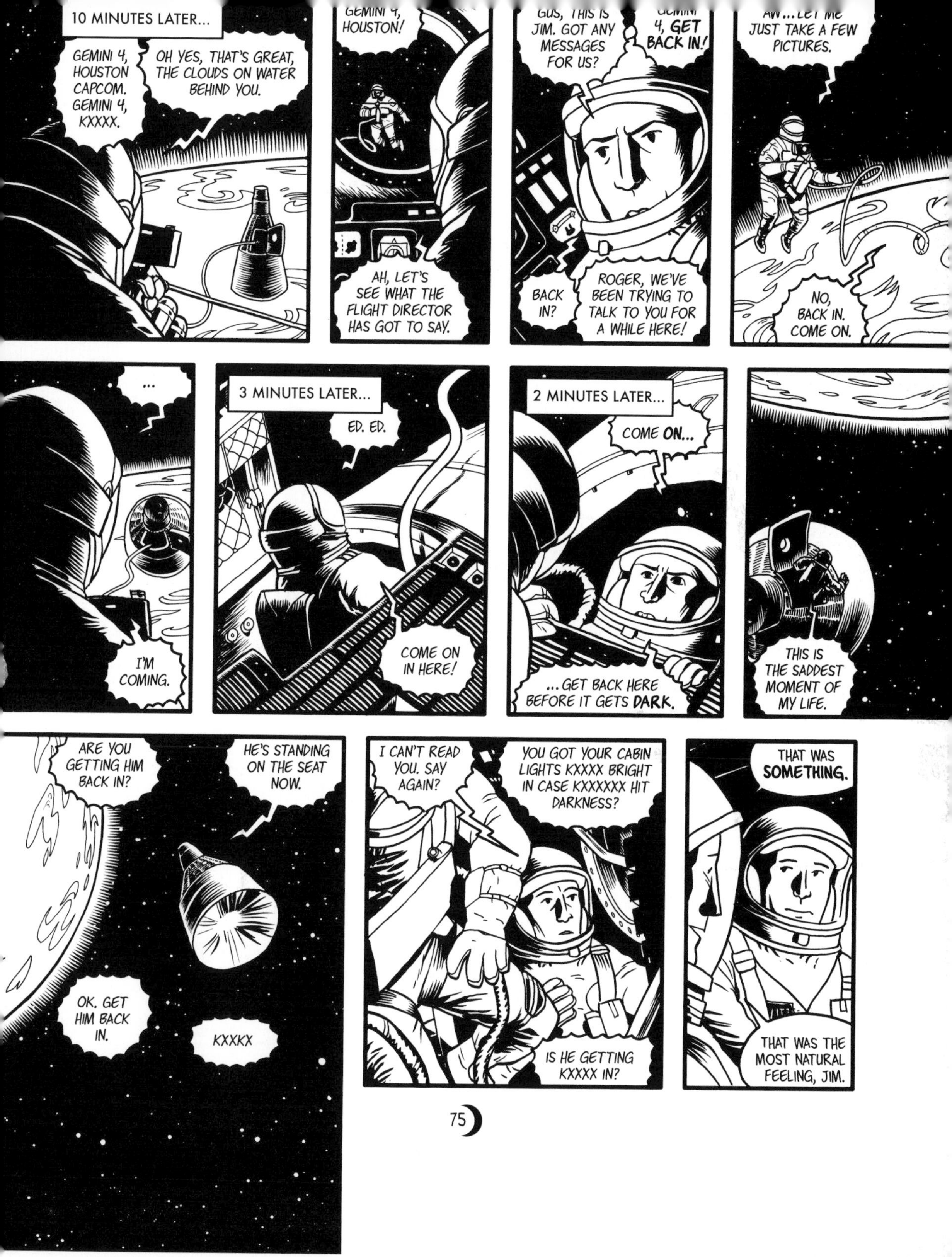
10 MINUTES LATER...
GEMINI 4, HOUSTON CAPCOM. GEMINI 4, KXXXX.
OH YES, THAT'S GREAT, THE CLOUDS ON WATER BEHIND YOU.
GEMINI 4, HOUSTON!
AH, LET'S SEE WHAT THE FLIGHT DIRECTOR HAS GOT TO SAY.
GUS, THIS IS JIM. GOT ANY MESSAGES FOR US?
GEMINI 4, GET BACK IN!
BACK IN?
ROGER, WE'VE BEEN TRYING TO TALK TO YOU FOR A WHILE HERE!
AW...LET ME JUST TAKE A FEW PICTURES.
NO, BACK IN. COME ON.
...
I'M COMING.
3 MINUTES LATER...
ED. ED.
COME ON IN HERE!
2 MINUTES LATER...
COME ON...
...GET BACK HERE BEFORE IT GETS DARK.
THIS IS THE SADDEST MOMENT OF MY LIFE.
ARE YOU GETTING HIM BACK IN?
HE'S STANDING ON THE SEAT NOW.
OK. GET HIM BACK IN.
KXXKX
I CAN'T READ YOU. SAY AGAIN?
YOU GOT YOUR CABIN LIGHTS KXXXX BRIGHT IN CASE KXXXXXX HIT DARKNESS?
IS HE GETTING KXXXX IN?
THAT WAS SOMETHING.
THAT WAS THE MOST NATURAL FEELING, JIM.

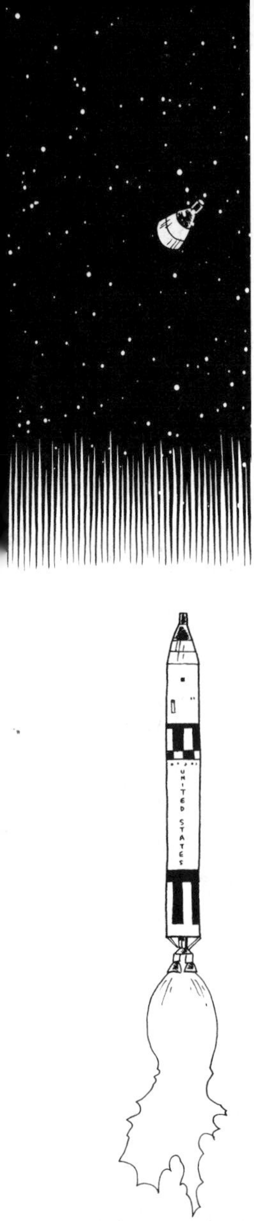

Titan II/Gemini 5:
September 21–29, 1965
T-Minus 3 Years, 9 Months, 29 Days
Flight duration: 7 days, 22 hours, 55 minutes
Motto: "8 Days or Bust" for this 120-orbit flight
Gordon Cooper and Charles Conrad

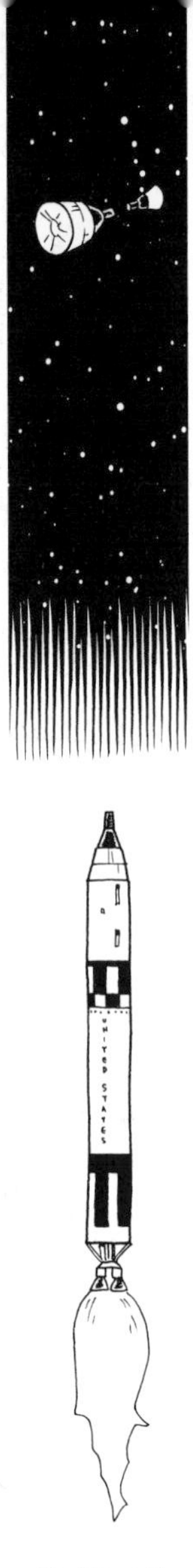

Titan II/Gemini 7:
December 4–18, 1965
T-Minus 3 Years, 7 Months, 16 Days
Flight duration: 13 days, 18 hours, 35 minutes
(enough time to complete a lunar expedition)
Frank Borman and Jim Lovell, who both brought books along

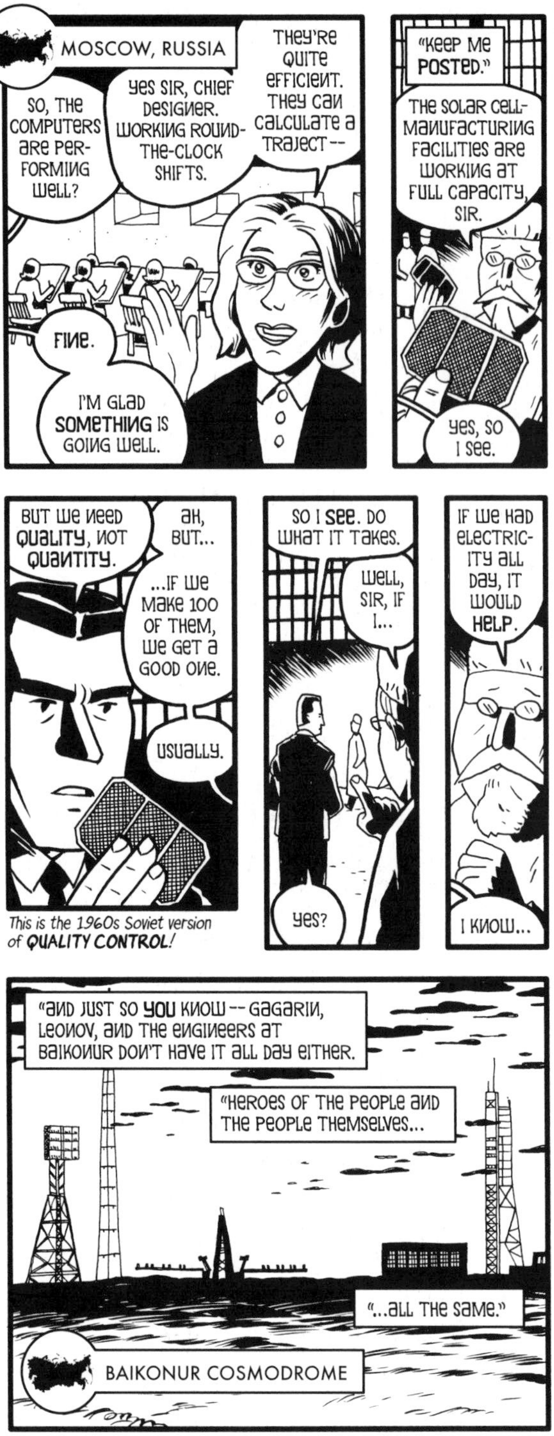

MOSCOW, RUSSIA
SO, THE COMPUTERS ARE PER-FORMING WELL?
YES SIR, CHIEF DESIGNER. WORKING ROUND-THE-CLOCK SHIFTS.
THEY'RE QUITE EFFICIENT. THEY CAN CALCULATE A TRAJECT--
FINE.
I'M GLAD SOMETHING IS GOING WELL.
"KEEP ME POSTED."
THE SOLAR CELL-MANUFACTURING FACILITIES ARE WORKING AT FULL CAPACITY, SIR.
YES, SO I SEE.
BUT WE NEED QUALITY, NOT QUANTITY.
AH, BUT...
...IF WE MAKE 100 OF THEM, WE GET A GOOD ONE.
USUALLY.
This is the 1960s Soviet version of QUALITY CONTROL!
SO I SEE. DO WHAT IT TAKES.
WELL, SIR, IF I...
YES?
IF WE HAD ELECTRIC-ITY ALL DAY, IT WOULD HELP.
I KNOW...
"AND JUST SO YOU KNOW -- GAGARIN, LEONOV, AND THE ENGINEERS AT BAIKONUR DON'T HAVE IT ALL DAY EITHER.
"HEROES OF THE PEOPLE AND THE PEOPLE THEMSELVES...
"...ALL THE SAME."
BAIKONUR COSMODROME

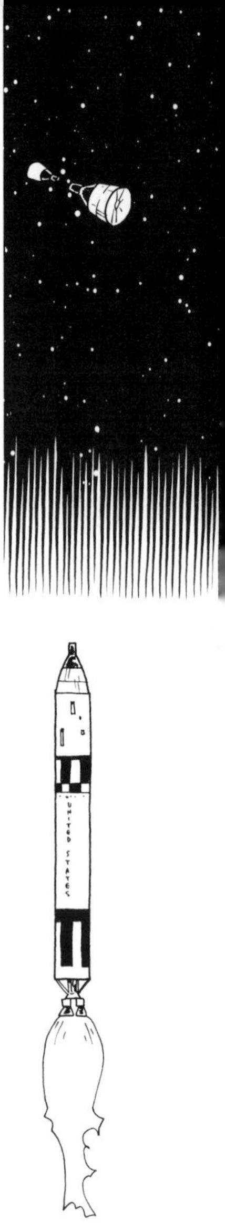

Titan II/Gemini 6A:
December 15–16, 1965
T-Minus 3 Years, 7 Months, 5 Days
Flight duration: 1 day, 1 hours, 51 minutes
Rendezvous with Gemini 7
Wally Schirra and Tom Stafford

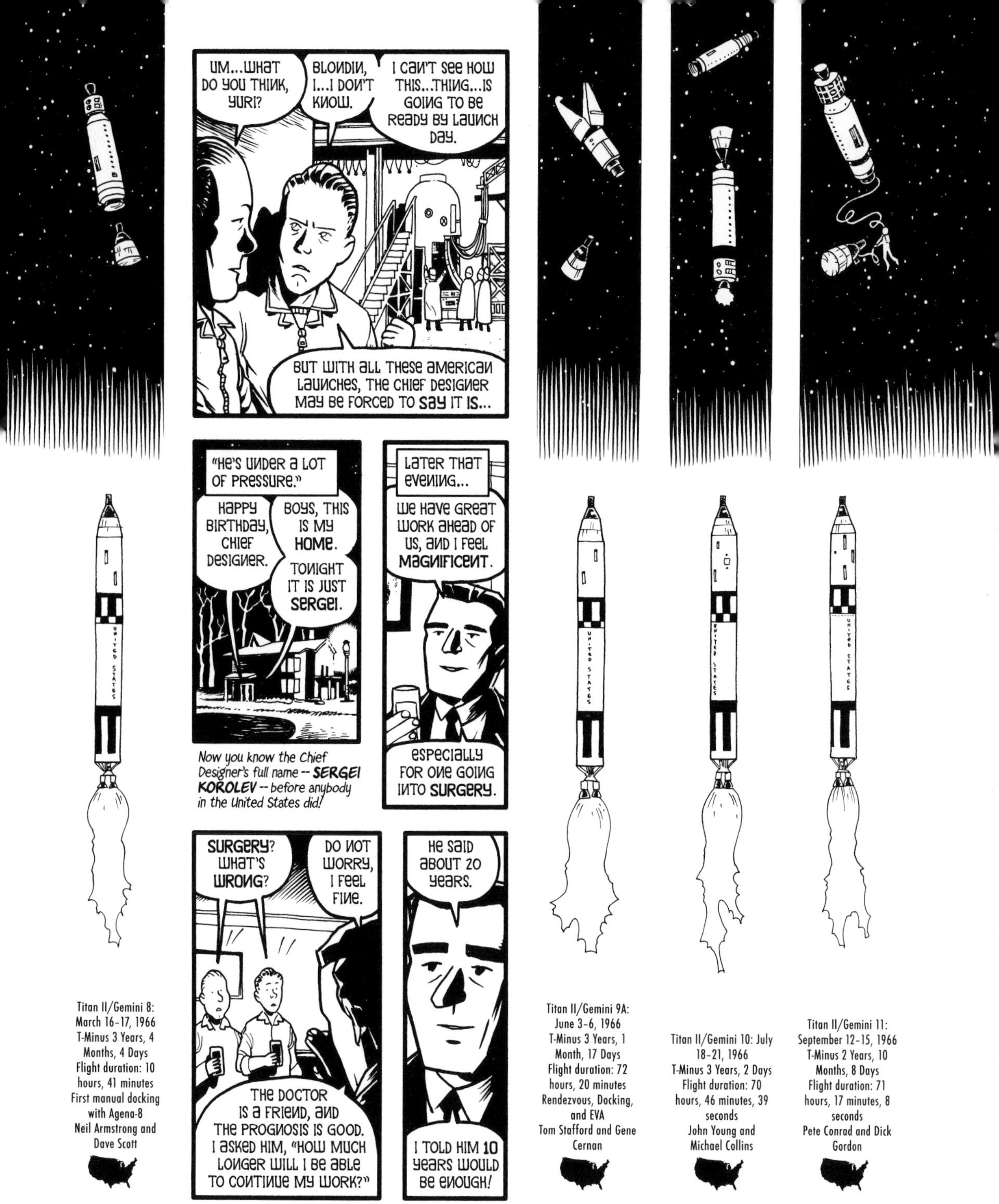
Titan II/Gemini 8: March 16-17, 1966
T-Minus 3 Years, 4 Months, 4 Days
Flight duration: 10 hours, 41 minutes
First manual docking with Agena-8
Neil Armstrong and Dave Scott
UM...WHAT DO YOU THINK, YURI?
BLONDIN, I...I DON'T KNOW.
I CAN'T SEE HOW THIS...THING...IS GOING TO BE READY BY LAUNCH DAY.
BUT WITH ALL THESE AMERICAN LAUNCHES, THE CHIEF DESIGNER MAY BE FORCED TO SAY IT IS...
"HE'S UNDER A LOT OF PRESSURE."
HAPPY BIRTHDAY, CHIEF DESIGNER.
BOYS, THIS IS MY HOME.
TONIGHT IT IS JUST SERGEI.
Now you know the Chief Designer's full name -- SERGEI KOROLEV -- before anybody in the United States did!
LATER THAT EVENING...
WE HAVE GREAT WORK AHEAD OF US, AND I FEEL MAGNIFICENT.
ESPECIALLY FOR ONE GOING INTO SURGERY.
SURGERY? WHAT'S WRONG?
DO NOT WORRY, I FEEL FINE.
THE DOCTOR IS A FRIEND, AND THE PROGNOSIS IS GOOD. I ASKED HIM, "HOW MUCH LONGER WILL I BE ABLE TO CONTINUE MY WORK?"
HE SAID ABOUT 20 YEARS.
I TOLD HIM 10 YEARS WOULD BE ENOUGH!
Titan II/Gemini 9A: June 3-6, 1966
T-Minus 3 Years, 1 Month, 17 Days
Flight duration: 72 hours, 20 minutes
Rendezvous, Docking, and EVA
Tom Stafford and Gene Cernan
Titan II/Gemini 10: July 18-21, 1966
T-Minus 3 Years, 2 Days
Flight duration: 70 hours, 46 minutes, 39 seconds
John Young and Michael Collins
Titan II/Gemini 11: September 12-15, 1966
T-Minus 2 Years, 10 Months, 8 Days
Flight duration: 71 hours, 17 minutes, 8 seconds
Pete Conrad and Dick Gordon

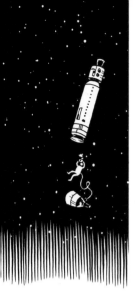

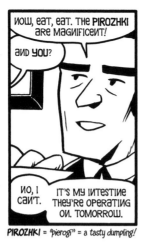

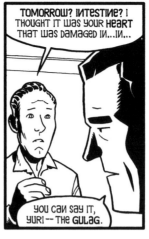

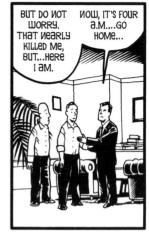

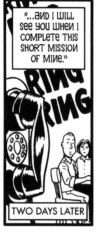

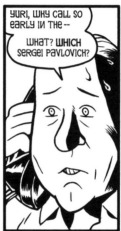

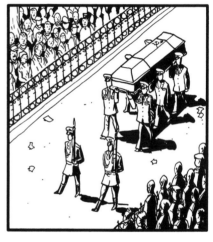

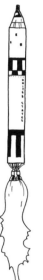

Titan II/Gemini 12:
November 11–15, 1966
T-Minus 2 Years, 8 Months, 9 Days
Flight duration: 94 hours, 34 minutes, 31 seconds
Jim Lovell and Buzz Aldrin

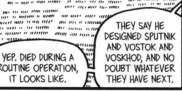

NOW, EAT, EAT. THE PIROZHKI ARE MAGNIFICENT!
AND YOU?
NO, I CAN'T.
IT'S MY INTESTINE THEY'RE OPERATING ON. TOMORROW.
PIROZHKI = "pierogi" = a tasty dumpling!
TOMORROW? INTESTINE? I THOUGHT IT WAS YOUR HEART THAT WAS DAMAGED IN...IN...
YOU CAN SAY IT, YURI -- THE GULAG.
BUT DO NOT WORRY. THAT NEARLY KILLED ME, BUT...HERE I AM.
NOW, IT'S FOUR A.M....GO HOME...
"...AND I WILL SEE YOU WHEN I COMPLETE THIS SHORT MISSION OF MINE."
RING RING
TWO DAYS LATER
YURI, WHY CALL SO EARLY IN THE --
WHAT? WHICH SERGEI PAVLOVICH?
SO THAT'S HIM?
AND HIS NAME WAS SERGEI KOROLEV.
YEP. DIED DURING A ROUTINE OPERATION, IT LOOKS LIKE.
THEY SAY HE DESIGNED SPUTNIK AND VOSTOK AND VOSKHOD, AND NO DOUBT WHATEVER THEY HAVE NEXT.
MORE LIES, I BETCHA. BUT MAYBE IT'S GOOD NEWS.
WHAT THE HECK ARE YOU TALKING ABOUT?
IF IT'S TRUE -- WHICH IT PROBABLY IS --
-- IT'S BAD NEWS.

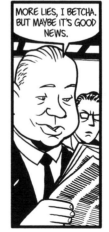

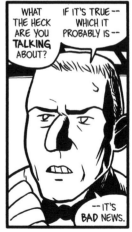

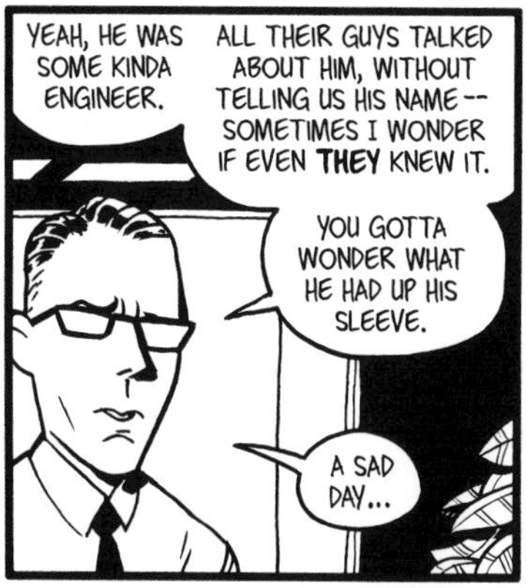
YEAH, HE WAS SOME KINDA ENGINEER.
ALL THEIR GUYS TALKED ABOUT HIM, WITHOUT TELLING US HIS NAME -- SOMETIMES I WONDER IF EVEN **THEY** KNEW IT.
YOU GOTTA WONDER WHAT HE HAD UP HIS SLEEVE.
A SAD DAY...

NASA engineers and astronauts met their ***SOVIET COUNTERPARTS*** *now and then. They all got along well -- they had a lot in common!*

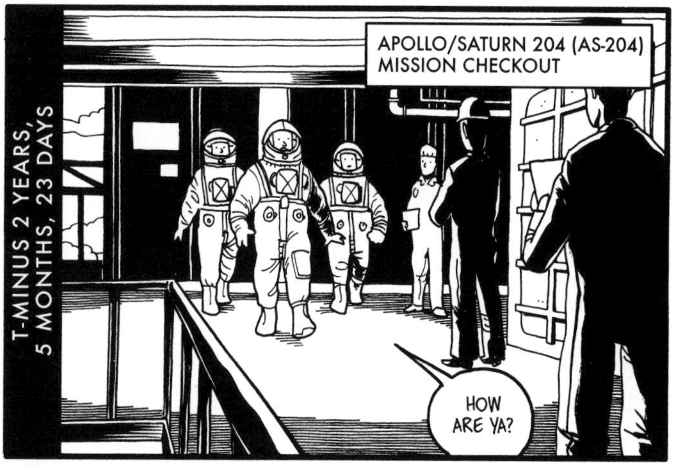
T-MINUS 2 YEARS, 5 MONTHS, 23 DAYS
APOLLO/SATURN 204 (AS-204) MISSION CHECKOUT
HOW ARE YA?

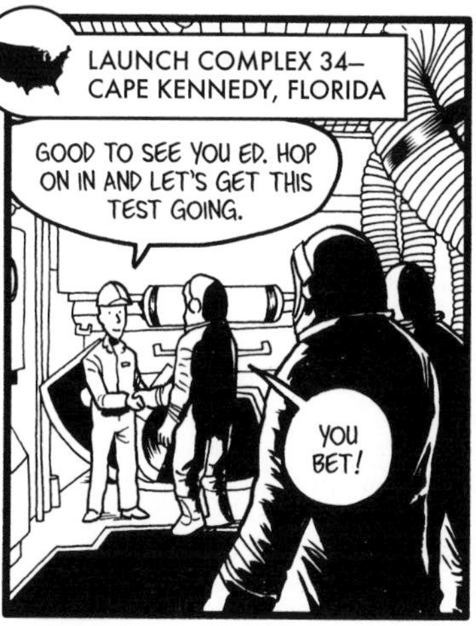
LAUNCH COMPLEX 34– CAPE KENNEDY, FLORIDA
GOOD TO SEE YOU ED. HOP ON IN AND LET'S GET THIS TEST GOING.
YOU BET!

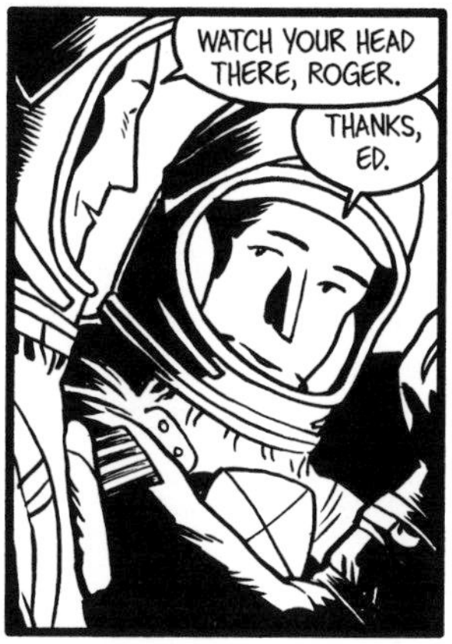
WATCH YOUR HEAD THERE, ROGER.
THANKS, ED.

ROGER CHAFFEE *= Apollo 1 Lunar Module Pilot*

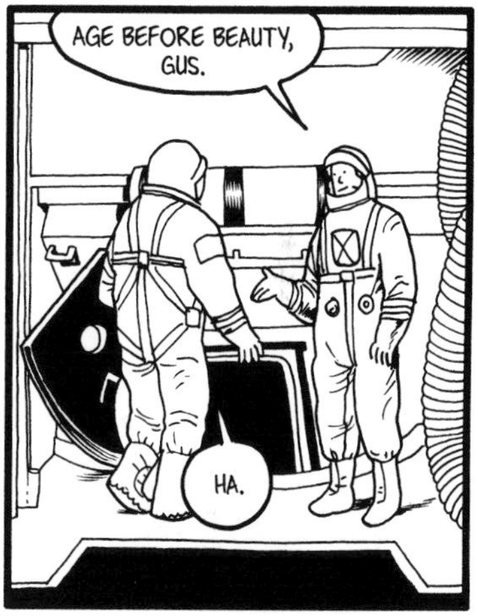
AGE BEFORE BEAUTY, GUS.
HA.

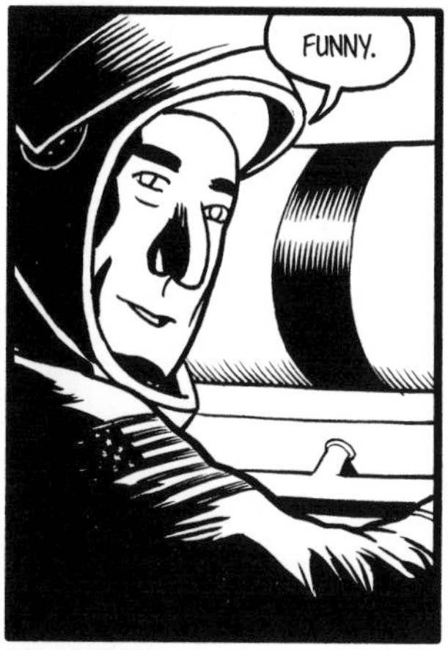
FUNNY.

GUS GRISSOM *= Apollo 1 Commander*

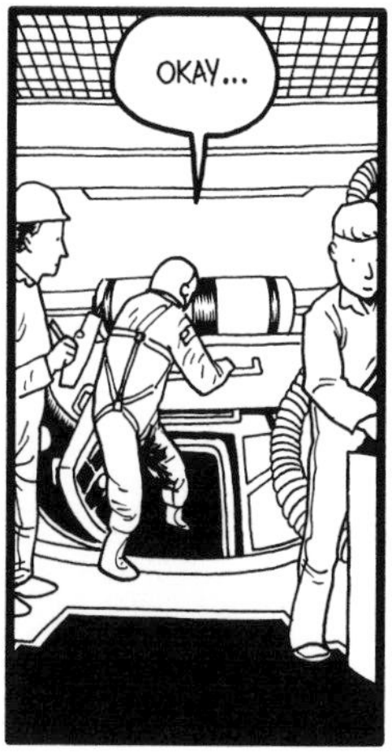
OKAY...

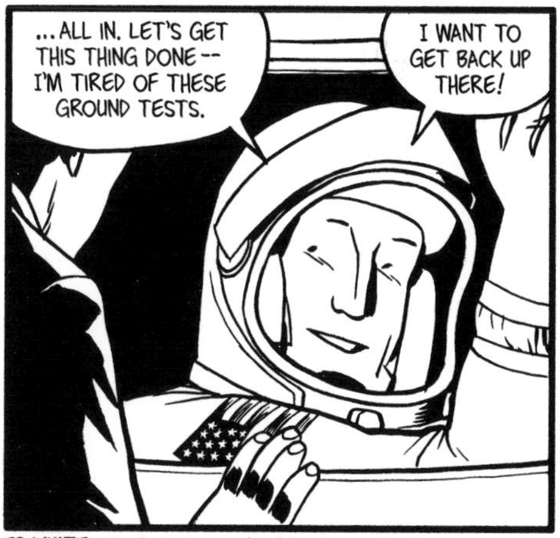
...ALL IN. LET'S GET THIS THING DONE -- I'M TIRED OF THESE GROUND TESTS.
I WANT TO GET BACK UP THERE!

ED WHITE *= Apollo 1 Command and Service Module Pilot*

HECK...

...I'LL SETTLE FOR GETTING HOME IN TIME FOR DINNER.

5 HOURS AND 20 MINUTES LATERS...

ANOTHER HOLD?

HOW KKKKKKXXXX GET TO KXXX MOON IF WE CAN'T TALK BETWEEN KXXXX?

APOLLO 1, THIS IS STONY -- HOW DO YOU READ?

STONY = Stu Roosa, CAPCOM for today's test

KKKKXX CAN'T HEAR A THING SCREEEE SAYING.

...I SAID...ARE WE GOING TO SKKRRX MOON KKKKXXXX TWO SKRRXX BUILDINGS?

SCREEEEE HOLD THE COUNTDOWKXX XXXXXX XXXX.

REMIND YOU OF ANYTHING, GUS?

YEAH, BUT YOU WERE **150 MILES UP** HAVING FUN IN GEMINI 4 WHEN I WAS YOUR CAPCOM.

THIS TIME WE'RE STUCK HERE ON THE **GROUND,** AND DOIN' NOTHING!

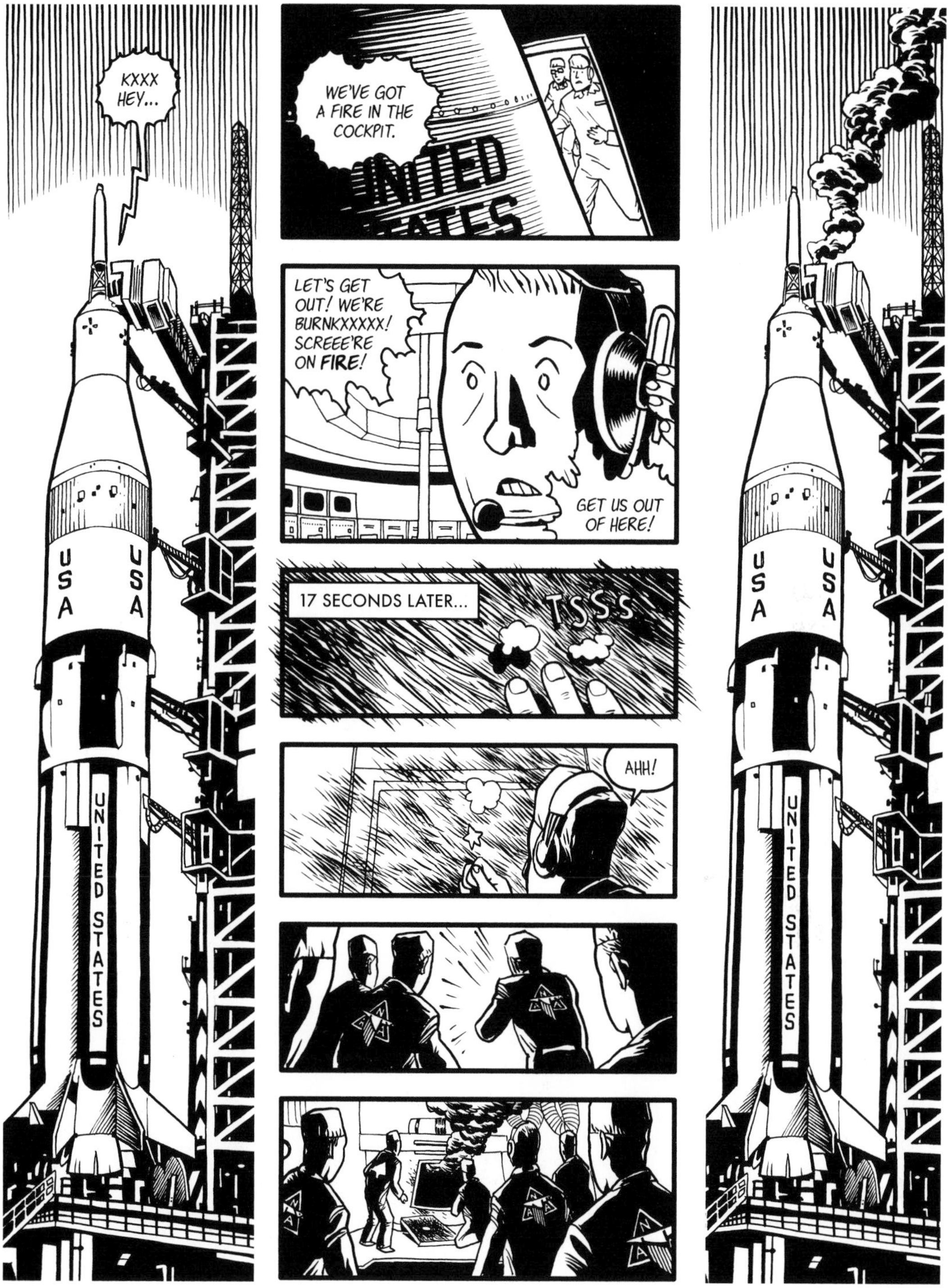
KXXX HEY...
WE'VE GOT A FIRE IN THE COCKPIT.
LET'S GET OUT! WE'RE BURNKXXXXX! SCREEE'RE ON FIRE!
GET US OUT OF HERE!
17 SECONDS LATER...
TSSS
AHH!

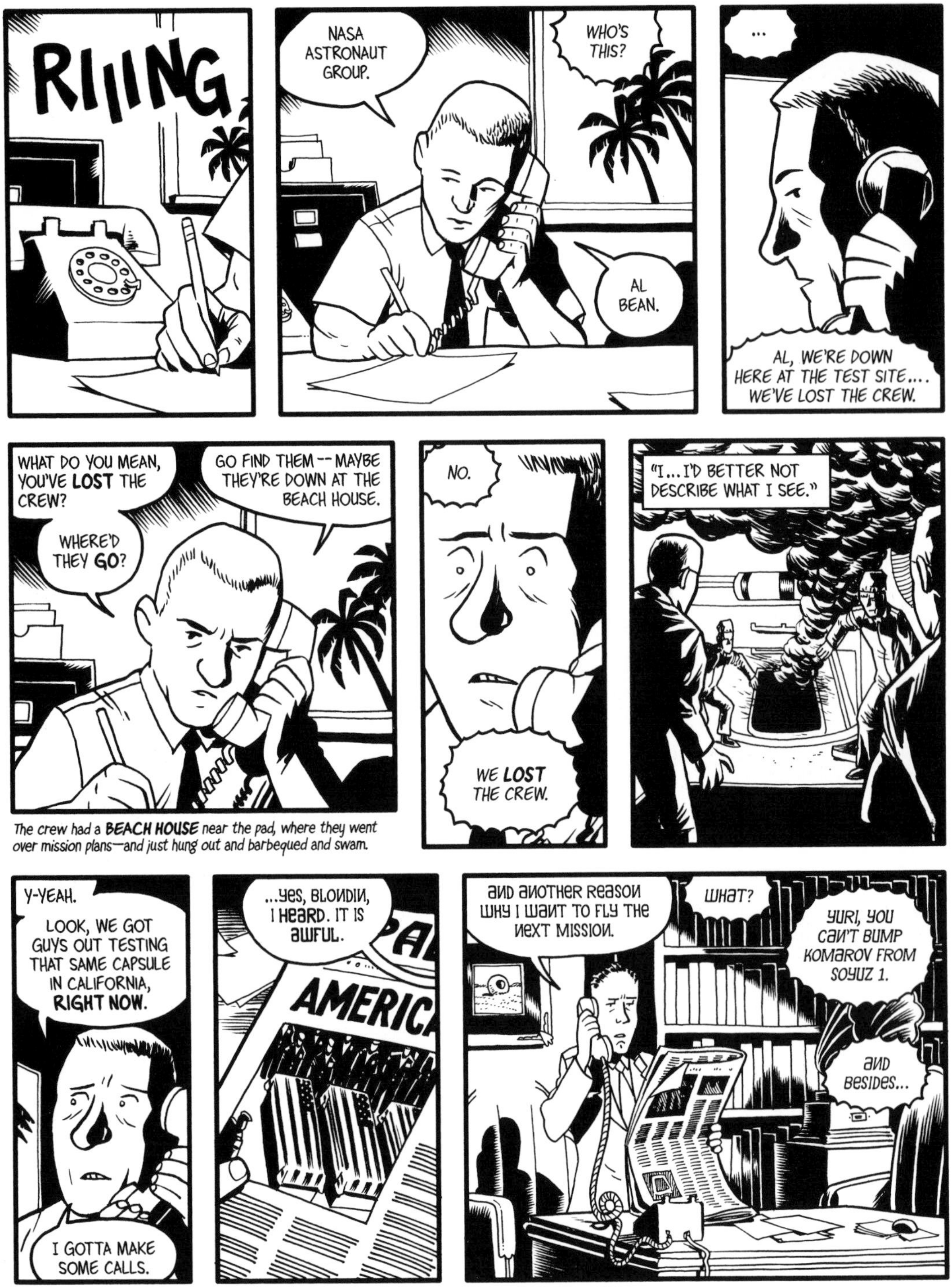
RIIING
NASA ASTRONAUT GROUP.
WHO'S THIS?
AL BEAN.
...
AL, WE'RE DOWN HERE AT THE TEST SITE.... WE'VE LOST THE CREW.
WHAT DO YOU MEAN, YOU'VE **LOST** THE CREW?
GO FIND THEM -- MAYBE THEY'RE DOWN AT THE BEACH HOUSE.
WHERE'D THEY **GO**?
The crew had a **BEACH HOUSE** near the pad, where they went over mission plans—and just hung out and barbequed and swam.
NO.
WE **LOST** THE CREW.
"I... I'D BETTER NOT DESCRIBE WHAT I SEE."
Y-YEAH.
LOOK, WE GOT GUYS OUT TESTING THAT SAME CAPSULE IN CALIFORNIA, **RIGHT NOW**.
I GOTTA MAKE SOME CALLS.
...YES, BLONDIN, I **HEARD**. IT IS **AWFUL**.
AMERIC
AND ANOTHER REASON WHY I WANT TO FLY THE NEXT MISSION.
WHAT?
YURI, YOU CAN'T BUMP KOMAROV FROM SOYUZ 1.
AND BESIDES...

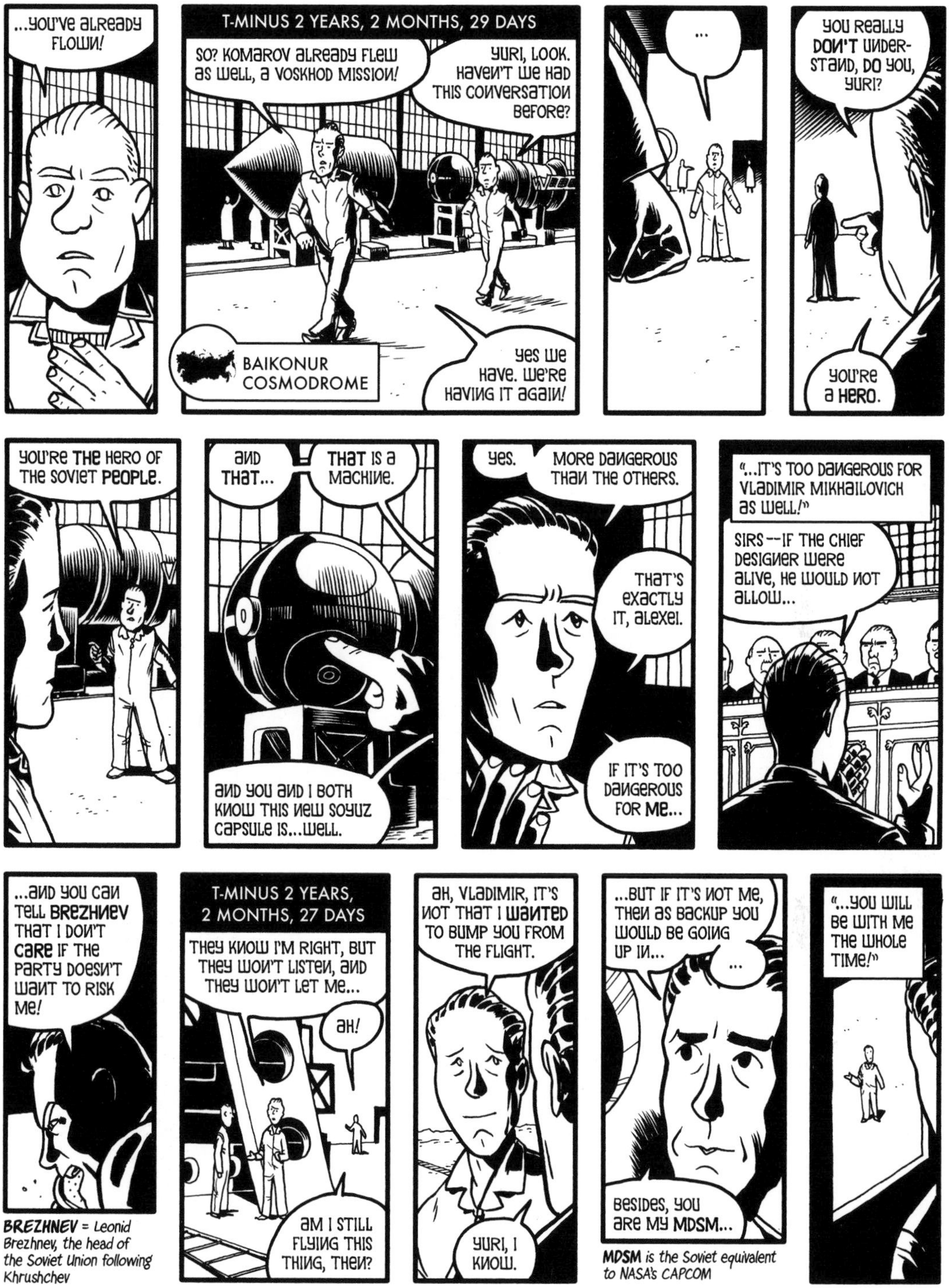
...YOU'VE ALREADY FLOWN!
T-MINUS 2 YEARS, 2 MONTHS, 29 DAYS
SO? KOMAROV ALREADY FLEW AS WELL, A VOSKHOD MISSION!
YURI, LOOK. HAVEN'T WE HAD THIS CONVERSATION BEFORE?
BAIKONUR COSMODROME
YES WE HAVE. WE'RE HAVING IT AGAIN!
...
YOU REALLY DON'T UNDERSTAND, DO YOU, YURI?
YOU'RE A HERO.
YOU'RE THE HERO OF THE SOVIET PEOPLE.
AND THAT...
THAT IS A MACHINE.
AND YOU AND I BOTH KNOW THIS NEW SOYUZ CAPSULE IS...WELL.
YES.
MORE DANGEROUS THAN THE OTHERS.
THAT'S EXACTLY IT, ALEXEI.
IF IT'S TOO DANGEROUS FOR ME...
"...IT'S TOO DANGEROUS FOR VLADIMIR MIKHAILOVICH AS WELL!"
SIRS--IF THE CHIEF DESIGNER WERE ALIVE, HE WOULD NOT ALLOW...
...AND YOU CAN TELL BREZHNEV THAT I DON'T CARE IF THE PARTY DOESN'T WANT TO RISK ME!
T-MINUS 2 YEARS, 2 MONTHS, 27 DAYS
THEY KNOW I'M RIGHT, BUT THEY WON'T LISTEN, AND THEY WON'T LET ME...
AH!
AM I STILL FLYING THIS THING, THEN?
AH, VLADIMIR, IT'S NOT THAT I WANTED TO BUMP YOU FROM THE FLIGHT.
YURI, I KNOW.
...BUT IF IT'S NOT ME, THEN AS BACKUP YOU WOULD BE GOING UP IN...
...
BESIDES, YOU ARE MY MDSM...
"...YOU WILL BE WITH ME THE WHOLE TIME!"

BREZHNEV = *Leonid Brezhnev, the head of the Soviet Union following Khrushchev*

MDSM *is the Soviet equivalent to NASA's CAPCOM*

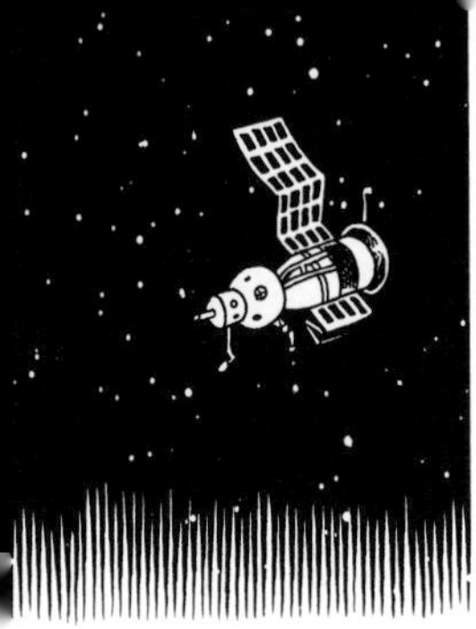

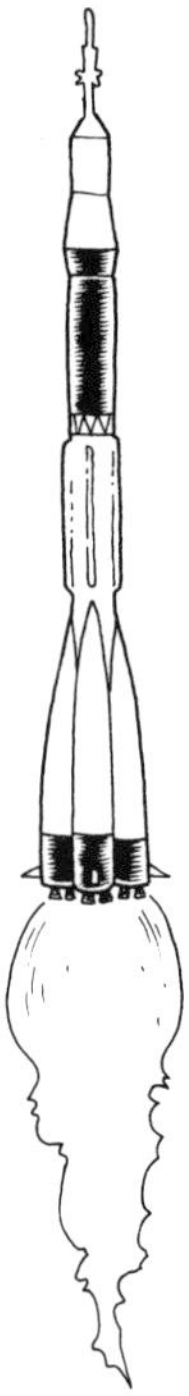

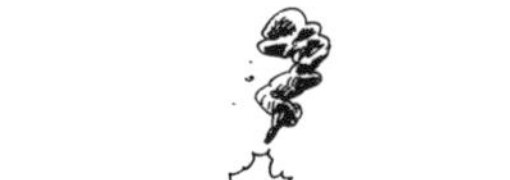

R7a/Soyuz 1: April 23, 1967
T-Minus 2 Years, 2 Months, 27 Days
Flight duration: 1 day, 2 hours, 47 minutes
Vladimir Komarov died when his solar panels, heat shield, retro-rockets, and parachute failed.

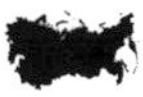

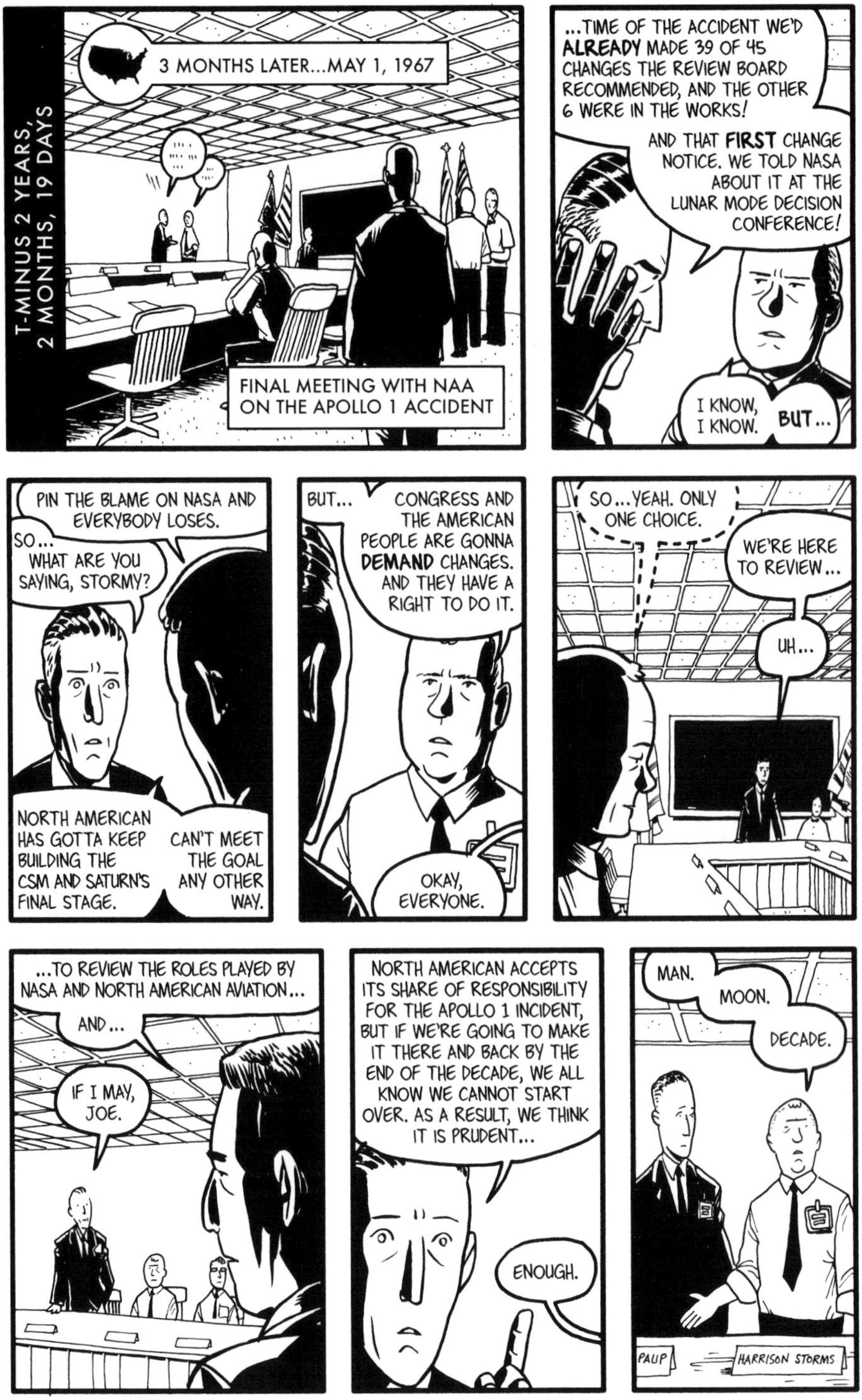
T-MINUS 2 YEARS, 2 MONTHS, 19 DAYS
3 MONTHS LATER...MAY 1, 1967
FINAL MEETING WITH NAA ON THE APOLLO 1 ACCIDENT
...TIME OF THE ACCIDENT WE'D **ALREADY** MADE 39 OF 45 CHANGES THE REVIEW BOARD RECOMMENDED, AND THE OTHER 6 WERE IN THE WORKS!
AND THAT **FIRST** CHANGE NOTICE. WE TOLD NASA ABOUT IT AT THE LUNAR MODE DECISION CONFERENCE!
I KNOW, I KNOW.
BUT...
PIN THE BLAME ON NASA AND EVERYBODY LOSES.
SO... WHAT ARE YOU SAYING, STORMY?
NORTH AMERICAN HAS GOTTA KEEP BUILDING THE CSM AND SATURN'S FINAL STAGE.
CAN'T MEET THE GOAL ANY OTHER WAY.
BUT...
CONGRESS AND THE AMERICAN PEOPLE ARE GONNA **DEMAND** CHANGES. AND THEY HAVE A RIGHT TO DO IT.
OKAY, EVERYONE.
SO...YEAH. ONLY ONE CHOICE.
WE'RE HERE TO REVIEW...
UH...
...TO REVIEW THE ROLES PLAYED BY NASA AND NORTH AMERICAN AVIATION...
AND...
IF I MAY, JOE.
NORTH AMERICAN ACCEPTS ITS SHARE OF RESPONSIBILITY FOR THE APOLLO 1 INCIDENT, BUT IF WE'RE GOING TO MAKE IT THERE AND BACK BY THE END OF THE DECADE, WE ALL KNOW WE CANNOT START OVER. AS A RESULT, WE THINK IT IS PRUDENT...
ENOUGH.
MAN.
MOON.
DECADE.
PAUP
HARRISON STORMS

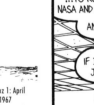

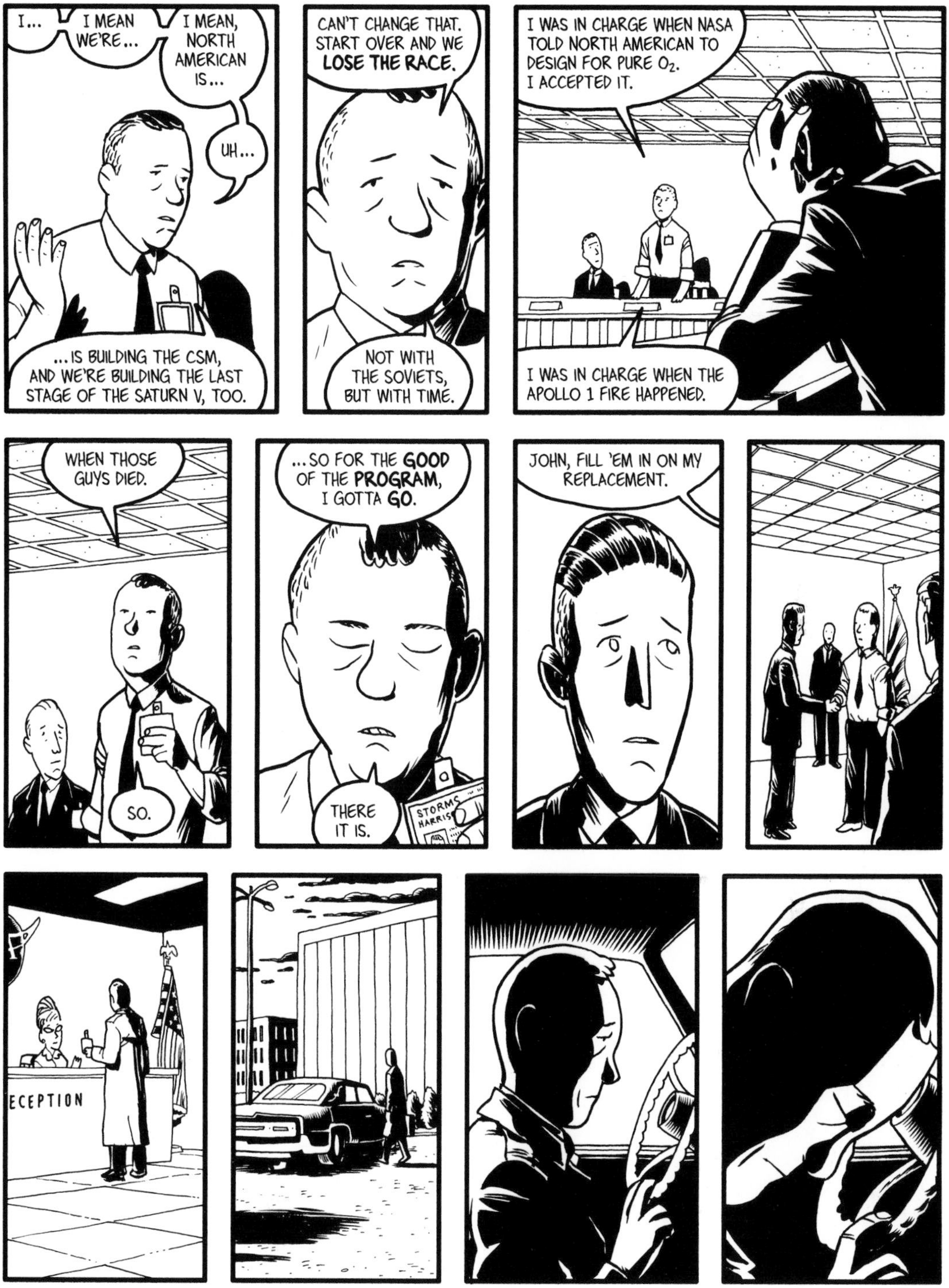
I...
I MEAN WE'RE...
I MEAN, NORTH AMERICAN IS...
UH...
...IS BUILDING THE CSM, AND WE'RE BUILDING THE LAST STAGE OF THE SATURN V, TOO.
CAN'T CHANGE THAT. START OVER AND WE LOSE THE RACE.
NOT WITH THE SOVIETS, BUT WITH TIME.
I WAS IN CHARGE WHEN NASA TOLD NORTH AMERICAN TO DESIGN FOR PURE O2. I ACCEPTED IT.
I WAS IN CHARGE WHEN THE APOLLO 1 FIRE HAPPENED.
WHEN THOSE GUYS DIED.
SO.
...SO FOR THE GOOD OF THE PROGRAM, I GOTTA GO.
THERE IT IS.
STORMS HARRIS
JOHN, FILL 'EM IN ON MY REPLACEMENT.
ECEPTION

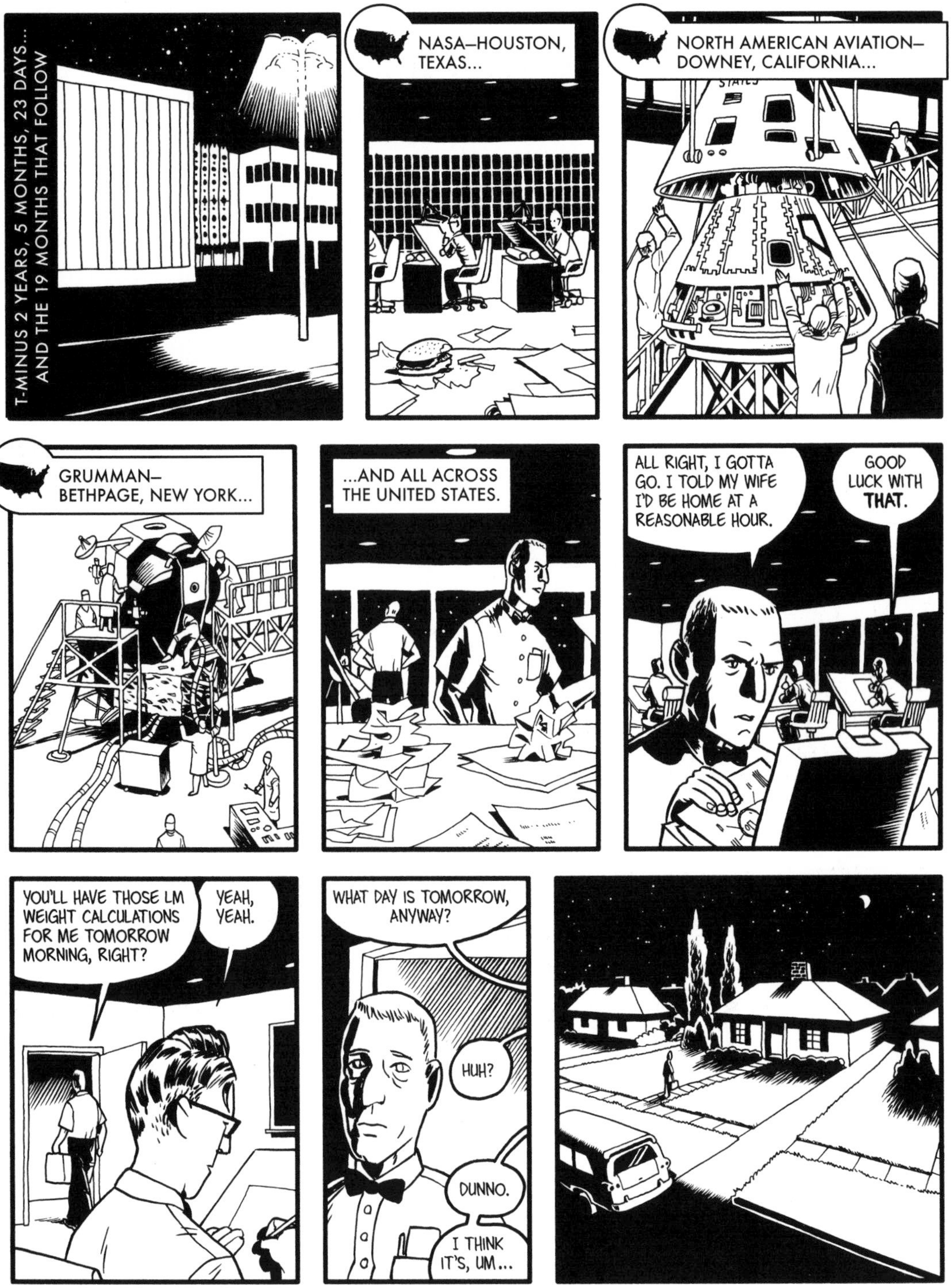
T-MINUS 2 YEARS, 5 MONTHS, 23 DAYS... AND THE 19 MONTHS THAT FOLLOW
NASA–HOUSTON, TEXAS...
NORTH AMERICAN AVIATION–DOWNEY, CALIFORNIA...
GRUMMAN–BETHPAGE, NEW YORK...
...AND ALL ACROSS THE UNITED STATES.
ALL RIGHT, I GOTTA GO. I TOLD MY WIFE I'D BE HOME AT A REASONABLE HOUR.
GOOD LUCK WITH **THAT**.
YOU'LL HAVE THOSE LM WEIGHT CALCULATIONS FOR ME TOMORROW MORNING, RIGHT?
YEAH, YEAH.
WHAT DAY IS TOMORROW, ANYWAY?
HUH?
DUNNO.
I THINK IT'S, UM...

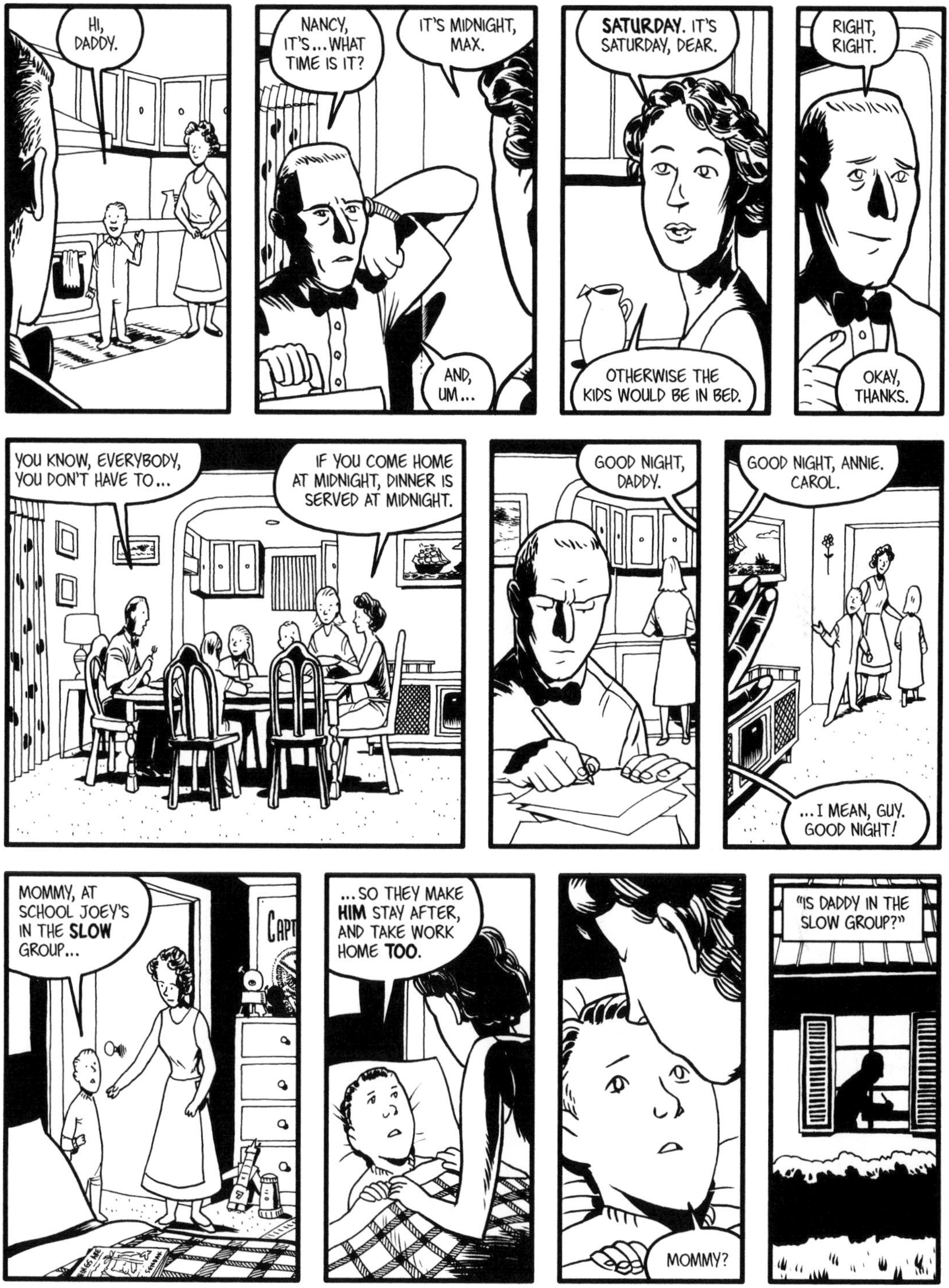
HI, DADDY.
NANCY, IT'S... WHAT TIME IS IT?
IT'S MIDNIGHT, MAX.
AND, UM...
SATURDAY. IT'S SATURDAY, DEAR.
OTHERWISE THE KIDS WOULD BE IN BED.
RIGHT, RIGHT.
OKAY, THANKS.
YOU KNOW, EVERYBODY, YOU DON'T HAVE TO...
IF YOU COME HOME AT MIDNIGHT, DINNER IS SERVED AT MIDNIGHT.
GOOD NIGHT, DADDY.
GOOD NIGHT, ANNIE. CAROL.
...I MEAN, GUY. GOOD NIGHT!
MOMMY, AT SCHOOL JOEY'S IN THE **SLOW** GROUP...
...SO THEY MAKE **HIM** STAY AFTER, AND TAKE WORK HOME **TOO**.
MOMMY?
"IS DADDY IN THE SLOW GROUP?"

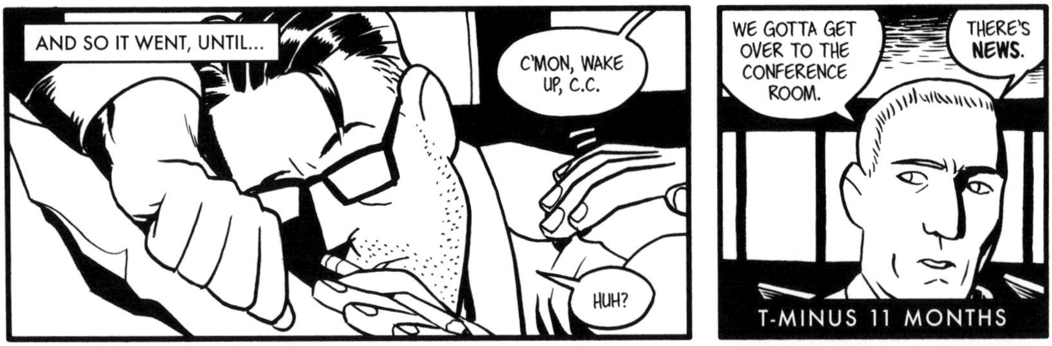
AND SO IT WENT, UNTIL...
C'MON, WAKE UP, C.C.
HUH?
WE GOTTA GET OVER TO THE CONFERENCE ROOM.
THERE'S **NEWS**.
T-MINUS 11 MONTHS

ALL UP

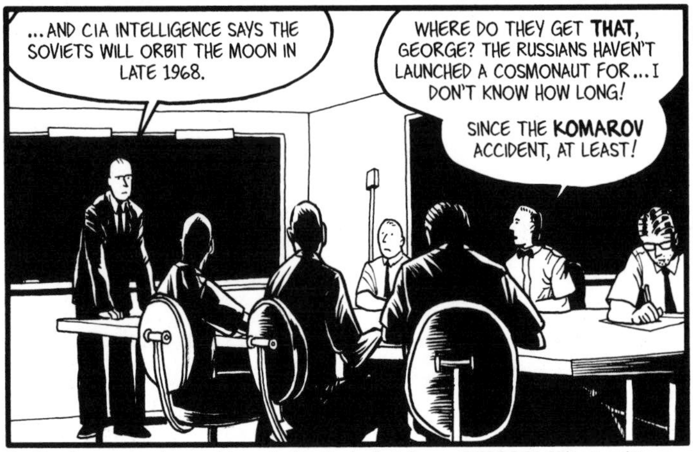
...AND CIA INTELLIGENCE SAYS THE SOVIETS WILL ORBIT THE MOON IN LATE 1968.
WHERE DO THEY GET **THAT**, GEORGE? THE RUSSIANS HAVEN'T LAUNCHED A COSMONAUT FOR... I DON'T KNOW HOW LONG!
SINCE THE **KOMAROV** ACCIDENT, AT LEAST!

Joe Shea became too depressed to work after the Apollo 1 fire, so **GEORGE LOW** *replaced him as head of the Apollo Spacecraft Program Office.*

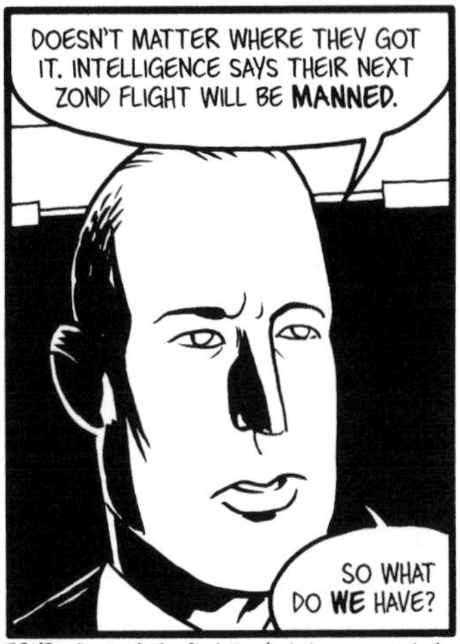
DOESN'T MATTER WHERE THEY GOT IT. INTELLIGENCE SAYS THEIR NEXT ZOND FLIGHT WILL BE **MANNED**.
SO WHAT DO **WE** HAVE?

ZOND *= "probe." The first Zond missions were robots.*

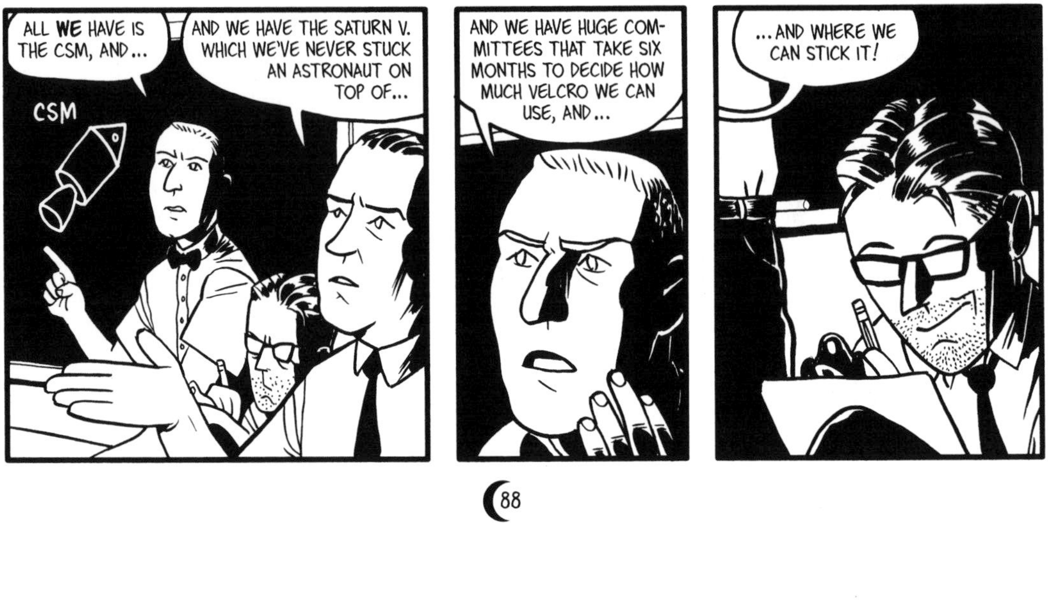
ALL **WE** HAVE IS THE CSM, AND...
CSM
AND WE HAVE THE SATURN V. WHICH WE'VE NEVER STUCK AN ASTRONAUT ON TOP OF...
AND WE HAVE HUGE COMMITTEES THAT TAKE SIX MONTHS TO DECIDE HOW MUCH VELCRO WE CAN USE, AND...
...AND WHERE WE CAN STICK IT!

AND NO **LM**.

AND NO SOFTWARE FOR THE LM LANDING COMPUTER.

DEKE SLAYTON = one of the original Mercury 7, and now NASA's director of flight crew operations. He decided who flew what mission.

OKAY, FINE.

WE DO HAVE GUIDANCE AND NAVIGATION COMPUTERS, THOUGH, ...

...AND WE WEREN'T GOING TO LAND ANYWAY. AT LEAST NOT **YET.**

BUT, WE'RE OUT OF **TIME.** IT'S "ALL UP" TESTING FROM NOW ON -- WE TRY A LOT OF THINGS AT ONCE, AND LEARN FASTER.

SO, WHAT'S THE CURRENT MISSION PROFILE FOR APOLLO 8?

TEST THE LM IN EARTH ORBIT.

C'MON, CHRIS. APOLLO 7 **ALREADY TESTED** THE CSM IN ORBIT, AND ...

...**WE. DON'T. HAVE.** AN **LM!**

I'LL SAY IT AGAIN: **ALL UP.**

ORBIT THE **MOON.**

THIS YEAR -- 1968.

"...CALL IT THE X MISSION."

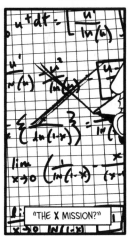

"THE **X** MISSION?"

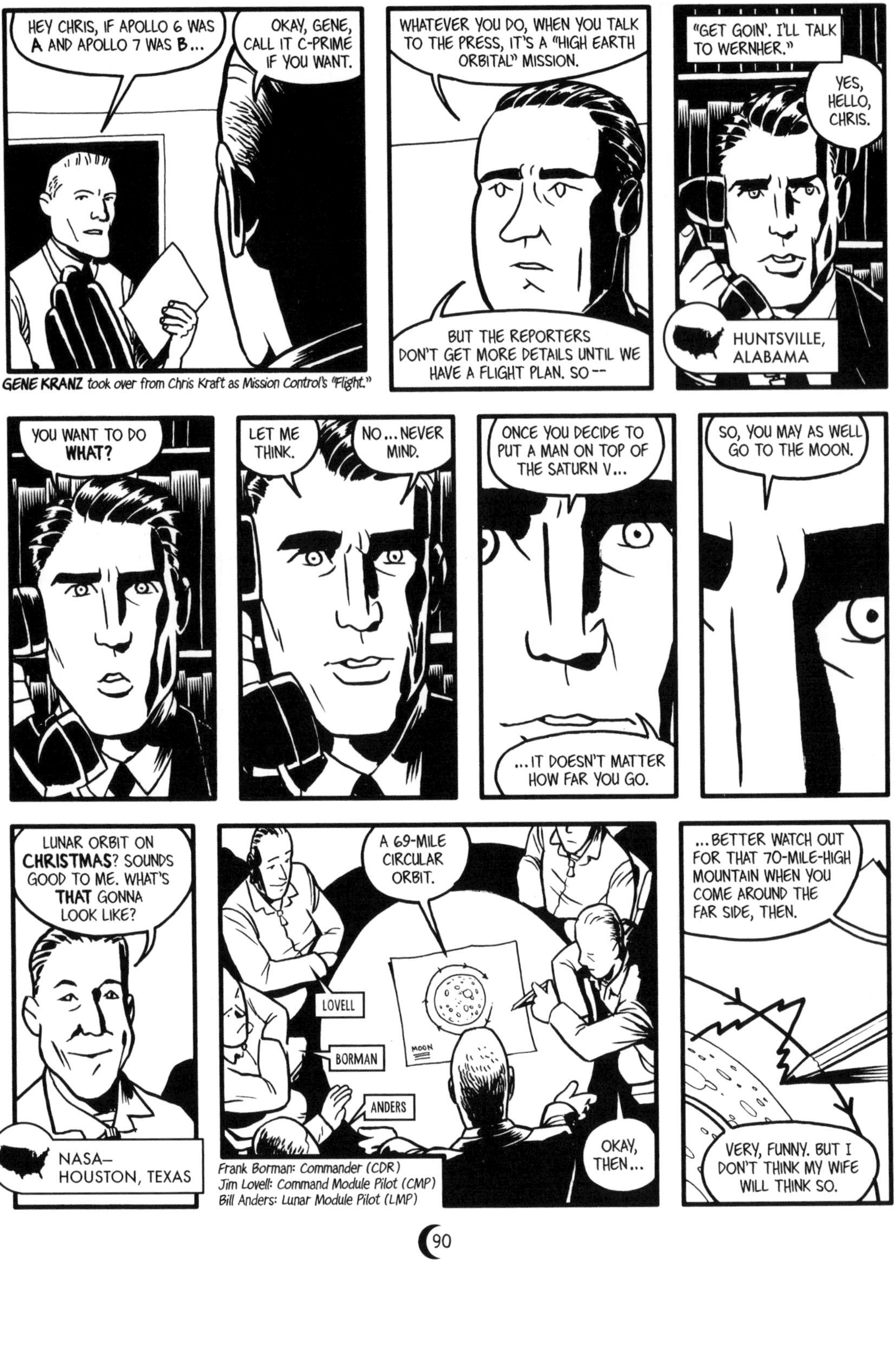
HEY CHRIS, IF APOLLO 6 WAS **A** AND APOLLO 7 WAS **B**...
OKAY, GENE, CALL IT C-PRIME IF YOU WANT.
GENE KRANZ took over from Chris Kraft as Mission Control's "Flight."
WHATEVER YOU DO, WHEN YOU TALK TO THE PRESS, IT'S A "HIGH EARTH ORBITAL" MISSION.
BUT THE REPORTERS DON'T GET MORE DETAILS UNTIL WE HAVE A FLIGHT PLAN. SO--
"GET GOIN'. I'LL TALK TO WERNHER."
YES, HELLO, CHRIS.
HUNTSVILLE, ALABAMA
YOU WANT TO DO **WHAT?**
LET ME THINK.
NO... NEVER MIND.
ONCE YOU DECIDE TO PUT A MAN ON TOP OF THE SATURN V...
...IT DOESN'T MATTER HOW FAR YOU GO.
SO, YOU MAY AS WELL GO TO THE MOON.
LUNAR ORBIT ON **CHRISTMAS**? SOUNDS GOOD TO ME. WHAT'S **THAT** GONNA LOOK LIKE?
NASA– HOUSTON, TEXAS
A 69-MILE CIRCULAR ORBIT.
LOVELL
BORMAN
ANDERS
MOON
OKAY, THEN...
Frank Borman: Commander (CDR)
Jim Lovell: Command Module Pilot (CMP)
Bill Anders: Lunar Module Pilot (LMP)
...BETTER WATCH OUT FOR THAT 70-MILE-HIGH MOUNTAIN WHEN YOU COME AROUND THE FAR SIDE, THEN.
VERY, FUNNY. BUT I DON'T THINK MY WIFE WILL THINK SO.

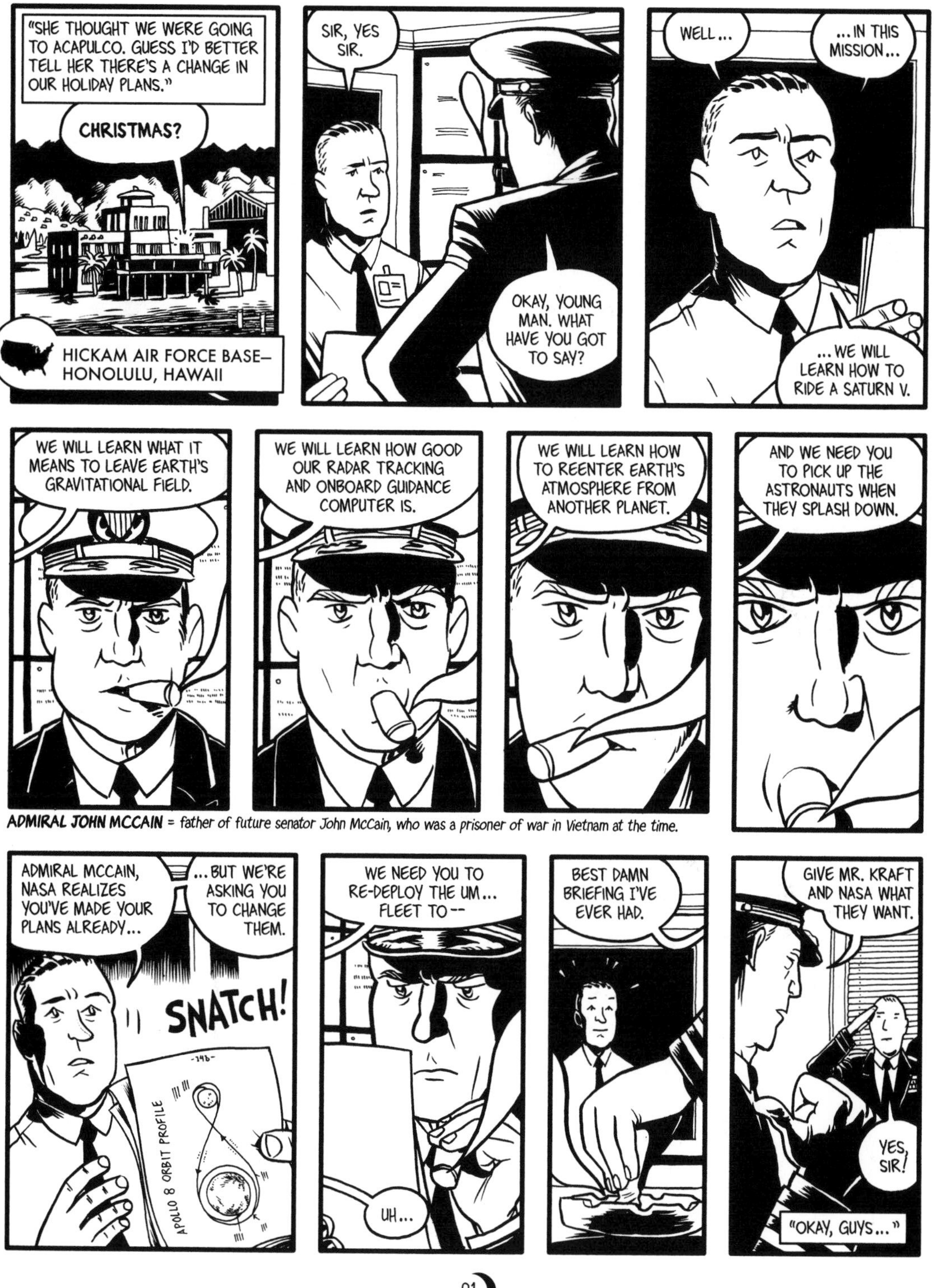
"SHE THOUGHT WE WERE GOING TO ACAPULCO. GUESS I'D BETTER TELL HER THERE'S A CHANGE IN OUR HOLIDAY PLANS."
CHRISTMAS?
HICKAM AIR FORCE BASE— HONOLULU, HAWAII
SIR, YES SIR.
OKAY, YOUNG MAN. WHAT HAVE YOU GOT TO SAY?
WELL...
...IN THIS MISSION...
...WE WILL LEARN HOW TO RIDE A SATURN V.
WE WILL LEARN WHAT IT MEANS TO LEAVE EARTH'S GRAVITATIONAL FIELD.
WE WILL LEARN HOW GOOD OUR RADAR TRACKING AND ONBOARD GUIDANCE COMPUTER IS.
WE WILL LEARN HOW TO REENTER EARTH'S ATMOSPHERE FROM ANOTHER PLANET.
AND WE NEED YOU TO PICK UP THE ASTRONAUTS WHEN THEY SPLASH DOWN.
ADMIRAL JOHN MCCAIN = father of future senator John McCain, who was a prisoner of war in Vietnam at the time.
ADMIRAL MCCAIN, NASA REALIZES YOU'VE MADE YOUR PLANS ALREADY...
...BUT WE'RE ASKING YOU TO CHANGE THEM.
SNATCH!
APOLLO 8 ORBIT PROFILE
WE NEED YOU TO RE-DEPLOY THE UM... FLEET TO--
UH...
BEST DAMN BRIEFING I'VE EVER HAD.
GIVE MR. KRAFT AND NASA WHAT THEY WANT.
YES, SIR!
"OKAY, GUYS..."

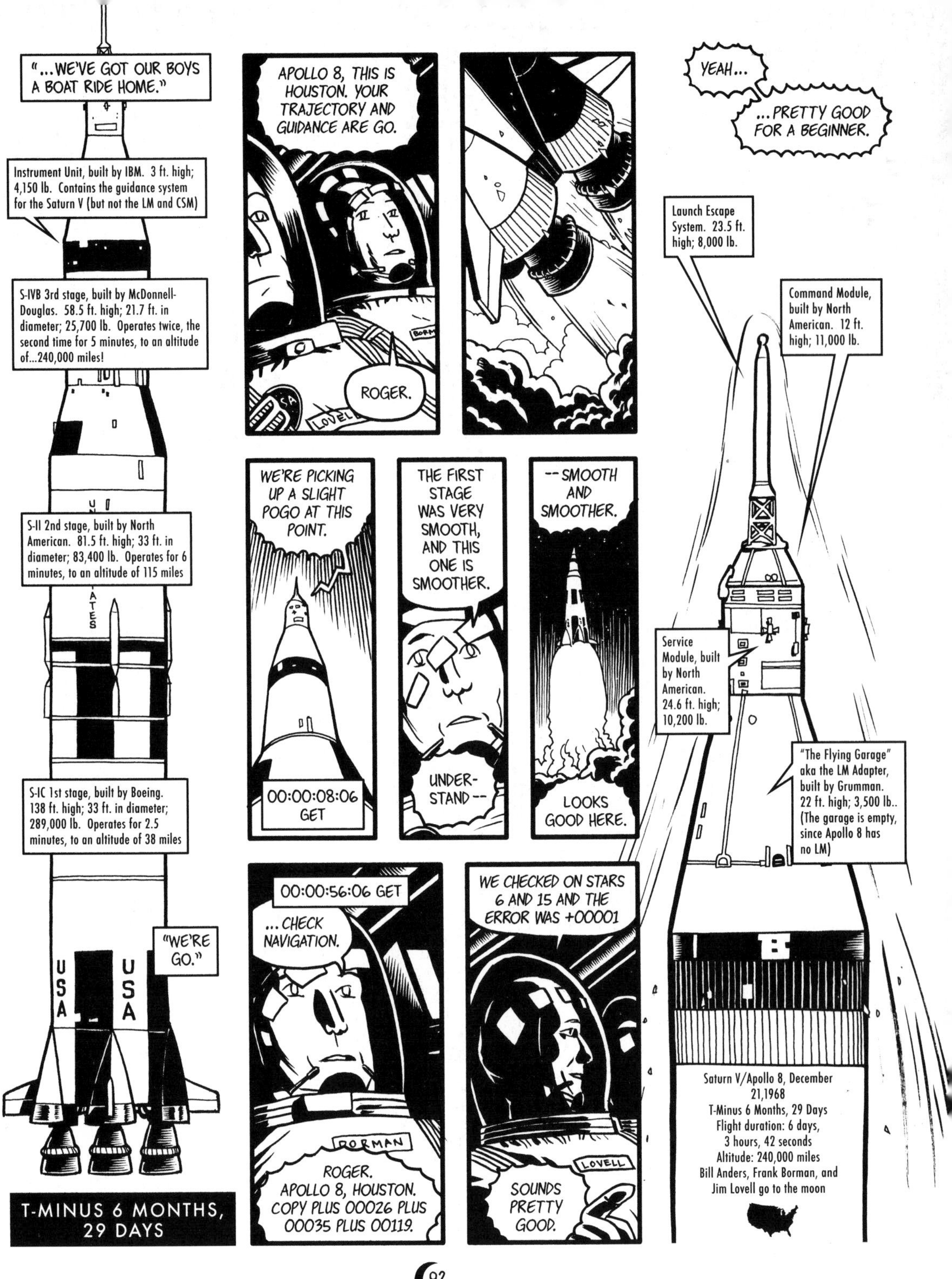
"...WE'VE GOT OUR BOYS A BOAT RIDE HOME."
Instrument Unit, built by IBM. 3 ft. high; 4,150 lb. Contains the guidance system for the Saturn V (but not the LM and CSM)
S-IVB 3rd stage, built by McDonnell-Douglas. 58.5 ft. high; 21.7 ft. in diameter; 25,700 lb. Operates twice, the second time for 5 minutes, to an altitude of...240,000 miles!
S-II 2nd stage, built by North American. 81.5 ft. high; 33 ft. in diameter; 83,400 lb. Operates for 6 minutes, to an altitude of 115 miles
S-IC 1st stage, built by Boeing. 138 ft. high; 33 ft. in diameter; 289,000 lb. Operates for 2.5 minutes, to an altitude of 38 miles
"WE'RE GO."
USA
USA
T-MINUS 6 MONTHS, 29 DAYS
APOLLO 8, THIS IS HOUSTON. YOUR TRAJECTORY AND GUIDANCE ARE GO.
ROGER.
LOVELL
WE'RE PICKING UP A SLIGHT POGO AT THIS POINT.
00:00:08:06 GET
THE FIRST STAGE WAS VERY SMOOTH, AND THIS ONE IS SMOOTHER.
UNDER-STAND --
-- SMOOTH AND SMOOTHER.
LOOKS GOOD HERE.
00:00:56:06 GET
...CHECK NAVIGATION.
BORMAN
ROGER. APOLLO 8, HOUSTON. COPY PLUS 00026 PLUS 00035 PLUS 00119.
WE CHECKED ON STARS 6 AND 15 AND THE ERROR WAS +00001
LOVELL
SOUNDS PRETTY GOOD.
YEAH...
...PRETTY GOOD FOR A BEGINNER.
Launch Escape System. 23.5 ft. high; 8,000 lb.
Command Module, built by North American. 12 ft. high; 11,000 lb.
Service Module, built by North American. 24.6 ft. high; 10,200 lb.
"The Flying Garage" aka the LM Adapter, built by Grumman. 22 ft. high; 3,500 lb.. (The garage is empty, since Apollo 8 has no LM)
Saturn V/Apollo 8, December 21,1968
T-Minus 6 Months, 29 Days
Flight duration: 6 days, 3 hours, 42 seconds
Altitude: 240,000 miles
Bill Anders, Frank Borman, and Jim Lovell go to the moon

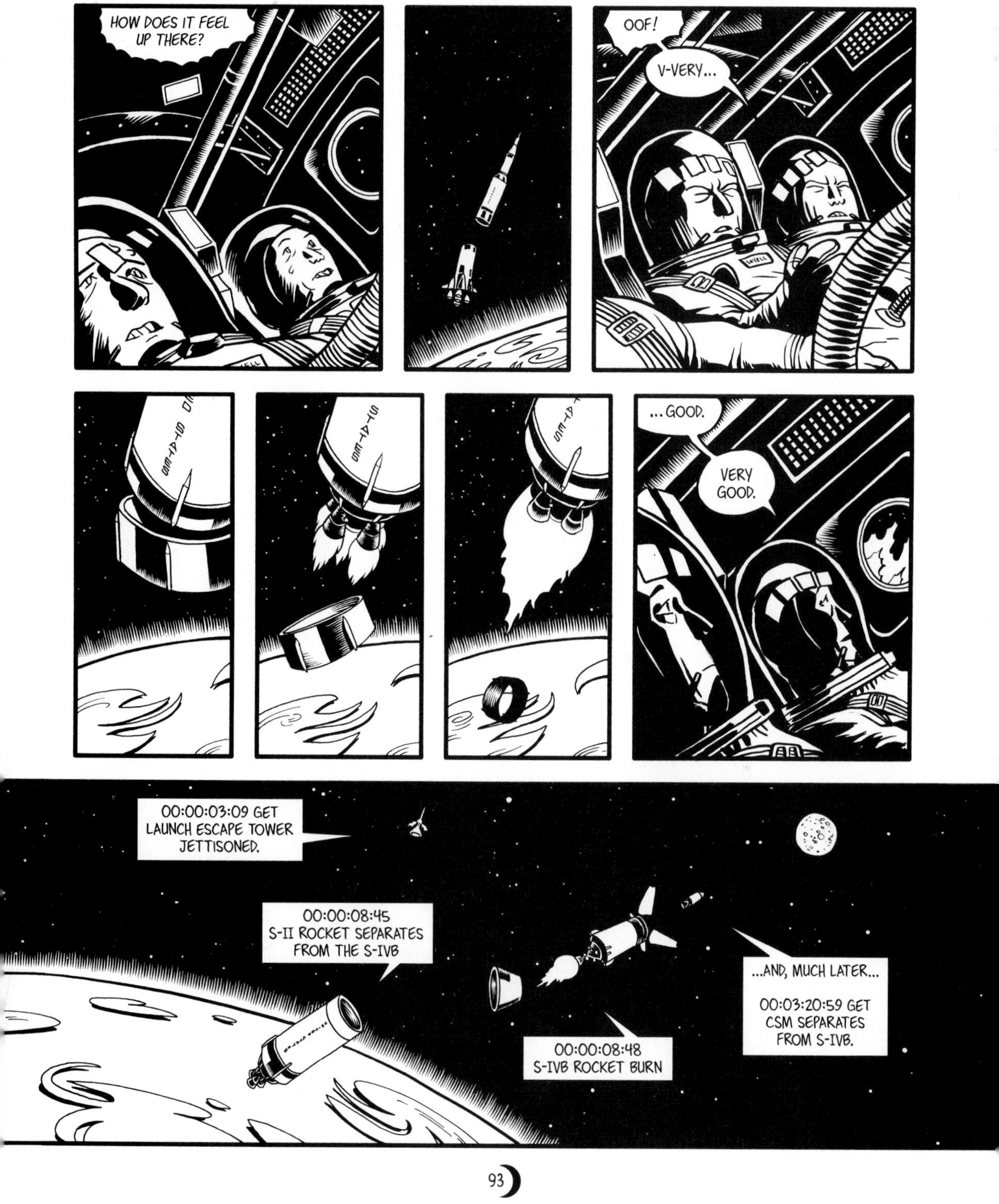

HOW DOES IT FEEL UP THERE?
OOF!
V-VERY...
...GOOD.
VERY GOOD.
00:00:03:09 GET LAUNCH ESCAPE TOWER JETTISONED.
00:00:08:45 S-II ROCKET SEPARATES FROM THE S-IVB
00:00:08:48 S-IVB ROCKET BURN
...AND, MUCH LATER...
00:03:20:59 GET CSM SEPARATES FROM S-IVB.

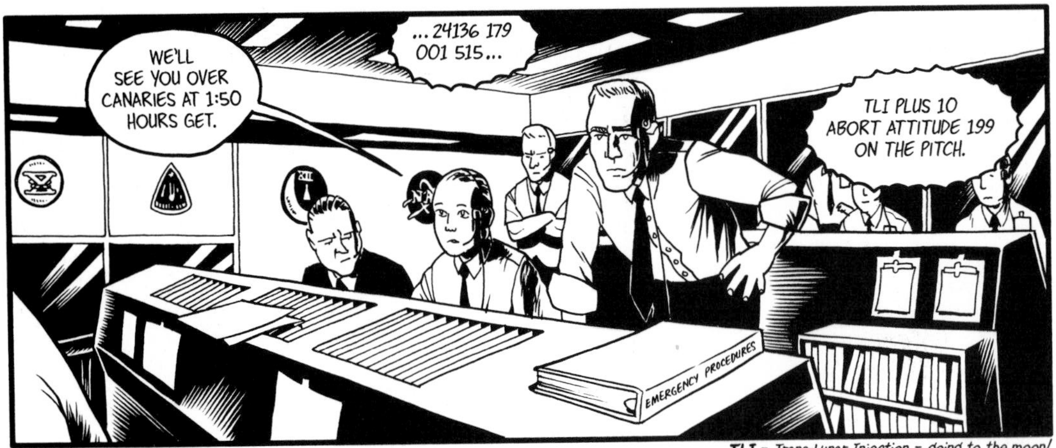
WE'LL SEE YOU OVER CANARIES AT 1:50 HOURS GET.
...24136 179 001 515...
TLI PLUS 10 ABORT ATTITUDE 199 ON THE PITCH.
EMERGENCY PROCEDURES

CANARIES = Canary Islands

TLI = Trans-Lunar Injection = going to the moon!

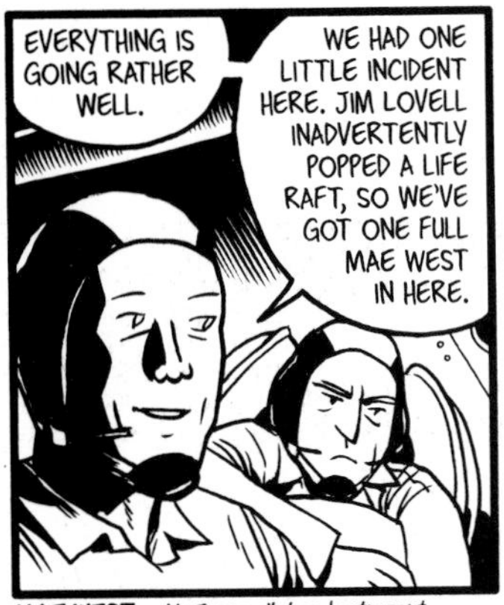
EVERYTHING IS GOING RATHER WELL.
WE HAD ONE LITTLE INCIDENT HERE. JIM LOVELL INADVERTENTLY POPPED A LIFE RAFT, SO WE'VE GOT ONE FULL MAE WEST IN HERE.

MAE WEST = Air Force pilot and astronaut nickname for a life vest (which Frank Borman mistakenly calls a raft).

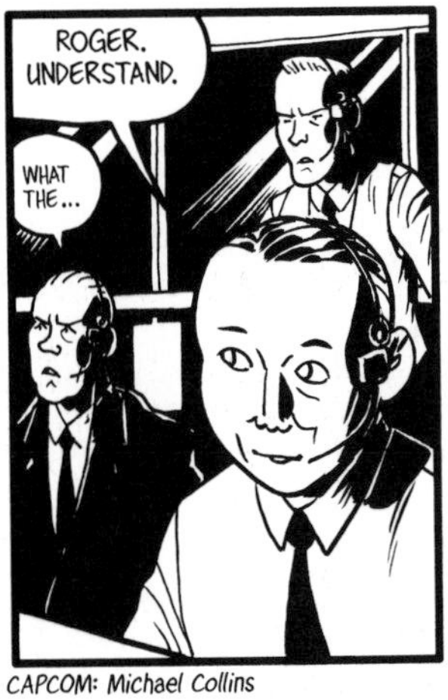
ROGER. UNDERSTAND.
WHAT THE...

CAPCOM: Michael Collins

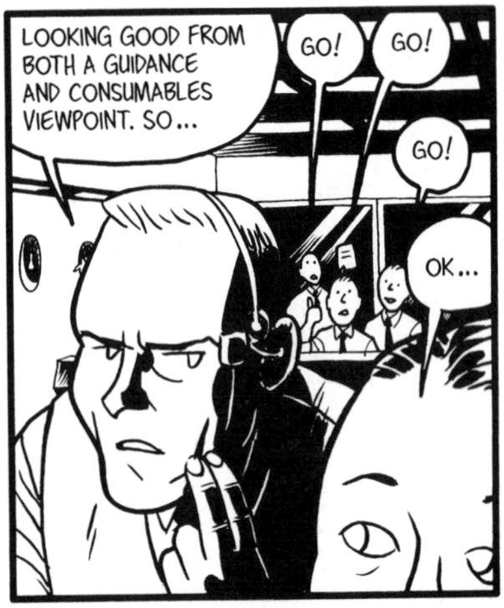
LOOKING GOOD FROM BOTH A GUIDANCE AND CONSUMABLES VIEWPOINT. SO...
GO!
GO!
GO!
OK...

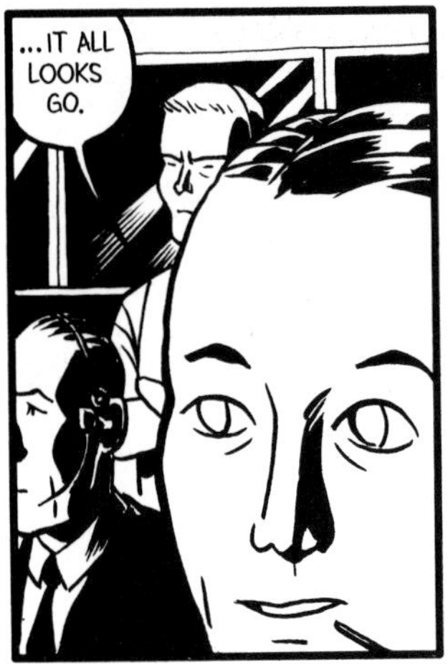
...IT ALL LOOKS GO.

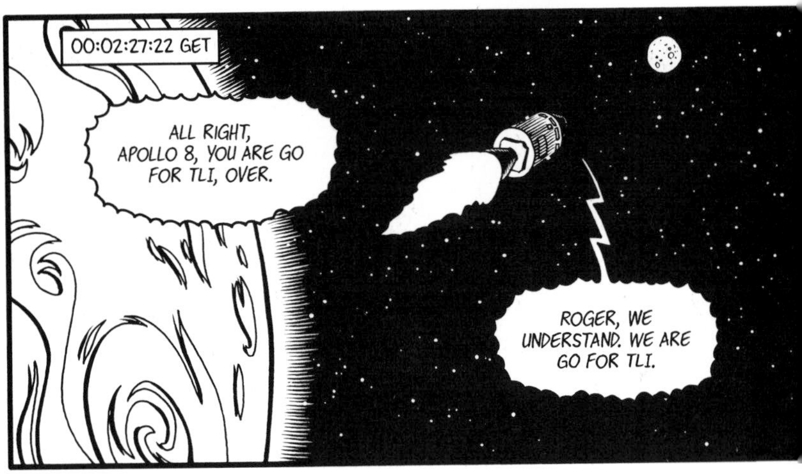
00:02:27:22 GET
ALL RIGHT, APOLLO 8, YOU ARE GO FOR TLI, OVER.
ROGER, WE UNDERSTAND. WE ARE GO FOR TLI.

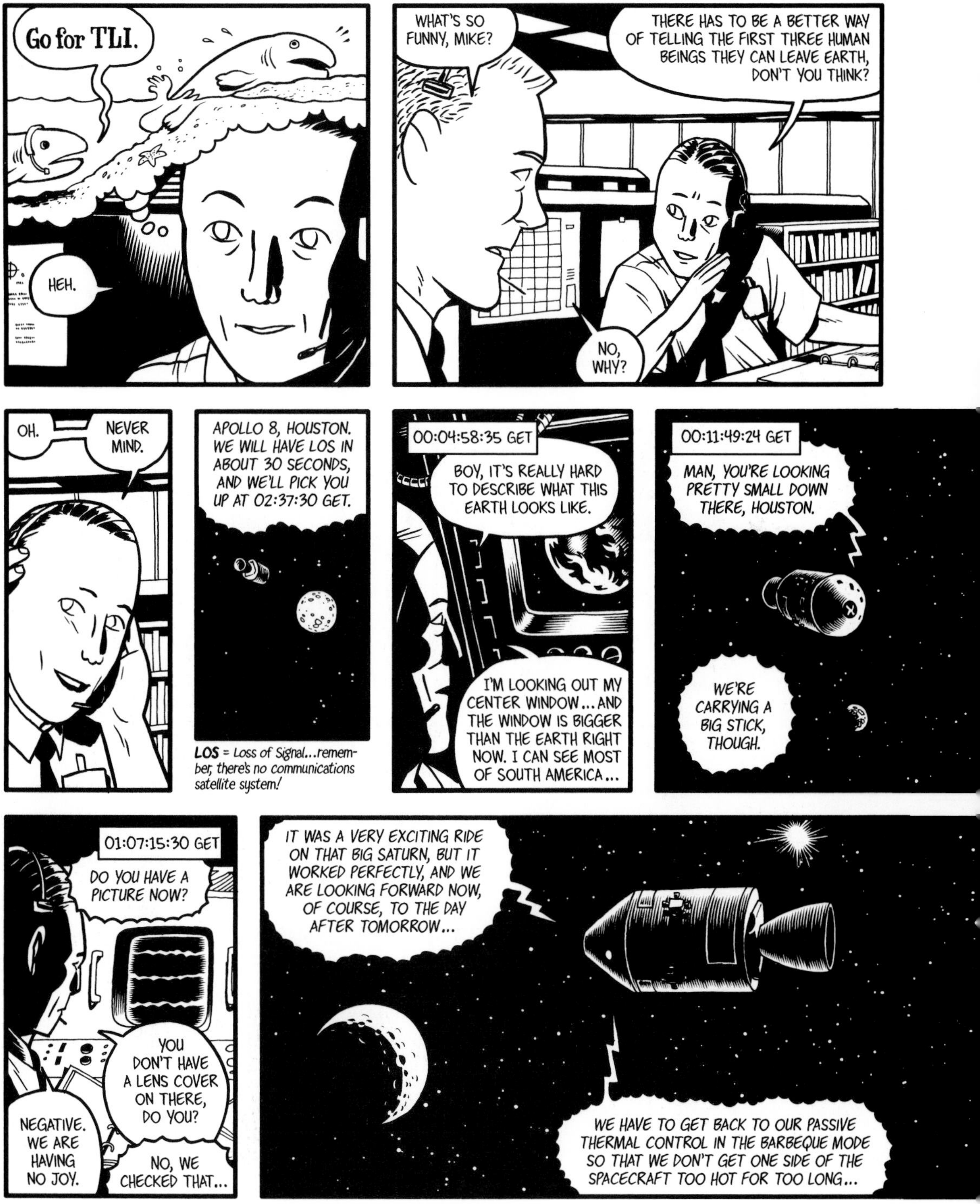
Go for TLI.
HEH.
WHAT'S SO FUNNY, MIKE?
THERE HAS TO BE A BETTER WAY OF TELLING THE FIRST THREE HUMAN BEINGS THEY CAN LEAVE EARTH, DON'T YOU THINK?
NO, WHY?
OH.
NEVER MIND.
APOLLO 8, HOUSTON. WE WILL HAVE LOS IN ABOUT 30 SECONDS, AND WE'LL PICK YOU UP AT 02:37:30 GET.
LOS = Loss of Signal...remember, there's no communications satellite system!
00:04:58:35 GET
BOY, IT'S REALLY HARD TO DESCRIBE WHAT THIS EARTH LOOKS LIKE.
I'M LOOKING OUT MY CENTER WINDOW... AND THE WINDOW IS BIGGER THAN THE EARTH RIGHT NOW. I CAN SEE MOST OF SOUTH AMERICA...
00:11:49:24 GET
MAN, YOU'RE LOOKING PRETTY SMALL DOWN THERE, HOUSTON.
WE'RE CARRYING A BIG STICK, THOUGH.
01:07:15:30 GET
DO YOU HAVE A PICTURE NOW?
YOU DON'T HAVE A LENS COVER ON THERE, DO YOU?
NEGATIVE. WE ARE HAVING NO JOY.
NO, WE CHECKED THAT...
IT WAS A VERY EXCITING RIDE ON THAT BIG SATURN, BUT IT WORKED PERFECTLY, AND WE ARE LOOKING FORWARD NOW, OF COURSE, TO THE DAY AFTER TOMORROW...
WE HAVE TO GET BACK TO OUR PASSIVE THERMAL CONTROL IN THE BARBEQUE MODE SO THAT WE DON'T GET ONE SIDE OF THE SPACECRAFT TOO HOT FOR TOO LONG...

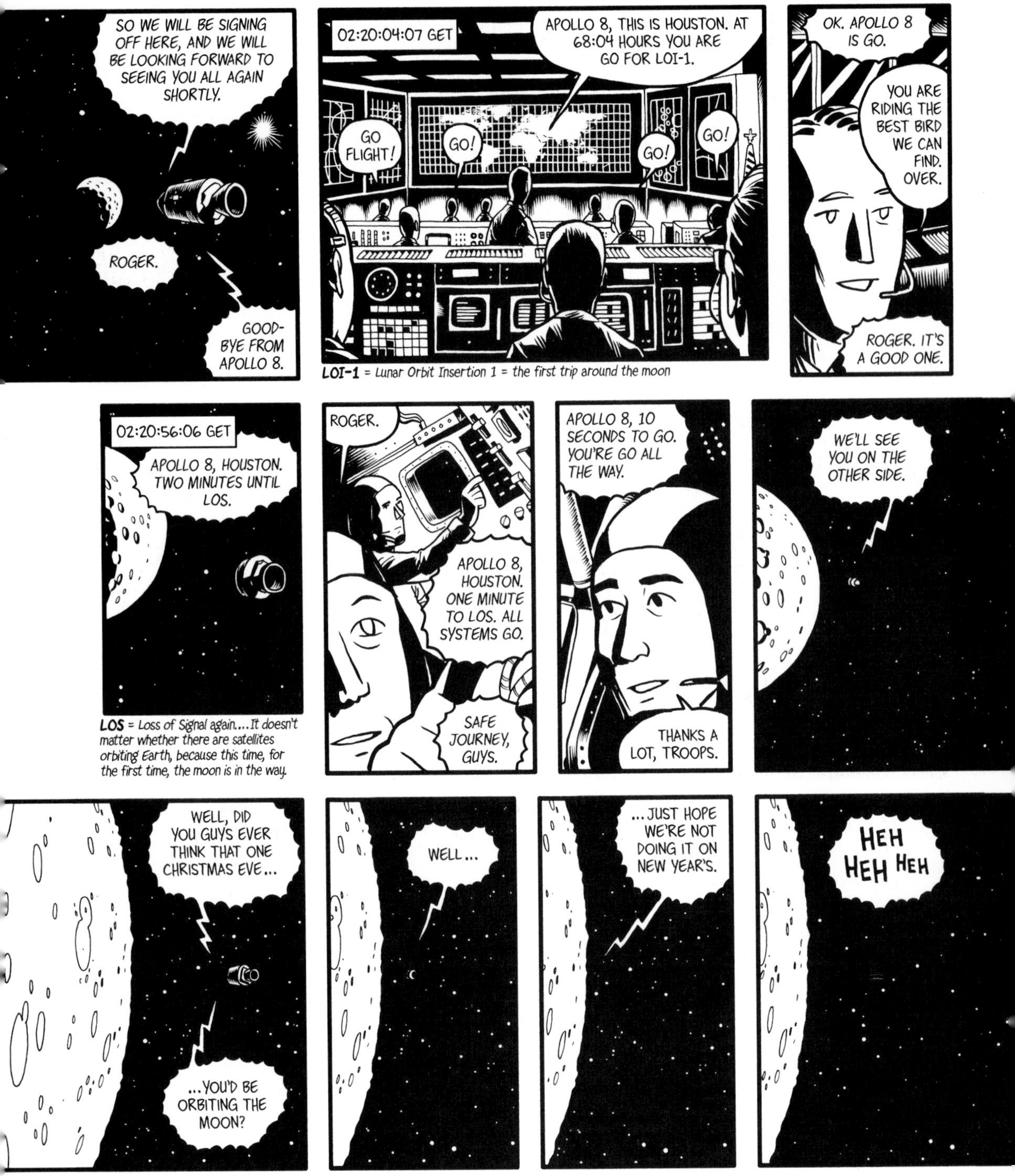
SO WE WILL BE SIGNING OFF HERE, AND WE WILL BE LOOKING FORWARD TO SEEING YOU ALL AGAIN SHORTLY.
ROGER.
GOOD-BYE FROM APOLLO 8.
02:20:04:07 GET
APOLLO 8, THIS IS HOUSTON. AT 68:04 HOURS YOU ARE GO FOR LOI-1.
GO FLIGHT!
GO!
GO!
GO!
OK. APOLLO 8 IS GO.
YOU ARE RIDING THE BEST BIRD WE CAN FIND. OVER.
ROGER. IT'S A GOOD ONE.
02:20:56:06 GET
APOLLO 8, HOUSTON. TWO MINUTES UNTIL LOS.
ROGER.
APOLLO 8, HOUSTON. ONE MINUTE TO LOS. ALL SYSTEMS GO.
SAFE JOURNEY, GUYS.
APOLLO 8, 10 SECONDS TO GO. YOU'RE GO ALL THE WAY.
THANKS A LOT, TROOPS.
WE'LL SEE YOU ON THE OTHER SIDE.
WELL, DID YOU GUYS EVER THINK THAT ONE CHRISTMAS EVE...
...YOU'D BE ORBITING THE MOON?
WELL...
...JUST HOPE WE'RE NOT DOING IT ON NEW YEAR'S.
HEH HEH HEH

LOI-1 = *Lunar Orbit Insertion 1 = the first trip around the moon*

LOS = *Loss of Signal again....It doesn't matter whether there are satellites orbiting Earth, because this time, for the first time, the moon is in the way.*

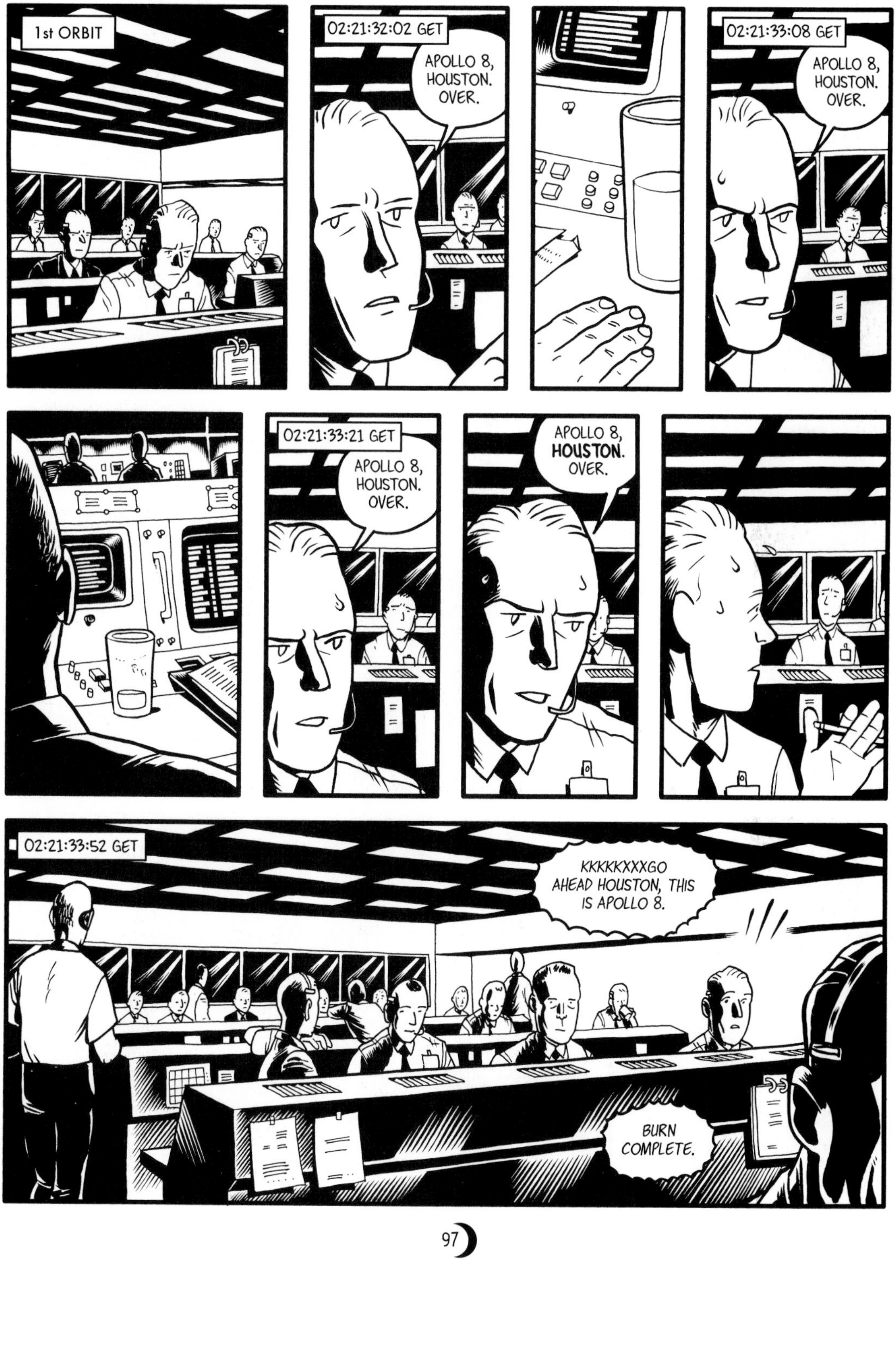

1st ORBIT
02:21:32:02 GET
APOLLO 8, HOUSTON. OVER.
02:21:33:08 GET
APOLLO 8, HOUSTON. OVER.
02:21:33:21 GET
APOLLO 8, HOUSTON. OVER.
APOLLO 8, **HOUSTON**. OVER.
02:21:33:52 GET
KKKKKXXXGO AHEAD HOUSTON, THIS IS APOLLO 8.
BURN COMPLETE.

APOLLO 8, THIS IS **HOUSTON.** ROGER.

...

GOOD TO HEAR YOUR VOICE.

ROGER.

BURN STATUS REPORT AS FOLLOWS: BURN ON TIME; BURN TIME 4 MINUTES 6-½ SECONDS; V_{GX} MINUS 1.4; ATTITUDE IS NOMINAL NO TRIM; V_{GY} WAS ZERO; V_{GZ} WAS PLUS 0.2; DELTA-V_C WAS MINUS 20.2...

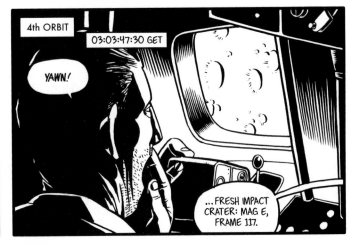

4th ORBIT

03:03:47:30 GET

YAWN!

...FRESH IMPACT CRATER: MAG E, FRAME 117.

WILL YOU GIVE ME A VERB 64, FRANK?

WHAT?

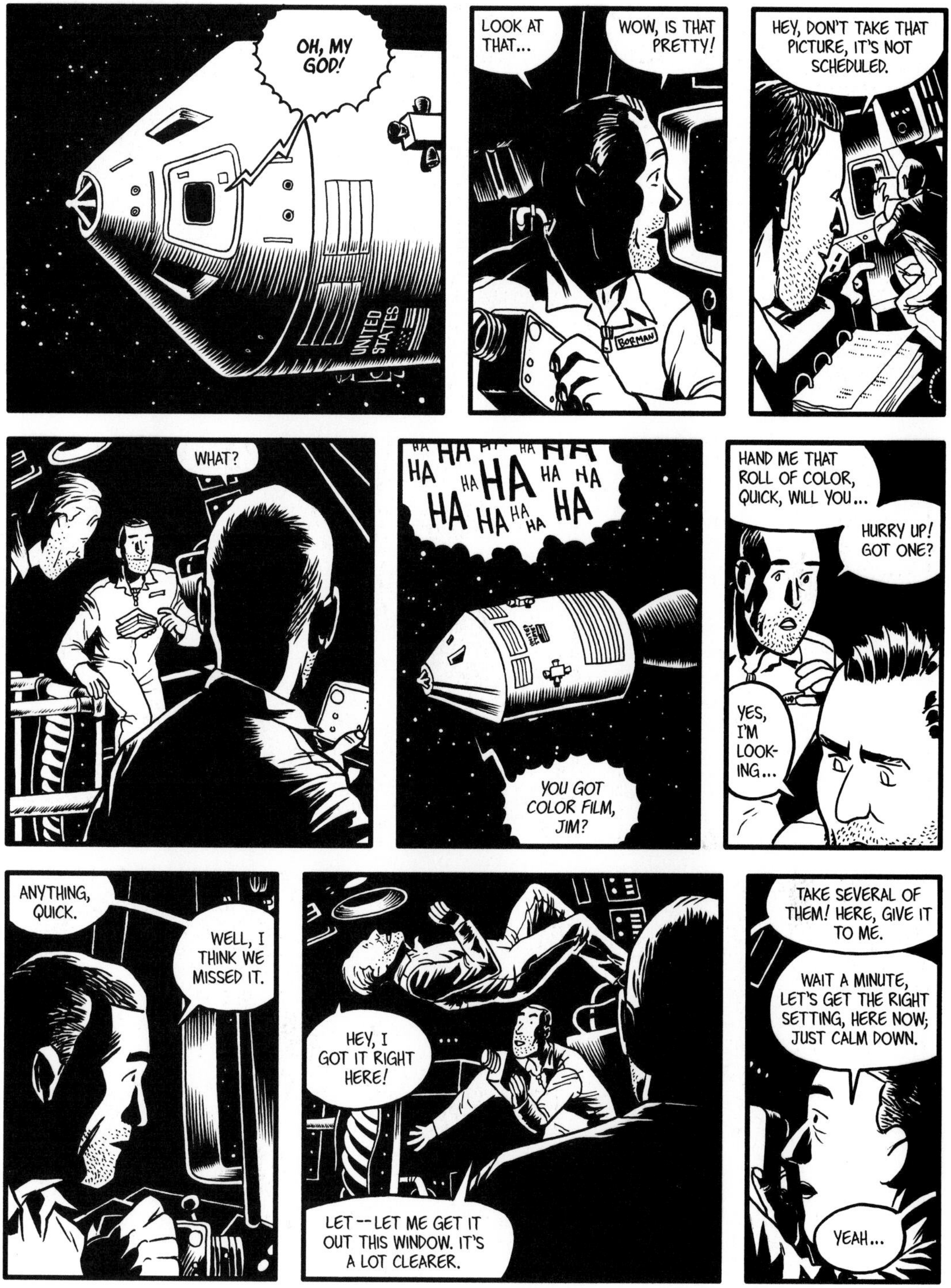
OH, MY GOD!
UNITED STATES
LOOK AT THAT...
WOW, IS THAT PRETTY!
BORMAN
HEY, DON'T TAKE THAT PICTURE, IT'S NOT SCHEDULED.
WHAT?
HA HA HA HA HA HA HA HA HA HA HA HA HA HA
YOU GOT COLOR FILM, JIM?
HAND ME THAT ROLL OF COLOR, QUICK, WILL YOU...
HURRY UP! GOT ONE?
YES, I'M LOOK-ING...
ANYTHING, QUICK.
WELL, I THINK WE MISSED IT.
HEY, I GOT IT RIGHT HERE!
LET--LET ME GET IT OUT THIS WINDOW. IT'S A LOT CLEARER.
TAKE SEVERAL OF THEM! HERE, GIVE IT TO ME.
WAIT A MINUTE, LET'S GET THE RIGHT SETTING, HERE NOW; JUST CALM DOWN.
YEAH...

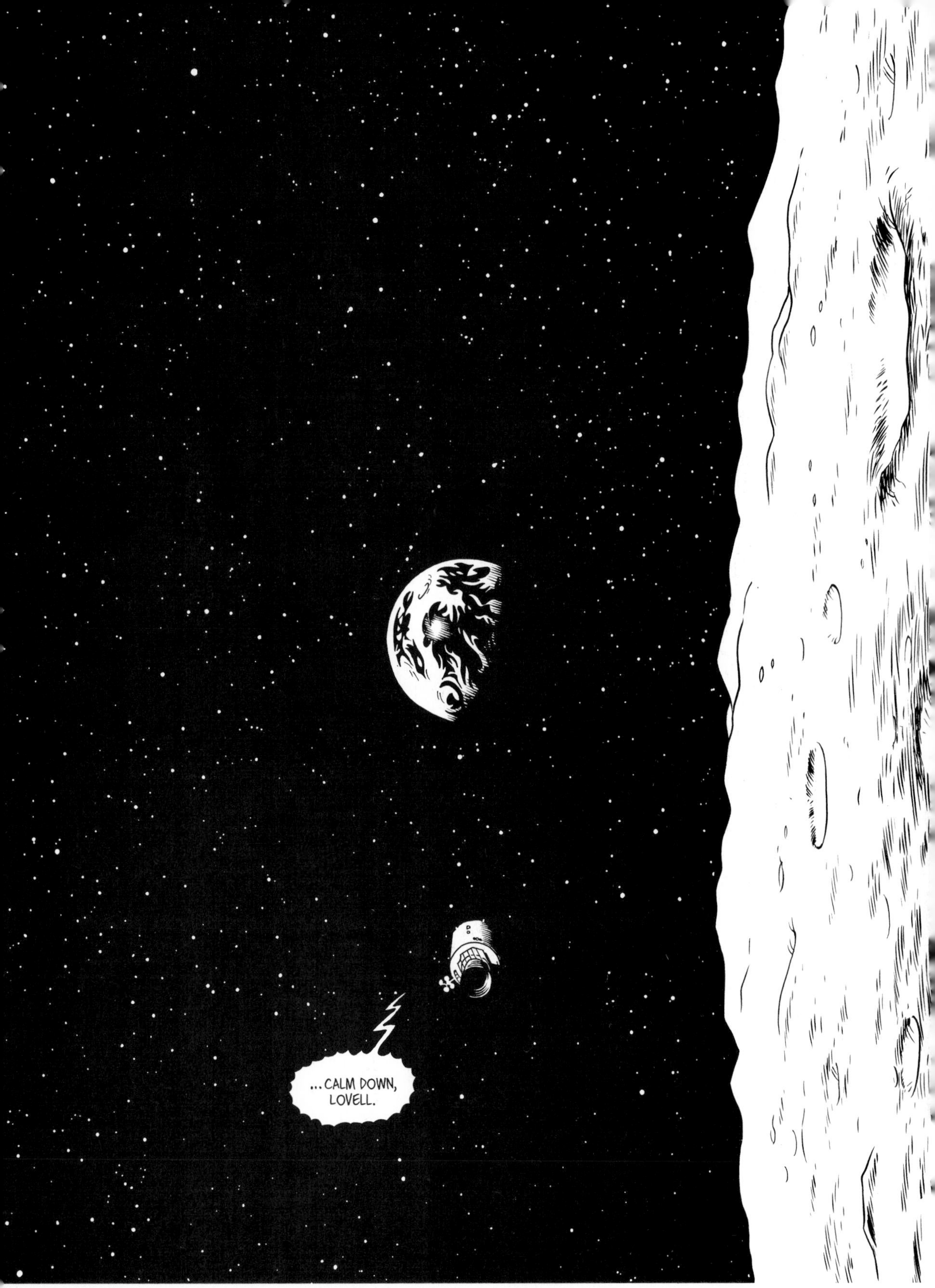
...CALM DOWN, LOVELL.

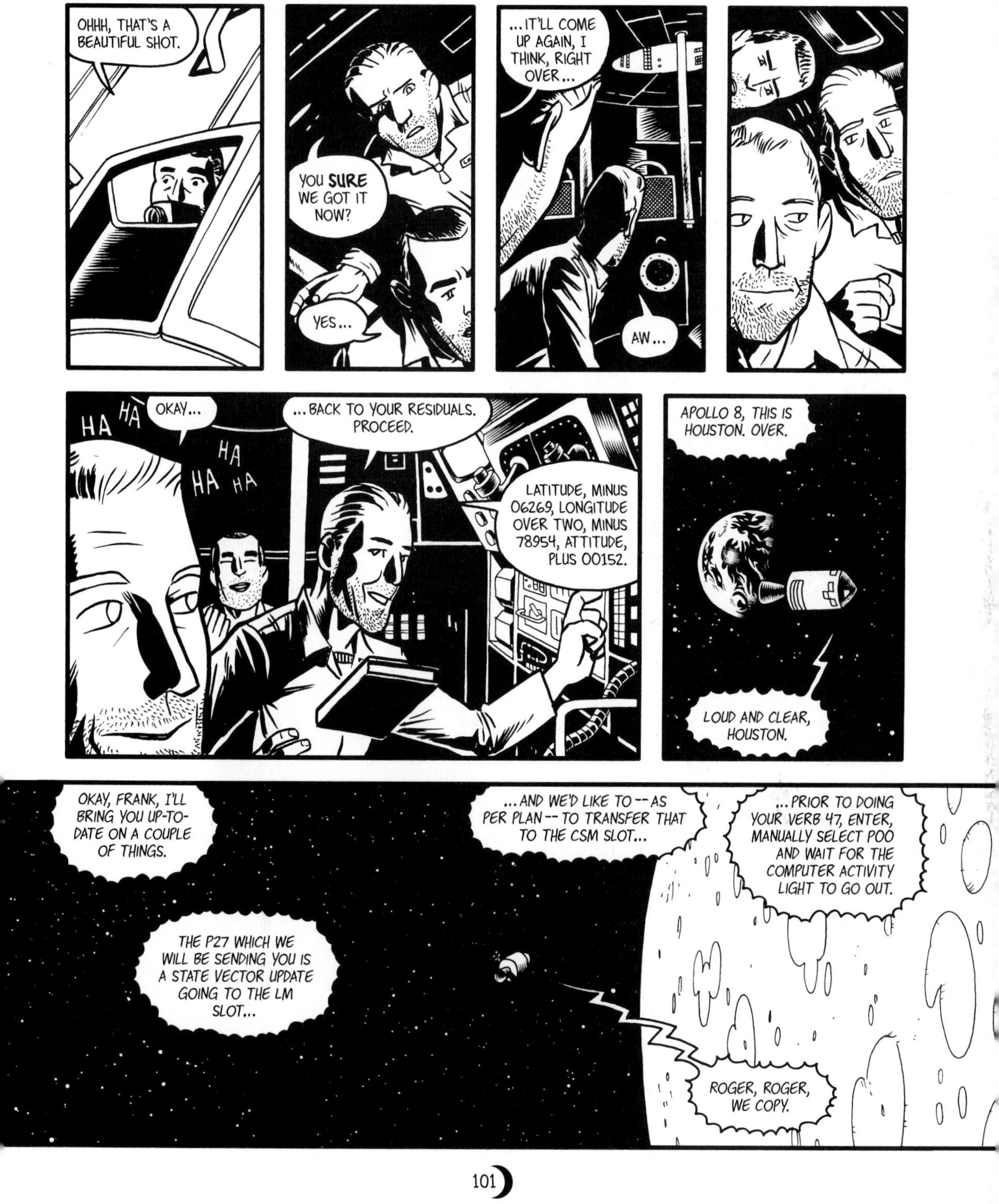
OHHH, THAT'S A BEAUTIFUL SHOT.
YOU SURE WE GOT IT NOW?
YES...
...IT'LL COME UP AGAIN, I THINK, RIGHT OVER...
AW...
HA HA
OKAY...
HA HA HA HA
...BACK TO YOUR RESIDUALS. PROCEED.
LATITUDE, MINUS 06269, LONGITUDE OVER TWO, MINUS 78954, ATTITUDE, PLUS 00152.
APOLLO 8, THIS IS HOUSTON. OVER.
LOUD AND CLEAR, HOUSTON.
OKAY, FRANK, I'LL BRING YOU UP-TO-DATE ON A COUPLE OF THINGS.
THE P27 WHICH WE WILL BE SENDING YOU IS A STATE VECTOR UPDATE GOING TO THE LM SLOT...
...AND WE'D LIKE TO--AS PER PLAN--TO TRANSFER THAT TO THE CSM SLOT...
...PRIOR TO DOING YOUR VERB 47, ENTER, MANUALLY SELECT POO AND WAIT FOR THE COMPUTER ACTIVITY LIGHT TO GO OUT.
ROGER, ROGER, WE COPY.

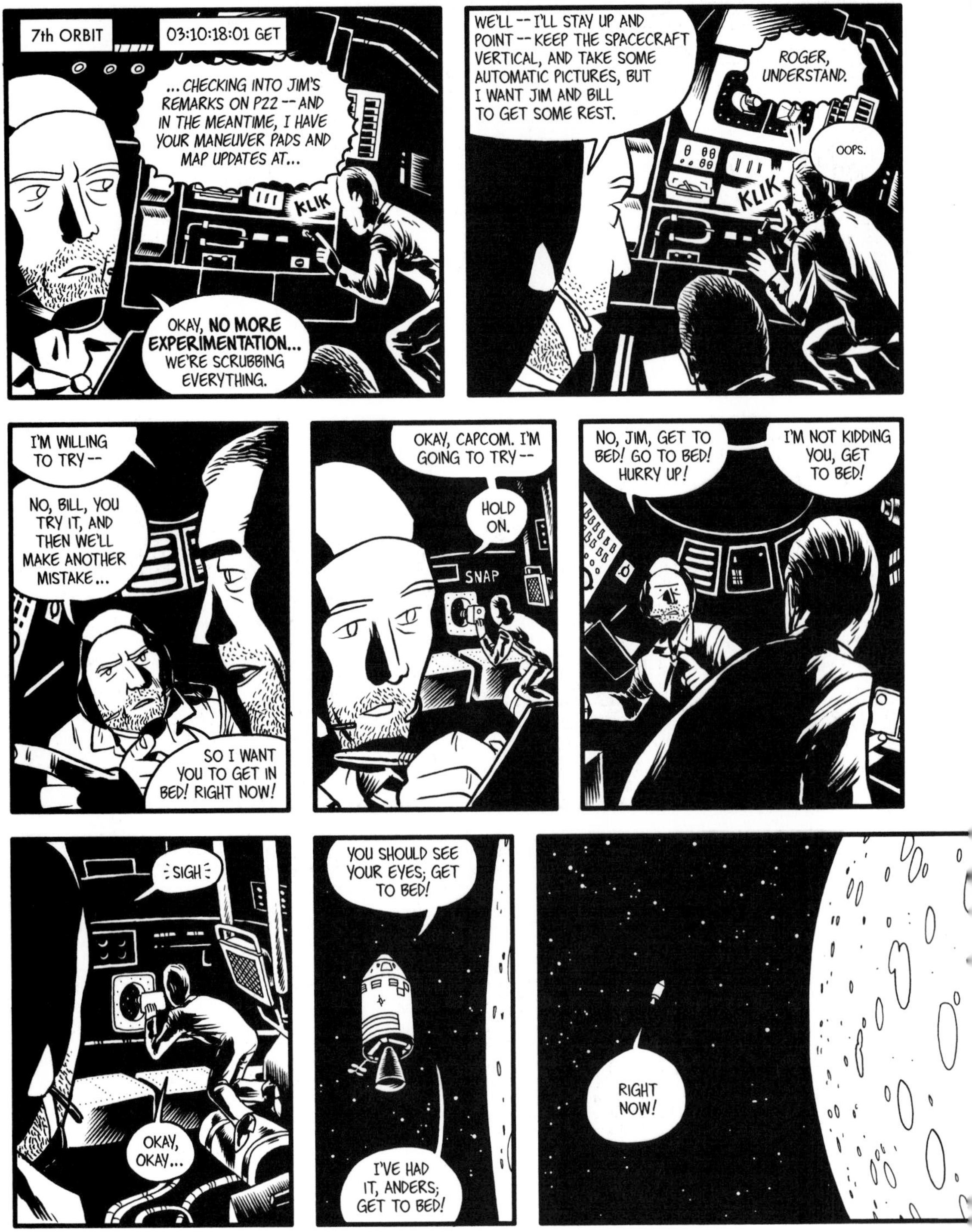
7th ORBIT
03:10:18:01 GET
...CHECKING INTO JIM'S REMARKS ON P22 -- AND IN THE MEANTIME, I HAVE YOUR MANEUVER PADS AND MAP UPDATES AT...
KLIK
OKAY, NO MORE EXPERIMENTATION... WE'RE SCRUBBING EVERYTHING.
WE'LL -- I'LL STAY UP AND POINT -- KEEP THE SPACECRAFT VERTICAL, AND TAKE SOME AUTOMATIC PICTURES, BUT I WANT JIM AND BILL TO GET SOME REST.
ROGER, UNDERSTAND.
OOPS.
KLIK
I'M WILLING TO TRY --
NO, BILL, YOU TRY IT, AND THEN WE'LL MAKE ANOTHER MISTAKE...
SO I WANT YOU TO GET IN BED! RIGHT NOW!
OKAY, CAPCOM. I'M GOING TO TRY --
HOLD ON.
SNAP
NO, JIM, GET TO BED! GO TO BED! HURRY UP!
I'M NOT KIDDING YOU, GET TO BED!
SIGH
OKAY, OKAY...
YOU SHOULD SEE YOUR EYES; GET TO BED!
I'VE HAD IT, ANDERS; GET TO BED!
RIGHT NOW!

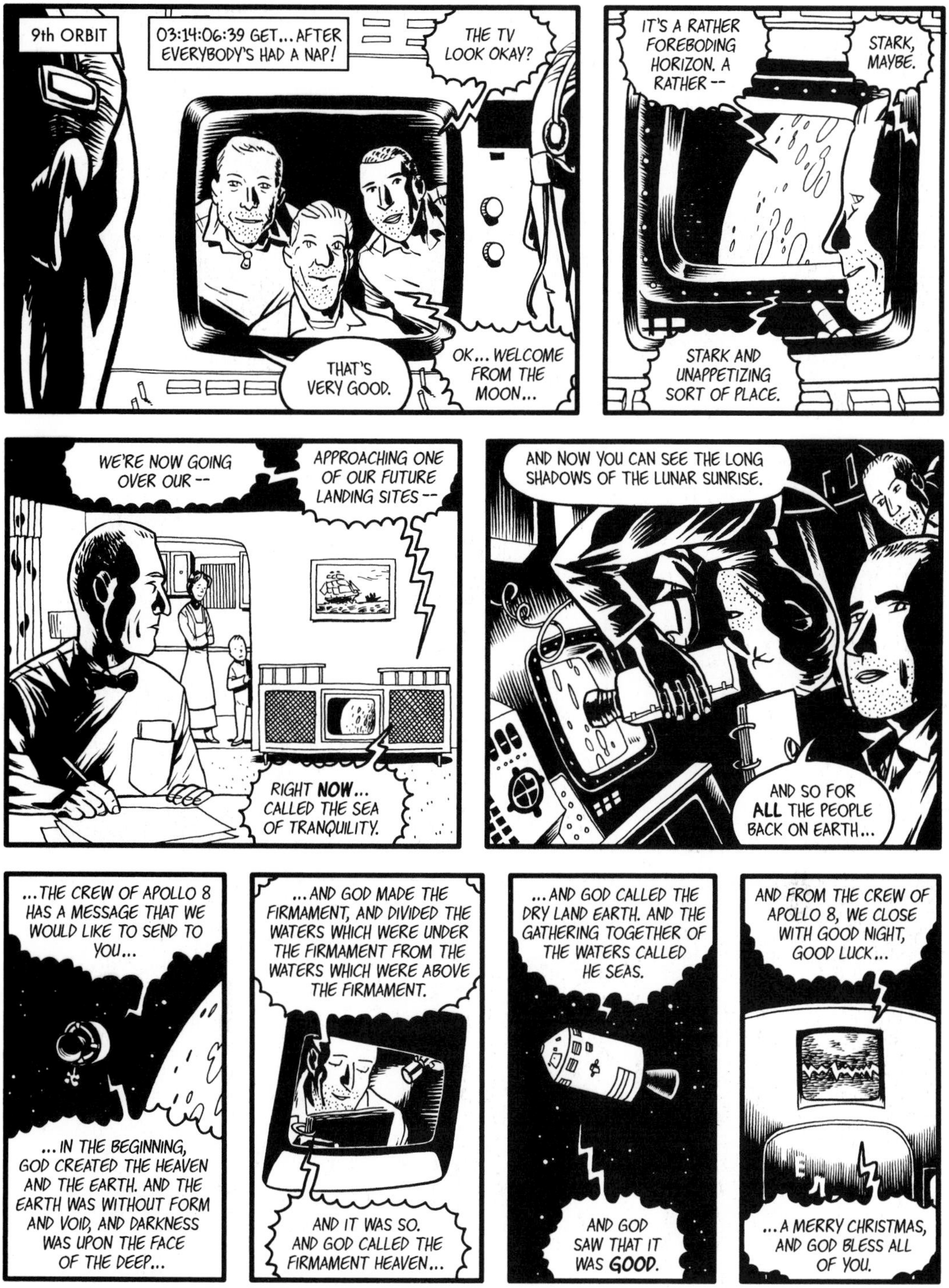
9th ORBIT
03:14:06:39 GET... AFTER EVERYBODY'S HAD A NAP!
THE TV LOOK OKAY?
THAT'S VERY GOOD.
OK... WELCOME FROM THE MOON...
IT'S A RATHER FOREBODING HORIZON. A RATHER --
STARK, MAYBE.
STARK AND UNAPPETIZING SORT OF PLACE.
WE'RE NOW GOING OVER OUR --
APPROACHING ONE OF OUR FUTURE LANDING SITES --
RIGHT **NOW**... CALLED THE SEA OF TRANQUILITY.
AND NOW YOU CAN SEE THE LONG SHADOWS OF THE LUNAR SUNRISE.
AND SO FOR **ALL** THE PEOPLE BACK ON EARTH...
...THE CREW OF APOLLO 8 HAS A MESSAGE THAT WE WOULD LIKE TO SEND TO YOU...
...IN THE BEGINNING, GOD CREATED THE HEAVEN AND THE EARTH. AND THE EARTH WAS WITHOUT FORM AND VOID, AND DARKNESS WAS UPON THE FACE OF THE DEEP...
...AND GOD MADE THE FIRMAMENT, AND DIVIDED THE WATERS WHICH WERE UNDER THE FIRMAMENT FROM THE WATERS WHICH WERE ABOVE THE FIRMAMENT.
AND IT WAS SO. AND GOD CALLED THE FIRMAMENT HEAVEN...
...AND GOD CALLED THE DRY LAND EARTH. AND THE GATHERING TOGETHER OF THE WATERS CALLED HE SEAS.
AND GOD SAW THAT IT WAS **GOOD**.
AND FROM THE CREW OF APOLLO 8, WE CLOSE WITH GOOD NIGHT, GOOD LUCK...
...A MERRY CHRISTMAS, AND GOD BLESS ALL OF YOU.

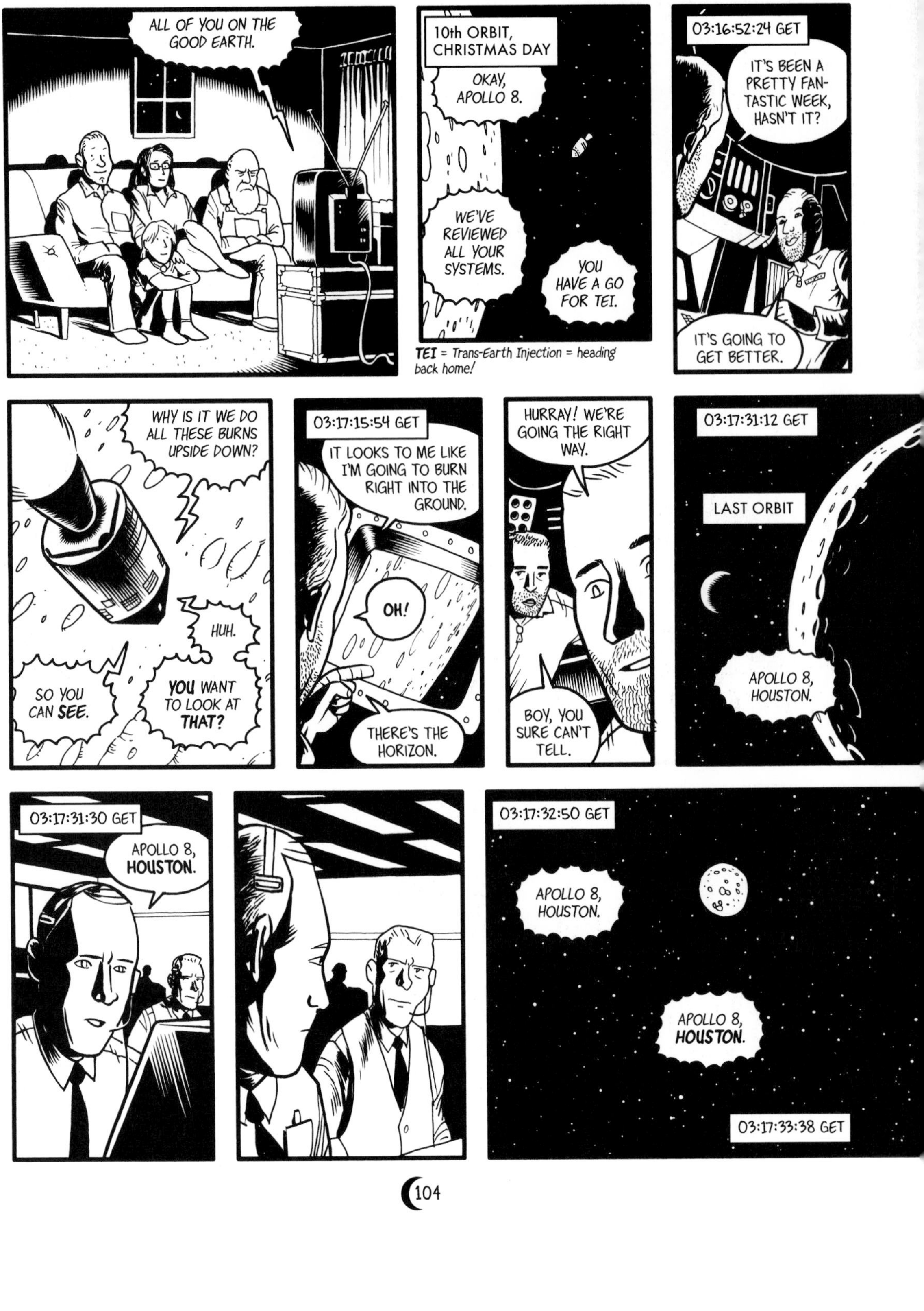
ALL OF YOU ON THE GOOD EARTH.
10th ORBIT, CHRISTMAS DAY
OKAY, APOLLO 8.
WE'VE REVIEWED ALL YOUR SYSTEMS.
YOU HAVE A GO FOR TEI.
TEI = Trans-Earth Injection = heading back home!
03:16:52:24 GET
IT'S BEEN A PRETTY FANTASTIC WEEK, HASN'T IT?
IT'S GOING TO GET BETTER.
WHY IS IT WE DO ALL THESE BURNS UPSIDE DOWN?
HUH.
SO YOU CAN SEE.
YOU WANT TO LOOK AT THAT?
03:17:15:54 GET
IT LOOKS TO ME LIKE I'M GOING TO BURN RIGHT INTO THE GROUND.
OH!
THERE'S THE HORIZON.
HURRAY! WE'RE GOING THE RIGHT WAY.
BOY, YOU SURE CAN'T TELL.
03:17:31:12 GET
LAST ORBIT
APOLLO 8, HOUSTON.
03:17:31:30 GET
APOLLO 8, HOUSTON.
03:17:32:50 GET
APOLLO 8, HOUSTON.
APOLLO 8, HOUSTON.
03:17:33:38 GET

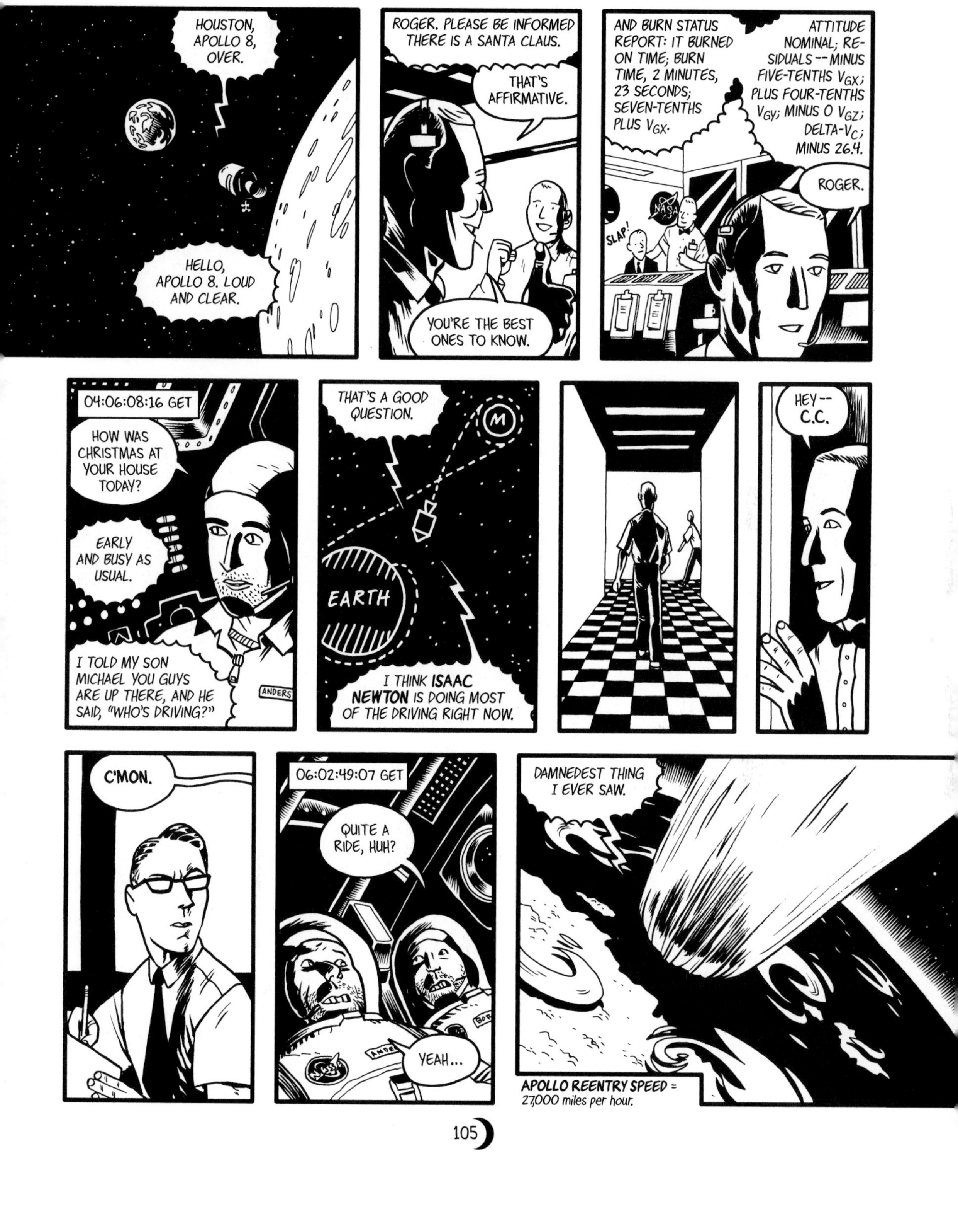
HOUSTON, APOLLO 8, OVER.
HELLO, APOLLO 8. LOUD AND CLEAR.
ROGER. PLEASE BE INFORMED THERE IS A SANTA CLAUS.
THAT'S AFFIRMATIVE.
YOU'RE THE BEST ONES TO KNOW.
AND BURN STATUS REPORT: IT BURNED ON TIME; BURN TIME, 2 MINUTES, 23 SECONDS; SEVEN-TENTHS PLUS V_{GX}.
ATTITUDE NOMINAL; RESIDUALS -- MINUS FIVE-TENTHS V_{GX}; PLUS FOUR-TENTHS V_{GY}; MINUS 0 V_{GZ}; DELTA-V_C; MINUS 26.4.
ROGER.
SLAP!
NASA
04:06:08:16 GET
HOW WAS CHRISTMAS AT YOUR HOUSE TODAY?
EARLY AND BUSY AS USUAL.
I TOLD MY SON MICHAEL YOU GUYS ARE UP THERE, AND HE SAID, "WHO'S DRIVING?"
ANDERS
THAT'S A GOOD QUESTION.
M
EARTH
I THINK **ISAAC NEWTON** IS DOING MOST OF THE DRIVING RIGHT NOW.
HEY -- C.C.
C'MON.
06:02:49:07 GET
QUITE A RIDE, HUH?
YEAH...
DAMNEDEST THING I EVER SAW.
APOLLO REENTRY SPEED = 27,000 miles per hour.

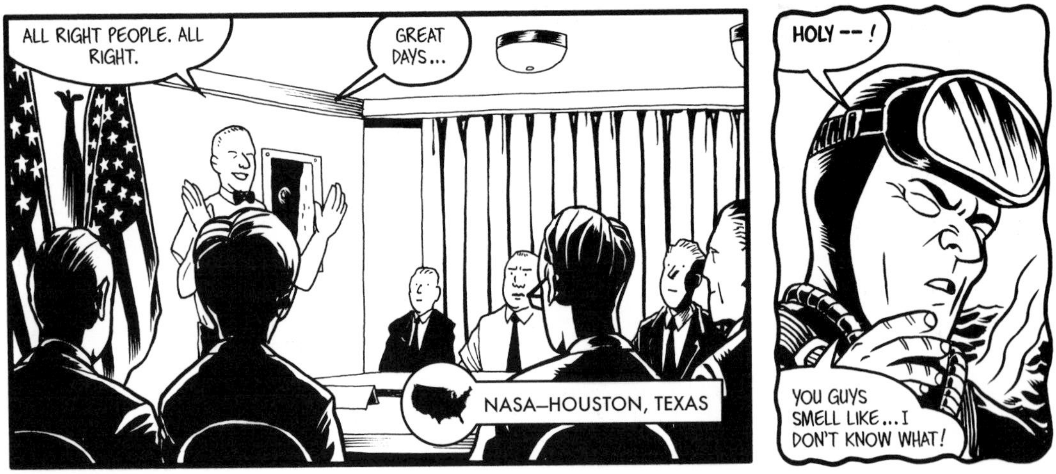
ALL RIGHT PEOPLE. ALL RIGHT.
GREAT DAYS...
NASA—HOUSTON, TEXAS
HOLY --!
YOU GUYS SMELL LIKE... I DON'T KNOW WHAT!

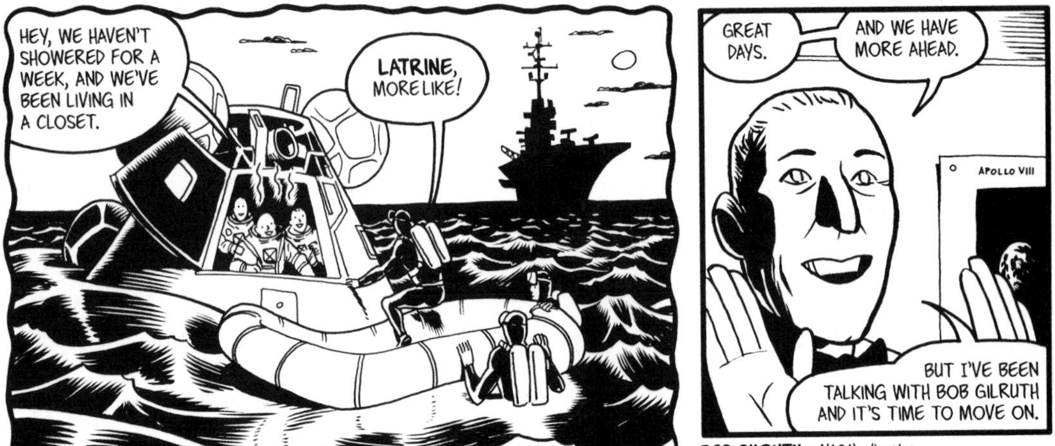
HEY, WE HAVEN'T SHOWERED FOR A WEEK, AND WE'VE BEEN LIVING IN A CLOSET.
LATRINE, MORE LIKE!
GREAT DAYS.
AND WE HAVE MORE AHEAD.
APOLLO VIII
BUT I'VE BEEN TALKING WITH BOB GILRUTH AND IT'S TIME TO MOVE ON.

BOB GILRUTH = *NASA's director*

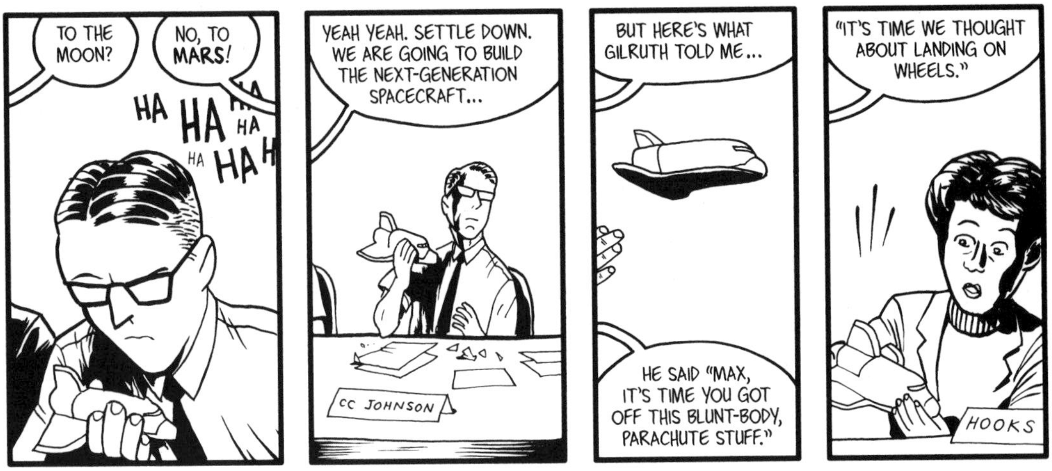
TO THE MOON?
NO, TO MARS!
HA HA HA HA HA HA
YEAH YEAH. SETTLE DOWN. WE ARE GOING TO BUILD THE NEXT-GENERATION SPACECRAFT...
CC JOHNSON
BUT HERE'S WHAT GILRUTH TOLD ME...
HE SAID "MAX, IT'S TIME YOU GOT OFF THIS BLUNT-BODY, PARACHUTE STUFF."
"IT'S TIME WE THOUGHT ABOUT LANDING ON WHEELS."
HOOKS

UNSUCCESSFUL

USSR: N1-L3: February 21, 1969
T-Minus 149 Days
Flight duration: 69 seconds, ending in an explosion

LATER, IN ANOTHER BUILDING...

A TV CAMERA? TOO HEAVY TO TAKE TO THE SURFACE.

IT'S FINE FOR THE CSM, BUT FOR THE LM? NO WAY CAN IT LAND WITH THAT.

AND OPERATING IT IS GOING TO TAKE UP VALUABLE ASTRONAUT TIME.

ARE YOU NUTS?

AMERICANS HAVE PAID OVER $20,000,000,000 FOR THIS.

AND YOU'RE NOT GOING TO SHOW THEM?!

...WEIGHT CURVE WON'T...

...FLIGHT PLAN IS ALREADY PACKED!

HOW CAN YOU EVEN THINK THAT...

...CRAZY, CRAZY, CRAZY!

NEIL? TV...YES OR NO?

ARGUE ARGUE ARGUE ARGUE ARGUE

ARGUE ARGUE ARGUE

NOD

YES.

UH...

ROGER THAT, NEIL.

SOUNDS GOOD.

YOU BET.

ABSOLUTELY.

MICHAEL COLLINS

NEIL ARMSTRONG

BUZZ ALDRIN

WHERE THE HECK ARE WE GOING TO...

GOTTA SCRAP PAGES 23-27 OF THE MISSION PLAN...

YOU KNOW HOW MUCH THAT THING WEIGHS?

YOU'RE CRAZY IF YOU THI...

IN ALL MY Y...

A LITTLE MORE SIMULATOR TIME, THEN. IS THE LM IN FLORIDA YET?

ON ITS WAY. WHAT ABOUT YOUR BIRD, MIKE?

107

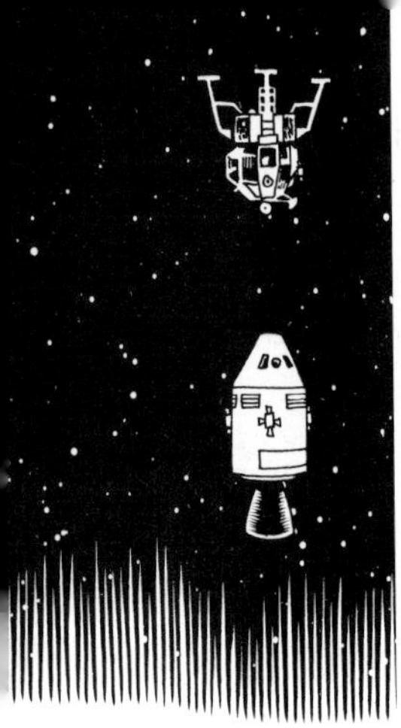

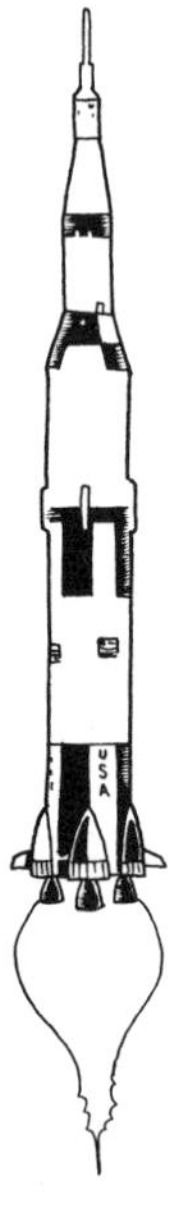

Apollo 9: March 3–13, 1969
T-Minus 4 Months, 17 Days
Flight duration: 10 days, 1 hour, and 54 seconds
First test of the LM in space, and docking it to the CSM
Jim McDivitt, Dave Scott, and Rusty Schweickart

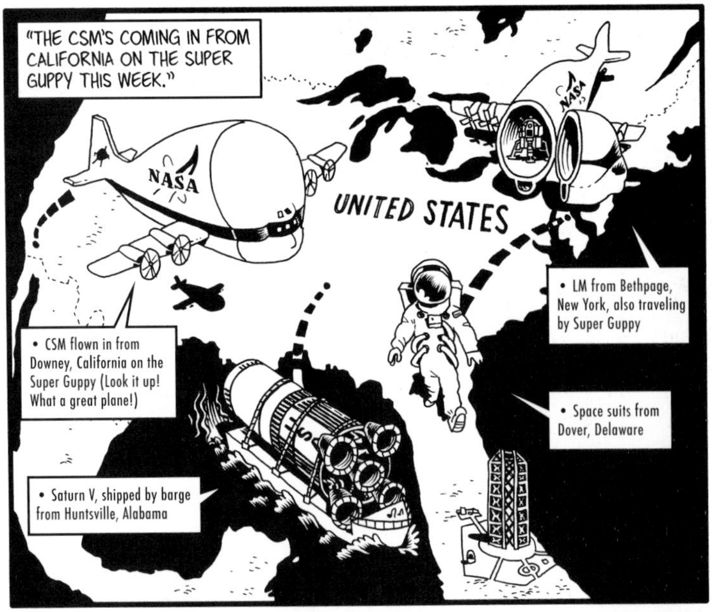
"THE CSM'S COMING IN FROM CALIFORNIA ON THE SUPER GUPPY THIS WEEK."
UNITED STATES
NASA
NASA
• CSM flown in from Downey, California on the Super Guppy (Look it up! What a great plane!)
• LM from Bethpage, New York, also traveling by Super Guppy
• Space suits from Dover, Delaware
• Saturn V, shipped by barge from Huntsville, Alabama

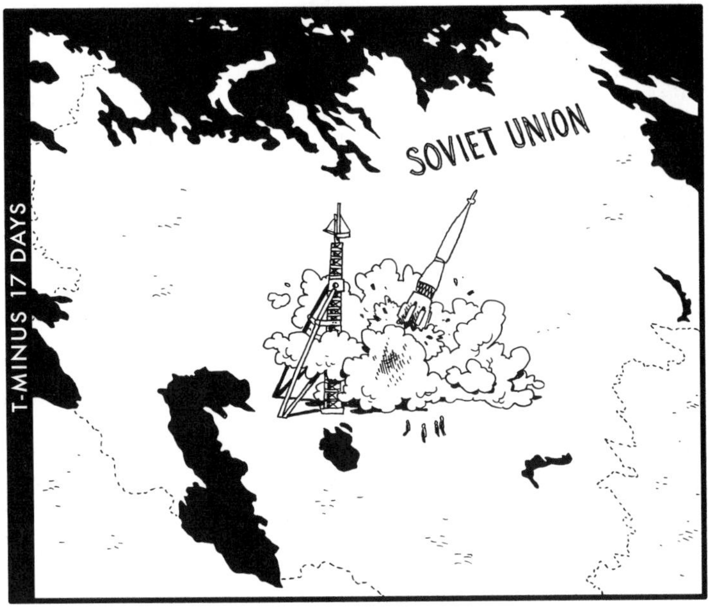
T-MINUS 17 DAYS
SOVIET UNION

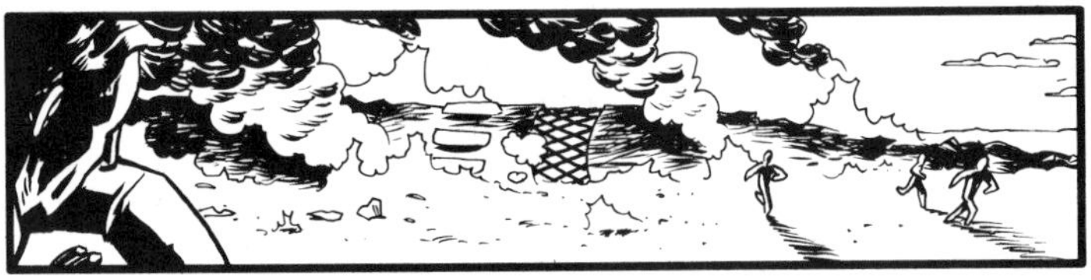

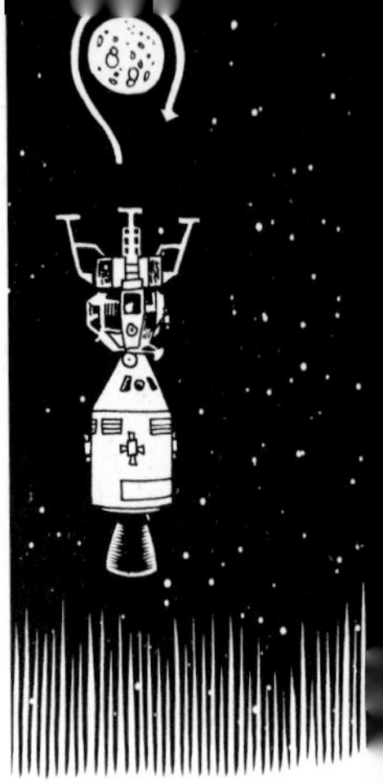

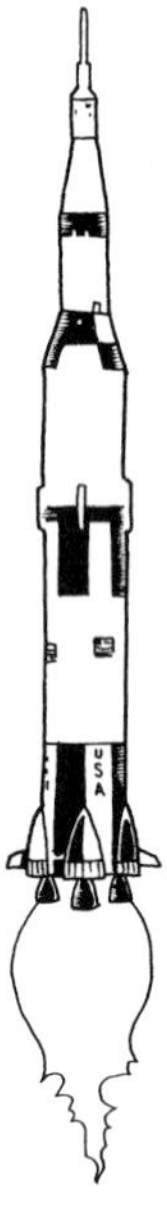

Apollo 10: May 18–26, 1969
T-Minus 63 Days
Flight duration: 8 days, 3 minutes, and 23 seconds, including more than 2 days in lunar orbit
The dress rehearsal to check out the landing site on the Sea of Tranquility.
Tom Stafford, John Young, and Gene Cernan

GET THE COMPUTERS OUT!
THEY'RE COMING.
KOFF! IF KOROLEV WERE HERE...
NO, NO... ...THE N-1 WAS HIS DESIGN.
SO THIS WOULD STILL HAVE HAPPENED.
BUT IT WOULD HAVE HAPPENED YEARS AGO.
SO IF SERGEI PAVLOVICH WERE HERE, PERHAPS I...WE...
MAYBE WE'D STILL BE IN THE RACE.

UNSUCCESSFUL

ONE WEEK LATER...
ALL COMPONENTS NOW ON SITE.
BEGIN COUNTDOWN FOR THE "G MISSION"...
JOHN FITZGERALD KENNEDY
1917 — 1963
...ON MY MARK.
SERGEI PAVLOVICH KOROLEV
1907 - 1966
AND...
VLADIMIR M. KOMAROV
1927 - 1967
START THE CLOCK!
LAUNCH COMPLEX 34
FRIDAY, 27 JANUARY 1967
1831 HOURS
DEDICATED TO THE LIVING MEMORY OF THE CREW OF THE APOLLO 1:
V. I. GRISSOM
E. H. WHITE
R. B. CHAFFEE
T-MINUS 6 DAYS

The countdown for ***APOLLO 11*** *-- the "G Mission" -- began on July 10, six days before launch.*

N1-L3: July 3, 1969
T-Minus 17 Days
Flight duration: 0 seconds...and 23 seconds later the rocket explodes, destroying their pad and tower and chance to land cosmonauts on the moon.

T-MINUS 4 DAYS, 13 HOURS, 20 MINUTES

CRYO TANK?

CRYO TANK.

CHECK.

NASA—CAPE KENNEDY—FLORIDA—1969

FLIP!

CLICK!

SWITCH!

FLIP!

TOGGLE!

MISSION CONTROL—HOUSTON, TEXAS

OKAY, FREDO. FUEL CELLS?

FUEL CELLS.

CHECK.

FREDO HAISE = Buzz Aldrin's backup Lunar Module Pilot for Apollo 11. His job is to prepare the spacecraft for liftoff.

DIAL!

SWITCH

TAP!

PUSH!

FLIP!

S-C-E TO MAIN.

GO!

S-C-E TO MAIN.

CHECK.

EDS TO MANUAL.

CHECK.

TOCK!

FLIP!

SWITCH!

FLIP!

SHIFT!

GO! EECOM. GO! GO! GO! GO!

SURGEON. NETWORK. GO! RETRO. GO! GO!

GO! GO! O&P. CONTROL. GO!

BOOSTER. GO! GO! TELMU. GO!

FLIP!

FLIP!

CLICK!

PUSH!

TICK!

GNC.

FAO.

GO!

GO!

INCO. GO!

SNAP!

FLIP!

TOGGLE

DEPRESS!

TOCK!

SWITCH!

FLIP!

FLIP!

CLICK!

PUSH!

HEY MAX, CHRIS...READY TO GO?

AFTER YOU, **FLIGHT!**

CHRIS KRAFT is now Max's boss

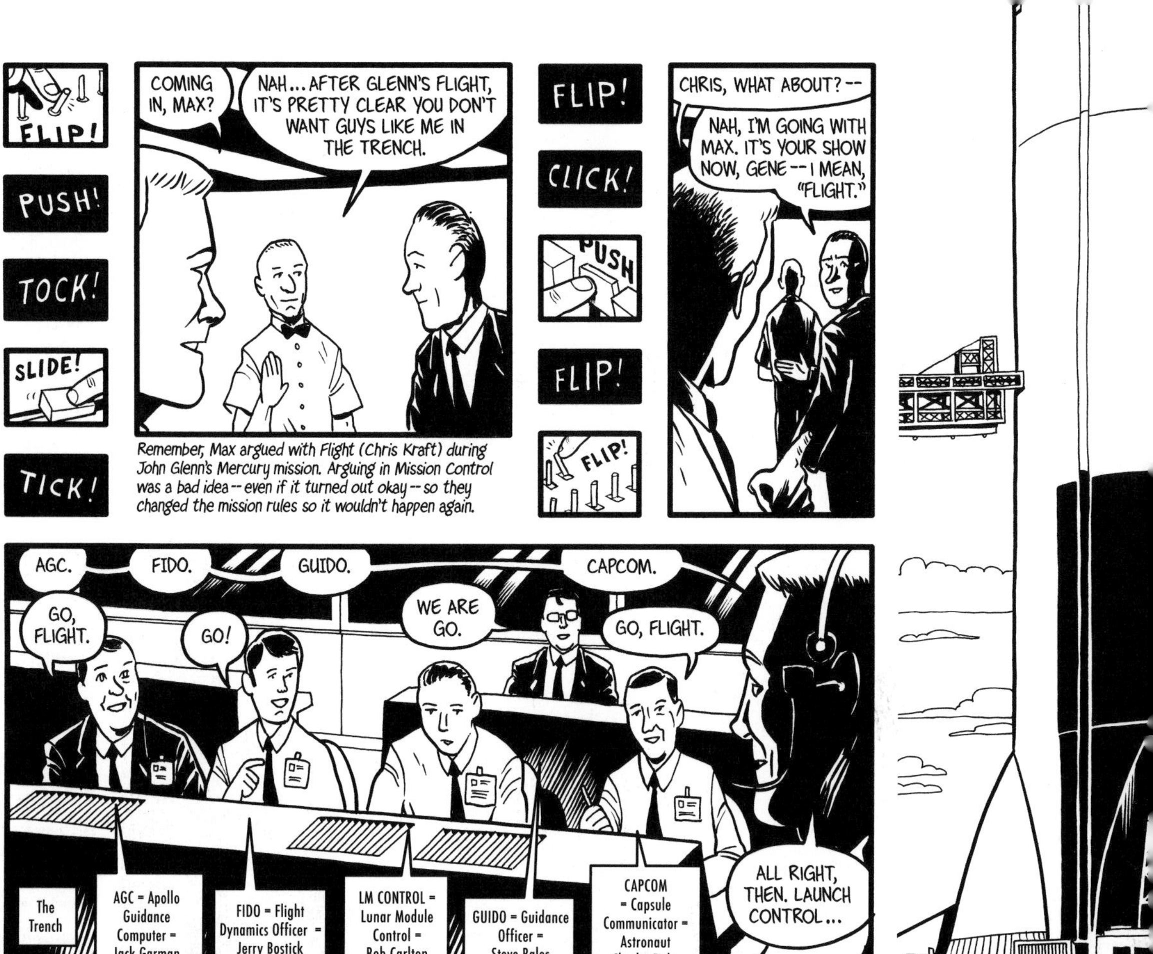
FLIP!
PUSH!
TOCK!
SLIDE!
TICK!
COMING IN, MAX?
NAH... AFTER GLENN'S FLIGHT, IT'S PRETTY CLEAR YOU DON'T WANT GUYS LIKE ME IN THE TRENCH.
Remember, Max argued with Flight (Chris Kraft) during John Glenn's Mercury mission. Arguing in Mission Control was a bad idea -- even if it turned out okay -- so they changed the mission rules so it wouldn't happen again.
FLIP!
CLICK!
PUSH
FLIP!
FLIP!
CHRIS, WHAT ABOUT? --
NAH, I'M GOING WITH MAX. IT'S YOUR SHOW NOW, GENE -- I MEAN, "FLIGHT."
AGC.
FIDO.
GUIDO.
CAPCOM.
GO, FLIGHT.
GO!
WE ARE GO.
GO, FLIGHT.
The Trench
AGC = Apollo Guidance Computer = Jack Garman
FIDO = Flight Dynamics Officer = Jerry Bostick
LM CONTROL = Lunar Module Control = Bob Carlton
GUIDO = Guidance Officer = Steve Bales
CAPCOM = Capsule Communicator = Astronaut Charlie Duke
ALL RIGHT, THEN. LAUNCH CONTROL...
"...WE ARE GO FOR APOLLO 11"
NASA—CAPE KENNEDY, FLORIDA
8 MILES LATER...
PAD 39A
T-MINUS 112 HOURS
THERE'S NOBODY HERE.
NASA
GOD... MAYBE THEY KNOW SOMETHING I DON'T!
WARNING

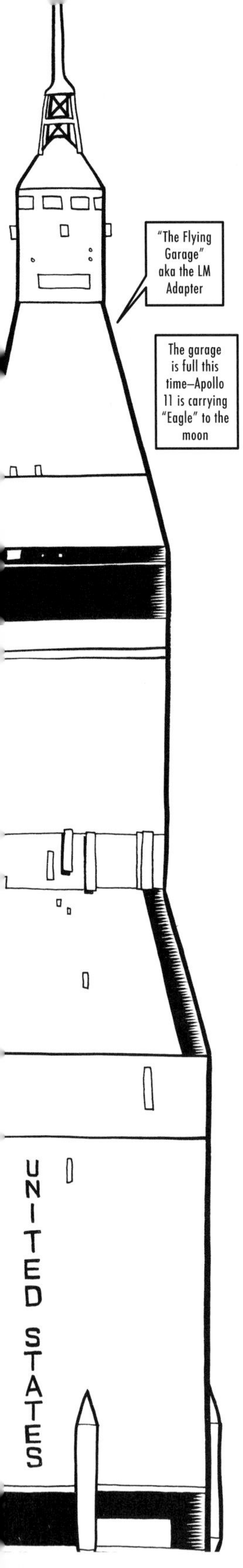
"The Flying Garage" aka the LM Adapter
The garage is full this time—Apollo 11 is carrying "Eagle" to the moon
UNITED STATES

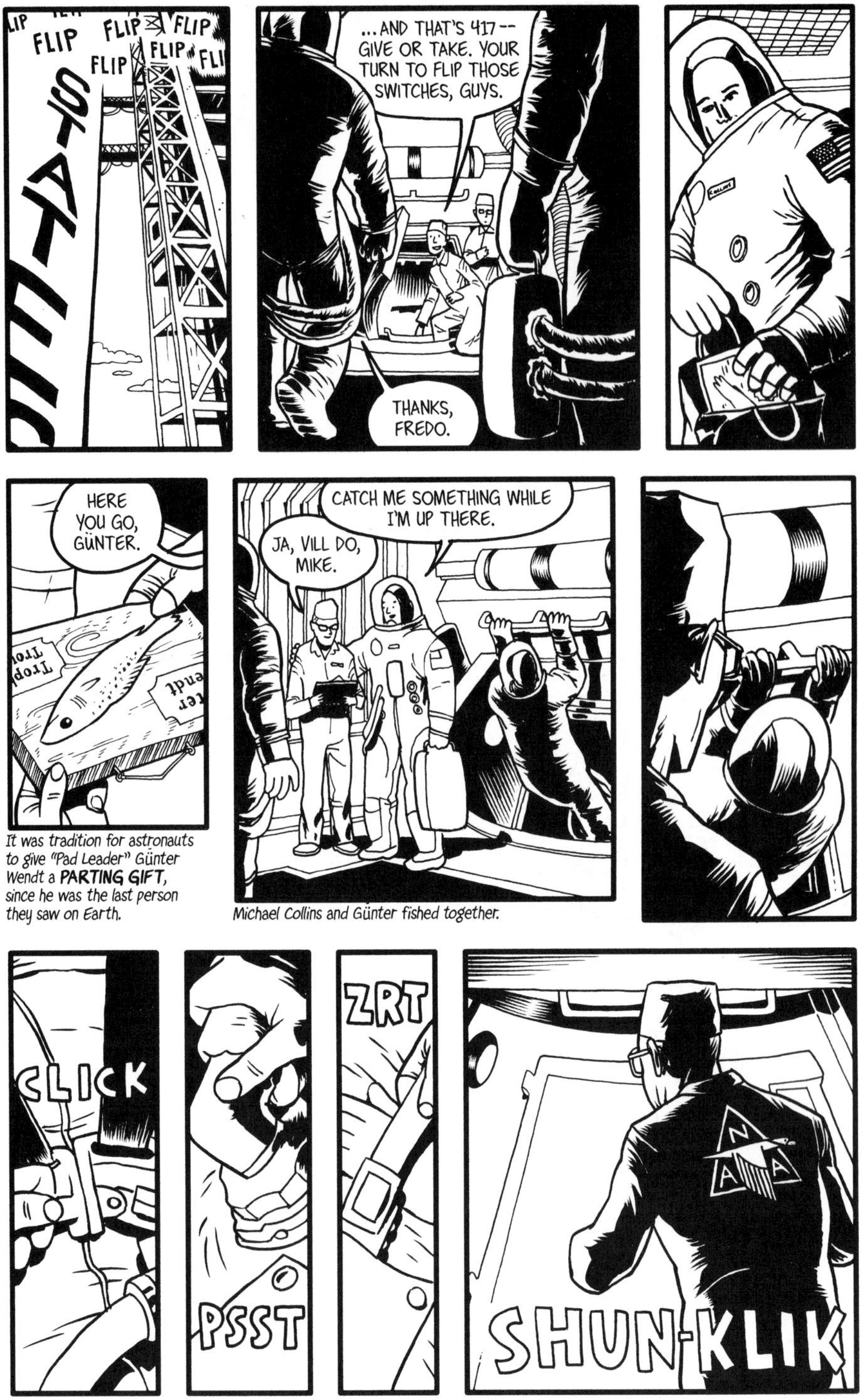
FLIP FLIP FLIP FLIP FLIP
...AND THAT'S 417-- GIVE OR TAKE. YOUR TURN TO FLIP THOSE SWITCHES, GUYS.
THANKS, FREDO.
HERE YOU GO, GÜNTER.
CATCH ME SOMETHING WHILE I'M UP THERE.
JA, VILL DO, MIKE.
CLICK
PSST
ZRT
SHUN-KLIK

It was tradition for astronauts to give "Pad Leader" Günter Wendt a ***PARTING GIFT****, since he was the last person they saw on Earth.*

Michael Collins and Günter fished together.

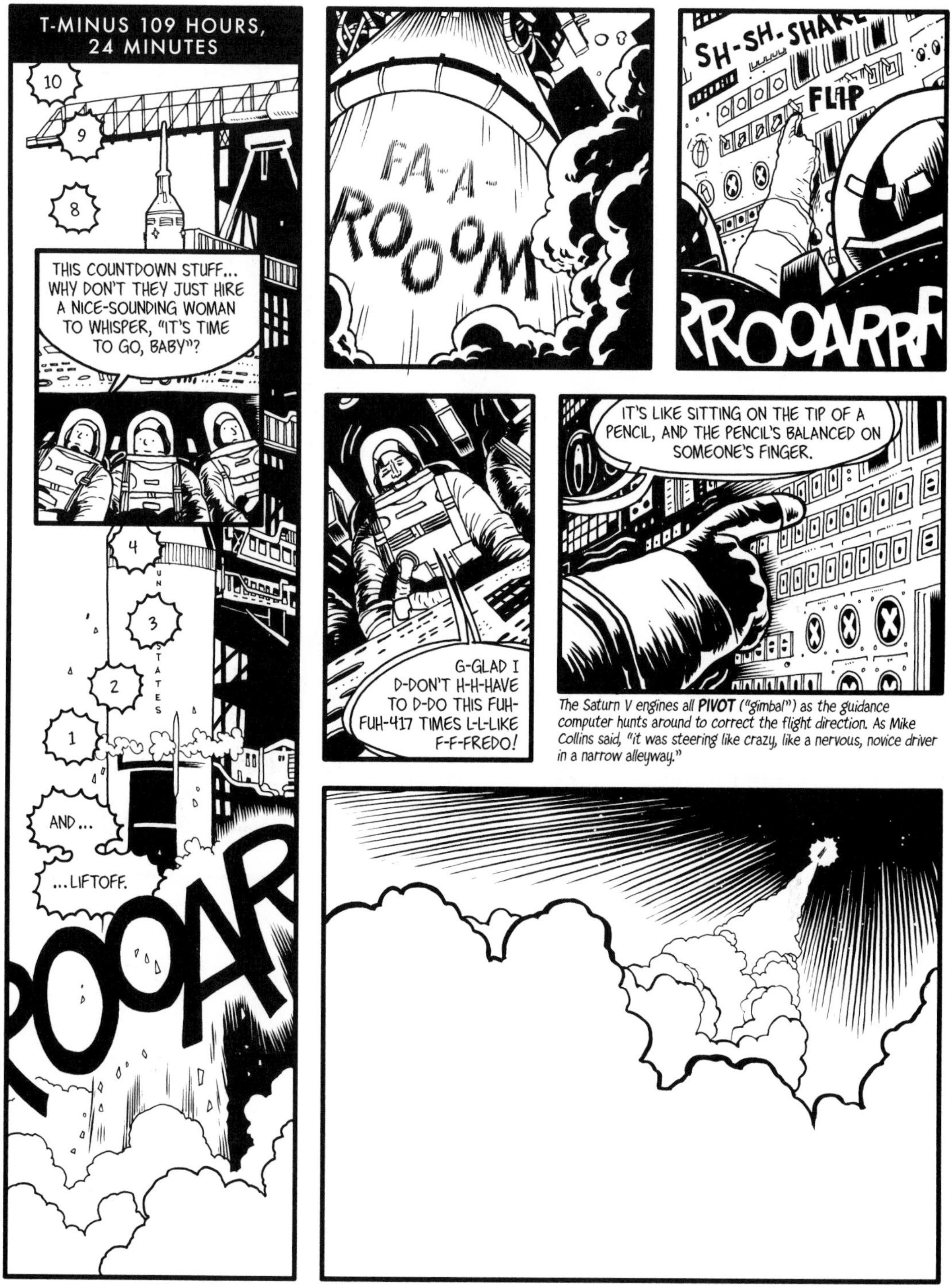
T-MINUS 109 HOURS, 24 MINUTES
10
9
8
THIS COUNTDOWN STUFF... WHY DON'T THEY JUST HIRE A NICE-SOUNDING WOMAN TO WHISPER, "IT'S TIME TO GO, BABY"?
4
3
2
1
AND...
...LIFTOFF.
ROOAR
FA-A-ROOOOM
SH-SH-SHAKE
FLIP
RROOARRR
G-GLAD I D-DON'T H-H-HAVE TO D-DO THIS FUH-FUH-417 TIMES L-L-LIKE F-F-FREDO!
IT'S LIKE SITTING ON THE TIP OF A PENCIL, AND THE PENCIL'S BALANCED ON SOMEONE'S FINGER.
The Saturn V engines all PIVOT ("gimbal") as the guidance computer hunts around to correct the flight direction. As Mike Collins said, "it was steering like crazy, like a nervous, novice driver in a narrow alleyway."

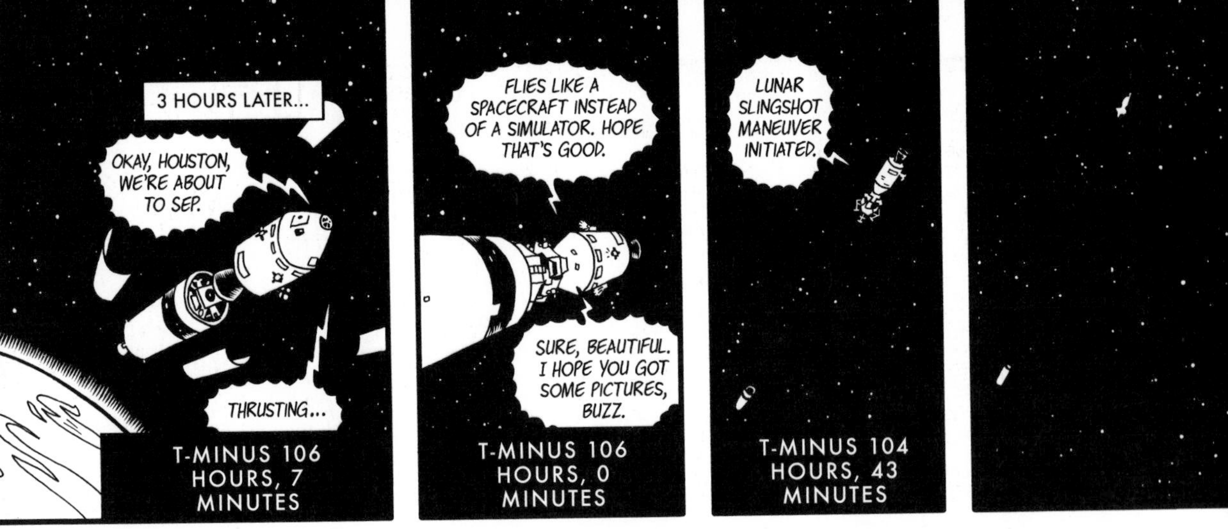
3 HOURS LATER...
OKAY, HOUSTON, WE'RE ABOUT TO SEP.
THRUSTING...
T-MINUS 106 HOURS, 7 MINUTES
FLIES LIKE A SPACECRAFT INSTEAD OF A SIMULATOR. HOPE THAT'S GOOD.
SURE, BEAUTIFUL. I HOPE YOU GOT SOME PICTURES, BUZZ.
T-MINUS 106 HOURS, 0 MINUTES
LUNAR SLINGSHOT MANEUVER INITIATED.
T-MINUS 104 HOURS, 43 MINUTES

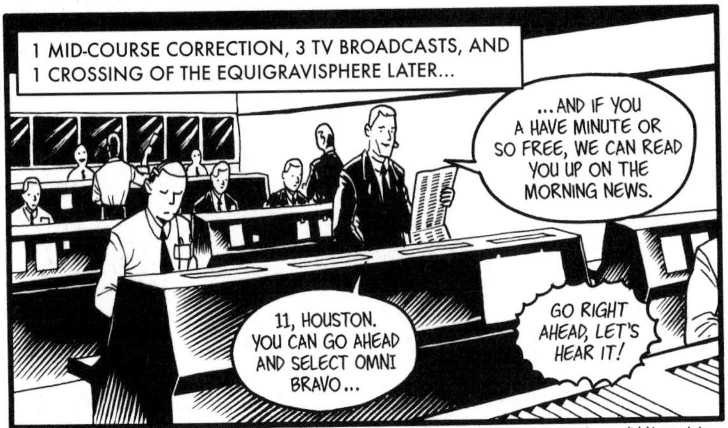
1 MID-COURSE CORRECTION, 3 TV BROADCASTS, AND 1 CROSSING OF THE EQUIGRAVISPHERE LATER...
...AND IF YOU A HAVE MINUTE OR SO FREE, WE CAN READ YOU UP ON THE MORNING NEWS.
11, HOUSTON. YOU CAN GO AHEAD AND SELECT OMNI BRAVO...
GO RIGHT AHEAD, LET'S HEAR IT!

EQUIGRAVISPHERE = *the point where the Earth's and the moon's gravity balance out. If you didn't want to come home, you could stop and balance there forever!*

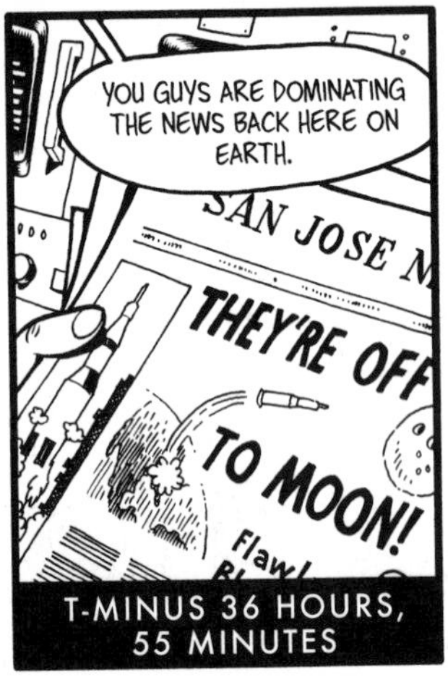
YOU GUYS ARE DOMINATING THE NEWS BACK HERE ON EARTH.
SAN JOSE M
THEY'RE OFF TO MOON!
T-MINUS 36 HOURS, 55 MINUTES

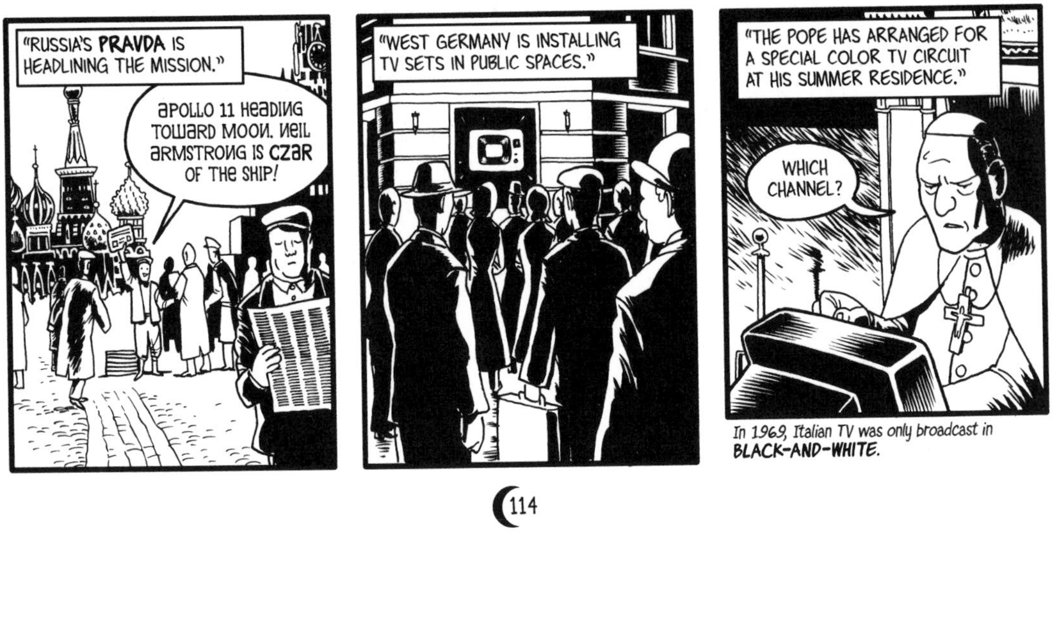
"RUSSIA'S PRAVDA IS HEADLINING THE MISSION."
APOLLO 11 HEADING TOWARD MOON. NEIL ARMSTRONG IS CZAR OF THE SHIP!
"WEST GERMANY IS INSTALLING TV SETS IN PUBLIC SPACES."
"THE POPE HAS ARRANGED FOR A SPECIAL COLOR TV CIRCUIT AT HIS SUMMER RESIDENCE."
WHICH CHANNEL?

In 1969, Italian TV was only broadcast in ***BLACK-AND-WHITE****.*

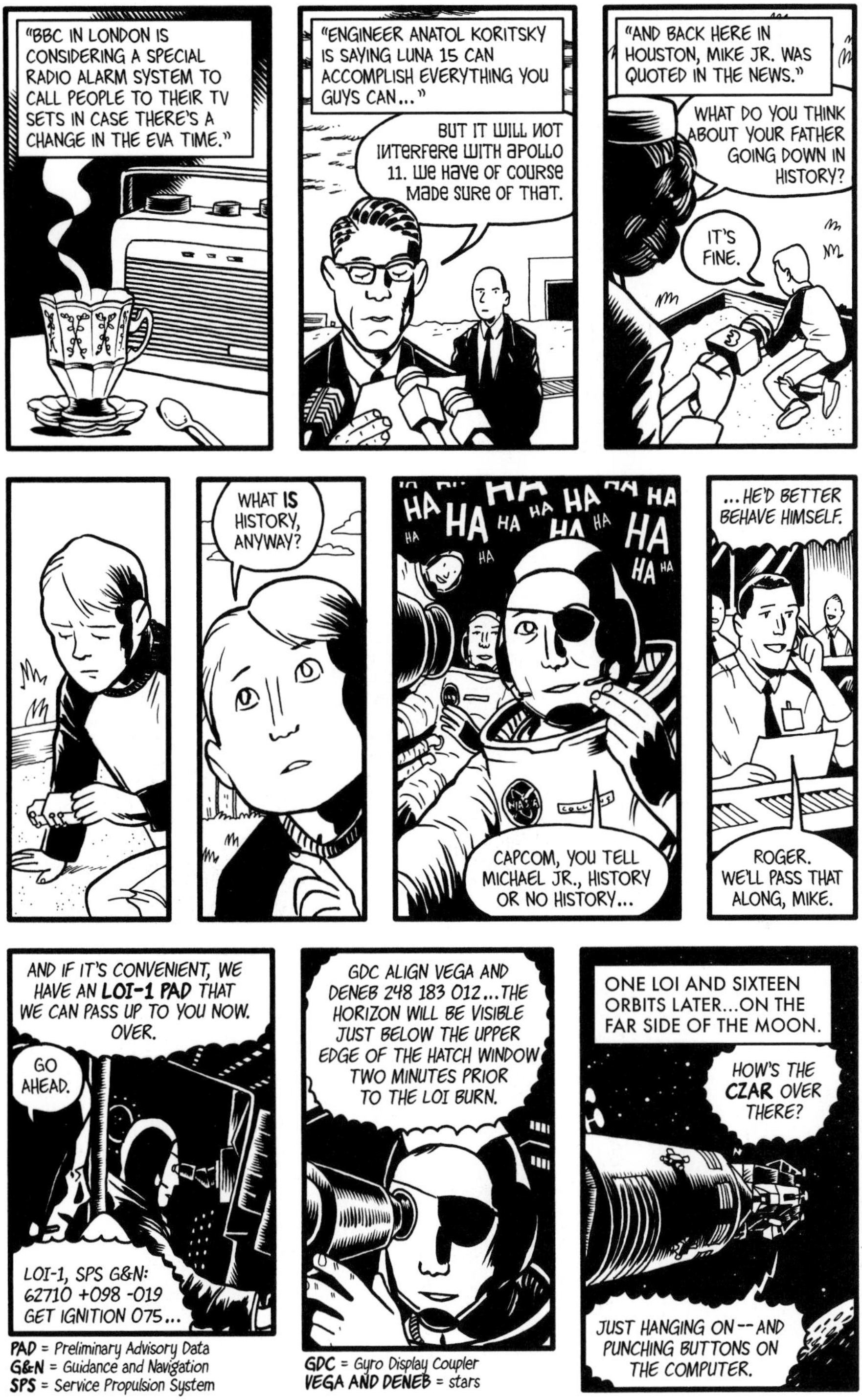
"BBC IN LONDON IS CONSIDERING A SPECIAL RADIO ALARM SYSTEM TO CALL PEOPLE TO THEIR TV SETS IN CASE THERE'S A CHANGE IN THE EVA TIME."
"ENGINEER ANATOL KORITSKY IS SAYING LUNA 15 CAN ACCOMPLISH EVERYTHING YOU GUYS CAN..."
BUT IT WILL NOT INTERFERE WITH APOLLO 11. WE HAVE OF COURSE MADE SURE OF THAT.
"AND BACK HERE IN HOUSTON, MIKE JR. WAS QUOTED IN THE NEWS."
WHAT DO YOU THINK ABOUT YOUR FATHER GOING DOWN IN HISTORY?
IT'S FINE.
WHAT IS HISTORY, ANYWAY?
HA HA HA HA HA HA HA HA HA HA HA HA HA HA HA
CAPCOM, YOU TELL MICHAEL JR., HISTORY OR NO HISTORY...
...HE'D BETTER BEHAVE HIMSELF.
ROGER. WE'LL PASS THAT ALONG, MIKE.
AND IF IT'S CONVENIENT, WE HAVE AN LOI-1 PAD THAT WE CAN PASS UP TO YOU NOW. OVER.
GO AHEAD.
LOI-1, SPS G&N: 62710 +098 -019 GET IGNITION 075...
GDC ALIGN VEGA AND DENEB 248 183 012...THE HORIZON WILL BE VISIBLE JUST BELOW THE UPPER EDGE OF THE HATCH WINDOW TWO MINUTES PRIOR TO THE LOI BURN.
ONE LOI AND SIXTEEN ORBITS LATER...ON THE FAR SIDE OF THE MOON.
HOW'S THE CZAR OVER THERE?
JUST HANGING ON--AND PUNCHING BUTTONS ON THE COMPUTER.

PAD = Preliminary Advisory Data
G&N = Guidance and Navigation
SPS = Service Propulsion System

GDC = Gyro Display Coupler
VEGA AND DENEB = stars

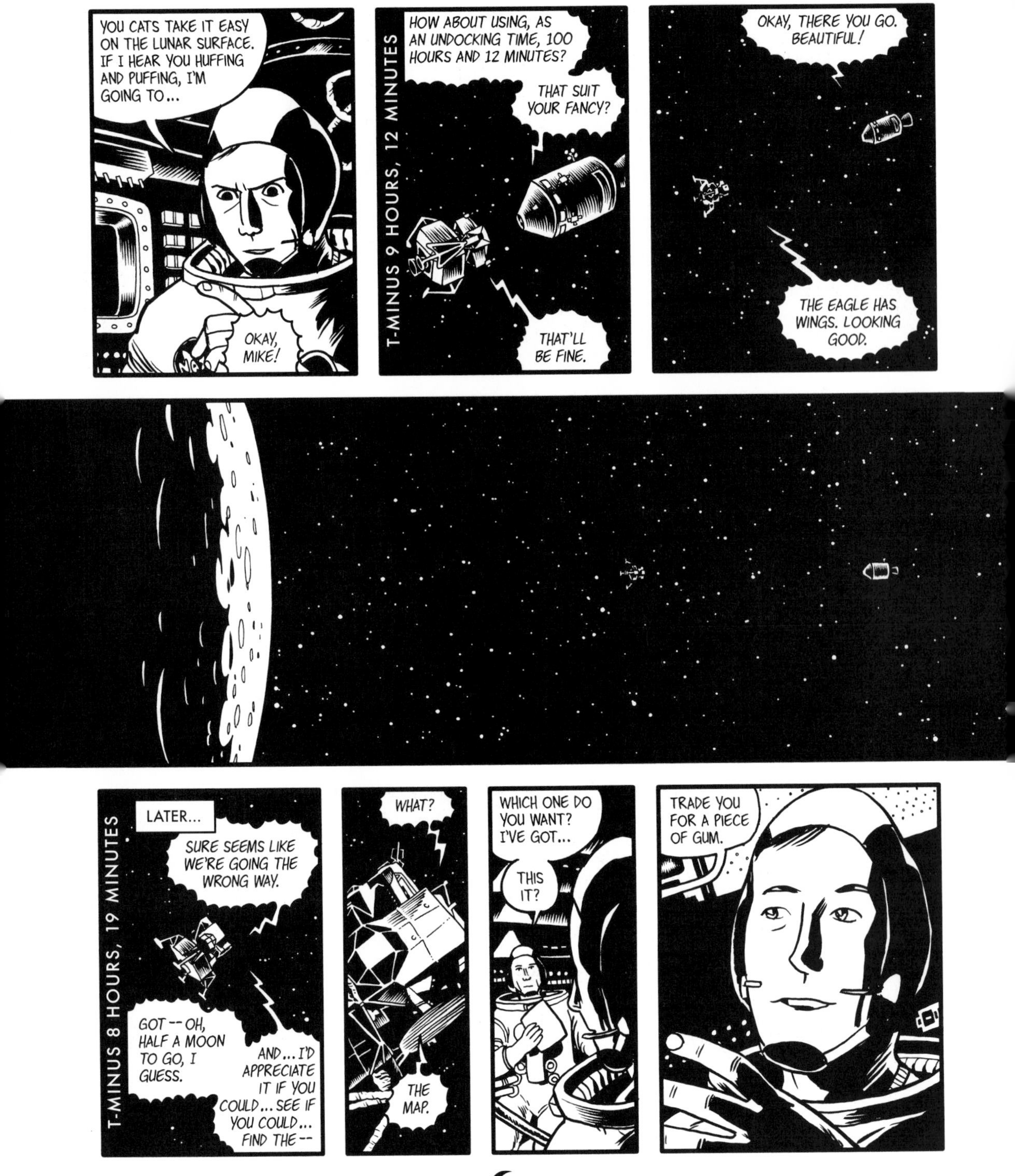
YOU CATS TAKE IT EASY ON THE LUNAR SURFACE. IF I HEAR YOU HUFFING AND PUFFING, I'M GOING TO...
OKAY, MIKE!
T-MINUS 9 HOURS, 12 MINUTES
HOW ABOUT USING, AS AN UNDOCKING TIME, 100 HOURS AND 12 MINUTES?
THAT SUIT YOUR FANCY?
THAT'LL BE FINE.
OKAY, THERE YOU GO. BEAUTIFUL!
THE EAGLE HAS WINGS. LOOKING GOOD.
T-MINUS 8 HOURS, 19 MINUTES
LATER...
SURE SEEMS LIKE WE'RE GOING THE WRONG WAY.
GOT -- OH, HALF A MOON TO GO, I GUESS.
AND... I'D APPRECIATE IT IF YOU COULD... SEE IF YOU COULD... FIND THE --
WHAT?
THE MAP.
WHICH ONE DO YOU WANT? I'VE GOT...
THIS IT?
TRADE YOU FOR A PIECE OF GUM.

T-MINUS 7 HOURS, 27 MINUTES
ALL RIGHT, LET ME...LET ME DO MY RAIN DANCE WITH THE DSKY HERE.
OKAY.

DSKY = Display/keyboard for the AGC
AGC = Apollo Guidance Computer, which all the astronauts loved...and relied on.

T-MINUS 6 HOURS, 54 MINUTES
HIT VERB 77?
OKAY. OMNI'S IN.

OMNI = Omni-directional antenna, which Buzz and Neil can point wherever they want.

COLUMBIA, HOUSTON. WE'VE LOST THEM.

THEY'VE LOST YOU...
...USE THE OMNI AGAIN.
ROGER. COPY.
...PGNS. WE GOT GOOD LOCK-ON. ALTITUDE LIGHTS OUT. DELTA-H IS MINUS...
PROGRAM ALARM.
IT'S A 1202.
...1202.
ACK!
PEOPLE?
WAIT. WAIT! WE... WE...
GOT A LIST, GOT A LIST, GOTALISTSOMEWHERE
SIMULATED THIS. YES. SOFTWARE ERROR, RIGHT? BUT IT'S NOT...
HOW MUCH FUEL IS LEFT?
20 SECONDS LATER...
GIVE US A READING ON THE 1202 PROGRAM ALARM.

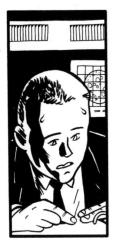

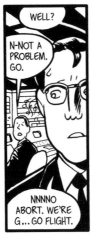

WELL?
N-NOT A PROBLEM. GO.
NNNNO ABORT. WE'RE G...GO FLIGHT.
WE GOT -- WE'RE GO ON THAT ALARM.
EAGLE, HOUSTON. YOU'RE GO FOR LANDING. OVER.
ROGER. UNDERSTAND. **GO** FOR LANDING. OVER.
OKAY...
3000 FE --
PROGRAM ALARM.
IT'S A 1201.
SAME TYPE. GO FLIGHT.
ROGER THAT, 1201 ALARM. WE'RE GO.
The **1202** and **1201 ALARMS** happened because Buzz had the landing and rendezvous computers both running (just in case), so the AGC's memory--barely big enough to hold four seconds of an MP3--struggled to keep up.
AGC, CONTROL. FUEL.
HOW MUCH LEFT?
60 SECONDS, FLIGHT.
OKAY... FLIGHT.
45 SECONDS.
OK. 75 FEET.
DOWN A HALF, SIX FORWARD.
30 SECONDS.
KICKING UP SOME DUST. 30 FEET, 2 ½ DOWN.
25 SECONDS.
20...19
MODE CONTROL -- BOTH AUTO.
DESCENT ENGINE OVERRIDE -- OFF.
UNITED STATES
ENGINE ARM-OFF.

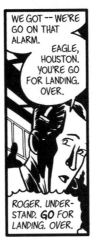

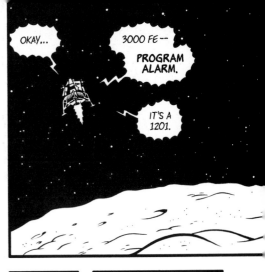

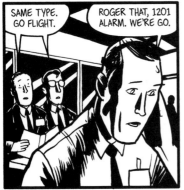

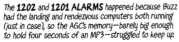

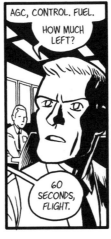

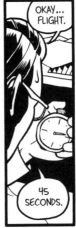

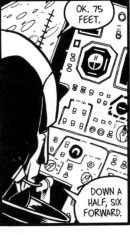

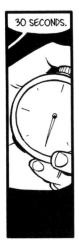

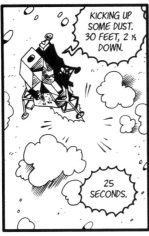

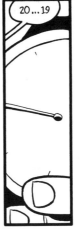

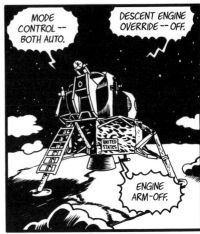

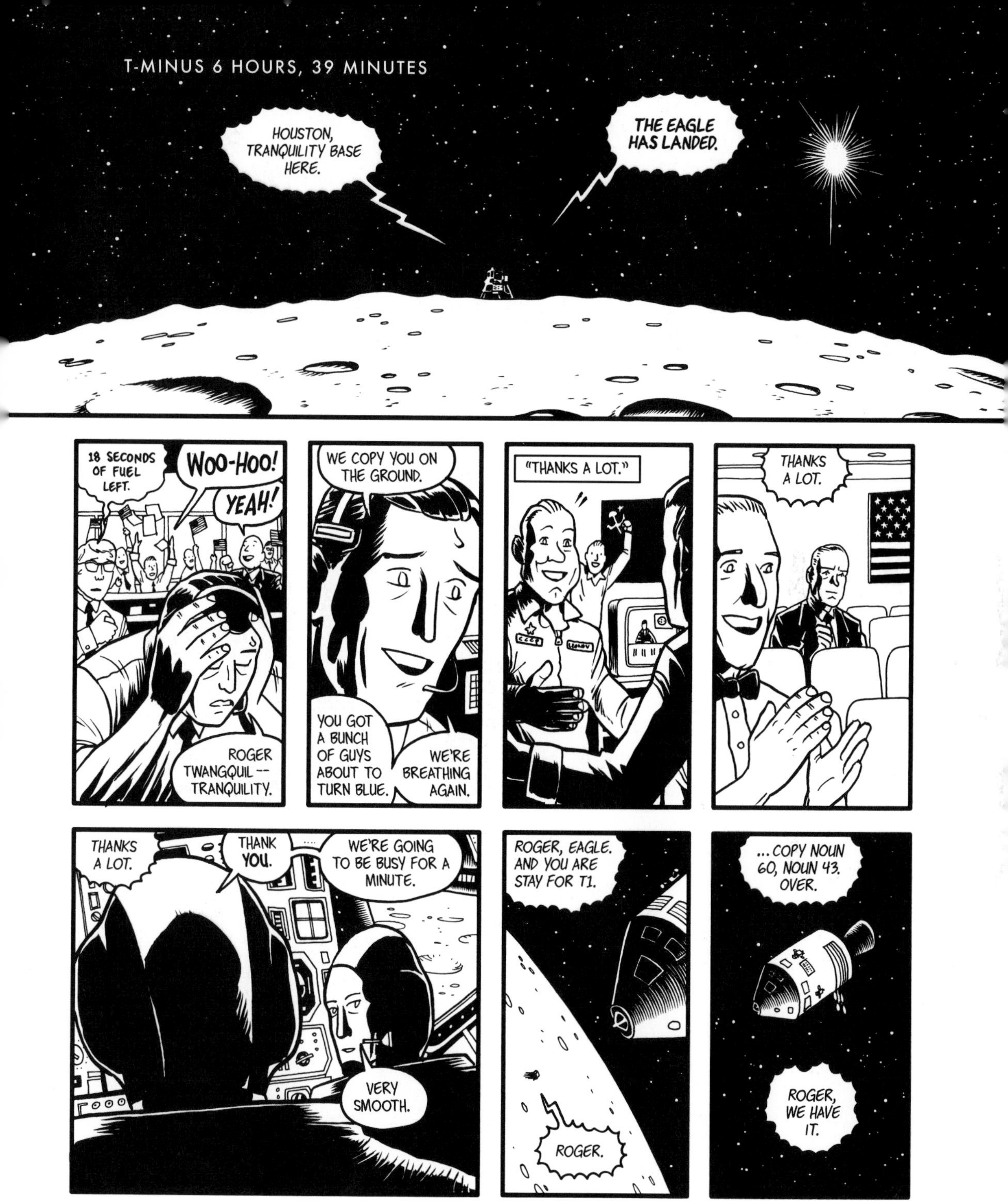
T-MINUS 6 HOURS, 39 MINUTES
HOUSTON, TRANQUILITY BASE HERE.
THE EAGLE HAS LANDED.
18 SECONDS OF FUEL LEFT.
WOO-HOO!
YEAH!
ROGER TWANGQUIL -- TRANQUILITY.
WE COPY YOU ON THE GROUND.
YOU GOT A BUNCH OF GUYS ABOUT TO TURN BLUE.
WE'RE BREATHING AGAIN.
"THANKS A LOT."
THANKS A LOT.
THANKS A LOT.
THANK YOU.
....
WE'RE GOING TO BE BUSY FOR A MINUTE.
VERY SMOOTH.
ROGER, EAGLE. AND YOU ARE STAY FOR T1.
ROGER.
...COPY NOUN 60, NOUN 43. OVER.
ROGER, WE HAVE IT.

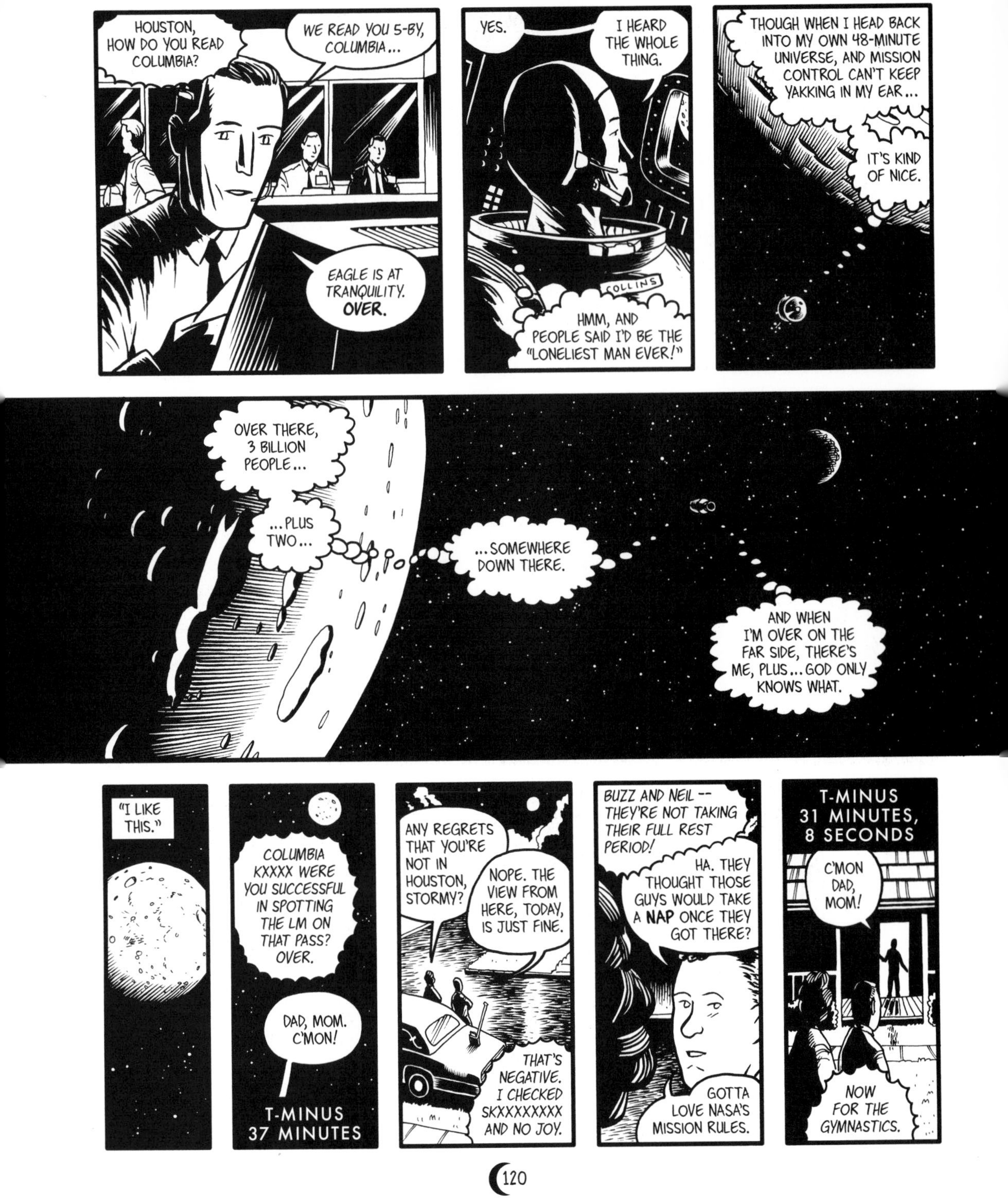
HOUSTON, HOW DO YOU READ COLUMBIA?
WE READ YOU 5-BY, COLUMBIA...
EAGLE IS AT TRANQUILITY. **OVER.**
YES.
I HEARD THE WHOLE THING.
COLLINS
HMM, AND PEOPLE SAID I'D BE THE "LONELIEST MAN EVER!"
THOUGH WHEN I HEAD BACK INTO MY OWN 48-MINUTE UNIVERSE, AND MISSION CONTROL CAN'T KEEP YAKKING IN MY EAR...
IT'S KIND OF NICE.
OVER THERE, 3 BILLION PEOPLE...
...PLUS TWO...
...SOMEWHERE DOWN THERE.
AND WHEN I'M OVER ON THE FAR SIDE, THERE'S ME, PLUS... GOD ONLY KNOWS WHAT.
"I LIKE THIS."
COLUMBIA KXXXX WERE YOU SUCCESSFUL IN SPOTTING THE LM ON THAT PASS? OVER.
DAD, MOM. C'MON!
T-MINUS 37 MINUTES
ANY REGRETS THAT YOU'RE NOT IN HOUSTON, STORMY?
NOPE. THE VIEW FROM HERE, TODAY, IS JUST FINE.
THAT'S NEGATIVE. I CHECKED SKXXXXXXXX AND NO JOY.
BUZZ AND NEIL -- THEY'RE NOT TAKING THEIR FULL REST PERIOD!
HA. THEY THOUGHT THOSE GUYS WOULD TAKE A **NAP** ONCE THEY GOT THERE?
GOTTA LOVE NASA'S MISSION RULES.
T-MINUS 31 MINUTES, 8 SECONDS
C'MON DAD, MOM!
NOW FOR THE GYMNASTICS.

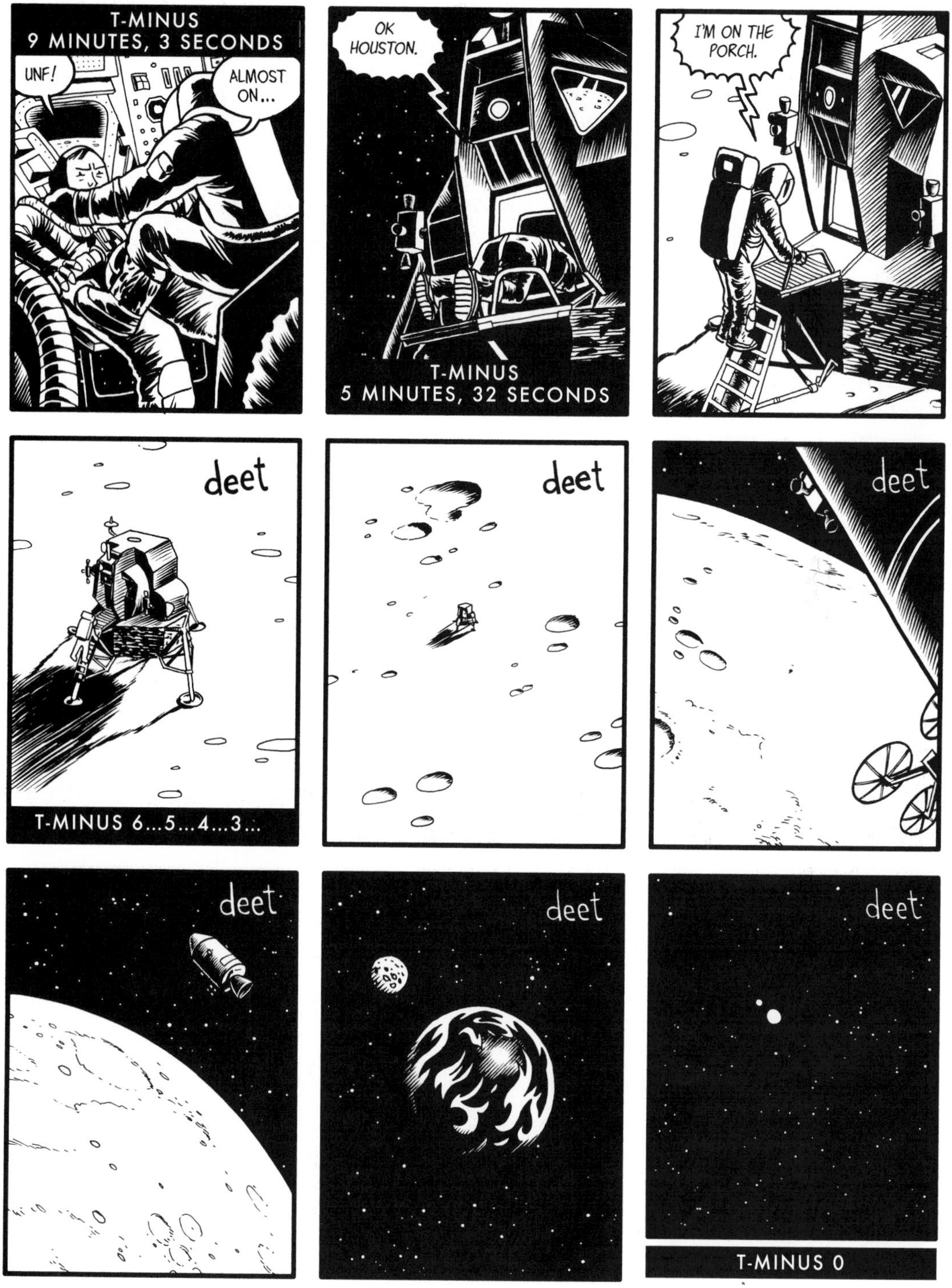
T-MINUS
9 MINUTES, 3 SECONDS
UNF!
ALMOST ON...
OK HOUSTON.
T-MINUS
5 MINUTES, 32 SECONDS
I'M ON THE PORCH.
deet
T-MINUS 6...5...4...3...
deet
deet
deet
deet
deet
T-MINUS 0

DID ALL OF THIS REALLY HAPPEN?

July 20, 1969

Yes...mostly! However, about 400,000 men and women worked on Mercury, Gemini, and Apollo—to show them all would've meant having more than 3,000 people on each page! So C.C. and Max are based on real NASA engineers Caldwell C. Johnson and Max Faget, but in our story they not only play their own parts, but also stand in for many other engineers and technical people as well. Similarly, we have Harrison Storms of North American Aviation say and do some things on behalf of other private contractors. And just like in the United States, thousands of people worked on the Soviet space program. Sergei Korolev was so pivotal, though, that he almost always spoke for himself. But just so you know, to make ***T-Minus*** we sometimes had to create some parts (scenes!) from scratch, imagining what people might have done, thought, or said so we could tell you the story more clearly.

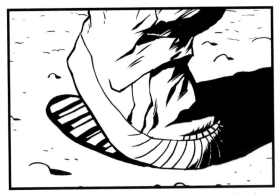

One small step: Neil Armstrong walks on the moon, the first of only 12 to do so.

DIG DEEPER

NASA's History Division has created sites called "Apollo Lunar Surface Journal" (*history.nasa.gov/alsj*) and "Apollo Flight Journal" which give detailed accounts of what the astronauts saw and did on their way to and from the moon, and while they walked and drove around on it. It's a work in progress, but the text, videos, and pictures that are there already are tremendous. The NASA Library at their headquarters in Washington DC has made many great publications on all aspects of space exploration, and the folks there were very helpful to us as well.

As great as it was to discover interesting stuff in libraries and book stores, reading mission transcripts (*www.jsc.nasa.gov/history/mission_trans/mission_transcripts.htm*), oral histories (*www.jsc.nasa.gov/history/oral_histories/oral_histories.htm*) and talking to people was the real thrill of making this book. We owe special thanks to astronauts Buzz Aldrin, Neil Armstrong, and Alan Bean for sharing their expertise, support, and encouragement.

Finally, if you want to read more comics about the space race, you can find out about the first dog in space, and Korolev as well, from Nick Abadzis' book *Laika* (New York: First Second, 2007). And you'll meet Ham, the first chimpanzee to fly in space, in Jim Vining's book, *First in Space* (Portland, OR: Oni Press, 2007).

The stack of books we read to make this one is more than ten feet tall, so there's much more for you to read, too. For a full list of the things we consulted to make this book, visit *gt-labs.com/tminus.html*.

THERE'S MORE TO SEE, MORE TO READ!

Chaikin, Andrew. *A Man on the Moon: The Voyages of the Apollo Astronauts* (New York: Viking Adult, 1994).

This book, the basis for the HBO Series *From the Earth to the Moon*, is long and complete, but it won't feel long. Since the book you're holding is only about the race through Apollo 11, we promised ourselves we would stop once we finished that chapter. But, we couldn't stop reading once we started. You won't be able to put it down either.

Collins, Michael. *Carrying the Fire: An Astronaut's Journeys* (New York: Cooper Square Press, 2001).

Our favorite book by an astronaut—others come close, but this is the best.

Gray, Mike. *Angle of Attack: Harrison Storms and the Race to the Moon* (New York: W. W. Norton, 1992).

The only book on Stormy that we know of. It reads like a mystery, even though you already know how it's going to end.

Harford, James. *Korolev: How One Man Masterminded the Soviet Drive to Beat America to the Moon* (New York: John Wiley & Sons, Inc., 1997).

There's a longer biography of Korolev out there, but it's written in Russian, so we couldn't read it. Korolev lived a hard life, and if he hadn't died prematurely, the space race might have been a photo-finish, and then shifted immediately to one focused on a Mars landing.

Scott, David and Alexei Leonov, with Christine Toomey. *Two Sides of the Moon* (New York: St. Martin's Press, 2004).

Alexei Leonov's first person account of his spacewalk and what happened afterward is the best part of this book...at least for us. He and David Scott tell so many great stories, though, that you may find a different favorite.

Spacecraft Films. *Apollo 8: Leaving the Cradle, Apollo 10: The Dress Rehearsal, Apollo 11: Men on the Moon, and Mission to the Moon.*

These DVDs compile NASA films and other video to give you a sense of what it was really like to be on a trip to the moon. If you're expecting iMAX, you'll be disappointed, but remember that there was no such thing as iMAX in the 1960s. There were no HDTVs or cell phones, Internet, or PCs either. In fact, *Mission to the Moon* will show you how they made computers back then, when it was all very new. Amazing! Spacecraft Films has produced cool DVDs on the Mercury and Gemini programs as well.

Murray, Charles and Catherine Bly Cox. *Apollo: The Race to the Moon* (New York: Simon and Schuster, 1989).

This book gives the most complete and readable account of the science and engineering that went into building the first spacecraft. If these stories won't get you interested in studying math, or taking apart your bicycle to see how it works, nothing will.

Smith, Andrew. *Moondust: In Search of the Men Who Fell to Earth* (New York: Fourth Estate, 2005).

If you want to know what it was like to grow up during the space race, and want to find out what the moonwalkers are doing now, this book will tell you. It's clear Smith had a great time writing it as well!

***In the Shadow of the Moon*. Directed by David Sington and featuring astronauts Buzz Aldrin, Alan Bean, Eugene Cernan, Michael Collins, Charlie Duke, Jim Lovell, Edgar D. Mitchell, Harrison Schmitt, Dave Scott, and John Young (THINKFilm, 2007).**

Rare footage and candid discussions of what it was like to train on, fly in, and land the Apollo spacecraft. Very cool.

AND NOW, BACK TO C.C., ON THE GOOD EARTH...

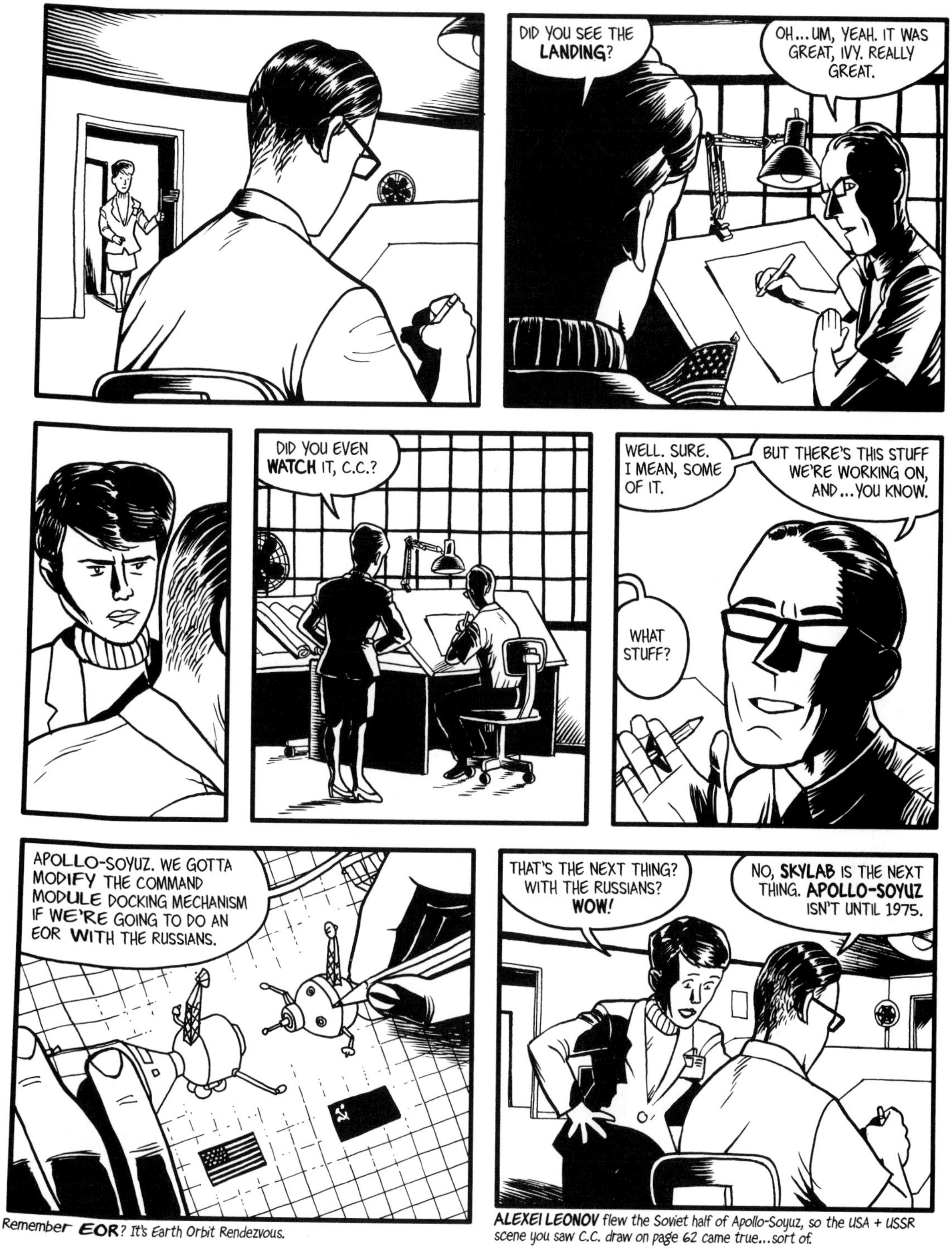
DID YOU SEE THE LANDING?
OH...UM, YEAH. IT WAS GREAT, IVY. REALLY GREAT.
DID YOU EVEN WATCH IT, C.C.?
WELL. SURE. I MEAN, SOME OF IT.
BUT THERE'S THIS STUFF WE'RE WORKING ON, AND...YOU KNOW.
WHAT STUFF?
APOLLO-SOYUZ. WE GOTTA MODIFY THE COMMAND MODULE DOCKING MECHANISM IF WE'RE GOING TO DO AN EOR WITH THE RUSSIANS.
THAT'S THE NEXT THING? WITH THE RUSSIANS? WOW!
NO, SKYLAB IS THE NEXT THING. APOLLO-SOYUZ ISN'T UNTIL 1975.

Remember ***EOR****? It's Earth Orbit Rendezvous.*

ALEXEI LEONOV *flew the Soviet half of Apollo-Soyuz, so the USA + USSR scene you saw C.C. draw on page 62 came true...sort of.*

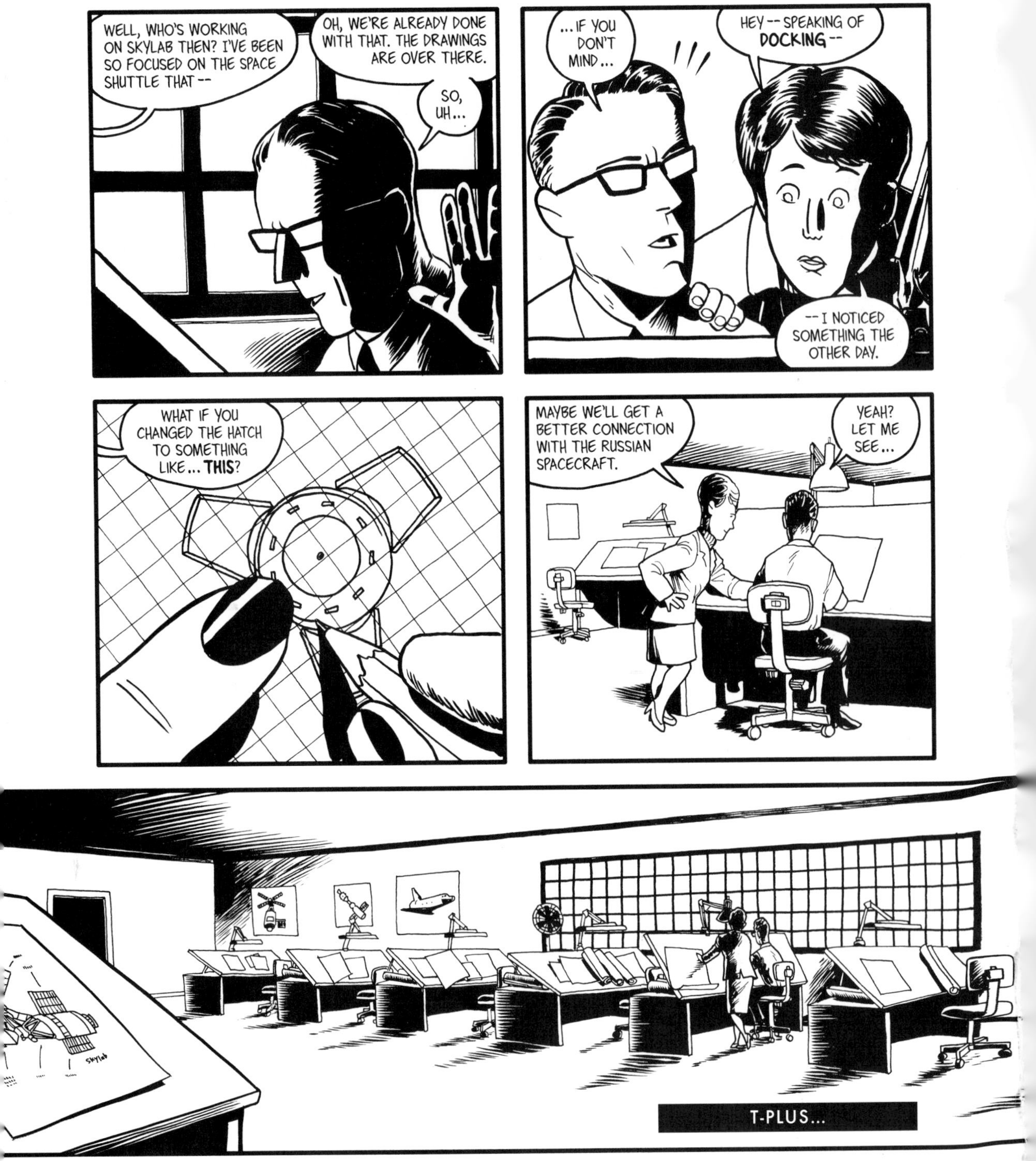
WELL, WHO'S WORKING ON SKYLAB THEN? I'VE BEEN SO FOCUSED ON THE SPACE SHUTTLE THAT --
OH, WE'RE ALREADY DONE WITH THAT. THE DRAWINGS ARE OVER THERE.
SO, UH...
...IF YOU DON'T MIND...
HEY -- SPEAKING OF **DOCKING** --
-- I NOTICED SOMETHING THE OTHER DAY.
WHAT IF YOU CHANGED THE HATCH TO SOMETHING LIKE... **THIS**?
MAYBE WE'LL GET A BETTER CONNECTION WITH THE RUSSIAN SPACECRAFT.
YEAH? LET ME SEE...
Skylab
T-PLUS...